THE GUY FROM JAMESTOWN

CHRISTOPHER DAVIES

First published in 2022 by Bloodhound Books.

www.bloodhoundbooks.com

Print ISBN: 978-1-5040-8187-0

'Everything of worth is found full of difficulties.'
– John Smith, *The Generall Historie of Virginia*

'I was always looking for a visual language that goes beyond the boundary of nations – and so I found gunpowder.'
– Cai Guo-Qiang

CHAPTER ONE

November 1st, 1605

It wasn't fair. None of this was fair.

He hated himself for thinking that way. The phrase itself was embarrassing, hyper-juvenile: *this isn't fair*.

Even as a child it had caused him trouble. Merely saying it would make his mother squirm and his father scowl. Those words, they told him, should never leave his lips. He was Francis Tresham: child of wealth, scion of nobility. No son of Sir Thomas Tresham – landowner, society man, confidant to the elite – should act like such a whining little maggot. '*Fair?*' his father would bellow, enjoying the moment, as though the joy of breaking the bad news was the only reason he'd ever had children in the first place. '*FAIR? Let me tell you about "fair", Francis. Life isn't fair. And if you think crying is going to change that, maybe you need your silly daydreams thrashed out of you.*'

Well. The old man had a point, hadn't he? Life was most assuredly *not* fair. And right now – the Year of our Lord 1605, the baby steps of a fearful new century – Francis and his people were very much aware of that.

The Treshams were Catholics – or Jesuits, or Recusants, or whatever other terms polite society could muster to avoid the C-word. And Francis had seen just how unfair life could be to followers of the One True Church. He had seen Catholics tortured and killed, the sanctity of Mass driven underground, churches purged of altars and vestments, Latin forbidden, priests decried as charlatans and made to hide in secret alcoves whenever the authorities came knocking. A venal crop of new Royals had forced the nation into Protestantism – and Catholics had been forced into a corner. Their very faith had been made illegal.

Francis had seen his father fight against all of this. Tresham-owned properties across the country were always open as safe havens for runaway Catholics, perfect hideaways for those who needed shelter from a regime that hated them. So, with all that was so deeply and utterly unfair in God's own England, Francis was loath to use the word. But what else *could* he think? Here he was: a loyal soldier for the Catholic cause, a man who had sacrificed much and was willing to sacrifice more... and now?

Now – all because he had stumbled into this accursed scheme; this 'gunpowder plot', he supposed you could call it – his integrity was being called into question. Worse than that: his very life was at stake.

The two men who were stood in front of Francis considered him a traitor. *That* was unfair. *That* was an injustice. *That* made him angry. And it was not advisable to make Francis Tresham angry.

Barnet. Francis could think of better places to die – but he could think of a lot worse too. At least the view was spectacular: an elevated vista over London, the highest point eastwards until the Ural Mountains in Russia. The name itself was Old English: bærnet, a land cleared by burning.

There were no fires here. Just the grey overhang of a November day, the threat of rain in the air, a tepid breeze fluttering the grass of the field he stood in. One of the men stood before Francis was called Robert. The other man was called Thomas. In the midst of this whole thing – the plot they were embroiled in – they were only ever referred to by their surnames: *Catesby* and *Wintour*, a stab at militaristic formality.

Francis found this strange. It just didn't feel right. The two men were family, after all. Thomas was more distant, yes – a quirk of marriage a few outlying branches away – but Robert was his *cousin*, for the love of mercy. And yet... they were acting like cavalrymen who had been bitterly forced into the same troop. Had they forgotten they were bonded by blood?

The grassland was open and empty: grand, impervious to minor human drama. They were isolated. There was no one nearby to whom Francis could call for help. This didn't really matter. How could he have explained what was happening anyway?

'How did you find out?' Wintour asked Catesby.

'Connections.' Catesby didn't look back to Wintour. He stared directly ahead at Francis, face locked in grim scrutiny.

'*What* connections?'

'Does it matter?'

'Yes. Yes, it does. If what you're saying is true...'

'Fine,' Catesby snapped. 'Ward. A message from Ward.'

'Saying?'

'Ward was the servant during a dinner in Hoxton. Some get-together organised by Lord Monteagle. Brother-in-law to our friend here.' Catesby pointed an accusatory finger at Francis. He glanced back to Wintour. 'You know who Monteagle is, don't you?'

'A baron. A lord.'

'Meaning?'

'I don't know.'

'*Meaning*,' Catesby was getting impatient, 'that he is a member of the House of Lords. Meaning that he would be present in the Houses of Parliament when...' He trailed off. He didn't need to finish the sentence. They all knew where it was heading.

When the dynamite we've planted in the cellar blows Parliament and everyone in it straight to Hell.

Catesby began to pace back and forth. Dirt and turf scudded up over his shoes. He didn't notice.

'Before the dinner,' Catesby said, 'Ward had been handed a letter. A note from a stranger in the street. He didn't get a good look at the man... but he heard his instructions right enough. Deliver this to your master. Ward did as he was told, naturally.'

'What was it?'

'A warning.' Catesby stopped pacing. 'A letter pleading with Lord Monteagle not to attend Parliament when it reopens.'

'How specific?' Wintour was trying to appear calm. He wasn't doing a particularly good job.

'Specific enough. No truly elaborate details... but it described the danger of a "terrible blow" in the making. One that would "appear from nowhere".'

Catesby and Wintour looked at each other for a moment, letting the implications settle. Then – slowly, in perverse tandem – they turned their gazes back towards Francis.

They eyed him up and down. Fishermen with an unknown catch.

'We were...' Wintour mulled things over, 'perhaps too hasty. In recruiting him to the cause.'

'Yes. We were.'

'We both knew of his... previous indiscretions.'

'Yes. We did.'

'We need to decide how to proceed.'

'Yes. We do.'

Francis could take no more. He had harboured a little hope that – left to discuss things between themselves – the two men would come to their senses. It wasn't to be. It was time to speak up.

'Listen to me.' Francis stepped forward. Catesby held out an admonishing palm: *You stay back, Tresham, or I will MAKE YOU stay back*. 'Please. Both of you. Just listen. I had nothing to do with this letter. You must believe me.'

Catesby nodded slowly. Assessing. Calculating. Then:

'Why should we *believe* you... when the better course of action would be to *hang* you?'

Ask him any other time, and he would have told you: *I'm not afraid to die.* And it was the truth. Francis was secure in his righteousness. He knew that everything he did served God and God alone, no small feat in a nation that loathed his kind. But... now? Facing his own mortality like this? He was terrified.

Shameful, really – but shame could come later. He needed to think. And talk. Fast.

'You know that I would never betray you,' he said, his breath hoarse and ragged. 'Not after all we've been through. Before and after this...' What could he possibly call it? This endeavour? Scheme? Enterprise? He settled on the obvious again. 'Plot.'

'You made your opinions clear from the start, cousin,'

Catesby said. 'You were quick to tell us we were walking into a disaster. You considered the whole thing a dangerous farce. You tried numerous times to make us reconsider our aims. Mr Wintour here' – a nod towards his companion, hanging further back – 'is correct. We shouldn't have dragged you into this. Something like this was bound to happen.' His anger was replaced for a moment with an intense sadness. A wall of regret. 'But now it *has* happened, cousin. And it must be dealt with.'

Catesby glanced back to Wintour. Francis deciphered their shared look: it was clear enough. They were cycling through the logistics: how to kill him, who should kill him, where to put the body. All the dark projections.

'You're right,' Francis said.

Catesby blinked. He was surprised. He hadn't expected an upfront admission. But that wasn't exactly what it was.

'I had my reservations,' Francis went on. 'I still do.' He gave a bitter snort. *Reservations* was an understatement. He had indeed told the others the plan was a maniacal one – and who exactly could blame him for doing so?

He was just like the others in many ways: just as full of hatred for the grubby little rulers of this 'kingdom'. Priests were reduced to scuttling like insects, their congregations turned into criminals. To strike at the foul heart of that beast was only admirable. But... *blowing up Parliament? Massacring hundreds of politicians and the King who ruled over them?* Francis had no mercy for the scum who would be killed – but he was afraid of the reprisals such a scheme would bring.

Say this plot was to succeed. What would happen to the Catholics in England then? Wasn't it likely that the boot on their neck would only press down harder... perhaps even choking them out altogether?

Francis had prayed. He had spoken to God. He knew that

Robert and the plotters were on the wrong path, no matter how furiously *right* their reasons were.

But. Still.

He would never stoop so low as to betray them.

And he most certainly had not written *ANY. FUCKING. LETTER.*

No. No. He calmed himself. That tone would not do. Such language was not fitting, such rage not productive. He may well be justified in losing his temper – he was being accused of backstabbing after all, the machinations of the lowliest rat – but he had to keep his composure. His anger was a cross to bear. Fury could feel good (so, *so* good) but it always got Francis into trouble. This was a lesson he had learned time and time again.

Anger wasn't necessary. He could be persuasive. Charming. *With your handsome looks and your smooth tongue, Francis Tresham*, his parents had said, *you could talk your way out of a lion's den.* They were right. He could convince anyone of anything. And that was when he was *lying*! Surely here... surely now... when he was telling nothing but the *truth*... he would be believed?

'Think about this,' Francis said, very slowly, very deliberately. 'What would I achieve by writing such a letter? I have voiced my concerns regarding your plan – yes, many times over – but only because I am worried that your talents and determination might be wasted.'

'What do you mean?' Catesby folded his arms.

'Within this plan,' Francis continued, 'I see eleven other men. Eleven men who can do *so much*, perhaps over *so many years*, to strike at the enemy. Yet I fear you are rushing headstrong into something that could kill the cause altogether.'

'Heh.' From a few feet away, Wintour gave a humourless laugh. 'I'm not sure I'm hearing this correctly. *You*, Tresham? *You*, stood there, warning others about getting "headstrong"?'

'Fair comment.' Francis nodded. 'I'll be the first to admit it. I'm a hypocrite. But let me tell you what I'm not.' He moved closer to the others. Catesby momentarily flinched – but decided to let him continue. 'I am not a traitor.'

A voice rumbled through Francis's skull again. Formless. Amorphous. Yet angry. Always angry.

And I most certainly did not write any letter, and I can't believe you would both have the gall to accuse me of something like that, and frankly I SHOULD GUT YOU BOTH LIKE A PAIR OF WRIGGLING EELS –

No. No. Calmness. That was the way forward. Calmness would have been the perfect preventative measure to some of the things Francis had done in the past: throwing his father's finances around like confetti, botched and ill-thought-out forays into rebellion, beating the life out of that pregnant woman when she owed him money (even though the thieving whore deserved every kick she got).

Calmness would have stopped Francis from going to prison several times over. Prison hadn't been much fun for a rich boy like him. Prison had done nothing for his temper.

He closed his eyes – and reopened them. A placid smile was etched across his face.

'I promise you,' he said. 'I am not the one behind this letter. And if you kill me today... you will be killing an innocent man.'

Catesby and Wintour stood in silence for a moment, taking this all in.

Their initial rush to judgement had subsided. Their certainty had wilted, their staunchness sapped. They both opened their mouths to speak at the same time – when another voice arrived, piping up as if to pluck the very thought out of their heads:

'I believe him.'

'I believe him,' said Guido Fawkes. 'And you should too.'

'What are you doing here?' Catesby asked.

Guido slowly approached. He was just like the other plotters on a surface level – smartly dressed, mid-thirties, shifty air compounded by a lifetime of looking over his shoulder – yet he also stood out from them: the tallest by a head or so, the one whose angular features were the most striking and severe. Despite all this, he was also the least formal. He held no stock in *Guido*. He was happy enough to be called *Guy*.

A few hours ago Guy had been in the borough of Westminster, dropping by the hideout he and his fellow plotters had established. Percy had been there – Thomas Percy, the one who had rented the property, a spot in sight of Parliament itself – sat alone at the table, looking worried. There was nothing unusual about that: these were worrying times. Their scheduled moment for destruction was mere days away: November 5th, a date they all hoped would never be spoken in casual tones again. All the plotters were fraught with anxiety.

But Percy looked particularly troubled. 'What's wrong?' Guy asked, taking a seat. 'What's right?' Percy snorted.

'Lots, actually. The merchandise is in place. The ceremony has suffered no delays. We've attracted no suspicion from the locals.' Guy paused while he was eating – a hunk of bread he had stashed in his bag for travelling. Sit-down meals were a rarity at the moment. 'Have some faith. God is smiling upon us.'

'Savour that.' Percy nodded at the bread. 'Could be your last.'

'Percy.' Guy glared. 'If we are to drag this nation out of the gutter, perhaps we could start by dragging your morale out of the gutter fir–' He stopped. Looked around. Frowned. 'Where are Catesby and Wintour?'

'Barnet,' Percy said.

'Oh. Lovely. Sightseeing, are they?'

'They are dealing,' Percy sighed, 'with Tresham.'

Guy froze. He knew what this meant. He had been hoping it wouldn't come to this.

'I assume you tried to talk them out of it?' Guy asked.

'I did my best.'

'Of course.' Guy got to his feet again. 'Tell you what.' He flung the bread over to Percy. It landed gracelessly in the man's lap. '*You* savour that. Some of us have work to do.'

Guy took a carriage to the outskirts of Barnet. It was money he winced at frittering away. Funds for the plotters were not particularly tight – but they needed to prepare for the potential aftermath of their plan, those days following the King's death when they would need as many resources as possible to continue their battle.

This was an allowable expense, he told himself. Necessary. Vital. Any in-fighting – or possibly something much worse – between the others and Tresham was the last thing they needed. It was too late to let personal grievances get in the way of destiny.

He *did* understand it. A little. Tresham was not a man who naturally attracted camaraderie. In any given group he would be the outlier, a natural martyr to wolf pack politics. Guy had met plenty of men like Tresham under his military command: outsider soldiers in the Low Countries and the siege of Calais, men whose precious air or haughty distance marked them out from the others. Guy always put his foot down, intolerant of any bullying. He may just have been a mercenary working for the Spanish Army, yes – but he was a mercenary who was *in command*, and any man who had signed up to defend the Catholic faith across Europe would be treated as an equal on his watch.

From nations afar back to his homeland: Guy still felt the same. Tresham was a pompous whelp yet he was *their* pompous whelp, a man who had helped fund not only their plot but had done much for Catholics over the years. He was on their side. That was good enough for Guy. He also knew – had heard stories – that Tresham harboured both a temper and violent tendencies. He wasn't keen to see those pushed. Something else he'd learned from the military: the quiet ones could be *absolute monsters* when their patience expired.

He hit his fist against the side of the carriage in frustration. There simply wasn't time for this nonsense. Why should he have to take charge like this? What was he, a schoolmaster whipping unruly pupils into shape?

Suddenly he was alone with his sadness. *School* was one of those words he knew he shouldn't think about – along with *youth* or *family* or *love*. All it did was trigger dark contemplation.

School. Had his son lived – survived beyond those first few seconds of life – he would have been starting school right about now. Or would he? Schools were now just Protestant indoctrination centres. Would Guy instead have dragged the boy into his own underground world, a life of home education and hideaways? Would his wife, Maria, have allowed such a thing?

Pointless questions. Moot what-ifs. Maria had died while giving birth in a Yorkshire infirmary ward. Their newborn – choked on a tangled umbilical cord – had left this world alongside her. Only Guy was left: filled with a rage against God until he realised what God wanted from him. Mysterious ways were often devastating ones: while Guy knew he would see

Maria and the boy again one day, he also knew he had work to do. He had a faith to defend. He travelled. He fought. He endured.

When Parliament exploded in a cleansing fire in just four days' time, the traitors in power would finally know what he had been working towards. It would be his message. His sermon of flames.

Catesby and Wintour and Tresham could do what they wanted once the deed was done. They could squabble like diseased pigeons until Judgement Day.

Until then?

They were on his time.

'Percy said you were here.' Guy approached Catesby and Wintour. 'He told me you had business to deal with.' He gave a dogged smirk. 'You know Percy. When he says *business*, he never means *good business*.' Guy looked over to Tresham: a figure of blunt dejection. 'Looks like he was right.'

'We have everything under control.' Wintour waved a dismissive hand.

'Do you now?' Guy's smirk faltered. Fine. He had tried to indulge them in fellowship: esprit de corps. Time for a more direct approach. 'Because it seems to me, gentlemen, like you're prepping a lynching party.'

'I take it you've been stood over there? Watching?' Catesby gestured towards the tattered brown-green overgrowth that sloped upwards towards the edge of the common, half out of view given their vantage point.

'Naturally.' Guy nodded. He was a born soldier in many ways – and one of them was observing the battlefield before he stepped out to fight. He had watched the three men for a while. Listened. Learned.

'How much did you hear?'

'Everything.'

'So you know about the letter. The one exposing the plot.'

'That's unfortunate,' Guy conceded. 'But...'

'But what?'

'As I said. I believe Tresham. He didn't write it.' Guy held his palms aloft. It was worth a go: one more stab at peacefulness. 'Think about it. Why *would* he? He said so himself, he's merely been acting out of concern in the past. You're family, he fears for your safety. Playing Judas wouldn't make sense.'

'So who is behind it then?' Wintour asked.

'That's a good question,' Guy said. 'We clearly have someone close to us who is less... committed than we thought.' He took a moment to think. 'What do we know about Monteagle?'

'I don't follow.' Wintour frowned. Catesby followed suit.

'How impulsive is he? How quick to act? Would he take this letter at face value or would he want to investigate further? Would he take it directly to the King or roundhouse someone else into doing it?'

'He's a placid type,' Catesby said. 'He'll hand it off, no doubt. Then the next person will hand it off to the next person. Three or four steps up the ladder until the King sees it.'

'That gives us time.'

'And the King is away. Hunting. He's not expected back for several days. At which point he'll...' Catesby trailed off once more, another sentence that didn't need completing. *At which point the King will head straight to Parliament... at which point the thirty-six barrels of gunpowder they had procured and stashed in the undercroft would blow him apart, along with every laughable 'dignitary' and every worm-souled lickspittle 'politician'... at which point the recusants would rise up and install a new Catholic Queen on the throne.*

They would take their country back. Take back control. Silence. They were all thinking it over.

But they were waiting for Guy to speak. 'We can still do this,' Guy said.

Catesby looked to Guy and then looked to Francis. He did it over and over, something that would appear comical were it not so foreboding – back and forth, back and forth. It was decision time. His gaze settled on Guy.

'Do you have any firm evidence that it wasn't Tresham?' Catesby gave a peculiar half-sneer. 'Or are you just going with a gut feeling?'

Guy slowly stepped forward until he was directly facing Catesby, not quite nose to nose but certainly closing in. If this whole thing came to blows, both men could put up a fight. They were both well versed in violence.

'Don't underestimate a "gut feeling",' Guy said, quietly, his eyes unmoving. 'You know... in certain circles... such a feeling can even be referred to as "faith". I trust you're familiar with the concept?'

'Very much so.' Catesby stared right back.

'Then we're in agreement.'

Silence.

Catesby nodded. Swallowed. Hard.

'Fine,' he said. He briefly glanced over to Francis. 'We take Tresham at his word. We do this. We continue. And we pray nothing comes of this letter. If anything *does*, Fawkes... it's on your head.'

He began to walk away, across the green, followed closely by Wintour. And with that, Guy Fawkes was left to handle Francis Tresham.

'Come on.' Guy clamped a reassuring hand on the man's shoulder. 'Let's go. We have a lot to do.'

Francis exhaled. He breathed for the first time in what felt like decades.

Once Fawkes had arrived on the scene, his own agency had devolved again – the accusers were once more talking about him as though he wasn't actually there. He no longer cared however. Fawkes had stood in his defence. Robert and Thomas – (*Catesby* and *Wintour*) – wouldn't hear out Francis's own pleas of innocence... but they certainly listened to Fawkes.

Guy and Francis began to follow Catesby and Wintour, two separate factions on the march. Had anyone seen them from afar, Francis mused, they might well have thought they were looking at four friends en route to the nearest tavern – not four dissidents embroiled in something that could change history.

Francis turned to look at Fawkes. The man who had just saved his life. His heart filled with gratitude.

This was a revelation. Truly.

How had he *not noticed* what kindred spirits they both were?

Francis had always silently respected the man from a distance – Fawkes was a hard worker, a good tactician, a famed mercenary with a history of battle, most of all a man dedicated to his God – but how had Francis not realised just how close in tenor they were?

Catesby and Wintour had been quick to point the finger at Francis, an immediate slide into suspicion. And what of the rest? How would they have conducted themselves? Francis did a quick mental inventory of the others involved in the plot, running their unforgiving faces through his head. Yes, yes... he had no doubt they would all have acted the same. They would all have accused him of writing that filthy letter. No hesitation, no compunction. No *faith.*

But... Fawkes.

Fawkes was different. Francis could see that now. 'Thank you,' Francis said. 'For believing me.'

'The truth is the truth.' Guy gave a half-shrug. This only edged Francis's hero worship up a notch. Guy was modest as well as principled: a true paragon.

The truth is the truth. And it was – it really *was*, wasn't it? A truth bestowed by God. Fawkes had been given a divine spark of faith; had within him the necessary insight to see that Francis was innocent. None of the others had. That meant that he and Fawkes were both on the side of the Lord. As for the others? No. They just *thought* they were on the same holy team.

'You're a good man,' Francis said.

'Thank you.' Guy looked a little taken aback – but recovered composure quickly enough.

Francis resisted the urge to laugh. Who could have predicted this? That – from an ordeal so nearly resulting in his death – God would have seen fit to present him with a new brother in arms?

His kingdom come. His will be done.

Up ahead Francis spotted Catesby and Wintour talking to each other, spewing sneaky huddled missives. He quickened his pace a little – just close enough to overhear them but just far enough not to be noticed.

'Fawkes is right, you know,' Wintour said. 'Let's be honest. Can you *imagine* Tresham composing a letter like that – much less delivering it safely and anonymously? The man couldn't find a hole in a whorehouse. Couldn't hit water if he fell out of a boat.'

'Yes.' Catesby snorted, amused despite everything. 'I suppose so.'

Francis gritted his teeth. Hanging back once again, he entertained himself briefly with visions of himself leaping on the pair of them, howling, jaw agape, taking Catesby first, sinking his teeth into the bastard's neck and tearing out a bloody chunk of throat before pouncing like a wildcat on Wintour, *laughing, his chin red and glistening, screaming you're next, you're next, YOU'RE NEXT–*

No. He had to settle down.

'Are you all right?' Guy asked. Frowning. Concerned. Francis suddenly felt a wave of self-consciousness.

He had kept those words inside his head, hadn't he? He hadn't been gleefully mouthing them out loud...? 'I'm fine.' Francis smiled. 'Considering.'

'Good. Listen, Tresham. This is merely an obstacle. One we shall overcome. In circumstances like these, men can find trusting each other very difficult. But once that trust is set in stone... then true change can be forced upon the world. You'll see.'

Guy continued to make his way across the grassland, powering ahead with a sense of renewed purpose. Lagging slightly behind, Francis resisted the urge to laugh again.

It was all so funny to him now. The irony was palpable. It *glowed*.

Before he had been dragged out to Barnet like a common thief to the gallows, Francis Tresham would never have dreamed of betraying his cousin and the others. But now his eyes had been opened: a Damascene flash. The way Catesby and Wintour had belittled him... accused him... humiliated him? These were not men of faith. They were not real Catholics. They were something else: imposters, frauds, costumed dogs at a gypsy circus.

Now Francis Tresham wanted his revenge. He stifled a giggle.

Forcing true change upon the world? Oh yes. That's exactly what I'm going to do.

He had a new ambition now.

With the noble exception of Guido Fawkes – his mortal saviour, his new-found ally in true belief – Francis Tresham was going to make sure that every godless bastard in this gunpowder plot got what they deserved.

CHAPTER TWO

November 5th, 1605

Guy Fawkes was kneeling.

It was one of the few things he knew for sure.

Other details were scant. He knew the time and date – it was the early hours of the morning on November 5th, a black prelude to a day that was only going to get worse. He knew that he had been hauled through to London to Whitehall Palace, gagged and bound and surrounded by armed guards. He knew that he had been stripped down to his undergarments, removed of the rosary beads and crucifixes that left no doubts as to his religion. The guards had muttered to themselves as they uncovered the scars that criss-crossed his torso, a faded lattice of war wounds and etched defiance.

Most of all: Guy knew that he had to stick to the name.

John Johnson. That was the title he had chosen. That was the name he had given when – merely an hour earlier – he had been seized while hiding in the bowels of Parliament, standing guard by the explosives that were set to reclaim the nation in a wondrous blast of Holy Fire.

He always had been John Johnson and always would be John Johnson. No one else. And when the man who was about to glide out of the darkness – emerging from the corrupted sanctity of his bedchamber – would stand above him and ask his name, *John Johnson* was the answer he would give.

It didn't matter that Guy was addressing royalty. King James was not *his* King, after all.

The King himself didn't look particularly regal. No one ever did at four in the morning. Despite being weary and bedraggled, however, James was still an imposing presence – and he knew it. The King was used to people shifting their eyes downwards and shrinking upon his approach. He likely couldn't imagine anything else.

Guy would be doing no such thing.

He stared up at James, unblinking and brazen. There was a glimmer of surprise in the King's eyes – but it soon vanished. He did not seem enraged at this prisoner's audacity. Instead, he seemed genuinely intrigued. And why not? He had never encountered anyone like *this* before.

'They tell me your name is Johnson,' James said.

Guy said nothing. James took the silence as a *yes*. Names really weren't the crux of the matter here anyway. What was truly important was:

'Your plan. Did you indeed intend to do what my men say? To set off those explosives?'

Once again, Guy said nothing. The King sighed.

'This will be a lot easier if you are honest and open,' James said. 'If you speak the truth.'

This was an out-and-out lie. Guy knew it and the King knew it. None of what followed for Guy could remotely be described as *easy*. What awaited him was almost certainly a demonic blood trail of assault and injury: imprisonment, torture, death, not to mention a million little miseries crammed within the spaces between.

This was almost incidental to Guy. The greatest torture – that Parliament would stay standing – had no competition from mere men. Indeed, it was telling that the King was dangling that word in front of him as an ersatz reward: *easy*. Easiness was no reward. Easiness should be spat at.

'My *plan*,' Guy finally spoke, every cadence fuelled by contempt, 'was to blow you back to your native mountains, you Scottish bastard.'

There was more than a glimmer of surprise on the King's face now. His eyes widened like saucers while his pupils tightened with anger. He managed not to gasp, however – he left that for a couple of the guards who were stood nearby, both unable to believe what they had just heard. In the hushed silence, Guy even heard one of the guards whisper something to the other. It was one word. A name. *Scaevola*.

Under any other circumstances, Guy would have taken the comparison as a compliment. Just like any other red-blooded man of fighting age, Guy knew exactly who Gaius Mucius Scaevola was: the legendary Roman youth who, when caught trying to assassinate an enemy leader had cried out, '*I came here as an enemy to kill my enemy, and I am as ready to die as I am to kill*.' The story went that Scaevola's bravery impressed the enemy so much that he was sent home unharmed.

Guy was not anticipating the same result.

'I see.' James was outraged by the slur, it was obvious – but he hid it well behind a smirking veneer. 'How very... bombastic. Are there any more specifics you would care to share?'

'Only that I wished more than anything to annihilate Parliament and everyone in it,' Guy said. 'And that I shall regret not doing so for the rest of my life.' *However short that may be.*

James nodded calmly. He lowered himself slightly, stooping to Guy's level – a move that inspired another quick gasp from the nearby guards – and put forth his next query. It was far more direct than the others.

'Why?' he asked.

Well, now. Wasn't *that* just the question?

The King undoubtedly knew the *overall* reason why. Guy had the same motivation of any Catholic recusant, assuming their boiling hatred for their oppressors matched his. What marked him out as different – along with his fellow plotters – was his willingness to *do something about it*.

Many so-called revolutionaries backed off when the genuine call to action came around. They made excuses as to why they could not stand up and fight. They fell back onto all the things they had to lose, unwilling to risk the safety of their livelihoods or their wives or their children. Guy was no such man. There was nothing that could be taken from him. There were no consequences he feared.

But, Guy suspected, that wasn't what the King wanted to hear, was it? No, no, no – His Majesty here doubtless yearned for all sorts of dramatic quirks and story arcs, didn't he, the sort of things that were crammed into one of those Shakespeare plays Guy kept hearing about?

Guy could have provided all this. Absolutely he could. He could have startled James with the revelation that he wasn't actually born a Catholic: that he converted from Protestantism illegally as a teenager, making the switch after the remarriage of his widowed mother, eventually realising that his grandparents – proud recusants who scowled at the idea of attending mandatory Protestant services – were true heroes in an evermore lightless world.

He could have reeled off countless other exploits. He had left England at the tender age of twenty-two, working as a mercenary for both the Spanish military and the Army of Flanders, fighting for the Catholic cause wherever he could. He had – unsuccessfully, sadly – petitioned the Spanish King to wage war against England, claiming he would rather see his nation invaded by sympathetic aliens than destroyed by home-grown savages.

If pressed, he could even have given James a definite turning point: the precise moment he knew that England's elites needed to be overturned. He was a boy of sixteen when – in York town centre – he had witnessed the execution via *peine forte et dure* of Margaret Clitherow, a woman convicted of harbouring Catholics and conducting forbidden Mass. He had watched as it took Margaret fifteen minutes to die, crushed alive underneath eight hundred pounds of stone. She had been stripped naked, laid upon a sharp rock that would break her back. She had been pregnant.

The whole debasing ritual was held on Lady Day, a feast day to mark the Archangel Gabriel's visit to Mary. This was very much a deliberate insult. Even though Guy had never met Margaret, he felt nothing but a thirst for vengeance on her behalf.

Guy would be sharing none of this with King James. The story of his spiritual awakening – and all his other defining moments – was only something he wanted his fellow faithful to hear. James did not *deserve* Guy's history, nor his justifications. One would not feed prime steak to a shithouse rat.

'I am telling you nothing,' Guy said.

King James continued to talk. Guy soon stopped paying attention. This was all performative nonsense anyway – simply a way that, when the story became public knowledge, the King and his lackeys could frame his involvement in a flattering way. *Did you hear? The King insisted on interrogating the prisoner himself – as soon as the man had been caught! He bravely held court and looked directly into the face of evil!*

Guy had made it very clear that he – or rather John Johnson, age, address and everything else unknown – would not be sharing any more details. Let the King wear himself out with his posturing and his blabbering. Guy knew what was coming next: he would be taken to the Tower of London. There he would experience agony beyond agonies, pain like he had never imagined. No matter. He would stay silent until they killed him. He had God on his side. He never doubted that would see him through.

Although... did he *deserve* the supportive presence of God?

He had utterly failed Him in his task, after all. He thought back over every step of the Gunpowder Plan, every vaulted obstacle and strategic coalition that had led to this moment: the first meeting of the conspirators in the Duck and Drake, the scheme being drawn up, the gunpowder being sourced, the tunnel dug underneath Parliament. Now the gunpowder remained exactly where it was, never to ignite, useless dust-like mounds heaped into barrels. The sight of Parliament going up in flames – birthing a new England – would never bless his eyes.

The letter. He should have taken it more seriously.

He had no doubt whatsoever that Francis Tresham was innocent of writing it. As weaselly and erratic as the fool was, he was a man of a certain loyalty. But Guy should have taken greater pains to find out who *was* behind it... yet he had been so punch-drunk on ambition he had let his guard slip.

Guy seethed inwardly. Had his hands been unbound, he

would have struck himself over the head. Throughout his entire military career he had worked by a fixed credo: *assumptions cost lives*. Now he had been stupid enough not to follow his own advice.

What of the others? As soon as word of disaster spread, he guessed that Catesby, Wright and Bates would immediately flee London, dashing their way along Watling Street before honing in on a fresh hiding place out of the city. The rest would surely make similar plans. Guy wished them all the best. It was entirely feasible – likely, even, it pained him to think – that they would be caught. Yet nothing leading to their arrest would ever leave his lips. Even with Death beckoning a bony finger from the corner of the room – Guy could practically see the cloaked fiend – he would never betray his brethren.

Soon enough, the King ceased his self-indulgent waffle: a small mercy, Guy thought, on an otherwise graceless day. Synchronised arms looped around his own. He was dragged out of the room. Out of the palace. Out to more guards and a waiting carriage.

The Tower was next.

Things got off to a peculiar start. Either they made a mistake – they wrongly thought that Guy would be intimidated by another display of authority – or they were trying to wrong-foot him, hoping that a softly-softly approach would ease his jaw a little.

He was questioned – he wouldn't dignify this feeble charade with the term *interrogation* – by the Lord Chief Justice and the Attorney General. Popham and Coke, their names were: influential figures among certain circles yet just two more brutally generic doormats to Guy.

Guy told them what was already extremely evident: that he had planned to blow up Parliament. When they questioned him slightly about his past, he allowed them a couple of insights, more because he pitied their fecklessness than anything else. He spared a few details of his time in Flanders and the Spanish Army, a couple of morsels for the starving mutts to pick at. He gave them no more.

'What if the Queen and the royal children had been present when you carried out your atrocity?' Popham asked.

'Then they would have been present,' Guy replied.

'And your fellow Catholics? A good number of them would likely have been caught up in the blast. How would you settle that account with yourself?'

'I would have prayed for them,' Guy said. It was the truth.

When it came time to sign his name on whatever meaningless paper they thrust in front of him, he wrote *John Johnson*. They put him in a cell where he slept fitfully on a stone floor – knowing that tomorrow would only bring despair, taking solace in the fact that his compatriots still might make it out of this whole mess alive... and then might devise some new and vengeful plot in his fallen memory.

The next day 'John Johnson' was taken to his first bout of torture.

Manacles were clamped around his wrists, extending from chains that were bolted from the wall. He was led up a small wedge of three or four steps – and then the steps were removed, leaving Guy dangling in the air, carrying his whole weight upon his wrists. It was incredibly painful, extraordinarily so – especially when the torturer rejigged proceedings to make the horror worse, leaving Guy suspended by only his thumbs for a few agonising hours.

He had heard men speak of torture before. He had heard many a pre-battlefield conversation. The trick, some said – as naïvely simple as it sounded – was to *place your mind somewhere else*, to seek respite in happier memories. For the first day's ordeal, at least, this worked for Guy. Or at least stopped him from spiralling into screaming madness altogether.

He transported himself back to Antwerp. He had found himself there a few years ago, in Hoogstraten, tasked with ironing out a mutiny from supposed Catholic 'comrades' in the Army of Flanders. He hadn't been successful – the mutiny had carried on for months and months, long after he was sent elsewhere – but amid the sieges and the suppression he did take the odd moment to admire the world around him.

Hoogstraten was a beautiful place. Guy would often look out at the flat strawberry-laden meadows and the calm tree-lined rivers and imagine dropping his armour and weaponry and just... vanishing into them completely. *I could so easily become more beast than man*, he would often think. Other times he would imagine his son playing in the fields, his wife chasing him around and laughing in delight. That mirage usually faded all too quickly, leaving him back on the cusp of battle again, a vagrant on foreign shores.

This was enough to get him through the first day. It was even enough to get him through the night in the cell the jailors mockingly nicknamed *Little Ease*: a cramped four-foot offering in which a man could neither sit, stand or lie. And – once more – whenever they gave him some papers to sign, he scrawled that self-same revolt at the bottom:

John Johnson.

The next day they put him on the rack.

With his ankles fastened to pulleys at one end and his wrists strapped to them at the other, Guy soon discovered that a day in the manacles was a feast of honey and ambrosia compared to this. As handles and ratchets and wheels turned... and his joints stretched and his cartilage snapped and his ligaments tore... and all throughout he couldn't tell which infernal noises were coming from the machinery and which were his screams... his torturer kept asking him the same question, over and over.

What is your name? WHAT IS YOUR NAME? WHAT. IS. YOUR. NAME?

Eventually – when those pastoral memory-trips to Flanders could serve him no further – Guy caved in. He gave his oppressors the name they wanted. When the next piece of paper came, the defiant shadow-figure of *John Johnson* had become the very real semi-carcass of *Guido Fawkes*.

As he was thrown back in the cell that evening – a hunched mass of sweat and pain – he allowed himself one self-congratulatory moment.

Fine: they had prised his real name out of him. It was not too much of a defeat – Guy was not invincible, after all. They could have their dismal little victory. By the time any investigative headway could be made from that name, the other plotters would be deep inside their new coven. What his imprisoners *really* wanted were details of the plot itself: the logistics, the locations, the men involved. And if they thought Guy Fawkes was going to give that information, they were in for a big surprise. Had Guy been able to laugh rather than merely cough and shiver, he would have.

The next day they took him to the rack again. And he told them everything.

It didn't even feel like *he* was the one spilling loose. The betrayal – the names, the places, *all of it* – seemed to come from a stranger's voice, one that forced itself out of his body. Tragically, however, Guy could only fool himself so much. He knew damn well that he was the one doing the talking. He was listing every man he had hoped would reshape the nation with him. Every name. Every detail.

Everything.

Guy Fawkes now lived in a world reduced to a nightmare. He was an entity made of pain.

It was during one of these frenzied eternities on the rack that Guy – internally, in a voice that would have shaken the walls had he been able to project it outwards – cried out for his saviour. He needed the hand of God to save him, now more than ever.

With his agony compounded by yet another twist of the rack, Guy kept reaching out to the Almighty. He waited for an answer.

And waited. And waited.

Finally, with his heart as broken as his body, he realised: no answer was coming.

CHAPTER THREE

1606

'You're a very lucky man, Mr Fawkes.'

He had taken it to be a slur. It was taunting mockery, a final slap in the face from someone who clearly enjoyed his job too much.

Attorney General Coke had been waiting for Guy on the upper floors of the Palace of Westminster. Guy wondered exactly why an armed escort had hauled him out of his cell that morning and dragged him here: to the very building he had failed to destroy as a 'free' man. Another jab at humiliation, maybe? Hadn't spending Christmas as a prisoner been enough? Hadn't making Guy enter 1606 behind bars given them sufficient entertainment?

Guy had naturally assumed that he would be taken to Old Palace Yard, where the crowds would be waiting to cheer on his execution. Instead, he'd been smuggled into a carriage and taken along the back roads of Eastcheap and High Timber, circling along Northumberland Street and through Embankment to arrive here. He'd been carried up multiple stairwells – he still found walking difficult after his torture sessions – and unceremoniously heaped into a wooden chair. The chair was placed before a large window, overlooking the ordered chaos down on Old Palace Yard itself.

It took Guy a moment to notice Coke. His once sharp senses weren't quite what they used to be. It took most of his concentration to grit his teeth and rally against the pain in his back. Coke had a strange analytical half-smile on his face, a far cry from his deadly serious visage when Guy had seen him last.

That had been three days ago: January 27th, almost three months after Guy's capture in the cellar of Parliament. Tresham, Grant, Morgan, Rookwood, the Wintours, Keyes, Bates, Digby: they had all been captured, just like him. The remaining others, Guy understood – including Catesby – were killed by gunfire in a last-ditch confrontation in Staffordshire. Coke had taken the stand for the prosecution at the plotters' 'trial' – a showy farce, nothing but a bogus formality before sending the accused to their deaths. Coke had also been the one to read out the punishment once the verdict had been delivered. Piecemeal fragments still rattled around Guy's brain: *to be strangled... then cut down... his bowels and inlayed parts taken out and burnt... his head cut off, which had imagined the mischief... his body to be quartered... his remains left to become prey for the fowls of the air.*

It was to be a fairly unpleasant morning, all in all.

So: yes, Coke's little aside about Guy being a *lucky man* was clearly an act of gloating. Coke had taken a unique loathing to Guy, it seemed, singling him out from among the other plotters. Now the man had arranged for him to be brought up here: a not so pastoral stop-off en route to his execution.

What the hell was going on?

'What...' Guy cleared his throat. He coughed and hawked. It had been around twelve weeks since his torture in earnest. He had only just regained the ability to speak – with great struggle, at that – around a fortnight ago. 'What am I doing here?'

'You're observing,' Coke said.

He nodded towards the window. Guy looked out to see the first of the day's dead-men-in-waiting being pulled towards the scaffold: Thomas Wintour, a ruined man, reaching the end of a two-mile odyssey of being dragged on a wooden bracket behind a horse. The crowd were excited. A precedent had been set: yesterday had already seen the execution of Digby, Grant, Bates and the other Wintour brother. This was the next instalment. Bigger. Better. A real showstopper.

Guy understood what was happening now. This was Coke's warped idea of a victory lap, one final triumphal sneer: he had granted Guy the best seat in the house to watch his brothers in arms die horribly... before he would be taken down himself to face his own end.

It was the theatre of the malign.

Wintour received his punishment. Grant followed afterwards, then Bates received his. Any hopes of a sympathetic executioner or merciful hand were immediately dashed – their deaths were slow and painful, their drawings stretched out, every physical slur accompanied by verbal tirades from the crowd. Upon cutting the heart out of the chest of each man – a high point which made the onlookers swell in jeering delight – the executioner would hold the still-beating mush aloft and yell: '*behold the heart of a traitor*'. Like clockwork it came: more jeers, more delight.

'Hmm.' Coke gave his assessment of the show so far. 'Somewhat disappointing after yesterday's exploits. Your man, Digby, showed particular spirit. Used his last breath to shout '*you lie*' when he was deemed a traitor. Impressive, really – to be so forceful when your own heart has just been torn out of your body. Takes a certain wherewithal.'

'I will not beg for my life,' Guy said.

'I do not expect you to.'

'Then why am I here?'

'I told you. To observe.'

As though in a play directed by Coke himself, the executioner thrust his arm aloft and beckoned for the final attraction of the day.

'*The traitor Guido Fawkes!*' he yelled.

For the fourth time that morning – once more pulled behind a horse – a man was being dragged towards the scaffold.

Guy's eyes widened.

'One of the quirks, I *suppose*, of public displays such as this,' Coke said, gesturing down towards the maelstrom, as though Guy actually needed any further encouragement to stare in disbelief, 'is that, from a certain distance, you really can't tell who is up there on the scaffold, can you? If you dress someone in the correct way... style their appearance just so... make sure that height and build are somewhat matched... then, really, when you think about it, *anyone* could step in and replace the poor devil facing punishment. The crowd won't know the difference. The executioners just want their payment and their lunch – no real preference as to what order. The King himself has more tasteful things to be doing than witnessing vermin meet their demise – so not even *he* would know. The only people who *would* know, I'd say, would be the select few intrepid souls who had orchestrated the whole affair.'

The man was untied from the bracket. To the massed vitriol

of the crowd – this was the big finale and they weren't going to hold back – he was prodded towards the platform.

'Who is he?' Guy asked.

'I don't know his name, I'm afraid. I wasn't the one who recruited him.' Coke gave a snort. '"Recruit" possibly isn't the right term. I wasn't the one who stumbled across the unfortunate bastard, let's just say that.'

The man staggered uneasily across the scaffold.

'The most I know,' Coke went on, 'is that he's a labourer from Gateshead. About your age. Fallen prey to the cancer. His entire body is riddled with tumours. He doesn't have long left. Of course, when he dies, his poor family will be left to fend for themselves. Not much in the way of a pension on those sort of wages, I hear. Unless...'

'Unless you promised to look after them.' Guy's head was foggy... but his strategic savvy was still in place. 'In exchange for...'

'In exchange for taking your place. Yes.' Coke took in the unfolding scene by Guy's side, as though they were two friends watching a musician ply his wares in a Pimlico tavern. 'That man is simply advancing his inevitable death. He takes on the mantle of Guido Fawkes and he takes control of his own demise. His wife, meanwhile, is granted a bursary of fifteen pounds a year for the rest of her natural life. Enough for her and her two children to live out their days very, very comfortably.'

The master of ceremonies read out the accusations – and then outlined the punishments that were now to be enacted. After each step of the bloody agenda ('*hang-ing, dis-embowelling, QUART-ER-ING*') the cheers of massed onlookers grew louder and louder.

The noose was placed around the man's neck.

'Right. Now. Let's see if he follows the advice we were kind enough to offer.' Coke watched as the man timed a fatal jump with the opening of the trapdoor, making sure that the force was such to snap his neck immediately. He gave a sternly satisfied nod. 'Good man. Gets it out of the way, you see. Once you're dead, you're dead. They're still going to cut his body apart, of course... you've got to please the audience... but at least now he won't feel a thing. *Get them before they get you*: it's common guidance shared between criminals should they ever face this kind of mess.' He looked to Guy. 'Mind you. I suppose this is all superfluous information to you, isn't it, Fawkes? I'm sure you would have done exactly the same thing, wouldn't you?'

Guy took in a deep breath. Torn musculature sent stabbing pains through his chest.

He wasn't going to die. Not today.

For some reason... he had been spared. 'Why are you doing this?' he asked.

'*Me*?' Coke smiled, shaking his head. 'I'm just a supporting role in all this. I'm getting paid to assist here. Paid quite handsomely. There's nothing more to it than that. Were it up to me, you'd be down there with the rest of your devil-spawn.'

'So who *is* paying you?' Guy was tiring of Coke's theatrics.

'As I told you. You're a very lucky man.' This was Coke's prompt: the moment he heard the door opening. He nodded to a new arrival and made his way to leave the room. 'Just *look* at you. Such influential friends.'

On the wall nearby, two shadows merged – Coke exiting, another man approaching. Guy recognised something in the footsteps of the newcomer: a certain gait, a distinct canter.

No, he said to himself.

Impossible.

Impossibility then turned to blunt reality. Stood right in front of Guy – looking as unharmed as the day he saw him last – was Francis Tresham.

'Hello, Fawkes,' Francis said.

'You're dead,' Guy told him.

It was a statement of bold fact, no agenda attached: the same way someone would casually say *you're bald* or *you're tall*.

Francis Tresham was no longer of this world. He had died on December 23rd while being held prisoner in the Tower. Guy had been informed by a laughing jailor two days later. 'Here's a Christmas present for you, Fawkes.' The man had smirked. 'One of your lot just croaked it. Name of Tresham. Know him well, did you? Doctor says he had some sort of bladder infection. Painful way to go... but, still, probably better than what you've got in store, isn't it?'

'I'm no ghost, Fawkes,' Francis said. 'Although I admit I'm a little paler than I used to be. Then again, aren't we all?'

'What's going on, Tresham?'

'I presume Coke gave you the layman's version. As of this morning – well, as of late last year in my case – you and I are officially dead. Every record kept in this country will show that Francis Tresham and Guido Fawkes are no longer among the living.'

'How...?' Guy winced. Another knife-twist of pain shot up his back. 'How did you...'

'I have resources,' Francis explained. 'My family is a very wealthy one, as I'm sure you know. My inheritance was not insubstantial. I might have been flippant with that money in the past, yes. But when it came to our capture I realised I could use it for the highest purpose of all. To buy our freedom.'

Guy shifted in his chair. The pain always intensified if he sat in one position for too long. Beads of sweat condensed on his forehead. He was finding it harder and harder to concentrate. But there were still questions to be asked... so many questions...

'The others?' Guy managed to ask. He craned his neck and

looked back out of the window – down to the vista below, where the crowds were dissipating, their thrills now abated, thousands of people tiredly sluicing back to their daily monotony. On the scaffold itself the assorted body parts and entrails were being collected, ready for display atop pikes on the outskirts of the city. As enshrined in law, they would stay there until the birds had feasted. 'I could see them. They were not imposters.'

'No.' Francis looked visibly upset, his thin, arched eyebrows meeting in the middle as he frowned, his piercing dark eyes softening for a moment. 'Regrettably not. Secretive dealings like this come at a hefty price. I would have dearly loved to save everyone. My fortune did not stretch that far. I had to make a difficult choice. I could only afford to spare myself... and one other.'

'You chose me?' Guy asked. 'Over your cousin? Your own blood?'

'I'll say it again. It was not an easy choice.' Francis sighed, lowering his head. He was silent for a moment. 'The obvious way forward would have been to save Robert, yes. My family, my kin. But I had higher considerations to deal with, Fawkes. This decision went beyond earthly concerns such as flesh and blood. I had to think: *who is the most spiritually bonded to me?* Who am I most aligned with when it comes to God? I believe that's you, Fawkes. You saved my life in Barnet that day. You trusted that I was on the one true path when the others did not. Who else could I save, if not for you?'

Francis was staring at Guy with a look Guy had never seen before: a fervent brotherly love, an awed connection, a sense that the rewards of Heaven were theirs alone. Guy was about to speak – to ask, not unreasonably, what the next step in Francis's master plan was – when he hunched over. A burning flurry throughout his torso was accompanied by something else: a deep *deep* itch.

Guy knew what this meant. His muscles were slowly beginning to heal. He hadn't paid any heed to his recovery before: healing had seemed like a wasted enterprise, considering the circumstances. Now he tried to straighten up, adjusting his frame, positioning the muscles correctly – when he was thrashed by another lasso-whip, one that set his nerves on fire. He hunched forward again, trying to vomit, gasping as he brought up nothing but bile. His vision turned white. The world faded back into view. The pain subsided. For now.

He felt Francis's hands gently clasping around his own.

'My God. What have you *been* through?' Francis had tears in his eyes. 'You must believe me when I tell you, my brother. Had I been able to save you from your torture, I would have. By the time I had been apprehended and managed to rope accomplices into my scheme... they had already set about you.' Guy noticed: Francis's tears were not those of sorrow. They were of happiness. Seraphic optimism. 'It's a testament to your strength that you made it through. Now we need that strength of yours to *grow*. You need to rest and recover. The next step in our journey will be a demanding one. Rewarding, too, of course.' He gazed off to one side for a moment, as though fixated on an imaginary horizon. The tears only welled further. 'So, *so* rewarding.' He looked back to Guy. 'But it will not be easy. Nothing worthwhile ever is.'

Guy tried to speak again – he wanted to know the exact details, the ins and outs, the military-grade specifics of whatever Francis had arranged – but he found that he couldn't.

'Come, Fawkes.' Francis put an arm round Guy's shoulder and helped the man to his feet. Dizzily, Guy just about managed to stay upright. Guy felt a sudden rush of anger – *this* was what those bastard torturers had done to him, taken a man who had fought bravely at countless battles across Europe and turned him into a woozy invalid. 'I'll help you outside.'

'Outside?' Guy said. It was little more than a hoarse whisper – but at this point just speaking at all was a victory.

'I have transport waiting. A carriage. It will take you to a safe house in Buckinghamshire. There you will take a few months to recover. I will come to visit periodically – I have much to do. But you will be tended to by good people, I promise. People who will nurse you back to full health and offer you all the spiritual nourishment you need along the way.'

'I...' Guy wheezed. No more words would come. 'I...'

'Please. Save your strength. I will reveal everything when you're good and ready.' Francis gave a reassuring smile, the kind a parent would give to a child who had just grazed their knee. 'But don't worry. You're going to like my plan, Fawkes. A lot.'

Francis was taking no chances. As soon as he sat in the carriage, a burlap sack was placed over Guy's head. While Coke had been right about Guy's face being unrecognisable to the average passer-by... it only took one person to change that. A one-in-a-million chance was still a chance.

So: Guy's head remained covered until he reached his destination – at which point one of his wordless escorts removed it for him. *Hurleyford House*, the signs read. It was the kind of manor for which the term *house* seemed a snub: a palatial estate amid several acres of land, a private many-roomed kingdom. Guy wondered who it belonged to. The Vaux family, maybe? Or some other super-wealthy benefactors? Francis moved in some very prominent circles – and he probably had numerous favours to call in. The three Cs in action: capital, collateral and connections.

Guy was weary from the journey. He was in pain from sitting still too long. Flanked by escorts, he uneasily made his way from the carriage to the property itself. Inside there was an ornate hallway and cavernous drawing room: wholly legitimate-looking, an ideal cover for any on-the-spot inspections.

In a tight corridor behind the drawing room there was a hidden doorway compartment. It could be unlatched via a series of ordered wall-panel presses. Going through that door took Guy to another level of the building entirely, a downstairs maze-like area of varying rooms that stretched the length of the entire property.

He noticed that his travelling escorts had gone. Now he was being helped along by a couple of kindly looking women – one younger, one older, maybe a mother and her daughter. They ushered him to a quiet room with a bed, desk and oil lantern. The temptation to lie down was almost overwhelming.

'You can sleep soon, my dear,' the older woman said. 'We just need to do this first.' The younger woman covered the end of the bed with some tattered-looking sheets, gesturing for Guy to sit there. He did. Then they went about cutting his hair and shaving his beard. Not too tired to feel shame, Guy suddenly realised how filthy he was. His hair was matted and likely lice-infested. The women hacked away at his knotted locks, leaving only a close crop. They undressed Guy and gently bathed him before drying him off. He sank back into the straw bedding. He exhaled a long sigh. He had forgotten what an actual bed felt like. If someone told Guy this was where he would lie for the rest of his life, he would have been content. More than that: he could happily die here. With that option not on the cards, he did the next best thing.

He slept.

Sleep was a revelation in itself. When he awoke after a solid twenty hours out cold, Guy felt so refreshed it was as though all his wounds had been healed. He tried to get out of bed. He immediately regretted it.

He was feeling better, yes. But better was a long way off from good. His muscles still burned. His joints throbbed. His back was on fire. His ankles and wrists were under constant barrage from invisible needles.

Guy was naturally a man of action. It took a couple of days for him to realise that this was his primary mission now: *doing nothing*. He slept. He ate, wholesome meals of stew and bread and ale that seemed like manna compared to the tepid gruel he'd suffered in the Tower. The food was delivered by an assortment of people who simply smiled and left it by his bedside. Guy wasn't offended by their silence. Having to talk back was an extra burden he just didn't need.

As the early days flowed past, Guy kept expecting a visit from Francis: some more details from him at least, a small concession towards explanation. The man never came. The days turned into weeks – but that was just fine with Guy. Rest and recovery took up most of his time. He began to familiarise himself with the day-to-day noises of the mansion around him: putting imaginary faces to the voices he heard regularly in the hallway outside, becoming attuned to specific time-of-day sounds like a pet on a feeding schedule. Most of the conversations were indistinct.

There was one man, however, who had a habit of conducting discussions right outside Guy's door.

Guy knew the type. This kind of man had no specific label, but his role was well known among certain Catholics: he was a fixer, a forger of records, a person you turned to when the authorities were closing in and your only recourse was a new name and new life entirely.

When Guy was able to walk without aid again – only a few steps across the room, yes, but that was an achievement in itself – he began to hover by the door and listen to the conversations.

'You leave in the morning,' the man was telling someone. 'Before sunrise. I have arranged transport. You'll go by the Thames at first. There are moorings here, towards the outskirts of the estate. You'll go to Hythe and on to Port Lympne. From there you're going north – Atherton, a mining town, three days away, maybe four. Once you arrive head to Chanters Farmhouse. You will be provided with new documentation and new dwellings. Work will consist of manual labour. Not best befitting a man of your education, I understand – but nothing else can be done.'

'Will I...' The other man sounded younger, a sprite with a jittery childish whine. 'Will I ever see my family again?'

'You know the answer to that.'

'I can't do it.'

'That is entirely up to you. But you also know that by staying near London you are putting your family at risk. At best, they could have their reputations destroyed. At worst... well. I don't think I need to elaborate on that, do I?' There was an anguished silence.

'I'll do it,' the younger man finally said.

'Good. The life of a true believer is not an easy one. Don't lose faith. You are a good man. Good things await you in time.'

The conversation faded as the two men drifted away. Guy tried to open the door – for some reason, he yearned to see what they looked like – only to discover that it was locked. His caretakers had figured that Guy would want to explore the grounds as soon as he was halfway able. They had been right.

He staggered back to the bed and lay down again. That was when the dark thought returned.

He didn't know precisely what it was. He couldn't put his

finger on what this bizarre inner voice was talking about. He just knew that... somewhere along the line... his torture in the Tower had not just sapped him physically.

It had snatched something from his soul as well.

I've got a revelation waiting for you, Guy, the voice said, more mocking than a thousand jailors. *Don't try to figure it out just yet. You're not ready. I'm waiting for the right moment to let you in on a big secret, you see... and when you guess what it is, you're not going to like it one bit.*

An instinctive rebel, Guy tried to disobey the voice. He tried to think harder, to decipher things. He had no luck.

Patience, Guy, the voice said. *Enjoy your innocence while it still lasts. Sleep, now. Sleep.*

So he did.

He dreamt of strawberry fields and still rivers.

More weeks went by. They became months. Guy grew steadier on his feet and stronger in his build. He could speak properly again. He began to exchange pleasantries with the people who brought him food. His favourite was a plump middle-aged woman named Mary: a doting sort whose bedside manner could quell the rage of a rabid fox.

'Come on,' Mary said one morning, pulling the sheets back. 'Up.'

'What?' Guy asked.

'You've been cooped up in this room too long.' She smiled. 'You're still going to be here a while longer – but we might as well give you the run of the place. Oh – and maybe see if you can't help out with some of the chores as well.'

The estate was no labyrinth – yet after so long in a single room it felt like a whole new world to Guy. There were around ten other bedrooms down in the cellar level. Their inhabitants fell into two camps: recovering invalids kept behind locked doors or fugitive Catholics staying here while they planned their next move. These men rarely shared names or even conversation: it was deemed more than enough to give a nod of greeting now and then, wordless affirmation that they were all in the same bind.

Guy had only been half-cogent when he saw the main property for the first time. Elements of Catholic paraphernalia – rosaries, statues, crucifixes, beads – took pride of place. They could be swiped away and hidden within seconds – yet the gesture still felt daringly blatant.

'You have had no inspections here?' he asked Mary.

'They have no reason to suspect this place.' She shook her head. 'We're well-prepared, of course, should we ever get a knock at the door. But God willing we've been fine so far.'

Fine so far. That put Guy's mind at ease. Indeed, the men and women here showed an efficiency that could put many an army unit to shame. Guy needed no instructions on how he could help out around the place: he immediately got to work on much-needed repairs, keeping the property clean, assisting with cooking and serving meals for his fellow haven-dwellers. While he was waiting for Francis to return – 'Mr Tresham will be back when he is good and ready, that's all I know,' Mary told him, and would say no more than that – it was a few weeks of domestic purgatory. Guy would be lying if he said he didn't see the lure of a homely life. It was quiet. Dependable. Predictable.

He felt himself improving physically day upon day, sometimes getting noticeably more agile within the space of a morning to an afternoon. He glumly realised that he would never be the same as at his peak – age had seen to that, even before his torture – but this was not something that concerned him often. He had bigger things to worry about.

He still couldn't shake that inner voice. That promise of a dark epiphany.

Oh, don't you worry, Guy, it would say to him. *It's coming.*

It seemed strange watching the date come and go: November 5th 1606, a full year since the plotters' scheme had been shot to hell. Guy had been at Hurleyford House for ten months now. It was, many on site remarked, the longest they had known anyone to stay – and that record was only growing by the day. He had almost forgotten what life was like beforehand.

As for Francis Tresham? He seemed a distant prospect too. Guy had almost given up hope of seeing him again when the man turned up unannounced one evening in early December. He stepped in from the foggy dusk, flanked by two burly-looking gentlemen. The two men were dressed in ordinary civilian garb – but their posture and stance was unmistakable. These men were trained guards and fighters, possibly military types. The carefully hewn bagginess of their clothes couldn't hide the truth from Guy's trained eye: they were both armed underneath, carrying weapons, most likely flintlock muskets.

Francis didn't bother introducing his two new associates. Instead, he headed straight over to Guy. He flung his arms around the man.

'Fawkes! My brother!' Francis stretched back from the hug, grinning wildly, taking in his first sight of Guy for nearly a year. 'You look better than I could have imagined! A different man!'

'I have recovered well,' Guy said.

'That you have!' His hand now clasped on Guy's shoulder, Francis turned to address the nearby house staff. 'We should give thanks. Everyone, come. Make preparations. I gave Father Willis word while on my way. He should be here soon.'

'Mr Tresham.' Mary cautiously raised her voice. 'I thought we agreed. To hold congress before it is fully dark is very risky–'

'It *will* be fully dark by the time Willis gets here, woman,' Francis snapped. He caught himself: a quiet rebuke under his breath for losing his temper. He gave an affectionate smile. 'Forgive me. Please. But what is this talk of "holding congress"? Let us call it what it is.' He clasped his hands together before saying the word: one he would not dare utter outside these walls. 'Mass.'

And so Mass was held.

Chairs were arranged into makeshift pews and an altar was improvised. Father Willis arrived roughly an hour after Francis had shown up. Guy vaguely recognised the man: he had seen him loitering around the safe house yet had no idea he was a priest. Now dressed in the splendour of his vestments, Guy wondered how he could have thought Willis was anything *but*: he was steeped in quiet dignity, an ambassador of fluid grace.

'Francis brought you here?' Willis asked Guy as they were setting up the room.

'Yes.' Guy nodded.

'The ladies say you are almost part of the furniture now.'

'They might be right.'

'That's not so bad.' Willis shrugged. 'The world outside gets darker every day. An extended sabbatical could be just the tonic.'

'You see much of the world outside?' Guy asked.

'Enough to know how grim things are. When I'm not here I harbour another safe house in Wapping Marsh. Just next to the central warehouse on Monza Street. You know London well?'

'Yes.' Guy knew London like a lover's body: the good, the bad, the taken for granted and – every now and then – the unexpected. Speaking of which: 'You're a trusting man, Father.'

'Am I?'

'You don't even know my name.' Guy handed Willis a neatly folded white corporal cloth. 'Yet you're sharing your secrets.'

'Oh.' Willis took the cloth and smiled. 'Not all of them.'

The ceremony began. Everyone present – the carers, the hideaways, Francis and his mystery entourage – was bowed in devout reverence. Guy was among them... at least until that inner voice came back.

With a dawning horror, Guy knew exactly what was happening to him.

No. He fought inside, trying to stem the voice. *No, no, NO–*

You needed to have this revelation at this moment, Guy, the voice said. *This had to take place now. It was the only time you could truly realise.*

You are the Devil, Guy countered. *You are the Devil inside me and I renounce your evil–*

I am merely a product of your own mind, the voice said.

You are the Devil, Guy tried again. *The Devil. And I will–*

You will do nothing, the voice said – and this was the final time Guy ever heard it speak. Its work had been done. *I am not the Devil. And you know precisely why.*

Yes. Guy did.

The world around him seemed to slow down, a blurry underwater reconstruction of real life. With mounting despair Guy took in the sacred rites that had always meant so much to him. The Liturgy of the Word. The Eucharist. The Epiclesis. The Anamnesis. *Everything.*

And he realised that he felt absolutely nothing.

It was a thread. He understood that now. It had started during his torture – and it had been unravelling ever since. While on the rack he had tried to reach out to God. He had been met with only eternal blackness. It had taken him until now to truly realise.

That blackness was *all there was.*

Tears of rage and regret formed in his eyes. He glanced over to Francis. The other man was also tearful – tears of love and allegiance to his Heavenly Father – and assumed that Guy was sharing the same zeal. He gave a smile of gilded fraternity. *We are united in faith,* he was saying.

He was wrong.

Guy now knew the truth. There was nothing awaiting him after this – no reward, no Heaven. There was no Hell. There was no Devil.

There was no God.

There was nothing.

Guy went to his room and fell into a dreamless sleep. Perhaps this was a moment of madness, he tried to tell himself. A test of his vision and loyalty.

When he woke up in the morning, he felt exactly the same. Empty. Bereaved. Adrift.

Someone knocked at his door. Guy slid out of bed and answered. It was Francis and his two travelling companions.

'Morning, Fawkes.'

'Morning.'

'I'm sorry to spring this upon you. But speed is of the essence regarding our departure.'

'Our departure?' Guy frowned.

'Get dressed,' Francis said. 'Get your things together.'

'I don't have any things.'

'Perfect.' Francis was holding something behind his back. He brought it round for Guy to view: a set of officious-looking documents. 'A very fitting attitude, I must say. All you will need now is *this...*' He tapped his finger against one of the papers. 'And whatever awaits you in your new land.'

Guy's eyes darted down to the documents Francis was clutching. The language was not English – but he recognised it. He could speak and read it well. This was why he understood the two men behind Francis when they glanced to each other and spoke in their native tongue.

'He seems distressed,' one of them said. 'Do you think he'll refuse?'

'He can't,' the other said. 'I don't think he'd dare try.'

One particular sentence on the documents stuck out to Guy. It seemed to shine and glow with prominence.

'You and I, Fawkes,' Francis said, nodding eagerly. 'We're going to Spain. We're going to join those who *really* want to protect the True Faith. No more half measures. No more hiding. We're on the winning team now.'

Guy looked at that sentence again. *Santo Oficio de la Inquisición,* it read. The Holy Office of the Inquisition.

CHAPTER FOUR

1606

After that meeting in Barnet – beginning with a false accusation of betrayal, ending with a vow that now he *would* become a betrayer – it hadn't taken Francis Tresham long to decide on his next course of action.

Francis had been recruited to the Gunpowder Plot quite late in the scheme. He knew that his cousin had only approached him due to his perceived wealth.

Francis had told Catesby a half-lie: he was no longer a man of huge means, he had insisted, after frittering away a good chunk of his father's inheritance. He could help them out... but he was no endless money-fountain.

There was some truth to this. Francis had indeed thrown his father's money around – a tradition that had started when the dour old bastard was still alive and had coughed up bail money for Francis on numerous occasions. But Francis was far from destitute. He'd managed to put aside a fair amount of funds over the years, as well as a good annual income from various dealings. He had been waiting until he was truly convinced of this plot to blow up Parliament before offering Catesby and co a *real* investment.

Francis – out of genuine concern, mind – had voiced his reservations about the plot... which led to him being blamed for this mystery letter exposing the plan... which very nearly led to his death. And yet: they all still wanted him to play along, after accusing him of the grossest betrayal? Those fools! Those sickening faithless imbeciles! Francis couldn't believe that he had once considered the men to be friends. Now he knew what they *truly* thought of him.

They had labelled him a turncoat, an apostate. So he labelled them right back. They were vermin. Scum. Lower than that: they were heretics.

Apart from Guy, of course. Guy Fawkes: the only one in that accursed bunch who was still marshalled by the light of God.

The only one worth saving.

Francis had had many dealings with Spain. His father had too, spying a Catholic kinship in a nation considered England's 'enemy'. Much illicit funding had been ferried from Spain to England under the Tresham family watch – all of which went towards undermining the Protestant oppressors and maybe even setting the groundwork for a Spanish invasion. The Treshams also sent much funding back to Spain: money to embolden and empower Spain's mighty Catholic institutions.

Francis had, therefore, visited the Spanish Embassy in London a number of times. The splendour of the place never failed to impress him: a huge rented town house complex just off

Ely Place. The Spanish Ambassador himself – a wiry, bright-eyed man in his forties named Baltasar de Zúñiga – was no less resplendent. His style was the embodiment of impractical yet elegant: pitch-black doublet and an impeccable millstone ruff collar.

'*Señor* Tresham.' Zúñiga smiled politely as Francis was ushered into his quarters. 'What a pleasant surprise. How may I help you today?'

'I think,' Francis said, 'I am the one who can help you.'

'Oh.' Zúñiga raised an eyebrow. 'Is that right?'

'I think... I can help lots of people.'

He was a practised storyteller. That was what his mother had always told him – although she had never really meant it as a compliment, more of a chastisement for his convincing lies. *You could use this talent of yours for so much more, Francis,* she had often said. Francis found this curious: what better talent was there than getting what he wanted?

He had Zúñiga rapt as he explained everything. He didn't go into the specifics of the plan – what it entailed, who was involved – but he made sure that the point was clear. He, noble and wandering Francis Tresham, just so happened to have unwittingly discovered a terrorist plot being devised in the name of England's Catholics. And he was deathly afraid.

'You worry,' Zúñiga summed up, 'that more damage may come to the nation's Catholics from this plot than any benefits.'

'Precisely.' Francis nodded.

'Why do you think this?'

'Ambassador,' Francis sighed, 'should this plot succeed, England's tirade against Catholics will surely escalate. I foresee more oppression. More punishment. Mass killings, even. Enforced exodus.'

'Then, why, might I ask, are you here talking to me rather than taking great pains to stop it?' Zúñiga folded his arms. 'I understand that you might be consigning those involved to death. But, if things are as grave as you fear, then that is a trade you must make. The good of the whole Catholic community takes precedence over these... misguided souls.'

'Things are not that simple.' Francis was now entering his play. If he could swing Zúñiga's favour, the next few moments could change his life forever. 'By accident I am further embroiled in this plan than I would like. To sabotage it now would mean throwing myself onto the fire.'

'I see.' Zúñiga slowly nodded. 'Well. We all have to make sacrifices sometimes. That's the surest evidence there is of a faithful man.' Francis couldn't help but notice that Zúñiga was idly toying with one of his gold sovereign rings as he said this. He felt anger growing.

Don't you lecture me on sacrifice, you DISGUSTING GARNET-BEDECKED HYPOCRITE–

He took a deep breath. Settled.

'I feel I have much more to offer the Catholic faith,' Francis said. 'Both myself and another of the plotters. If the authorities were to exclude us from any punishment, we would happily devote our lives to strengthening our community.'

'You would bribe the authorities?'

'I would persuade them.'

'By means of money.' Zúñiga glared.

'For many men there are no better means.'

'And where would this money come from? You are a reasonably wealthy man, *Señor* Tresham, but this is beyond your finances, I feel.'

'The money would come from the Kingdom of Spain, of

course. A wise investment to oversee the future safety of England's Catholics.'

'You ask a lot.'

'I am not done asking.' Francis saw the surprise in Zúñiga's eyes – but kept on going before the ambassador could interrupt. 'This other plotter and I. We would no longer be able to stay in the country. But we could begin new lives in Spain. We could use our faith and our talents – both of which are manifest – to serve the Catholic Church in the greatest way possible. By devoting ourselves to one of Spain's proudest institutions.'

Francis didn't need to say the word. Zúñiga saw where this was going. 'You wish,' he said, 'to join the *Inquisición*?'

'Yes, Ambassador.'

Zúñiga closed his eyes and rubbed his temples.

'*Señor* Tresham,' Zúñiga said after a long moment. 'Why would I – why would *Spain* – agree to this?'

'You are widely seen as the protectorate of Catholics in England.' Francis straightened up to his full height, hoping to make his final selling point as compelling as possible. 'It is a well-deserved reputation. It is also your Holy Duty. I would loathe to see you reject either of them.'

'And if I refuse?' Zúñiga's glare was unyielding.

'Then this plot will go ahead. And you, in a roundabout way, will be responsible for the untold future misery of thousands of English Catholics.'

Zúñiga lapsed into silence again.

'Joining the *Inquisición*,' he finally said. 'You understand it is not a holiday, *Señor* Tresham. It is not a mercenary contract you can fulfil and then depart. It is a lifelong act of fealty. A commitment like no other.'

'I know this, Ambassador.'

'And your friend?'

'I believe he knows this too.'

Zúñiga sat back in his chair. He pushed the tips of his fingers together, lost in contemplation.

'Has anyone ever told you, *Señor* Tresham,' he asked, 'that you are one of the most arrogant men alive?'

'Now and again.' Francis gave a thin smile.

Zúñiga remained still for another moment – then threw his hands back in the air, like he was quite literally tossing any caution to the wind.

'Very well,' he said. 'Let's do it.'

Francis made his next move.

He never actually found out who wrote the letter of betrayal in question. A couple of potential suspects sprung neatly to mind. It could have been Monteagle's sister, a woman with her ear forever to the recusant network. It could have been Edward Oldcorne, a priest known in dissident circles for his nosiness.

Whatever. Francis had no real interest in who had opened the barn so the horse could bolt. What interested him most was *what that letter could do for him*. It was out there now: so how could he seize upon this gift?

Francis was also an acquaintance of Thomas Ward, the initial recipient of the letter... who had passed it on to his master, Lord Monteagle. The trouble was: Monteagle was a man who would no doubt stay quiet. He was a tremulous and meek soul, someone who had no desire to implicate himself in the world's larger dramas. Well – he was out of luck. Francis could not afford for Monteagle to keep that letter to himself – or even dawdle in the slightest in passing it on. He had to provoke Ward into spurring Monteagle on.

The provocation itself came with the pointed end of a steel blade, jabbed against the flesh of Ward's lower back in a darkened alleyway. With his face shrouded, Francis gave Ward some very direct instructions.

'Speak to your master,' Francis hissed. 'Impress upon him the importance of the letter and its contents. Insist that he takes it to the King immediately. If you don't, your family will be finding your body for weeks. Am I clear?'

It turned out that, yes, he was very clear.

With the letter now hopefully en route to the King, Francis took his airs of persuasion and applied them liberally to the necessary targets: Popham, Coke, a selection of nobody bit-players in the Tower of London who he nonetheless needed to convert. Some were hesitant, even outraged, threatening to alert the authorities. That all changed when the subject of money came up. Francis had a signed yet secret declaration given to him by Ambassador Zúñiga, a promise of huge funds to see this scheme through.

Francis laid down the agenda. He set out the timetable. He put forth his requirements.

When the mass arrest of the plotters took place, he was to be included among them. A cover story would be concocted about him being imprisoned in the Tower of London. A *later* cover story would then emerge, telling the world about the tragic death of one Francis Tresham. Francis mulled over his possible method of demise before he hit upon the perfect one – a strangury, a fatal blockage of the urinary tract. Very appropriate. Catesby, Wright, the Wintours: what more were they worth to him than a stream of piss?

The arrests came. The plot was foiled. Francis was surprised to see exactly how much the story captured the public imagination. On the night the news broke, many across London were burning effigies of the plotters, setting them ablaze in an act of celebration. Francis didn't approve. It was an undignified outburst; gratingly modern. At least, he assured himself, it would never catch on.

Francis engaged very little with the rest of London over the next few months. He sailed to and from Spain a few times, setting down the groundwork for his reinvented life over there, meeting with representatives of the church and the *Inquisición*, charming them into malleable pawns. In the midst of his travels he made sure that he was back in London for the execution of the plotters: he wouldn't miss *that* for the world, after all, and he also wanted to be there to ease Guy through the first stage of his liberation face to face.

More travels followed: further meetings with Spanish dignitaries and religious leaders. By the time Francis had finished bolstering the reputation of Fawkes and himself, the *Inquisición* was eagerly awaiting the conscription of these two fine young men.

Francis often dreamt about how history would perceive him and Fawkes. *They are among the greatest Englishmen to draw breath*, citizens of a future Catholic nation would say. *And yet... they had to flee their homeland.* The irony would amaze many; astonish every schoolroom in the country.

History would be kind to him. No, no – more than kind. It would swoon. It would fawn.

Oh, history would kiss the feet of Francis Tresham. And rightly enough.

Guy was a master at assessing situations quickly: evaluating threats, tallying up the odds, ticking off every possible getaway route.

He had no intention of following Francis's plan. The whole demented scheme was madness. Guy had been expecting something hare-brained from Francis, yes – but this was truly startling.

Talking could provide no route out of this, however... no matter how slick Guy's song and dance could be. The two men accompanying Francis had clearly been sent to ensure Guy's co-operation. And while Guy could hold his own Spanish-wise, he knew that no words would deter them from their mission.

He would need to pick his moment to get out of this. That moment was certainly not now.

'I hope your silence is one of joy rather than alarm,' Francis said. His grin was full of certainty... but it was starting to flex a little at the edges. Guy knew Francis was only seconds away from fielding an uncomfortable question: *have I made a mistake? A most grievous error?*

Is Fawkes less of a brother than I thought?

Guy never held much stock in drama or theatrics. He considered the whole thing folly, a lofty game. But – returning Francis's triumphant smile with one of his own – he stepped into a performance that would set the Globe Theatre alight. 'Joy, of course.' Guy laughed, flinging his arms around Francis. The Spaniards backed off, slightly uncomfortable at such a display of affection. *Good,* thought Guy. *The more distance between them and I, the better.*

Francis, meanwhile, had no such hesitation – now laughing wildly too, he returned the hug. 'What else could it be? Lead the way, brother. Lead the way.'

The curtain of the carriage was drawn. Guy didn't care: he was not in the mood for sightseeing. He was instead listening to Francis, sat directly across from him, jabbering excitedly while the two Spaniards sat in wary silence.

'We'll do this for the others,' Francis was saying. 'For their memory. We might not have been able to change the way things are here in England... but we can uphold the righteousness of our faith overseas. We'll be more powerful. We'll have authority. Command. We'll have no need for gunpowder, brother.'

Guy said nothing. He just nodded enthusiastically, pretending to be swept away in awe at Francis's plan. The man's religious fervour was weirdly admirable. He may have been a lunatic but he was a convicted lunatic. Unlike Guy, of course – and how exactly would Francis react if he found he was sharing a carriage with a freshly minted non-believer?

Guy envied the man. While other Catholics had a loathing for atheists, he had always pitied them – and, now he was lost in unbelief, he realised truly *how* pitiable they were. Was this it for him? An earthly struggle and then just... nothingness?

One thing was for certain: he was not swearing lifelong fealty to *any* inquisition, Spanish or otherwise. Even the old Guy had had his reservations about them: wondering if their brutality was more of an affront to the Holy Spirit than a campaign of preservation.

He had already given up his faith. That was a tragedy. But he was *damned* if he was going to relinquish control of his life... his fate... his *direction*.

However Guy was going to live now, it was not going to be under the warped guidance of Francis Tresham.

It was unmistakable: the summertime heat-stench of Billingsgate docks, the cooked sewage of the Thames forming an almost walkable crust. Countless vessels of varying sizes bobbed in the filthy water. New arrivals stepped onto English land and immediately winced at the smell: handkerchiefs being raised to mouths by pampered ladies or softened-with-age military captains.

Dock workers rolled their eyes in disdain.

Guy wondered how he must appear to these toiling dockhands: a man of privilege or a salt-of-the-earth type like them? Then he realised: they thought absolutely *nothing* about him. Things were going just as Francis had planned. As they departed the carriage and made their way through the bustling throng, Guy understood that the quartet – him, Francis, Spaniard One and Spaniard Two – posed no special sight. They were just more people among the crowds, the next best thing to invisible.

Guy glanced around. The two Spaniards flanked him closely. They were perhaps not fully alarmed about the prospect of him dashing off – but they had clearly considered it. Guy felt his heartbeat begin to quicken – he probably *could* still make his way through if he really wanted to – but rationality soon overcame rashness. The crowds were too tightly packed together. He wouldn't make it far. The time wasn't right. Yet.

'I've arranged passage on a vessel called the *Guadiana*,' Francis outlined. 'It's a Portuguese supply ship. We'll be at sea for five days before it drops us off in Spain en route, a covert stop at Puerto de Vigo. Not the most comfortable ride – but you're a man of some fortitude, aren't you, Brother Fawkes?'

'Absolutely,' Guy said. He could see the Spanish guards on either side of him, blurred entities in his peripheral vision. They were a little further away now. But still too close. 'When do we set sail?'

'In about ten minutes,' Francis said, flashing Guy an artful smile.

'You've certainly timed this well,' Guy said.

'Oh. You know me. Never a man to labour plans when the

here and now will do. Some say that patience is a virtue. I say that efficiency is. Don't you agree?'

'Absolutely,' Guy said again. But he wasn't really listening. He was instead stretching his neck back to look up as they approached the *Guadiana* itself – their erstwhile transport, a sturdy-looking vessel framed against an uncharacteristically sunny London sky. Nearby dockhands assisted the crew in rolling barrels of copper and tin up the gangway and to the main cargo hold.

Others carried huge crates packed with raw wool and cotton.

Francis looked slightly irritable as the four of them stood and waited for the gangway to clear. Eventually it did – and, with a flourish of the requisite boarding papers from Francis's hand, they made their way on board.

It happened in the crew quarters. It was the only place it could happen: the one moment where a deadly risk was at least salvageable.

In the middle of a voyage, the quarters – stretching out below deck, wedged beneath a low ceiling that would surely be the bane of any taller crewmen – would be fully occupied, packed both night and day. With the men all up on deck preparing to embark, it was completely empty. Francis had asked the captain if he and his party could take a look at the quarters for themselves. The captain had simply shrugged: *you're paying your passage fair and square, you can dance around them singing 'Patty-cake' if you want to.*

'Not as cramped as I had expected, actually,' Francis had mused, sizing up the space. 'Obviously I've taken pains to secure us the best lodging. We may be sleeping near the crew but we certainly don't have to suffer the same indignities.' Guy heard one of the Spanish escorts – both of whom had joined them in the quarters – lean over to his accomplice and mutter a mocking appraisal: *the stupid arsehole thinks he's on some sort of floating tavern.*

It was enough of a distraction.

Guy's body didn't co-operate at first. He hadn't expected it to – which is why he put more force than usual behind the punch.

His fist connected fiercely with the Spaniard's jaw. The man's head slammed against the nearby wood-panelled wall. He slumped to the floor immediately, out cold. Guy allowed himself a second of surprise – he was rusty, he'd expected to need another punch or two – before he arched round to face the other Spaniard. Instinctive muscle memory took over. The other Spaniard was just able to reel off a grimace – *I knew you were going to be trouble, Englishman* – before Guy swung a fist at his face too. The man staggered backwards. Guy wasn't relying on luck this time: he needed to make *sure* the man was unconscious. He clamped a fistful of the man's hair, yanking his head forward and slamming it hard against the opposite wall.

Guy quickly reached into the man's overcoat and pulled out the musket. He whirled around, pointing it directly at Francis.

Francis was stunned. Stupefied.

But not for long.

A dark understanding fell over his face.

Guy could see: Francis was angry with himself for misjudging things. But he was far, far angrier with Guy.

'Not one step closer.' Guy held the musket in Francis's direction.

'You've made that very clear,' Francis said.

'I mean to vacate this ship. Now.'

'I don't think I can allow that, brother.' Francis made the word *brother* sound like *demon*.

'I don't care for what you allow. I'm leaving.'

'Don't care for much, it turns out, do you, Fawkes?' Francis gave a bitter smirk. 'Not loyalty. Not reason. Certainly not God. Let's draw a line from this to... whatever comes next, shall we? What exactly do you hope to gain?'

'I am leaving.' Guy didn't have time to play Francis's games. 'Do not try to stop me.'

'One word.' Francis raised his eyes to the ceiling of the quarters, as though he could perfectly see through to the decks above. 'That's all it will take. I just have to shout and a dozen men will be down here. You're a fine soldier – if not slightly dilapidated these days. But I still don't think the odds would be in your favour, do you?'

A second passed – or was it a century? Guy tensed his hand around the musket.

Francis opened his mouth, letting out a full-throated bellow like an animal's mating display:

'GET DOWN HERE NOW! FAWKES HAS–'

He said nothing more.

Guy fired. He shot straight at Francis's head. Francis was thrown back by the impact, his body lying in a smouldering pile of debris.

Guy immediately turned tail. He vaulted over the unconscious Spaniards. He ran onto the deck. He dropped the musket as he went. Why bother keeping it? If he needed to reload, he wouldn't have time.

Guy emerged into commotion. Many had heard Francis's attempted call for help – but it had coincided with another shout, a firmer and louder bellow from the harbour master:

'DEPARTURE!'

The ship was casting off.

Guy pelted across the deck, barging into crewmen, pushing them out of the way. The first rumblings of motion already shook the whole vessel; the gangway was long retracted by now. But the docks were still close.

Guy could still make it back.

A number of smaller crates had been bound and stacked on deck, lesser priority cargo that the crew could stow away once the voyage had begun. Guy scrambled up on top of them, hoping they would give him the vertical boost he needed – when the stack collapsed beneath him, boxes splintering, his feet losing their way.

He was falling. He had been pitched over the side.

Ah well, he thought. *I was going that way anyway.*

He slammed into the murky Thames. The broken crates followed, each one crashing into the water with ten times the force of Guy's impact, a miniature tidal wave now sluicing inland. Large wooden slats and heavy sacks of food supplies landed on Guy, weighing him down, threatening to drag him under. He kicked furiously, the first time he had used his legs like that in months, ignoring the pain as he forced his way back to the surface.

Muffled underwater sounds became clear in a rush of air. Guy caught the odd snippet where he could: there were many puzzled outbursts about *a mad crewman flinging himself overboard...* but most of the yelling was focused on the destroyed cargo: the value lost, money turned to muddied gulch.

Taking a deep, *deep* breath – again, something his body had not done in months and which made his lungs burn in protest – Guy submerged himself, unable to see a thing as he pushed away and took off swimming. He went on for as long as he could, completely unaware of where he was going. Eventually he could hold his breath no longer. He broke through to the surface, taking a rasping wheeze. He sloshed around, relieved to find that he was now some distance from the frantic docks – but still close enough that a wandering eye might spot him.

Taking another breath, he plunged under the water again. He let the current carry him along. The next time he emerged he was further away still, the maelstrom almost out of sight, the departing *Guadiana* now just a receding shape on the water.

Before too long he felt safe enough to swim towards the bank. He dragged himself out of the water like some primeval slug emerging from the mire. He coughed, vomiting, bringing up copious amounts of river water.

Woozily getting to his feet, soaking wet and stinking with a noxious tang he worried no bath would ever remove, Guy took in his surroundings. The area was empty and overgrown – but the noise of the city could be heard not too far away. Buildings peeked above the bushes and foliage. And the smell was distinct too. Sewage. Ammonia. Tobacco.

He took a moment to reflect.

Guy's head filled with recollections: a eulogy for the past year. He thought about the choices he could have made; how things could have been different; how it might even have been better to die a true believer than limp on as a faithless wretch.

He soon cast all that aside. He looked in the only direction that mattered. Ahead. Forwards.

He knew exactly where he had to go next.

Wapping Marsh. Just next to the central warehouse on Monza Street. You know London well?

Guy headed to Wapping, following the river. At first he worried that he might attract undue attention – but soon remembered that he looked like a staggering vagrant fresh from a fight, hardly a rarity on the streets of London.

Wapping Market was about as busy as it got during the day, bristling with lunchtime verve: maybe the closest that the city really got to a sense of camaraderie. Guy had no time to take in the mood. He was honing in on his destination. He recognised the safe house well enough from Willis's description. He made his approach and–

He backed off.

Even with the secluded side-street entrance, it was still too busy to risk heading inside. He didn't want to put any of the safe house dwellers in danger. Besides – would anyone even answer if he started rapping on the door while the streets were so crowded?

He hung back. He could wait.

And then – providence on a day that had been sorely lacking, good fortune from a well Guy presumed had long run dry – he saw the man he was looking for anyway.

Father Willis. Out here, on the streets, he was – naturally – a different man, his faith kept well under wraps. Guy briefly wondered how Willis masqueraded in the 'outside world': posing as a merchant or a tailor maybe, non-committal asides to make money while he secretly followed his true calling.

Guy watched Willis from afar. He was fairly certain he knew what the man was doing. Safe houses often relied on reports from daily observers: trusted denizens who could occasionally sweep the nearby area for signs of detection or jeopardy. Willis was giving off the sheen of an everyday nobody – but he was on a reconnaissance mission.

This was when he spotted Guy.

He didn't recognise him for a split second – and when he did it took all his self-possession not to gawk like a floundering goldfish. Father Willis glanced around and then gave a subtle shake of his head, his wide eyes sending a message: *I don't know why you're here... but you can't go inside the safe house. Not now. Not yet.*

Guy returned the gesture. He shook his head too: *I know, I know. But that's not why I'm here.* Guy turned the shake into a nod: a slight one aimed at the door of the Prospect of Whitby, a nearby tavern.

Guy headed in. If he had been invisible on the streets outside, he was a complete nonentity here: just one more mess among the daytime drunks. His clothes were dry now. The river stench lingered, of course – but one septic bouquet simply mingled with all the others.

He took a seat. He suddenly realised: he couldn't buy a drink as he had no money. He was about to figure this out when a murky glass of ale was placed on the table before him.

'Smile,' Willis said, barely moving his lips. He sat opposite Guy, clutching a drink of his own.

'Excuse me?' Guy asked.

'*Smile.* We're old friends. Catching up.' Willis gave Guy an exaggerated slap on the shoulder: a show for any unwanted onlookers. 'Raising a glass together after many years apart. Enjoying a reunion. Isn't that right?'

'Right.'

'So *smile,*' Willis hissed. 'Look the part.' Guy gave his best fake smile. Willis winced in disapproval. 'On second thoughts, don't. Let's just pretend you're ambivalent about seeing me.'

'I can carry ambivalent.'

'You would be wise to *carry* yourself out of here. Good God, man, why are you back in the city? Are you insane?' Someone strolled by the table, a little too close for comfort. Willis laughed loudly as though Guy had just told an uproarious joke. He waited until the passer-by was out of earshot. 'Your friend,

Tresham, had arranged passage out of London. Is that not the case?'

'Of sorts.'

'Well?'

'Passage didn't work out. Not for me anyway.'

'And your friend?'

'Not my friend.' Guy took a long gulp of his ale. It was good. The best he had ever had. Maybe he should hit the pub half-drowned more often.

'I see.' Willis mulled this over. He lowered his voice even further. 'I'll admit it. I have no real affection for Francis Tresham. He is well known around our circles. His money and his assets are always useful. Yet I've always felt that he is something of a... loose cannon.'

'*Was* a loose cannon,' Guy said.

He let the implication hang in the air.

'He's dead?' Willis asked.

'Yes.'

'By your hand?'

'My *forced* hand.'

Willis didn't quite know how to react. He stared at the foam in his ale for a moment. He looked back up, seeking to mollify this horror in the only way he knew how. That would involve something exceptional: a word, a concept, a ritual. His voice was now even lower. Willis could not speak it lightly – and yet, even said quietly, the term shimmered with reverence.

'You seek confession?' he whispered.

'No,' Guy replied. 'I seek a solution.'

Willis did not want to continue the conversation in the tavern. Leaving together – with Willis still playing up the *two old friends* act, talking loudly of 'seeing some more old haunts' – they glided silently away from the pub and walked over to Wapping Park.

'I'm not sure what solution I can offer,' Willis said.

'Of course you are.' Guy watched as a squirrel darted up a nearby tree. So simple: the life of a mere animal. So unfettered. 'I know who you are. I know what you do.'

'Hardly surprising.' Willis snorted. 'You were in the room when I conducted Mass.'

'I'm not talking about that,' Guy said. 'I mean your *other* hidden pursuit.' Willis kept playing dumb. Guy didn't have the patience for this – but from Willis's inflexible face he could tell the man would not yield just yet. 'All right. Fine. Let me ask you a question. Have you ever had one of those moments where everything just fell into place?'

'Several.'

'Then you'll appreciate this,' Guy said.

He told Willis of his time recovering in Hurleyford House: those months spent swimming in and out of lucidity as he lay in bed. He mentioned a voice he came to recognise: an unseen man who often passed his room in the corridor outside, always discussing new identities with fellow recusants, helping those in need to abandon their present lives.

The realisation had taken way too long. Guy had been too preoccupied with his inner demons during the Mass to notice. It was only when he had been stood on the banks of the Thames a few hours ago – reflecting, thinking back – that his addled mind had finally spat out the truth.

Guy wondered how he could have missed something so obvious.

The voice. Willis's voice. It matched. He was that man in the corridor.

'Ah,' Willis said. '*That* hidden pursuit.'

'You assist people. Give them new names, new lives.'

'You just *had* a new life. You threw it away.'

'That would have been no life,' Guy said.

'And what exactly do you think I have to offer?' Willis asked. 'You think you're going to head up to York and step into the shoes of the local gentry? Maybe flutter across to Devon and rub shoulders with the local landowners? The lives I can offer are often mere shadows of what came before. They are desperate avenues. Princes to paupers, gentry to genuflectors. People who sever all ties, ditch everything they know. People who are left with only their faith to carry them.' He raised a sceptical eyebrow. 'How far, say, do you think your faith could carry you, friend?'

Guy said nothing.

'Listen,' Willis went on. 'I have no great bounty of opportunities to offer. What is it that parents say to their fussy children at the dinner table? *You'll get what you're given.*'

'So do it,' Guy said. 'Give me something. I have no money now but I can pay you later, I'm a man of my–'

'I don't do this for *money*.' Willis looked as though the very word left a foul taste in his mouth. 'I do it because I have no other choice. It is who I am, for better or worse. If I can help someone to continue living – to keep on expressing their love for God, no matter how and where – then it is my duty to do so.'

Willis stopped walking. Sighed.

'My networks have gone quiet,' he said. 'Word from the North is slower than usual. The West Country too. The type of vacancies I would usually have in England are thin on the ground.'

'How thin?'

'Honestly? Non-existent. Of course, if you were to speak to me this time next week, I could have a hundred new openings.

They come, they go. You never can tell. But I get the impression you're looking for something a bit more immediate. Correct?'

'Correct.' Guy nodded.

'Bad luck. England has nothing.'

'Scotland? Wales?'

'Also nothing. Not that I would advise either option anyway. I've had previous set-ups around those parts. Many of them have gone awry. The borders are a nightmare. The locals are resentful and suspicious – eager to shop any Englishmen to the authorities. It can be riskier heading there than outright heading overseas.' Willis stalled, struck by a thought. 'Speaking of which...' He trailed off, hesitant.

'Yes?'

'It's a long shot. But I might just have something of interest to you.'

'I'm listening,' Guy said.

'Have you ever heard,' Willis asked, 'of the Virginia Trading Company?'

CHAPTER FIVE

1606-1607

If I stayed out here long enough, the woman wondered, *would I forget my own name?*

It was the kind of question she liked to ask herself: nicely abstract, something to ponder over. It was possible, she guessed. If she remained out here, isolated for years – no one to talk to, only the longleaf pines and palm-sized moths for company – her name might well slip from her memory. To say it out loud would merely be to make a sound. No context. No meaning.

She wasn't entirely sure she would miss it.

No one back in her village would understand. They would laugh at her weird fixation, maybe then berate her for having such a wandering mind. They would say it was a testing distraction sent from *Okeus* himself, something to drag her away from weaving or planting corn or gathering firewood... or whatever mundane task she was supposed to be satisfied with.

Her family would frown. Her friends would mock. Her

husband's reaction would be twofold: a scowl when in company, a raised hand when in private. The first was not always guaranteed. The second was. And that was when hearing her name hurt the *most*: when he snarled it between strikes, punctuating each syllable with his fist.

So: let the world take her name. Let the shrub oaks and the red cedars absorb it. Let the river sweep it away. Let the wolves hunt it down. Let the raccoons bite and squabble over the carcass.

She was defective. Everyone knew this, even those who were nice enough to hold their tongues. At first she had worried that her disappearance might be selfish, an act of stroppy nihilism. Now she knew: it was an act of love. It was generosity. Her departure would be a blessing for the Paspahegh. They had no need for her and she had no liking for them. Maybe her whole presence as well as her name would vanish from the world... wiped from the collective memory of the *Tsenacommacah*.

But.

She could not disappear yet.

There was one person she needed to see: the only person who had ever mattered to her. She didn't know exactly how far away that person was right now... only that they should be near. They had arranged enough meetings at this very spot to ensure they could both find their way here blindfolded.

There was no rush. The person would come.

She just had to wait – and, really, what greater pleasure was there than *doing nothing*? What felt better than leaning back against the bark of the overhanging yellow pine, closing her eyes, immersing herself in the sounds of the forest – so much sweeter than the bickering chatter of her people – and just *being*... even for a moment or two?

There was a shift in the air. Slight at first... but then tangible.

It was not her imagination, no matter how hyperactive that could be. No, this was real: the wind picking up, the scent of bloodroot and dry grass now laden with distant dread.

Where was it coming from? Why was it coming to *her?* What was it a harbinger of?

It was gone as swiftly as it had appeared.

She heard footsteps approaching: soft, delicate, barely crunching the leaves that scattered the floor. Lighter than light. Unmistakable.

She smiled. *That girl could walk on water if she wanted to,* she thought. *She could tiptoe through the clouds and not a raindrop would fall out of place.*

She opened her eyes. She had company.

And for that brief moment – as unbelievable as the idea could seem to her anymore – Odina was happy.

Guy was no stranger to seafaring... but this journey would be like no other. All his previous expeditions had taken place as himself: Guido Fawkes, mercenary, soldier, devoted Catholic. This voyage was stripped of all such decoration. 'You can choose a name,' Father Willis had told him.

'Is that standard procedure?' Guy had asked.

'No.' Willis had laughed, despite himself. 'Look. This isn't a case of carefully placing you in an established community. There are no existing records we need to consider. You're going to be part of a ship's manifest, nothing more. A deckhand, lower orders. Somewhere between the rats and the ship's cat in terms of rank. No one's going to think twice about your clerical paper trail or your criminal history. This is about as fresh as fresh starts get. So – pick a name. Any name.'

'John Johnson,' Guy said.

He had already gotten used to the pseudonym. Plus... he felt it was now more appropriate than ever.

It sounded like a nobody.

The logic was sound then: he was treated like a nobody, just as he wished. When Willis had outlined the whole enterprise to him – the ultimate destination of a ship named *Susan Constant* and its sister vessels *Godspeed* and *Discovery* – Guy had worried at first.

'Are you sure no one's going to check up on me?' Guy asked. 'This whole thing sounds very... *prestigious*.'

'Hardly.' Willis had snorted. He reconsidered. 'Well, I mean, *yes*, if you look at the smaller picture. In that case, it does sound illustrious, doesn't it?'

It certainly did: three ships with a totalled crew of 104, their aim to lay down a permanent settlement in the New World and act as a centre of commerce for the Virginia Trading Company. The vessels would then spend their days crossing back and forth across the Atlantic, leaving a gaggle of fresh colonists to build a stable community while they were gone.

The ultimate goal? The prized commodity? Something far loftier than Raleigh and his tobacco or Drake and his sanctioned piracy. Gold. The Company was betting on an untouched surplus of the stuff to be mined: a Precious World as well as a New one.

Damn right it sounded illustrious.

'Then what's the bigger picture?' Guy asked.

'Ever the pertinent question.' Willis oddly seemed to be enjoying this. Priesthood was clearly in his blood – he was a man who liked to dish out a sermon, no matter who the audience was. 'My contacts tell me that only around thirty of the passengers could be labelled *gentlemen.* The others are bog-standard commoners. No women either, of course. Apart from a cluster of pampered types, we're looking at a crew of hardened, wizened souls – men who will tend to the deck when at sea and tend to the land upon arrival. They will be tilling the soil and scavenging food and God knows what else. For many of them, the same thankless drudgery they would be doing in their home towns – thousands of miles away. So think about it. What kind of men would sign up for a deal like that?'

'Those with nothing to stay behind for,' Guy answered.

'Precisely.'

'How did you come across all of this?'

'Pure chance. A friend of a friend within the company. This isn't the most commonplace scenario, as I've pointed out. The question is – is it one you would like to take advantage of?'

Guy did not have to think for long. 'Yes,' he said.

Three ships, 104 passengers, one ultimate vision: to bring a little piece of England to the New World and turn it into a very profitable one.

It was not the sort of motivation that had ever driven Guy. For him travel had always been an act of service: committing himself to a greater cause. And now he was... *what?* Bereft. Causeless.

He was content, then, to adopt the Company's needs in lieu of his own. They wanted rough and disposable men – and 'John Johnson' fit the bill with guttural aplomb. Willis provided him some scant documentation. He told Guy when and where the voyage was departing. They said their goodbyes.

'Try not to mess this up,' Willis told him. 'You're already one new life down. Losing two would be careless.'

'You don't deal with return customers?'

'No. Nor do I do refunds.' Willis was about to walk away – but he couldn't just leave it at that. He was a shepherd forever tending to a flock. 'I hope you find some peace out there. Some freedom.'

'I hope so too.' Guy stuffed the papers inside his tattered jacket. 'Assuming I make it.'

'Why wouldn't you?'

'Things happen at sea. People perish.'

'Nothing freer than death.' Willis gave a weak smile. It was either a look of faint hope or wordless pity. No matter how much he thought of it in the future, Guy could never figure out which.

Despite his talk of uncertain sailing – Guy had been at sea many times over, and people did indeed perish, often in extremely painful ways – he had every intention of making it through the voyage intact. He would eventually step onto dry land. New land. He would awake from a lifelong dream of England.

And then he would... *what?*

The New World was an enigma to everyone – yet Guy had received a greater education on the topic than most. During his days in the Spanish military and the Army of Flanders he had heard stories from men who had spent time there. The Spanish had long seized the opportunity to explore the region. They had established settlements already. There was St Augustine in *Pascua Florida*. There was *La Villa Real de la Santa Fe* in New Mexico. The dispatches from each place were mostly the same:

tales of back-breaking work, stories of trying to find some grounding on new and uncooperative soil.

Guy had also heard talk of the natives: people whose ancestors had long since adopted the land as their own. They could be civil but they could also prove suspicious – and violent. The natives might have used an alien tongue but they shared a common language with the Europeans: they did not take kindly to their territory being invaded. Military leaders had been surprised by this. Rank-and-file soldiers had not. That was always the way: generals and gentlemen were so often educated out of their common sense.

What struck Guy most was the impression of scale. The men who had seen the New World could barely put into words the wide-open lack of confines, the paucity of brokenness. This was a continent fit to be named Eden: a land of both bounty and anonymity.

The Company could keep their gold, if they found any. Guy's first priority when he stepped upon that foreign soil would be to disappear.

An atheist is lower than a beast, he had once heard said – and Guy fully intended to follow that path. He would vanish into a new wilderness. Like an animal driven by nothing but the need for motion.

Yes. Like a beast.

Beasthood, however, was a long way off.

The *Susan Constant* and its two siblings set sail from Blackwall on December 20th. Guy had no real desire or need to make friends on board – he was going to abandon these people as soon as they made landfall, after all – but, at the same time, he didn't fancy the idea of four months without conversation. It would also have been impossible: the *Constant* was about a hundred feet long and twenty feet wide, sardine-can packing for the seventy-one men on board. The other ships fared even worse: they had fewer crewmen but were much smaller.

So: Guy said his hellos and waited for the journey to begin in earnest. It was always difficult to gauge a man by handshake alone, Guy figured. True rapport came from working together – and there would be plenty of that in the coming weeks. Ample time to find out who was worthwhile company.

Except... things didn't quite work out like that.

The *Susan Constant* was just off the coast of Kent before it came to a standstill. The captain – a weathered man in his forties named Newport – had taken stock of the weather and made the costly decision to drop anchor, waiting out an impending storm. The *Godspeed* and the *Discovery* followed suit. The wider ocean was tantalisingly just out of reach.

Guy had a lot of time for Newport. He respected the man right from the start. That was a boost: nothing was harder than taking orders from a man you held in contempt. Guy had travelled with many feckless captains in his time, barely capable types whose managerial antics on land could never prepare them for the harsh realities of the sea. Newport was a sailor to the core: a captain-for-hire privateer who had lost an arm while raiding Spanish freighters.

'We'll be moving again by tomorrow,' Newport had told his men. 'The day after at the latest.'

They remained still for six weeks.

One storm became many. A perfect maelstrom of cyclonic conditions kept gale-force winds howling up the Channel, bitter winter fury that allowed no one to pass.

No one held any grudges against Newport for his inaction – there was no other sensible thing to do – but life on board the stilled *Constant* became a peculiar microcosm. There was work to be done – but not enough work to keep idle minds busy and hands fully occupied. The food stocks took a dangerous hit before the ships had even cleared Dover. The crew felt more isolated and adrift than they would in the middle of the Atlantic. Nothing embodied the lure of land more than the things that still seemed so *close*: taverns, markets, carriages, women.

In the midst of all this was an almost literal Pandora's box. Before setting off, the Company had placed a number of papers inside a sturdy lockbox on the *Constant*. The notes inside – a mystery to every single person on board, no matter how high their rank – contained the names of six people randomly selected to be the 'council leaders' of their New World settlement. *The instructions are to be opened within four and twenty hours of arrival at your destination*, the Company had stated. *And not before*.

Yet – as even the beginning of the ocean voyage seemed further away – the crew's patience dwindled. What was the point of waiting, even if the Company had insisted upon it? What could they do about it if the box was opened anyway? And wouldn't it actually be useful to know who was doing what once they arrived in the New World?

Talk began to spread. Half-plotted notions of defying orders and breaking open the box fluttered around the *Constant*. Inevitably, Newport soon caught wind of them – and promised the noose to anyone who even *thought* about the matter from thereon in.

And so the box was forgotten.

For a while.

Factions were formed. Social class was the first great divider. In the past Guy had always managed to stride neatly between worlds: he had known money without having great wealth, he had known hardships without ever being destitute.

On the *Constant*, however, 'John Johnson' was very much a man of the lower orders. Guy initially bristled at this – but soon learned it was the best camp to be in. The alternative was to be one of the 'high-born' gentlemen who strode about the ship like Narcissus reborn. Any reminder that they were on a galley rather than a grand chateau – having to sleep near the crew, abiding by set meals, breathing the same air as the rabble – was met with a sneer or a sigh.

Boldest among braggarts was one Edward Maria Wingfield, the sole Virginia Company investor on board: a man who viewed the crew around him as disposable tools rather than fellow travellers. He was notable as the only name anyone *knew* would be in the lockbox: the company had guaranteed him the role of President long before departure.

When Wingfield looked at Guy, it was as though he was looking right through him, dismissing a grubby pleb in favour of dreamier horizons beyond. From what Guy learned, Wingfield had also seen combat – soldiering in the Low Countries, taking forts and garrisons, no mere song and dance. Unlike Guy, however, he had ditched battle for more comfortable pursuits: a stint as an MP in Parliament, a prestigious role as a school governor, forays into business.

Below the gentlemen were the deckhands and labourers – and what of them? Some had simply drifted into the gig seeking money. Some were enthused about leaving England behind and starting afresh in the New World. A handful were a mixture of the two. Herd and Garret were bricklayers. Laydon and Laxon were carpenters. Dods and Love were former soldiers. And so on and so on.

Whenever they asked what John Johnson's story was, Guy threw out a tale he had cobbled together: he was a ruined labourer turned petty criminal, out of jail and yearning for a new life. It was the unremarkable background of an unremarkable man. The crewmen believed him.

Apart from one.

There was another man – similar age to Guy, similar temperament, similar air of displacement between social tribes – whose mask occasionally slipped. Guy could see hints of suspicion. The man clearly thought there was more to the history of 'John Johnson'.

Was this man maybe a recusant, a Catholic on the run? Was he honing in on Guy out of some strange kinship? Was he – Guy felt his stomach lurch at the thought – another Francis Tresham?

He needed to find out more. Guy started with his name. The man was called John Smith.

What would he admit to? What secrets would he shed? None.

As civil as Guy planned to be with his crewmates – a necessity rather than a nicety – he wasn't looking for a new confidant. Not now, not ever. And yet – on a stilled vessel where conversation had dwindled into grunts and nods – John Smith turned out to be something of an intellectual godsend.

Guy could no doubt have held his own in conversations with the 'elites' on board – but they avoided him like a social plague. John Smith was of a similar mind, Guy could tell: a man smart beyond his humble beginnings, someone who had the temerity to make a break for the fence. Men like that could always spot one another. In certain situations their lives depended on it.

'I hear you're another John,' Smith said to him one morning.

'You heard right.'

Smith had an abundance of stories to tell... and he seemed happy not to demand any in return. This arrangement suited Guy perfectly. Either when working on deck or supping a glass of heavily rationed rum in the quarters, Smith always had an anecdote to share or a narrow escape to recount. Guy began to suspect a lot of this was embellished – but he didn't mind. The stories were hugely entertaining. They were also, at least, grounded in truth: there were details Smith could not know unless he had served extensively in combat. He might not have been the hero he was painting himself to be... but Guy had no doubt that Smith was a brave man. He would rather have him as an ally than a foe.

Smith had been a mercenary too, fighting for a litany of causes: serving with the French army, taking up arms against the Ottoman Turks, somehow finding his way to Romania amidst a bloody feud between nobility. Battle after battle, each with a twist of fate to savour.

'I was at Limbach,' Smith recalled. 'Under siege from the Turks. We needed to provide a distraction. We used string, cloth and powder – created a pretty picture against the night sky, let me tell you. We made the bastards think a couple of thousand flintlocks were firing–'

'Matchlocks,' Guy interrupted. It was an offhand correction. Instinctive.

'Excuse me?'

'Matchlocks,' Guy said, still unthinking. 'Flintlocks wouldn't light up like that. It couldn't have been...'

He realised what he had done.

Smith paused. A smile slowly broke out on his face.

'Well now,' Smith said. 'What did you say your story was again, John Johnson?' His smile had a tinge of victory – but no malice. 'Seems odd to me that a simple labourer would know so much about weaponry.'

Guy took a moment to gauge Smith's expression. Eventually he smiled back. Smith was no traitor. He was not going to use this knowledge as leverage or bait. He just enjoyed digging beneath the surface.

In short: he was no Francis Tresham.

'It would be odd, wouldn't it?' Guy said.

'Theoretically,' Smith went on, 'a man who knew that kind of thing would likely have seen battle in Europe. Spain, for instance. Wouldn't you say?'

'I suppose I would.'

'And this man, *theoretically*...' Smith couldn't help but smile wider. 'Would this man have taken up arms for the land of his forefathers... or for the Kingdom of *España*?'

'I couldn't possibly say,' Guy replied.

He instantly regretted it. Whatever his exaggerations, Smith was obviously a man who had rallied against the Spanish cause. Guy should at least have stayed on neutral territory. He cursed himself. What the hell was he thinking?

'I see.' Smith nodded slowly. 'Well. I'd also say that – on a mission like this – men would be wise to disregard such past differences. I would say that new factions take much greater precedence over old ones. Would you say that too, Mr Johnson?'

'I would.'

'Good.'

Smith had one particular favourite story. Whenever he heard someone moaning about the difficult living conditions on board the *Constant*, he would pull out his trump card: recalling how he had once been taken slave after being captured by the

Crimean Tatars. He was brutalised and tortured before escaping, eventually making his way back to England through an arduous trek across Russia, Africa and Northern Europe.

'Comfort is a very relative notion,' he would say. 'Always remember that. And always try to be grateful for what you have.' The crewmen from the lower decks would nod sagely at this. The gentlemen in charge did not share the same reaction. Wingfield in particular was no longer hiding his contempt for Smith – dismissing such pieties with a scowl.

'You should be careful,' Guy eventually told Smith.

'Of what?' Smith frowned.

'Upsetting our "betters".'

'Wingfield's a cretin.'

'Yes,' Guy said. 'But he's a powerful cretin.'

'Newport too. A buffoon.'

'Newport has decency in him. He's not a man I would personally choose as captain but...' Guy sighed. 'Choice seems to be very thin on the ground.'

'I never pegged you for a bootlicker.'

'And you shouldn't. I'm just saying – you're a man who has been in enough fights. You must know that some aren't worth picking.'

'And what about the fights *you've* been in, John Johnson? Maybe one day you'll see fit to share those memories with me?'

Guy said nothing.

Guy's kinship with Smith had other benefits. Smith had had more time to prepare for the voyage than Guy – and had packed away a few luxuries to make the Atlantic passage more bearable. Among these was a stash of books that Smith stored beneath his straw hammock. While the other crewmen preferred to take solace in booze and card games, Guy didn't hesitate to work his way through Smith's mini-library.

Smith had well-worn copies of *Don Quixote* and *The City of the Sun* and *The Kingdom of the Slavs* among others. There were also books Guy had once refused to read – would have advocated burning, in fact – which he now pored over with a fresh gaze. He had heard of *Naometria* before: Simon Studion's long-winded treatise on why the papacy must be destroyed. Guy had once considered this the work of the Devil. Now, leafing his way through the pages, he just found the whole thing merely... depressing. Was this all a godless existence had to offer?

Nonetheless, he read it cover to cover.

Guy had seen mutinies before. He had never spearheaded one – although he had often been tempted to – but he had certainly been caught in the middle of many. He knew what they looked like: blood-spattered and bitter, the revenge of the mistreated upon the clueless.

What John Smith did? No. That was no true mutiny in Guy's eyes. *Rebellion*, maybe – yet what was there to do about idiocy other than rebel against it?

The ship's chaplain had fallen sick. Robert Hunt was – naturally – a full-blooded Protestant roped into the mission to provide spiritual guidance. When Hunt was struck with a fever, Smith was among the men who tended to him. In the worst throes of delirium, Hunt had spoken of his past: an affair he had had with a young servant girl. The story spread. Soon Hunt was decried as a hypocrite and a bad omen, someone whose presence on board would bring ill luck.

Smith had fought hard against these accusations, getting into numerous fights. He was loath to see that Wingfield and Newport did nothing to stop the unrest – and soon lost his patience. He decided that he would fare better in charge. He began to formulate plans – with a small group of supporters – to make that happen.

Newport and Wingfield got word of these plans. They didn't react well. Wingfield in particular had every reason to put his boot on Smith's neck. Smith was a direct threat: at best a ruffian who could undermine him, at worst a constant source of minor humiliation. Wingfield had Newport's ear – and Wingfield's bankrolling of the entire operation meant that power overstepped principles every time. He insisted Newport charge Smith with plotting mutiny under maritime law.

This meant two things. Firstly, Smith would be consigned to a makeshift brig for the remainder of the journey: walled in by oak struts and heavy supply sacks.

Secondly – at the first suitable opportunity come landfall – Smith would be put to death.

'In hindsight,' Smith said to Guy from his new prison, ever-deadpan even in the face of execution, 'I should probably have listened to you.'

Guy ventured down to the brig a couple of times a day to talk to Smith and generally check in on him – occasionally even sneaking the man extra rations or smuggling down one of Smith's prized books. While conversing with prisoners wasn't forbidden, most of the other crewmen had distanced themselves from Smith. Guy wasn't one of them: he was willing to trade a little social status in the name of intelligent conversation.

This finally warranted the attention of one particular man, who approached Guy one morning with his hand outstretched:

'Johnson, isn't it?' He gave a warm smile. 'Hard to believe we still haven't spoken properly. I'm Hunt. Robert Hunt. I'm–'

'I know,' Guy said. 'The ship chaplain.'

'That's right.'

'I trust you're feeling better? Fully recovered?'

'Yes. Thank you. Touch-and-go for a while there... but I made it through.'

Hunt was a harmless enough soul, if not a little cloyingly naïve. The crewmen had quickly forgotten about Hunt's minor 'scandal' and turned their frustrations elsewhere. As such Hunt mainly inspired a mixture of indifference and slight pity. The crew rolled their eyes whenever Hunt cornered them for a sermon or daily 'lesson'.

'I've seen you speaking to the prisoner,' Hunt went on. 'That hasn't particularly bolstered your popularity on board.'

'I can live with that,' Guy said.

'It takes a strong sense of will to do something like that. To offer companionship to those who have been exiled. I'm aware of how Smith stood up for my name. I'm glad that someone like you is able to ease his suffering. You seem like a man in touch with the Spirit.'

'Rum.'

'Excuse me?'

'The spirit I'm in touch with.'

'Ah. I see.' Hunt gave a tolerant chuckle. 'May I call you John?'

'Go ahead.'

'John.' Hunt's forearm tightened around the Bible he forever had clutched to his chest. 'Are you a man given much to prayer?'

Guy hesitated. Part of him wanted to tell Hunt the truth: *no, Father, it's as useless as jabbering to the ocean and expecting the Kraken to appear.* He didn't. Guy couldn't risk developing a reputation as some sort of godless freak. So he dulled his ire:

'In my own fashion,' Guy said.

'Your own fashion?'

'Worship is of equal strength in private as it is communal.' Guy had said this once before: during the Plot, back when Catesby had asked him why he seemed to prefer praying in solitude than in a group. Guy had wholly meant what he said back then. Now – they were just mere words. 'I find the ability to reflect in peace gives me a closer bond with the Almighty.'

Hunt took on a look of contemplation. Guy realised that he'd done the specific opposite of trying to shoo the man away: he had now convinced Hunt that he was an intellectual sparring partner.

'I shall look forward to talking to you more, John.'

'Wonderful.' Guy strained a grin.

It soon got to the stage, however, where even a dialogue with Hunt would be a welcome reprieve from boredom. Guy had now made his way through Smith's book collection multiple times.

'Exhausted the library, have we?' Smith asked him during one of their conversations in the brig.

'I'm afraid so.'

'No you haven't.'

'What?'

'Look under my hammock. Near to where the other books are kept. There's another volume under a loose oak board. Something you might find useful.' He shuffled closer to his 'window': a gap in the heaped sacks. 'Did you ever hear of Hernando de Soto?'

'No.'

'An explorer. He went on several excursions to the New World about seventy years ago. Died trying to cross an uncharted river in 1542. Anyway, between travels, he wrote a book called *Chronicles*. Even now, it's about as comprehensive a guidebook to the region as we have.'

'Like... geography? Climate? Wildlife?'

'All that and more. He also had several encounters with the local savages. Turns out that "savages" isn't an entirely accurate term. They are not without customs or wisdom. He managed to compile a good amount of written work on their language, a dialect he labelled Algonquian.' Smith coughed. The stale air of his cell was getting to him. 'Here's the thing, Johnson. We can assume that wherever we land in the New World there will be savages nearby. We will need to communicate and trade with them. We can *also* assume that their dialect will be similar to Algonquian.'

Guy couldn't help but smile.

The sly bastard.

'This book,' Guy said. 'It would give one person a distinct advantage over the rest of his colonists, wouldn't it?'

'The penny drops.'

'And you want me to bring it down here for you?'

'Why bother?' Smith snorted. 'It looks like my time in the New World is going to be awfully short.' Guy felt a stab of remorse – despite Smith's jocularity, he was still sentenced to death. He was still set to go down in history: the first man hanged in a nameless land. 'I suspect it could come in very useful to you, however.'

Guy agreed. Wherever he disappeared to, the land would undoubtedly be populated by savages – or, at the very least, he would stumble across some of them on his exodus.

He dug out *Chronicles* from Smith's hiding place and stashed it away near his own hammock. No one else seemed to care about what Guy read – but nonetheless he took great pains to hide it from view, only immersing himself in de Soto's knowledge when he was alone.

Guy began to familiarise himself with the Algonquian tongue, swirling new phrases around under his breath, trying to figure out the punctuation of words he could soon be speaking for real.

Maškihkyiwi. Grass. *Ešpaxkweyawi.* Trees. *Sipiwehsehsi.* River. *Pematesiweni.* Life.

Nepwawiweni. Death.

His vocabulary grew. Soon enough he could form sentences. Soon after he was holding court in imaginary Algonquian conversations, whispered under his breath.

The voyage went on.

The first hints that arrival at the New World was forthcoming – was actually *possible* – came with a stop-off at Dominica, a balmy and sweet-smelling Caribbean island that offered the grateful crew a yield of fresh fruits and tobacco.

'What's it like out there?' Smith asked Guy, once the crew had reboarded.

'Nice.' This was all Guy could say. He didn't want to burnish Smith's suffering any further. It wasn't just *nice* out there. After several months cooped up on the *Constant*, it was close to paradise. The air. The sky. The reassuring ballast of terra firma. The *world*.

'Yes,' Smith said quietly. 'I expect it is.' He swallowed, managing to break his cracked lips into a smile. 'Still. Not long now, is it?'

'No,' Guy quietly said. 'Not long at all.'

And it wasn't.

On 26th April the *Susan Constant,* the *Godspeed* and the *Discovery* drifted into an area previous explorers had named Chesapeake Bay. The crew of each vessel crowded onto deck as landfall beckoned. Low-lying land stretched to the horizon to the west, set against a vast inland body of water to the north.

A land as God made it, Guy heard Chaplain Hunt mutter

in awe.

They made it to shore. They headed inland slightly, tracking past tree-laden meadows and freshwater streams. Just over a hundred men were assembled on the soil, forming their first bond with the land that was now their home. They looked out to the surrounding treeline, all sharing the same thought: were they already being watched?

The moment ended soon enough. President Wingfield made an address to the gathered men, announcing that the dirt they stood on was now claimed in the name of the King. He gave it a name. He birthed a colony. He called it *Jamestown.* And now Jamestown had matters of state to attend to.

Guy could see from Wingfield's slavering officiousness: the man had actively been looking forward to carrying out Smith's sentence. Smith himself was retrieved from the brig and dragged across the soil, barely able to walk.

A noose was constructed and flung over a strong-looking tree branch. Smith looked around, taking in the natural surroundings, inhaling the untainted air. Most of the other men could not meet his gaze. Guy held his head high. Smith gave Guy a thankful nod of acknowledgement – and farewell.

'John Smith,' Wingfield began, pacing back and forth. 'In accordance with maritime law, you are guilty of the crime of mutiny. Your sentence, to be carried out forthwith, is to be hanged by the neck until you are dead. The citizens of Jamestown are gathered today to witness your punishment, as well as the newly-established council–'

He stopped.

The council had not yet been formed.

Or rather – it had not yet been announced.

'Captain Newport,' Wingfield called out. 'Before we proceed. Please fetch the lockbox containing Company Orders and councillor names.' Newport nodded for a subordinate to carry out the task, who returned soon after clutching the sealed box. Newport unlocked it, pulling out the neatly folded papers.

'"The Virginia Trading Company hereby delegates the role of councillors to the following six men".' He began to reel off the names. '"Firstly, as established prior to departure, Mr Edward Maria Wingfield will be President. The other councilmen are named as follows".' Newport cleared his throat. '"Captain Christopher Newport. Mr Bartholomew Gosnold. Mr John Martin. Mr John Ratcliffe. Mr George Kendall. And..."'

Newport faltered.

'Well, Captain?' Wingfield frowned. 'Out with it.'

'"The final council member",' Newport said, '"will be Mr John Smith".'

Silence fell over the new community; the settlement's first ever moment of communal shock. Newport cleared his throat again and continued to read. Wingfield's face was contorted with disgust.

'"The Company takes great pains to point out",' Newport went on, '"that all previous misdemeanours that may have occurred at sea are to be disregarded. The council is duty-bound to work together and set down new laws, boundaries and instructions".'

Silence fell once more. Until something broke it.

It began as a struggling wheeze. It grew louder: a recognisable bout of laughter. Smith may have looked like a vagrant stowaway – but he was now as triumphant as any monarch.

'You play by the book, Wingfield,' he said between rasping laughs, 'and soon enough the book plays you.'

'Silence!' Wingfield snapped. This only made Smith laugh harder – and a good number of the other men followed suit. Sensing open rebellion, Wingfield gave them all a deathly glare. Some stopped. Some continued. Guy was among the latter.

Wingfield caught sight of Guy.

I'll be watching you, his stare said.

Likewise, Guy thought.

'Enough of this nonsense,' Wingfield bellowed, as though the whole charade had been someone else's idea. He gestured for a couple of men to take the noose down from the tree. They did so. He then waved a hand at Smith. 'Untie him.' He watched as a few crewmen unbound Smith's knotted wrists. 'See, Smith? Some of us actually abide by principles. It's nothing to do with *being played*, as you put it. It's more to do with *being a man*.'

'Whatever you say, President Wingfield.' Smith rubbed at his sore wrists. 'Any more orders?'

'Yes, as it happens. Let's stop messing around and get a move on. We have a lot of work to do.'

This, it turned out, was truer than anyone could imagine.

Collecting firewood had been the first point of order. While most of the new councilmen stepped back – eager to detach themselves from the concerns of common labour – Smith made sure to pitch in, heading into the outskirts of the unexplored forest with the others.

He and Guy were tackling a large oak when:

'Johnson.'

'Yes?'

'Your plans,' Smith said. 'I don't believe we've discussed them.'

'I don't believe I've mentioned them.' Guy stopped to catch his breath. 'Who says I have plans anyway?'

'Don't take me for an idiot. You're not like the others. I doubt you have any intent on staying in Jamestown longer than you have to. Look, as far as I'm concerned, no one here is bound by law. If a man does not intend on sticking around, that is not my concern.' He sighed. 'Although...'

'Although what?'

'I am on the town's council. I have a new role to fulfil. And I happen to think I will be very good at it. Although...'

'*Although* again.'

'I will need a good foundation to build on. You're a smart and resourceful man, Johnson. Whatever background you're hiding has made you that way.'

'So,' Guy said, 'what are you suggesting?'

'Not a suggestion. A question.'

'Then ask it.'

'Would you be willing to delay your... *plans* for a few weeks? Just long enough to help me whip this place into shape? Once I have Jamestown in some semblance of functioning order, then you'd be free to run off wherever you want. What do you think? Would you be willing to help me out of a sense of debt? I did provide you with ample reading material, after all.'

'As I recall, Smith,' Guy grunted between swings of his axe, 'I was the only one who didn't let you rot alone in the brig. Maybe *you* are indebted to *me*.'

'True.' Smith nodded. 'In that case... would you be willing to help me out of a sense of friendship?'

Guy stopped chopping for a moment.

The wilderness was going nowhere. His scheme to disappear into it could wait a little while.

Besides – even beasts needed allies, didn't they?

'Yes,' Guy said, taking up the axe again. 'I think I would.'

'Excellent.' Smith beamed. 'In the meantime... I suppose I had better start reading *Chronicles*. Turns out those language skills might come in handy after all.'

CHAPTER SIX

1607

Bitterness? Yes.

Anger? Yes.

Resentment? Oh *yes*.

There were certain characteristics adopted by members of the *Inquisición*. Inquisitors were generally outcasts from wider society: men who had shunned the frivolities of normal minds, hotly casting aside any other distraction to protect their faith. And when it came to this checklist of shared qualities... Francis Tresham had them all.

All but one.

There was one thing about Francis Tresham that marked him out from his peers very firmly indeed.

His face.

Francis had seen Fawkes hoist the musket. He never thought the man would go through with it – but he did.

Francis's world had turned into a bright-white firestorm of pain before he dropped into empty darkness. When he came to later – gummily blinking open his one remaining eye – his agony was countered by surprise.

Despite Fawkes's best efforts, Francis was very much still alive.

There was a doctor on board the *Guadiana*. He wasn't exactly a man at the top of his field but he knew enough to keep Francis comfortable. Francis was plied hourly with as much laudanum as supplies could bear. His head was wrapped daily in fresh bandages. During each redressing he always spotted a couple of crew members loitering around in the background, eager to catch a glimpse of his hideous injuries. Lost in a near-perpetual haze, Francis began to find the gawkers funny. *It's carnival time, boys*, he used to slur between laughs. *Get a good look while you can today, because I'll be tripling the ticket prices once the scabs start to pus.*

In moments of lucidity – awake at night on the swaying ship with only pain for company – Francis would swear revenge on these men. Who did they think they were: these *ingrates*, these *barbarians*, finding joy in the disfigurement of a superior man? When the morning came, however, the desire had usually faded. Francis only had the energy to maintain one burning vendetta.

Guido Fawkes.

Fawkes had gotten away – and presumably survived. Crewmen relayed that Fawkes had vaulted overboard and swam back into the cesspool of London: a rat now lost among rats. It had been too late to turn the *Guadiana* around – and Fawkes would already have been miles away by the time they could safely step back onto the docks.

In a way, the betrayal hurt Francis more than his injures

(but only just). Fawkes was a modern-day Judas Iscariot. No, no, Francis madly simmered and boiled: he was worse than that. Many said that the Devil himself had possessed Judas and spurred his evil actions. Not so with Fawkes. He was a demon in his own right.

No context would ever redeem him.

Francis also found his anger turning inwards. There was no point denying it: he had been taken for a naïve fool, the kind of lamblike simpleton who offered up easy prey to the con men around Cripplegate and Shoreditch. Had it been a test? Had the Lord expected Francis to spy out Fawkes's intentions? Was this his punishment for failing?

Or... was Francis *supposed* to fall victim to Fawkes's treachery? If so, what was the meaning of that?

What was the next phase in the grand plan?

Immune to Francis's turmoil, the *Guadiana* sailed onwards.

Luck. It was a word the ship's doctor had often used. It was *luck* that the musket shot hadn't been two inches or so to the right – and had merely blown off a fragment of Francis's skull rather than spreading brain matter all over the quarters. It was *luck* that the lead pellets had mostly embedded themselves into the woodwork – with a smaller smattering lodged into his shoulder and neck. It was *luck* that the explosive blast had only burned through the flesh on the left-hand side of his scalp, merely singeing the hair on the other side instead. It was a shame that Francis's left eye could not be saved – that it had been smeared like jellied pulp across the nearest panelling – but it was *luck* that the other eye escaped completely unharmed.

But... when he looked in the mirror... Francis didn't feel very lucky.

Francis's wounds had healed in the months since the attack – as well as they ever could. Roughly one half of his face looked the same as ever: skin that always seemed so youthful, lustrous hair that Francis took deep pride in. The lower left-hand side of his face formed a hostile boundary: skin turning redder, scar tissue running outwards in criss-cross lines, chunks taken out of his lips and jaw.

Then there was the upper-left side of his face: an upwards swipe from a hellhound. Puckered pink flesh swarmed around the impact point, a giant cauterised cleft. Veiny cartilage and sinews stretched around and atop the left of Francis's half-bald scalp. An insulting tuft of untouched hair formed an island above his ear. A desiccated flap of skin hung over where his left eye had once been. A useless crater lurked underneath.

Some luck.

Some fucking luck.

Francis, however, was a man of utility at heart. He could mope around, lost in self-pity – and, yes, he did do plenty of that – or he could figure out what the next step in God's plan was.

None of this was accidental. Francis grew more and more convinced of that with each passing day. A sign would come soon. But while he was waiting for direction or enlightenment... he would also make the most of his resources.

Francis saw how the world reacted to him now. Children caught sight of his mangled features and began to cry. Grown men and women shuddered in revulsion or pity. He had been stripped of his beauty – like a woman of Zion, her finery snatched away by the Lord – and ditched his vanity. He had once used his handsome looks to sway people. Now he had a different weapon in his arsenal. So: his horrible appearance inspired fear, did it? His very looks could make others tremble?

Fine. Fine and well.

That was a very good thing for an Inquisitor.

'The book,' Francis said, leaning over the man who was hunched on a splinter-laden wooden stool. 'I know you have it. Numerous people have said it is in your possession. Are you trying to tell me they are *all* lying? What possible reason would they have to do that?'

'I... I...' the man stammered. 'I...'

'You...' Francis moved in closer. '*What?*'

'I... I... I...'

'You have it. The book. Hidden well, apparently – and for that I congratulate you. But that's the last pleasantry I can offer you. You need to admit it. You need to confess.'

The man gave one more strangled attempt at speech – before letting out a meek sob instead. Francis resisted the temptation to roll his eyes (or his *eye*, he grimly reminded himself). The man here – Hortuño, his name was – was typical Galician stock. Oh, he was just Galicia through and through: ever the swaggering brute when down the local tavern or flirting with a farmer's daughter... but a simpering wreck when faced with the authority of the *Inquisición*.

He was in possession, the accusations went, of the *Catechism* – a heretical volume by a rogue archbishop called Carranza. Possession of the volume was bad enough – but word had got around that Hortuño had been preaching from it, sharing criticisms of the *Inquisición* and their procedures. Hortuño would end up with an unpleasant amount of jail time or a hefty fine if convicted – which was getting off lightly when compared to the recent case in Pontevedra.

Fourteen heretics had been burned at the stake. Those who repented before death had had their necks snapped first. Those who didn't went to the stake fully conscious. It was the only case of such magnitude Francis had been involved with; the only time he had felt he was truly defending the faith. He yearned for more of them. Clamping down on rule-breakers like Hortuño carried some reward... but it never felt quite enough.

And yet: he did what he could. He put his all into every single interrogation. That was where his face worked to his advantage. Interrogation subjects felt the innate need to flinch when Francis loomed in close to them, eye to eye – and yet they couldn't. They had to take in that visage in all its 'glory': the scarred freakishness of a man who looked to be beyond reason.

Francis had already tried to start some rumours among the local peasantry. He had planted the seed of a story: that one sinner had almost broke free from his bonds while aflame at the stake... and Francis had leaned in to restrain him as he burned, wordless and stoic as the fire took half his face and scalp, determined beyond mortal concerns to see the wicked punished. He wondered if the story was spreading well. He would put an ear to the ground – his one good ear – to check in on it soon enough.

Hortuño was trying to look down at the floor.

'Look at me,' Francis insisted. 'I need you to see how serious I am. I am not a man to underplay things. Look at me. *Look at me.*'

Hortuño did. He whimpered.

Francis felt something by his shoes. Liquid seeping around the outside of his soles, spreading from beneath Hortuño's chair. The man had pissed in his own breeches.

Now we're getting somewhere, Francis thought.

There was a knock at the interrogation-room door. Francis gave Hortuño a reproachful look – *be thankful for the interruption... for now* – and went to answer. The man on the other side was Brother Garcia, a fifty-something fellow Inquisitor with gaunt features and dull brown eyes: almost as dull, Francis often thought, as the lack of fire within the man's spirit.

'Brother Tresham.' Garcia's pronunciation of his surname always irritated Francis. *Treth-em.* Over-deliberate inflection: *TRETH-em.*

'Yes?'

'A moment, please?'

Francis stepped outside. He and Garcia headed to a small courtyard. It was just after noon: hot and sunny, but not yet the feverish blaze mid-afternoon would bring. Francis had enjoyed the change in weather at first: good for his mood, good for healing his scars. Soon, though, he grew to dread the heat. It was just another burden. A daily disappointment.

And here was another disappointment: Garcia, and all those like him. So few of the other Inquisitors seemed to share Francis's zeal. Older ones like Garcia had seen their drive for action sapped, happy to enforce their regime with pen and parchment rather than hands-on influence. They favoured bureaucracy over beatings. It made Francis sad.

'How is it going?' Garcia asked. 'With Hortuño?'

'I'm making progress,' Francis said.

'To what end?'

'Excuse me?'

'Is this really the best use of the *Inquisición's* time?' Garcia raised an eyebrow. 'Chasing up on a relatively minor infraction such as this?'

'I... I...' Francis spluttered. He realised: he sounded just like Hortuño, strapped to that chair. He was desperately struggling to justify himself to *Garcia*, of all people.

'Don't worry about it too much.' Garcia gave a smirk.

Francis recognised both the smirk and the tone. There was an unspoken – but widely displayed – sense of superiority from the other Inquisitors. Francis had fully expected that he would need to prove himself: he was a foreigner, after all, and had joined up in a very unusual way. But he hadn't bargained on *this* either: the constant spectre of non-acceptance.

From his very arrival in Spain, Francis had been defined by failure. He had promised to bring over another loyal recruit for the *Inquisición* – yet the man had betrayed Francis, attacking him and leaving him for dead. No internal *Inquisición* punishment had been doled out for this gross mistake. It was clear just by looking at Francis that he had suffered enough punishment already.

'I'd hardly call this just an "infraction",' Francis protested. 'He is reported to be holding a copy of Carranza's book, Brother Garcia. The *Catechism*. Are we to begin labelling such heresy as "minor" from now on? Perhaps we should stop investigating reports of blasphemy altogether?'

'Do as you will, Brother.' Garcia's smirk remained. 'Just don't be afraid to call on me should you need further consultation.'

Here's some consultation for you, Francis wanted to scream. *When I've finally climbed up every rung of the ladder... when I am IN CHARGE of this organisation... lazy bastards like you will be treated no differently than common heretics... and I will gleefully be the one to tie you to the post and LIGHT YOU ON FUCKING FIRE MYSELF–*

'I'll bear that in mind.' Francis smiled. 'Now – what can I help you with?'

'I just wanted to let you know,' Garcia said, his face scrunching as though the very idea of Francis *helping him* was impossible. 'There's been an arrest. Over in England. I understand you asked to be informed of any such developments via our spy networks.'

'That's right.'

'And you mentioned a couple of names. Catholic brothers and sisters who you wanted to keep an eye on.'

'Yes.'

'One of them popped up. Taken by the authorities around a fortnight ago, we believe. Convicted of numerous counts of banned worship, distribution of literature and harbouring recusants.'

'Who?'

'Name of Willis.'

Name of Willis indeed.

Edward Willis, the documentation revealed. *Date of birth: 15th October 1571. Location: London and Buckinghamshire. Previous criminal accusations: none. Physical description: brown-haired, fair complexion, slight.*

The details had been hastily copied from official documentation but were still legible. Spain had legions of spies in England who were highly adept at hurriedly duplicating Catholic arrest records and smuggling the papers out of the country. Mistakes were rare. So Francis had every reason to believe that, yes, Father Willis had been caught harbouring two escaped recusants.

Francis had always had a lot of time for Willis. They were hardly close but – as men who moved in the same dissident circles – they were almost duty-bound to know each other. Willis was perhaps on the weaker side – a naïve man of useless pacifism – but Francis had always been willing to overlook these flaws. He was a warrior by proxy. That was good enough for the cause.

When Willis was caught he had been in the process of putting together new identities for the two fugitives. The authorities had then 'persuaded' him to reveal the names of those he had helped in the past. He had held out for a while under torture, the records stated. But only a while.

Soon enough he had relented. Copied and attached right here was a list of recusant names that had been extracted. Francis scanned the list, his heart beating faster as he did so. While he'd been idly curious about Willis's activities from afar, there was only one real reason he had requested updates on the man. It was a hunch.

Soon enough, it was confirmed.

Fawkes had stayed in Hurleyford House, where Willis was a regular visitor. It made sense, then, to assume that Fawkes knew of Willis's trade... and would have tried to hone in on the man following his escape. Willis would no doubt have helped Fawkes if he had asked for it. Unbridled empathy: the man's Achilles' heel.

The list compiled the new names Willis had sourced for people, as well as the towns or cities they had fled to. Willis tried to know as little about his 'clients' as possible, meaning that original names were generally not available – but the information here was still a goldmine to the right people, name and place after name and place. *'Alexander Letts' relocated to York. 'Margaret Treacher' relocated to Hull. 'Russell Jones' relocated to Bolton.*

'John Johnson' relocated to Virginia.

There was an asterisk alongside this one, extra details also scrawled nearby. *Recusant was given to the care of the Virginia Trading Company. Not to be pursued. Virginia missions are not to be interfered with by royal decree.*

Francis's hand quivered as he held the page. He had heard of the planned mission to forge a settlement in the New World – mainly because it was the sort of thing his Spanish allies also kept a keen eye on.

Willis had never sent his charges scurrying off overseas before – but it was feasible that he could have contacts in the Virginia Trading Company. And the timing was just right, wasn't it? The right schedule for an opportunistic rat like Fawkes to hop on board.

But... *John Johnson?*

Would Fawkes really be that brazen? He was legally a dead man, of course – but surely he would have *some* caution in using that name again?

Then Francis understood. He understood everything. It was a direct insult to him.

Fawkes clearly thought that Francis was dead. He thought that his cowardly musket attack had blown Francis's brains out. This was simply Fawkes laughing at him. Dancing on his grave. Tomb desecration without a tomb.

But.

Could Francis be sure?

Could he be *absolutely certain* that Fawkes was hiding out in Virginia? Francis closed his eyes and delved into silent prayer. He needed an answer. It came almost immediately: flowing through him, a feeling, a certainty.

Of course it was Fawkes.

Francis felt invigorated. He had a purpose now. How would he follow it? He didn't know yet. This would be a monumental undertaking – and he was only at the beginning.

He went back to the interrogation room. He would continue to think things over as he dealt with the prisoner. Hortuño let out an audible moan as Francis walked back in.

With a bit of perseverance and imagination, Francis figured, maybe he could get Hortuño to confess to something bigger than simply hiding a book. Maybe something that could merit the appliance of torture.

His mind always worked better when his hands were busy.

And busy hands were at work elsewhere.

He may have agreed to stay behind and help construct the settlement – but Guy was dreading the interpersonal nonsense that would go along with that, the divisions that had formed on board the ships now taken one step further. There would be arguments. Fights. Violence.

It came as a pleasant surprise, then, that there was very little of that. Everyone was too busy building their new home to squabble over it. Decisions were swiftly made, directions promptly given, tasks delegated and followed.

They had decided to make the settlement upon a marshy peninsula around fifty miles up the newly christened James River. They had yet to make contact with the natives… but that wasn't the main worry. Attacks from any would-be Spanish settlers were a top concern. The plot offered good defensive ground should they come calling.

The initial fort was constructed reasonably quickly: a structure of around an acre, a triangle of palisaded wooden walls around a storehouse and small domiciles. It was no impenetrable stronghold but it would do for now. Even Wingfield was impressed.

'A fine start,' he had said, surveying the work. 'I have every confidence we will make England's heart swell with pride.' Everyone noticed something: the use of the term *we*. Whatever further hard graft was coming, Wingfield and his elites would most assuredly not be part of it.

The more pragmatic types – Smith included – knew the importance of establishing a good food supply. The colonists were going through their remaining supplies at an alarming rate. Yet self-appointed men of leisure seemed happy to munch their way through dwindling reserves as they put their focus on cosmetic matters – like the building of a church.

Rather unsurprisingly, Chaplain Hunt was fully on board with the latter 'priority'. Until he had a chapel to call his own, however, he had been conducting daily services outdoors, with his congregation sat cross-legged on the grass like schoolchildren in a morning assembly. Guy played along: said the right words, went through the right motions. He soon felt a growing worry from most of the men: *if we don't start to seriously think about how we eat, no higher power is going to come and save us.*

Some more eager colonists had carried out a couple of rudimentary hunting expeditions. Spying the foxes and mink and raccoons who roamed around the treeline of the forest, they took their muskets and went to work. They managed to get lucky now and then – but muskets were inherently close-range weapons, noisemakers that sent anything nearby scattering after a first shot. To reload a second shot took around fifteen seconds.

Some men tried to put traps together. They never worked. Many colonists might have been rough and ready when it came to hard labour or fighting... but none of them had any experience when it came to living solely off the land. The animals soon began to seep into Guy's dreams – but he wasn't catching them or eating them. He was running alongside them, of non-human form himself, darting with a pack of wolves or civets into the darkened forest.

Following another one of Chaplain Hunt's outdoor sermons – during which stomachs audibly rumbled and tempers visibly frayed – Smith came over to sit next to Guy.

'You've seen them,' Smith said. 'Haven't you?'

'Yes.'

It hadn't just been local wildlife teeming around the edge of the woodland. Human eyes had been peering out at the new settlers too. They were difficult to spot – but even they couldn't help stepping on the odd snapped twig or rustling through leaves. The natives had been watching them. A lot.

'They're interested in us,' Smith said. 'They should be. We're on their land.'

'What do you suppose is going through their heads?'

'They're taking their time,' Guy said. 'No sudden moves. Getting the measure of us.'

'Maybe,' Smith mused. 'I think they might pity us.'

'What?'

'They could survive off this land with their eyes closed. Then the pale man turns up and... yes, he can put a fort together quickly. But he can't *do anything else*. Can't eat. His weapons might sound fearful... but men can't dine on fear. Their bows and spears put our muskets to shame. They're skilled hunters, expert fishermen. It's all they know from birth. If I was them... looking at this feckless bunch... *I* would pity us.'

'What about the rest of the council?' Guy asked. 'What do they say?'

'Wingfield is Wingfield. He views these people as little more than wildlife or fauna. He holds them no ill will, of course. I suppose that's to his credit. He says we should make efforts to engage with them in future.'

'How magnanimous.'

'Quite. In the meantime, however, he's content to let them watch.'

'They'll be watching us starve,' Guy said.

'That they will.'

'What about the others?'

'Well.' Smith stretched out a little. 'You were right about Newport. He has his head screwed on more firmly than the rest. He thinks we should be talking to these people. Trading with them, ideally. At the very least learning something from them.'

'I assume Wingfield didn't take that well?'

'What on God's earth could WE learn from THEM?' Smith put on his best impression of Wingfield: spittle-flecked mimicry. It was surprisingly good. 'No. He hated the very thought. Thankfully, however, Jamestown is not a dictatorship. Not yet, anyway. Newport put forward a motion. The council voted. It was approved.'

'What motion?'

'A voyage upriver. A small crew will unpack and assemble one of the shallop boats we stored on the *Constant*. We'll be gone for a week or thereabouts. We'll try to make contact with any natives we come across. I mentioned that it could also be useful in determining nearby gold deposits. Funnily enough, Wingfield warmed to the idea after that.'

'Who's going?'

'Newport's on board. I am too. As for the rest... I'm scouting for other crewmen today. Four, five more, maybe.' He idly pulled up a fistful of grass, opening his palm, letting the brown-green strands float off in the breeze. 'Here's the thing, Johnson. If there were anyone intent on trekking off by himself into the New World – perhaps even thinking of doing so shortly – a little expedition like this would make for ideal reconnaissance. Would you happen to know of a chap like that?'

They were silent for a moment.

'I can ask around,' Guy said.

'You do that.' Smith got to his feet. 'And if you find someone? Tell him that we're setting off tomorrow. The first light of dawn, down by the riverside.'

The first light of dawn. Down by the riverside.

The assembled crew was a decent selection. Guy hadn't spoken much to the other men – Tyndall, Archer, Percy and a surgeon named Wotton – but he knew them to be reliable and honest. That was a relief.

The plan was fairly straightforward. They would take the shallop upriver until they found the river source itself or a rumoured mountain range and lake. Any contact would be treated as an opportunity to forge new relationships. They had goods for trading and weapons for defending themselves. They had bedrolls which they would unfurl at night and sleep close to the riverside, ready to leap back on the shallop should danger arise.

On the first day they saw nothing of note and encountered no one else. While the natives could indeed have been tracking them from out of view – following their progress, whispering between themselves as this unusual vessel crept along – the crew simply watched as greenish-brown scenery drifted by. Low-lying meadowland began to roughen slightly; cobblestone-like rocks and higher peaks emerging as time passed. They came across a colony of wild turkeys. They ate.

On the first night they pulled over by a small islet on a looping bend in the river. They built a small fire and sat and talked: mainly observations about the day's travel, predictions for what might lie ahead. Every now and then talk turned to the new settlement itself. Archer had a few less-than-complimentary things to say about Wingfield – before he caught himself. He glanced to Newport with widened eyes. He had assumed that Newport and Wingfield were close: comrades in elitism. Newport's knowing smirk implied exactly the opposite. 'Don't worry about me,' he said. 'My ears are closed.'

Time passed. Talk trailed off. They left the embers of the fire smouldering and bedded down for the night. Guy lay on his back, staring up at a crystalline patchwork of stars, waiting until the others were asleep. It was a knack he had from years of experience: he knew the sounds of crewmen out cold, the settled air of nothingness.

He took in a deep breath. Smith had summed things up well. This was the perfect opportunity to test the waters, literally and otherwise. This was the ideal scouting expedition, a surveyor's dream.

Yet it was something else too.

They were around eighteen miles upstream by now, Guy estimated. Should a man make headway into the dark woods that surrounded them, he could easily make a further ten to fifteen miles inland by the time dawn broke. He would be virtually impossible to track, especially given that the land was unmapped.

When would another chance like this come along? Reconnaissance was all well and good.

But this was also the moment Guy could finally disappear.

'I suppose that's that then,' Smith said.

Guy winced. He had done his best to stay quiet – packing up his bedroll with stealth verve – but hurriedness had made him complacent. The other crewmen remained asleep. All but Smith.

Guy froze on the edge of the clearing. He slowly turned around to face Smith. The moon briefly emerged from behind the thick cloud cover, illuminating them both for a moment.

Guy slowly held up his hands, resigned to circumstance. 'Come on.' Guy sighed. 'You must have expected this.'

'Yes.' Smith nodded as the moonlight vanished again. 'I just didn't think it would happen on the first night.'

'It's as good a night as any.'

'I suppose.'

Faraway animals chittered and howled in the distance. Water gently sloshed at the riverbank.

'Well?' Guy asked.

'Well what?' Smith frowned.

'How this plays out is up to you.'

'Meaning I could wake the others? Detain you? Stop you from leaving?'

'Something like that.'

'Maybe I could stop you myself.'

Another brief glimmer of moonlight pierced the clouds. It dulled almost as soon as it brightened. Guy quietly tensed himself. He clenched his fists, digging his feet into the soil. He hadn't wanted it to come to this – but he was prepared to fight his way to freedom if necessary.

He'd been imprisoned before. It wasn't his style. 'I wouldn't advise it,' Guy calmly said.

Smith remained still. Poised or perhaps not. Guy couldn't tell. 'One question,' Smith said. 'If I may.'

Guy glanced over to the huddled sleepers: the silhouetted crewmen who looked like heaped cargo sacks, snoozing mounds that lay twenty or so feet away. Any of them could stir. At any moment.

'Make it a quick one.'

'What *are* your plans out there, John Johnson?' Smith asked. 'What does a lone wanderer like you intend to do with himself?'

Despite everything, Guy couldn't help but give a weary smile.

'Smith, I have no plans. I have no agenda. I have no scheme, no stratagem, no tactics, no proposition. I am a man without an aim, an outline, an idea or an intention. I simply intend to be John Johnson no longer. What I may become is of no concern right now.'

Smith took this all in.

Guy cast another glance at the sleeping others – their shapes still rising and falling with each snored wheeze.

'You do realise,' Smith said, his whisper remaining level. 'Whatever you intend to vanish from... whatever John Johnson may have done that you wish to excise from history... it is already gone.' He raised an arm and pointed: the instinctive inner compass of a natural explorer. East. Way, way east. 'It is five thousand miles that way. It is never ever coming back. It is no longer part of you.'

That's the problem, Guy wanted to say. *Nothing much IS part of me these days.*

'I wouldn't expect you to understand,' Guy said.

'I see.' Smith looked out into the pitch-black forest. 'You're a resourceful man, Johnson. A survivor. But none of us know what is out there. There could be predators vying to make you their prey. Aggressive natives who would ensure your first contact is also your last. You may not find any water sources. You may not find anything to eat or hunt. You may last but a few days on your path to nowhere.'

Another fleeting shard of moonlight. It came. It went. 'Then I last a few days,' Guy said.

'Very well.' Smith gravely nodded. Guy felt his heartbeat slow a little: this was the final approval he needed, the clinching proof that Smith definitely wasn't going to raise the alarm.

'What will you tell the others?' Guy asked.

'I'll tell them I woke up in the night. I saw you sneaking away. I tried to stop you but I stumbled while running after you. There was no way I could catch up with you but... as I lay there, you shouted one thing. You said: *don't try to find me. I want no part of this colony.* Something like that should remove any incentive to chase after you. Why try and stop a man who fled of his own accord? If some fool wants to vanish and ensure there are more supplies for the rest of us – then so be it.'

'That should work,' Guy said.

'It's only half a lie anyway.' Smith sighed. 'Moment of decision, Johnson. No second chances. If you leave, you leave. I'm a relatively forgiving man... but I doubt the other colonists would welcome you back if you decide to return.'

'I understand.'

'Very well.' Smith looked out into the darkened forest again. 'Then...' He used the Algonquian translation. His grasp was far from perfect – but then neither was Guy's. '*Eškwešamwa. Ešpahamwa.*'

Onward and upward.

Guy turned and faced the darkness. Before he made another move he had one final compulsion. One last thing to say. He half-turned back to Smith. 'Jamestown will fare well without me,' he said.

'That may be.' Smith nodded. 'But it would fare a lot better with you.' Guy had no answer to that.

He made his way into the forest.

He hadn't been entirely truthful with Smith. No scheme, no stratagem: right for the most part, yes, but Guy had at least sketched out some notion of what his first night as a New World hobo would entail.

Guy knew that the land here was mainly pine barrens. Such territory was ill-suited for animal life – meaning encounters with bears and wolves were unlikely. He would be able to sleep soundly enough atop the fine sugary dirt. He had a waterskin and enough food to last him four days – eight if he really spaced out supplies. He was confident of finding edible plants and potable water sources once he left the barrens.

He would aim to walk a crescent-like path inland for the

next week and then slowly make his way back out to the river, at which point – no matter how fruitful or otherwise their expedition had been – Smith and company would have headed back to Jamestown. Newport was a man who lived and breathed strict timekeeping: the shallop would be back at the colony when scheduled.

Guy slept beneath an overhanging pine copse the first night. He carried on walking for most of the second day. It was the first time he had been alone in as long as he could remember. He inhaled deeply.

He felt good.

He slept in a similar spot the second night. When he awoke and carried on trekking, he felt even better. His emptiness was a blessing rather than a burden. As the land unfurled around him, he was becoming an entity without self, flowing with the natural order of things. He could forget about humanity and civilisation and religion and Jamestown – about everything – and turn into something new.

There was, he realised, the possibility of something like peace in his future. And then, on the third night, he found something truly unexpected.

He found a woman.

When he first spotted the hunched yet lithely poised figure, a primal part of his brain thought it was a crouching wildcat. That illusion was soon dispelled.

Wildcats didn't build fires.

Guy emerged from the undergrowth.

He slowly walked forwards, holding his hands aloft in – he hoped – a display of harmlessness. He awkwardly tried to balance a couple of things: holding the woman's gaze while also scanning the area for any other people.

She looked over to Guy with wide eyes, half-illuminated by the fire. She was around his own age, he guessed: mid-thirties, with coffee-brown skin, tawny hair tied into a single braid with a rounded fringe, saucer-like pupils filled with apprehension. She shrank into herself, protective, tucking her hands into her deerskin mantle. She hadn't called out to a fellow native; hadn't tried to share a look or signal with someone hidden nearby. She appeared to be alone.

She was as isolated as he was.

This didn't mean she wasn't a threat, however. She was short and slim but not waiflike: she had a taut body forged from physical exertion. One deep cut from a hidden blade could be all she needed – a gash across an artery and Guy could bleed to death here in the wilderness, a weak and whitened mess days from help. He took another cautious step forward.

The woman flinched. For a moment Guy thought she was about to take off running – but she couldn't help herself from staring at him. They were equally fascinated by each other.

It had been a while since he read *Chronicles*. But he could do this. Just about.

'Kawin manači,' he said, gently speaking the Algonquian words for No Danger. He didn't quite get it right. His phonetics were muddled up... but it was close enough for the woman to get the gist. She looked at Guy's empty hands: visible, weaponless. She looked at his clothes: peculiar, foreign, yet no apparent threat. She raised her own hands in a mirrored gesture.

'Kawin manači,' she said back. It was a start.

Guy took some more faltering steps forward, each movement watched with hawk-like intensity by the woman's wide brown eyes. He stood on the other side of the fire. He gestured to an empty patch of ground: *may I?* He stooped to sit.

She let him.

They sat for a moment. They stared at each other's faces above the flames.

Guy could only wonder what she thought of him. The woman opposite was striking, aged by hardship yet also curiously ageless, strong and tenacious – yet with an air of sadness based around miseries unknown. He was leafing through his internal dictionary – trying to find something to say – when to his surprise she spoke first, a lilting tone of her own language:

'You are with them.'

Guy understood. *Them.* The new arrivals. The strange men who had come from across the ocean.

'Yes,' Guy replied in faltering Algonquian. 'I am.'

'Why are you here?'

You had to ask, didn't you? Guy thought.

'We are here to...' He struggled to find the right words. 'To explore and learn.' Once again, his translation wasn't exactly right – it was closer to *find and see* – but the woman understood. *Finding* and *seeing*: there were few more universal notions than that.

Guy pointed a finger at himself. He jabbed a digit at his own chest. 'John,' he said. 'My name is John.'

He regretted it not half a second later. John? He had introduced himself as John? He knew why: it was instinct after months of lying. But here he could be Guy again. Or any name he wanted.

Still. It was irrelevant now. It had been said. He was John.

'Ch-awn,' the woman said, turning the word over. For a moment Guy thought he saw a tiny smile at how strange it sounded. The woman copied his finger-jabbing gesture, pointing at her own breastbone. 'Odina.'

'Odina?'

'Odina.' She frowned. Something was bothering her, a thought she had perhaps been too surprised by Guy's appearance to consider. 'Wait. You know our language? You can speak our tongue?'

'A little bit, yes,' Guy said. Another close-but-understandable effort: yes, I know some of your words.

'Do all of your people speak our tongue?'

'No. Only two of us.' No. Two alone can do. 'And... where are your people, Ch-awn?'

'Far away, I think. Days from here.' Near they are not. Days must be travel. 'But they are not my people anymore. I have left them. I am alone now.' My people I not belong. Now I go from them. Now I be alone.

Odina reached down for something nearby. She shuffled around to one side of the fire, closer to Guy, not entirely trusting but more confident now. She held something out for him. It was dried fish wrapped in a pond leaf. It was warm, heated over the fire to draw out the tenderness.

'You are hungry?' Odina asked.

'Thank you.' Guy took the fish. Hesitant at first, he bit into it. It was delicious. It tasted of the carp he used to catch as a boy in York: the bounty of his juvenile fishing excursions to Redwood Lake.

Odina watched him eat. Then:

'Ch-awn. Why did you leave your people? And where did you all come from in the first place?'

'That is a long story,' Guy said. To know the story will take time.

'I would like to hear it.'

'Very well. But tell me first, Odina. Why are you out here all alone? Where are your people?'

There was movement nearby. Noise. Rustling. Hushed chatter.

Guy quickly turned to look at the treeline. Whoever the people were, they were closing in.

Had this all been some sort of trick? He turned back to face Odina – She had vanished.

Through sheer chance, Guy caught sight of her, nestling her way into the nearby red cedar foliage, camouflaging herself the way only a native could. She spotted him looking at her. She gave a panicked gesture, flitting her hand back and forth – quick, come and join me over here, quick, please, you need to HIDE – before the new intruders arrived, hacking their way through the dense surroundings.

Odina looked at Guy with begging eyes. An unspoken plea not to reveal her whereabouts.

Whoever was here... Odina was very, very frightened of them.

There were three men. Three natives. Two of them seemed barely into their twenties while the other one – the natural-looking leader – was perhaps in his mid-forties. Guy initially wondered if they could be father and sons. As they emerged further into the clearing, it seemed unlikely: they looked too different from each other for any close family ties. They wore the same clothes – loincloths, mantles, buckskin sandals, their heads shaved on one side and the hair pinned under a deer-tail roach on the other. They clutched the same weaponry. But... apart from that... they varied too greatly to be relatives.

What did unite them was their sheer amazement.

Their spears aloft, they slowly parted from each other, working in sync, a time-honed hunting pattern working on muscle memory. Guy was now on his feet by the fire. He had his hands up once more. Open. Empty. Free of danger.

He glanced to and fro between the three men as they circled him closer. The oldest man was now the nearest. He squinted, cocking his head, as though making sure this pale apparition was not a mirage. They spoke to each other in faster, more clipped tones than Odina had – but Guy could still more or less follow.

'One of them,' the eldest said.

'They stay outland.' The taller of the younger men sounded nervous. 'The white men. They keep to the marshland. Don't they?'

'Perhaps they're getting braver,' the shorter one piped up.

'Or stupider.' The eldest one had not taken his frozen stare off Guy for a moment. Guy noticed that all three of them were carrying supplies of food and water: not the kind of stuff someone would bring if they were staying close to home. They had travelled at least a day from their village. A trip with purpose. Looking for something.

Or someone.

'He will not be alone,' the eldest man said. 'Others will be near. Maybe they're trying to set a trap for us. Spread out. Look for them.'

'No!' Guy yelled out, a sudden burst of Algonquian. 'Wait. I'm alone here. There's no one else. The fire is mine, the camp is mine.'

If the three men had looked amazed before... they now looked like babies watching a meteorite shower.

It didn't last long.

With incredible speed, the elder man whipped out a blade and soon had it pressed to Guy's throat.

'You know our tongue?' the man said.

'Yes.' Guy swallowed. His neck bulged, his flesh pricking against the tip of the knife.

'How?'

'Some of my people have been here before. They learned

things. I learned from them. My people some men come early. They find. I find too.'

The elder man took a moment. He kept the knife pressed against Guy's jugular.

'You understand us well?' he asked.

'Yes. Better than I speak.'

'I never met your kind before, white man. But I know those who have. They often do not have good things to say.'

'Those were not my people,' Guy said.

'I do not care. You should keep your differences to yourselves. Away from us.' He relaxed his grip on the blade a little. 'We have seen your settlement by the river. Watched you building. You seem to have made that your home. So why are you out here alone?'

'I left.'

'You left?'

'The men there are honourable and mean you no harm,' Guy said, unsure of exactly how true this was, 'but I have no wish to stay with them. I want to make my own way in this land.' Men over there are true and of no danger. I am not of them. I wish for myself to find world. The eldest native mulled over the scrambled sentences. He lowered the knife. The two younger men now had their bows aimed squarely at Guy. Guy stayed as still as he could.

No one said anything for a while. The tallest of the younger men eventually spoke up, addressing the eldest:

'Wowinchapuncke says that we are to take any of the foreigners directly to him, if we encounter them directly.'

'I know what Wowinchapuncke says,' the eldest snapped, giving him a withering sneer. 'But Wowinchapuncke also doesn't know that we're out here, does he? Or why we're out here. Would you like to be the one to explain everything to him?' The man shut his mouth.

Wowinchapuncke is a leader, Guy thought. An authority. Someone these men are scared of. Someone whose boot is forever on their necks.

Some things really are the same the world over.

'If we never saw him,' the smaller one ventured, 'we would never have to bring him to Wowinchapuncke.'

'My thoughts exactly,' the eldest said.

He gestured for the younger men to lower their bows. They did so. He pointed his knife in the air, using it as punctuation as he addressed Guy.

'If you do see your people again,' he said, 'tell them a reckoning is coming. Tell them we are biding our time before we respond to your invasion. Tell them they still have a chance to leave. Barely.' He put the knife back in his mantle and walked away. The others followed. As the eldest led them to the opposite end of the clearing – taking them back into the forest on whatever mission they were on – he turned back to Guy. 'And if you don't see your people again? If you decide to keep travelling on your own? We won't have to worry about you. You won't survive a day out here, white man.'

He spat on the ground. The three natives left.

The natives had gone. They weren't coming back.

Guy finally exhaled.

He jumped slightly as a rustling noise came from nearby. He settled when he saw who it was: Odina, emerging from the red cedars, flushed with a mixture of relief and uncertainty.

'They are gone,' Guy said.

'I can see that.'

'They were looking for you.'

'Yes.'

'Why?'

'That,' Odina said, 'is my long story.' She made her way over to the fire again, glancing into the surrounding darkness just to make sure the men were gone for good.

Whatever her story was, she had no intention of sharing it right now. Maybe she was waiting for Guy to reveal his first – in which case she would be waiting a while. Guy also went back to the fire, sitting on the ground again.

'Will they be back?' Guy eventually asked.

'No.' Odina stared into the fire. 'They have almost found me before. But they never retrace their steps. Their time is limited on each trip. They can only search so far.'

'How long have you been running from them?'

'Long enough.'

'And if they do catch you? What then?'

'Nothing good.' She prodded at the fire with a stick, reigniting some of the embers. 'Are all your people this curious?'

'Some of us.'

'That can be a dangerous thing. Askook is a terrible man – but he was right. You should all leave. There will be trouble otherwise.'

'Askook?' Guy frowned.

Odina paused. She flung the stick to one side, irritated. She had revealed something she didn't want to reveal. Guy twigged: Askook. That was his name. The eldest of the natives.

'No more questions, Ch-awn,' Odina said. 'Please.' She slowly regained her composure. She closed her eyes and took a deep breath. Opened them again. 'But... I thank you. For not telling them where I was.'

Guy nodded. No more questions: that seemed like a fair approach. Guy had ventured into this land to be reborn, hoping to leave the concerns of humanity far behind. That was a pledge he intended to keep.

But.

He was tired.

'You say they never come back,' he told Odina. 'But they might. This time. I could camp here tonight. To protect you.'

Odina finally looked away from the fire again. A thin smile tugged at the corners of her lips.

'To protect me?' she asked. 'Or to sleep near my fire?'

'Maybe both.' Guy smiled back.

'Then I accept your offer. But as soon as dawn arrives, I will be moving on.'

'So will I.'

'Where to?'

'I don't know,' Guy said. 'What about you?'

Odina didn't answer. Another unwelcome topic broached. Guy let it go. He reached over for his bedroll – which, thankfully, the three natives had been too distracted to tear apart and pillage – and began to unpack it. He noticed Odina watching him. She found the whole thing perplexing. Guy held the bedroll out for her.

'Do you want it?'

Your chivalry is going to cause you a cold night, he told himself. Luckily for him Odina had her own sleeping arrangements. She nodded over to it: a sturdy leather mat unrolled upon a lattice of leaves and branches.

Guy had no idea whether he would be able to sleep. He was willing to try. He settled onto his back, watching the smoke from the fire curl into the starry sky, wondering if the night would eventually take him.

Serendipity. That was what lesser minds would have called it.

Francis knew better than that. He knew that such fortunate

twists were interventions, rewards from above. And frankly – not that he wanted to question the divine plan or anything – he was damn sure he was overdue a reward.

The Grand Inquisitor was visiting Galicia. A sturdy man named Acevedo who had been in the role for four years now. Acevedo had expressed a desire to keep a closer eye on his charges than previous leaders. As such, around three times a year, he headed out on a short tour of various Inquisición bureaus.

Francis had no great respect for Acevedo. He viewed him in the same light as the rest of the Inquisición. He was the leader of the lazily faithful, the figurehead of an institution that could achieve true Crusade-era glory but had chosen to sink into complacency instead. Francis had heard stories of the Inquisición in days gone by. It was like comparing a warrior in his prime to a senile old geriatric.

Francis had put in a request for a face-to-face meeting with Acevedo upon his visit... but had soon found out this was unnecessary. Acevedo had taken particular interest in Francis – this curious English interloper – and wanted to speak to him anyway. As he strode to meet Acevedo, Francis spotted other Inquisitors watching him with a jealous eye: why, exactly, did *this* specimen get called to a special meeting when so many others did not?

A couple of guards ushered Francis into Acevedo's temporary chambers. Acevedo himself was indulging in a late lunch. Age hadn't been especially unkind to Acevedo so far – but the way he lived was bound to destroy his body eventually.

Acevedo finished off a grilled swordfish fillet and put the remains on a plate, alongside the remains of some sweetened cheese and stuffed eggs.

'I'm honoured to see you, Grand Inquisitor.' Francis bowed.

'Bow not to me, but only to God,' Acevedo said, wiping his

fingers clean. He chuckled. 'Although I'd be lying if I said I didn't appreciate the gesture.'

'Few merit the gesture as much as you, Grand Inquisitor.' Such enforced smarm did not rest easily with Francis – although he was very good at it.

'Sit, sit.' Acevedo gestured for Francis to take a seat at the table. He did so. 'How are things, Tresham? Life in Galicia is to your satisfaction?'

'My satisfaction is unimportant,' Francis said. 'My work is what I should be judged on. And, if I may say so myself, I feel I have been doing an exemplary job.'

He reined himself in slightly. 'Forgive me, Grand Inquisitor. I did not wish to sound arrogant.'

'No need to apologise.' Acevedo waved a dismissive hand. 'Modesty is a virtue, yes. But when it comes to holy service, achievements should be celebrated. You *have* been doing good work here, Tresham. Your fellow men are quick to confirm this.' Acevedo's eyes briefly flitted over to the plate of leftovers. Francis kept up his veneer of deference – but inside it was crumbling quite quickly.

Still hungry, are you?

Still want some more swill, you greedy FUCKING PIG?

'I am glad to hear that,' Francis said.

'As am I.' Acevedo looked back. 'I was worried at first, you know. Following that incident before you left London, I was concerned that you would feel the need to... prove yourself to a greater degree. Nothing can tamper a man's work more than a sense of inadequacy. I am pleased to say that I see none of that in you. Despite the horror of what happened to you' – he at least had the grace to steer clear of the word *disfigurement* – 'you have managed to keep a level head on your shoulders. You are to be commended.'

'Thank you, Grand Inquisitor,' Francis said. 'Although...' He intentionally trailed off.

Here we go, Francis thought. 'Although... what?' Acevedo asked.

'Nothing, Grand Inquisitor.'

'Come on now, Tresham. Out with it. What troubles you?'

'Well... my fellow Inquisitors here in Galicia have a very established set of routines. They have worked with each other for many years. I fear that I might be acting as something of a burden. An obstacle thrown into a device which was functioning perfectly well.' He hunched forwards slightly. 'I suppose, Grand Inquisitor... I'm saying that my talents could be better used elsewhere.'

'Are you now?' Acevedo was surprised. Few recruits were forthright enough to talk to him like this.

'I am. Yes.'

'And what exactly did you have in mind, Tresham?'

Francis told him.

The background details were mere illumination; details that Acevedo already knew but which would bolster Francis's cause.

Francis talked about how the *Inquisición* had been branching out to the New World in recent decades, setting up outposts in regions colonised by Spain. Since conquering the Aztecs around eighty years previously, Mexico had become a great resource of trade and wealth for the Spanish. Settlements thrived in Yucatán and Veracruz and Tenochtitlan – now renamed Mexico City. New international factions of the *Inquisición* emerged in these places. Not even a century had passed before the heathen Aztecs were a mere memory. Catholicism had not just gained a foothold. It *was* the foothold.

So: Mexico was en route to becoming a wholly Spanish domain. Further north, however – in the more unexplored regions of what they called *America* – things were far less certain. It was a source of both fear and embarrassment to Spain that England was making good headway while they were floundering. Only a few noble exceptions could help set things right: in particular, *la Florida.*

'Florida?' Acevedo asked. 'That is where you wish to go?'

'*San Augustin*,' Francis said. 'Yes. Grand Inquisitor. We have had established territory there for many years now. We have been working hard to spread the one true faith. We have even seen success in converting the locals. But – just like here in Spain – that faith will need protecting, especially if we have plans to expand further north. What better place would there be for a base of operations than *la Florida*? It could become the *Santo Oficio de la Inquisición* for the New World.'

'So.' Acevedo mulled this all over. 'You not only wish to relocate to Florida for *Inquisición* business. You also wish to become de facto regional leader for an entirely new faction.'

'Yes.'

Acevedo continued to think about this... and then burst into laughter. He clapped his hands together.

'You know,' he said. 'Ambassador Zúñiga said you were something of a character. Now I can see... this was actually an understatement.'

Francis gave a gentle laugh. He had to play this carefully. There was definitely camaraderie in the air... but Acevedo still had to feel in control. Francis couldn't afford to overstep his mark.

'My apologies again, Grand Inquisitor. I should be more humble.'

'Once again, arrogance can be forgiven if it is warranted.' Acevedo's amusement had subsided. 'You're right about *la*

Florida, to some extent. We haven't particularly had an easy ride with the natives but a few of them have opened their hearts to the Almighty. Most of the others know enough not to cross our path, even if they refuse the gift of conversion. A few remain violent and troublesome but their number is dwindling. It's nothing compared to the danger the natives pose further north. You know that the English are founding a settlement there, don't you? Some foolish enterprise in the land they call Virginia?'

'No,' Francis lied.

'It doesn't sound like a clever move.' Acevedo gave a contemptuous smirk. 'But you should never interrupt your enemy while they're making a mistake, yes?'

'Wise words.'

'Trust the English not to learn any lessons from history – even if it is *our* history. You're familiar with the Ajacán Mission, I take it?'

'Yes, Grand Inquisitor.'

'Anyone travelling to that part of the world should ask Alonso de Olmos how things worked out.'

'Indeed they should.'

Alonso de Olmos had become something of a notable public figure, despite his attempts to continually evade attention and live out a simple life. Almost forty years ago – 1570, to be exact – a rather foolhardy pair of Spanish priests had embarked on their ill-fated Ajacán Mission, an attempt to bring Christianity to the natives of the Virginia Peninsula.

Alonso de Olmos had been a young servant boy enlisted into the small party. He was also the only survivor of a massacre from the natives. For reasons best known to themselves, the savages had taken Alonso in, placing him under the care of their tribal chief. Two years later the crew of a Spanish supply ship decided to go on a revenge mission. Twenty natives were slaughtered. Alonso was rescued.

Alonso had stories. Lots of stories. The natives had treated him as one of their own. He had learned their language and adopted many of their customs. Upon his return to Spain he had been earmarked as a novelty guest for high-society soirées, someone who could regale the rich and pampered with his remarkable adventures. He wanted absolutely nothing of the sort. Lost between cultures, Alonso became a recluse. He now lived in Castile, a middle-aged man eking out a living as a labourer. No wife, no children. A curiosity to local children and a beacon of gossip for chattering old ladies.

'The English are welcome to that region,' Acevedo said. 'At least for now anyway. Let them take the brunt of the violence and horror. We can look at more strategic conquests in the meantime. Maybe head in there to clean up afterwards.' He frowned. Contemplative. 'Although you are right, Tresham. Florida would be a good location for a new *Inquisición*.' He tapped his fingers on the table thoughtfully. 'Assume I was to agree to this. To send you out there to establish a bureau. You understand that this is not a simple undertaking? Firstly, the *Inquisición* will need to arrange transport–'

'The *Magdalena*,' Francis said.

Interrupting the Grand Inquisitor: now *that* was risky.

'Excuse me?'

'I do not seek to offend you, Grand Inquisitor,' Francis went on. 'But I have taken a couple of liberties. Firstly, I have spoken to contacts in the navy. A military vessel named the *Magdalena* will be departing in just under a week for Florida, carrying supplies and reinforcements. There is sufficient room on board.'

'Interesting. And what–'

There was a loud, resonant knock on the chamber doors.

'Enter,' Acevedo said.

One of the guards poked his head through the door, looking equal parts confused and sheepish.

'Grand Inquisitor,' he said. 'There is someone here to see you.'

'Can you not see that I'm busy? Tell him to wait.'

'He claims that he has been summoned to be part of this discussion. Between you and your present guest.'

'What?' Acevedo looked incredulous. 'Who *is* this?'

'This, Grand Inquisitor,' Francis spoke up, 'is my other liberty.'

Summoning Alonso de Olmos had not been difficult. All it took was a letter affixed with the *Inquisición* seal, passed on through organisational hands until it reached the governor of Castile... and then Alonso himself. Saying no to an official *Inquisición* summons would be unthinkable, even for a man so disengaged from society.

'Your Grace.' Francis made the introduction as the new arrival was shown into the room. 'This is Alonso de Olmos.'

Alonso was a weary-looking man in the throes of a difficult middle age. His thick coppery hair had receded to a sparse balding crown. His strong frame had succumbed to flabby slackness. He looked like any other interchangeable peasant one might find on a ride between Candeleda and Calatañazor.

He was now facing the Grand Inquisitor. Unsurprisingly, he looked terrified.

'The further we expand, we may encounter some more difficult resistance from the savages,' Francis said. 'A shared tongue would be most useful for opening the natives' hearts to the glory of God – or at least for persuading them to get out of our way. Who better to assist me than a man who can communicate directly with the savages?'

The room was silent for a long moment.

'Allow me to understand,' Acevedo finally said. 'You were so sure that I would agree to your scheme that you brought de Olmos here in advance?'

'Yes,' Francis replied.

This was it. The moment where Acevedo would either agree to things – or explode in outrage.

'Remarkable.' Once more, Acevedo laughed and clapped his hands. 'Very well. You have my approval. You can carry the seal of the *Inquisición* over to Florida and continue your devotion to duty there.' Acevedo then turned to look at Alonso, as though the man was little more than an afterthought. 'And you, *Señor* de Olmos. You are hereby formally requested to join an expedition.'

'Requested?' Alonso managed to stammer.

'Ah.' Acevedo shrugged. '*Requested... ordered...* they both mean the same thing around here.'

Alonso was still left in dumbstruck silence as Francis led him from the chambers. They walked out into a courtyard. Francis was about to start explaining things in earnest when:

'No.' Alonso stopped in his tracks.

'Excuse me?' Francis stopped too.

'I said *no*. I won't do it. Whoever you are... whatever help you want from me... I refuse.'

'Do you think it is particularly wise to refuse orders from the *Inquisición*? From Grand Inquisitor Acevedo, no less?'

'You listen to me.' Alonso stepped forward until he was almost nose to nose with Francis. He may have been long past his physical peak... but he was still a somewhat imposing man.

Francis suddenly realised: Alonso was the only other person

who had not even blinked when confronted with his disfigurement.

Maybe he had seen much worse.

'The *Inquisición* is a fearful prospect, yes,' Alonso said. 'But it is not above the law. You may think I'm a nobody but I have my connections. I can speak to some powerful people. They could put a stop to this game of yours.'

'And when they fail? When the Grand Inquisitor's orders still stand?'

'Then I'll get on your boat.' Alonso somehow moved in even closer. 'I'll sail with you. And then, when we're in *la Florida*, I'll speak to the governor. Did I mention I'm acquainted with him too? I met him at a function a few years ago. A quick word with him and I'll be on the next boat back. I'll make your whole mission a complete waste of time. Once again, you may think that I'm some sort of nobody–'

Francis held up his hand.

'Are you happy, Alonso?' Francis asked.

'Happy?'

'Yes. Happy. Cheerful. Joyous. Leaping out of bed every morning, thankful for the wonders inherent in a bright new day. Are you *happy*?'

'Of course not.' Alonso snorted. The notion seemed utterly ridiculous. 'Who is? Happiness is for the wealthy and the gilded.'

'Then isn't that the solution,' Francis asked, 'to become wealthy and gilded?' Alonso froze. Francis took a step back. Breathing room.

'Go on,' Alonso said.

'I couldn't care less about Florida. Nor the *Inquisición*. What I care about is using their resources. You and I can head over on the *Magdalena* and then leave town at the first available opportunity. We'll go on a journey. A couple of weeks and we'll reach Virginia. Should we stumble into any natives there, your linguistic talents will be most useful.'

'Virginia?' Alonso nearly choked in disbelief. 'Why in God's name would I ever want to go back there?'

Francis unveiled it: the carrot for the donkey.

'Because,' Francis said, 'the English are also there. And word is they're digging for gold. Lots of gold. The kind of gold that two enterprising fellows like us could sneak in and take for ourselves.'

Alonso stared at Francis. Assessing his honesty.

'How much gold?' he asked.

'Enough to make terms like *wealthy* and *gilded* look like curse words scrawled on a whore's bedroom wall.' Francis gave an exaggerated sigh. 'Now. I'm getting tired of this back-and-forth. Are you with me? Or are you against me?'

Greed glistened in Alonso's eyes. Just as Francis had known it would.

'I'm with you,' he said.

CHAPTER SEVEN

1607

Guy's eyes snapped open. He remained still.

They were back. The three men. The natives. They had returned to take Odina... and also to deal with him.

He listened, trying his best to filter out the background noise from the surrounding forest. It was the very cusp of dawn, the pink-skied prelude to sunrise. The birds were twittering merrily. Guy blocked them out and honed in on a different noise.

Odina. Odina was talking to someone. He couldn't make out what she was saying... but there was sadness in her tone.

Was she pleading with the three men to spare her? Was she begging for forgiveness, whatever her transgression had been? Guy cursed himself for having fallen asleep. He should have made good on his promise.

Protection.

Still. It wasn't too late.

He just had to get the measure of things.

Listening further, Guy still couldn't make out any definitive words... just the cadence of muted conversation. This was when the revelation came. The men hadn't returned. Odina wasn't speaking to them.

The voice that conversed with Odina – similar pitch, light yet urgent – was female. She was talking with another woman.

Wait. No. Not a woman. A little girl.

The world was going to end. Odina had always known this.

Everyone else knew it too. The Prophecy had been given around seventy summers before her birth. When Odina was growing up, there had been a few elder men and women among the *Tsenacommacah* who could remember life before the doom-filled vision – and as they died off one by one over the years, soon no one could imagine life without the Prophecy hanging over their heads. Some took it more seriously than others. Many tried to claim that it was open to interpretation; that a trickster god like the Great Hare was playing some warped game. They never sounded entirely convinced. It seemed like they were just looking for comfort in the darkness.

The Prophecy had come, as all such things did, as a dream vision. The originator's name had long been lost to history. All that was known was a woman had entered a *hobbomak* rock circle and reached out for spiritual insight. She had got it. The vision itself was clear: the tribes of the *Tsenacommacah* would endure three incursions from invading white men. They would defeat the white men twice. The third time the white men would triumph. And that would, the vision said, be it: the end of the world.

The use of the term *world* confused many. What exactly did it mean? The world entire... or just the world of the

Tsenacommacah? Odina had little time for such distinctions. To the tribes of the *Tsenacommacah* – the Paspahegh, the Pamunkey, the Mattaponi, the thirty-plus others – the region *was* the world entire. It didn't matter if the lands beyond the ocean were preserved after the downfall: the Real People and all their traditions would be gone forever.

The Prophecy could not be ignored. Two such invasions had already taken place. One had been around twenty summers back, when the white men had built a settlement they called *Roanoake*. There had followed another less successful effort a few years after that. Both invasions had been repelled.

But this meant the third was coming.

So: the people of the *Tsenacommacah* looked to their leaders for guidance. Each tribe looked to a local leader they called a *weroance* – who in turn all looked to the Great Chief Powhatan for stoic inspiration.

Thankfully, Powhatan had never been short of that. While he was certainly getting no younger – he was an old man now, having been born shortly after the Prophecy was delivered – he still commanded a sense of fear and respect like few who ever lived. He had inherited a leadership of six tribes from his father.

Through a lifetime of conquering he claimed more than thirty: the Powhatan Alliance, fifteen thousand souls across a hundred and sixty villages.

Regular tithes and gifts to Powhatan – crops, animals, jewellery – were an essential part of life. They were necessary to maintain his benevolent grace: protection, leadership, favour. No one ever questioned or resented this. Minor skirmishes aside, existence in the *Tsenacommacah* was almost universally peaceful. Yes, the chiefdom was said to have personal conflicts, just like any family – Powhatan's younger brother Opechancanough was reportedly bitter of his sibling's status – but this posed little threat to the established order.

For the first twenty years of Odina's life, Powhatan remained an abstract figure. Her life revolved around her own tribe: the Paspahegh, a self-contained society. Likewise, the Prophecy was rarely spoken of in an everyday sense. The Paspahegh and the wider *Tsenacommacah* tribes led ordinary quotidian lives: hunting, fishing, agriculture, homemaking. The Prophecy did not stop the other Gods from making their presence known: a malicious spirit could regularly see to a weakened harvest or spate of infant deaths. In truth, life was often too fraught to worry about what the far future might hold.

Odina had been surrounded by uproar since her birth. The youngest of six other siblings – all brothers – she had soon learned that most of the womanly duties of the family fell upon her. Since she had first learned to walk she had been drafted into a litany of domestic busywork: weaving, cooking, harvesting crops, an endless list.

She often watched with bitter jealousy as the other girls in the village – those with only a fraction of the homely tasks to carry out – played with each other while she was stuck inside. Her mother would not let her go out to play until she had finished every little chore. Sometimes this meant not going out at all.

The inevitable happened: Odina grew more and more detached from the other girls. She was envious of their freedom and lightness of spirit – but she was also slightly contemptuous at how easily they could crumple into tears. *So a bite from a harmless ribbon snake is enough to make you cry?* she would often think. *How would you handle REAL problems?*

Unconventional as it was, Odina's best friend as a child was a slightly older boy named Askook. Both quiet and reserved, they immediately spotted each other as natural outsiders. Just as Odina didn't get on with the other girls, Askook was a natural misfit when it came to the Paspahegh boys. Shy and awkward, Askook was not helped by his bug-eyed demeanour and gangly frame. He had also been denied the physical dexterity of his peers. As was Paspahegh tradition, Askook had to 'earn' his breakfast every day: his mother would throw a clump of dried moss in the air which Askook was expected to hit with an arrow. A terrible archer, Askook went hungry most mornings.

'Everyone is good at something,' he lamented to Odina one day. 'Everyone but me. Rowtag is a fine all-round hunter. Pilan could strike a spear into the head of a flower from miles away. Elsu might as well have been born with a bow in his hands. But me? I have *nothing*. I can do *nothing*.'

'You'll find your talent,' Odina told him. 'You'll become great at something one day. Just wait.'

'Do you really think that?' Askook asked.

'Yes,' Odina lied.

'You shouldn't tease him like that,' Odina's mother said to her, after overhearing the two talking.

'What do you mean?'

'He is older than you. Old enough to start thinking of a future bride. It is clear he has you in mind.'

'We are just *friends*,' Odina protested.

'If you say so. I hope he thinks that too.'

Odina grew further into her teens. Her envy of the other girls took a massive turnaround: the other girls were now jealous of *her*. It wasn't difficult to figure out why. Odina had always been blessed with fair looks but had now blossomed into a beautiful young woman. She was now the subject of lots of male attention: young men who made no attempt to hide their lust, sadder and older men who covertly stole glances whenever she walked by. Her brothers now grew fiercely protective of her. Fights broke out on an almost daily basis.

Askook escaped such violence – mainly because Odina's brothers were too busy laughing at his fecklessness to see him as a threat. Odina's blood cycle had arrived, meaning she was now a marriageable prospect. Tradition meant that any suitors were to approach a potential wife and their family with gifts: bundles of fish or meat or plant delicacies. If the gifts were received without any fanfare, the suitor usually got the message: the girl was not interested.

Askook didn't get the message. Ever.

When it got to the point where the gifts were ridiculously extravagant – when Askook was likely taking food out of his own family's mouths – Odina's mother issued a warning again.

'You have to put a stop to this.'

'I haven't *done* anything,' Odina said.

'Precisely. You haven't told him that you are not interested in him. You have simply let this continue.'

'But he must *know* I'm not interested! I haven't responded to any gifts, any advances. He must know!'

'Men never do,' Odina's mother said, as though it was the most obvious thing in the world.

Odina then knew: like it or not, the burden was on her to shut this mess down. She would do this tactfully, she told herself as she went to meet Askook the next morning. She would be graceful and kind. He might have become a nuisance but she did not want to upset him more than necessary.

As she ventured to Askook's home, she noticed there was something of a fuss in the village. Askook's name was being thrown around – and another word was being mentioned too. *Huskanaw*.

Oh no, thought Odina. *Oh NO*.

The *huskanaw* was a ritual used to determine the 'elite'

among Paspahegh men. Those who passed the *huskanaw* would be entitled to high-status positions such as councillors when they matured. It was a gruelling ordeal: boys would be poisoned with toxic plants and sent into the woods to survive for a couple of months in a state of fevered madness. Older men known as 'keepers' would occasionally intervene to deliver beatings. If the boys lasted long enough without giving up, they had passed. It was something that only the truly strong and determined could endure.

In other words: Askook didn't stand a chance.

Odina prayed she was not too late to dissuade Askook. Her prayers remained unanswered. By the time she found him he was surrounded by keepers in the village square, preparing himself for the *huskanaw*. He gave Odina a look that confirmed her worst fears.

I am doing this for you, his eyes said.

There was no way she could talk him out of it. The *huskanaw* was now underway. He took the concoction and immediately clutched at his stomach. The keepers led him into the forest.

Maybe I have underestimated Askook, Odina tried to convince herself as she watched him go. *Maybe he is capable of this after all. Maybe he'll last the* huskanaw *and prove all the doubters wrong.*

Askook gave in three days later.

He staggered into town, already having dropped dangerously in weight, bruised, quivering arms outstretched, eyes glazed over with hallucinogenic horror, dried spittle on lips that could only form three words:

Please. No more. Please. No more. Please. No more.

Askook was taken to recover the way all *huskanaw* failures were: he was subject to a humiliation ritual, placed in a latticework cage in the village square, left to drift slowly back to sanity. It was a bad enough ritual for most rejects. For Askook it was a thousand times worse. Everyone had always said he was feeble and inept. Now they had living proof.

Odina occasionally passed the cage while on her daily chores. Askook gazed out at her with sorrowful eyes. She tried to give him a reassuring smile. His expression remained vacant. *He's not himself*, Odina thought. *Not yet. The toxins are still working their way out of his body.* Sure enough, day by day, Askook's eyes became more lucid – if not less distraught.

Poisoned or otherwise... something within him had changed.

It wasn't just the Paspahegh boys who took growing interest in Odina. Every now and then the tribe would have a visitation from Powhatan's men: part diplomatic envoys, part reminder of who was *really in charge*. She had noticed these men eyeing her up, often muttering between each other. She had thought nothing of it until her parents called her into the house one day.

They were waiting, sat on the floor, glum-faced and awkward.

'You know about Chief Powhatan?' her father asked.

'Yes.' Odina frowned. What kind of question was *that*? Of course she knew about him. It was like asking if she had heard of the river or the birds. As her father's expression grew wearier, she understood: he was merely trying to lay the groundwork for what came next.

'You are aware of his... marital situation?'

'Yes.' It was another obvious question. Powhatan had had many brides in the past and – assuming his body was strong enough to see through a few more difficult winters – he would have many more brides in the future.

Surrounding tribes in the *Tsenacommacah* did not just

offer material tithes to Powhatan. Every now and then Powhatan would select a young woman to become another of his wives. It was always a temporary arrangement: the woman would briefly go to live with the Powhatan tribe, bear the chief a child, raise the child for a few years in her own village... until the Powhatans took it away to be raised as their own. The mother would never have contact with the child again.

In return the woman – and her family – would be guaranteed a life of comfort. They would never go hungry. They would never lack shelter. The woman herself would be permitted to remarry, forging a new union with whoever she wanted – and that man would be allocated certain privileges too.

'Powhatan has...' Her father struggled. 'He has...'

Odina's mother gently put her hand on his.

He wanted to deliver the news – but she gave him a look that implied she should take over. He sullenly agreed.

'You are to become Powhatan's bride,' her mother told Odina. The words sounded so surreal: a voice that had once sung her lullabies was now plotting out her future. 'Powhatan's men will come to collect you at dawn tomorrow. Don't cry, Odina. Please don't cry.'

Don't cry: it was like asking her to stop thinking or breathing. She wept as her parents reeled off the platitudes, sentiments she was already familiar with. Yes, this would strengthen bonds between the Paspahegh and the Powhatans. Yes, she would be part of a proud tradition that kept peace within the *Tsenacommacah*. Yes, it would only involve the sacrifice of a few years of her life – the use of her body, the utility of her womanhood – and she would be 'free' once more. This was all objectively true – but that didn't matter. *It was supposed to happen to other people*. This wasn't the kind of responsibility that should be weighed upon Odina's shoulders. She was just a simple Paspahegh girl.

'Everything will be fine,' her mother said, stroking a reassuring hand along her face.

Odina pretended to believe her. She managed to quell her tears. While she was indeed a simple Paspahegh girl... she was also the girl who refused to cry like an infant when struck by the miseries of life.

She had strength. Resilience. Fortitude.

Now she was going to use them like never before.

Powhatan's men came. They took Odina away. She said goodbye to the people she would not see again for a while – her family among them – and watched as the village became little more than a distant speck on the river.

Not a word was said on the journey to the Powhatan village. The men had done this many times before: bringing Powhatan a new bride was as mundane a task as whittling an arrow.

Odina arrived in the Powhatan village to little fanfare. Exact numerical accounts differed – but Odina soon learned that she was around the seventieth wife Powhatan had taken. What was to be a life-changing rite of passage for her was treated as an annual quirk of the climate. Older Powhatan villagers spoke about Odina's arrival like they would a repeat harvest or change in the weather.

Marriage season again. Time moves so fast these days.

Powhatan himself, some whispered stories went, had made the mistake of falling deeply in love with some of his previous temporary brides – which made the inevitable split painful. As such, Powhatan had learned to invest very little emotion in his wives. They were there to bear his children and forge familial bonds across the *Tsenacommacah*. Nothing more. This was not to say he was a mean or unpleasant man. It just meant that both the bride and Powhatan had no illusions about the arrangement: it was a union of functionality, a set-up alien to love.

This suited Odina just fine.

The less complicated things were, the better.

She was introduced to Powhatan on her second day in the village. She moved into his household that same night. A tall and lean man in his eighth decade, he exuded power: hands that had once crushed the life out of countless throats, eyes that had stared hard at dying rivals, faded scars etched in a pattern of battle wounds. He would have been easy to mark out as a chief had he been clad in everyday villager clothing – never mind the regal garments he swathed himself with.

He told his other wives – four women who also inhabited the household at the same time – to leave him and Odina alone. They meekly obeyed, departing almost as one.

'This must seem strange,' Powhatan said.

'Yes.' Odina nodded.

'I understand that. It will come to seem normal soon enough. You have nothing to worry about. I am a good man.' This attempt to sound gentle should have seemed ridiculous – yet for some reason it *didn't*. Odina believed him. Powhatan didn't need displays of bravado or brutality. Not anymore. He had long since paid his dues in that department. 'You will be well taken care of. I do not ask that you pretend to adore me or love me or even *like* me. I just ask that you respect me and carry out your service to the *Tsenacommacah*. You will be part of a great legacy, as will your child. But during your time here you will need to obey me and live by the customs of the village. Do you understand?'

'Yes,' Odina said again.

'That is good to hear. Now...' His eyes betrayed a glimmer of embarrassment. 'I need you to tell me about something.'

'Of course.'

'Your cycle. Your blood. When you are at your most fertile.'

So Odina told him.

She had not done it before. Powhatan did not even ask if she had. They both knew the answer.

It hurt. She bled. And then – she lapsed into nothingness. She let her mind detach from her physical body while her flesh went through a passionless ritual. Odina had been nervously awaiting this moment: the night when Powhatan would say *it's time*. She had been scared. Had she known that *this* was what it would be like – a moment of sharp pain followed by the weight of an old man heaving on top of her, his scarred back looking almost vulnerable as it shone with sweat in the half-light – she would have told herself not to worry.

It will not be pleasant. It will not be unbearable. It will just... be.

She could imagine that this – the motions, the rocking, the closeness – could feel nice if it was with someone she liked: a handsome lover, a boy closer to her own age. Yes: it could be wonderful under those circumstances. Hopefully she would find out one day.

Powhatan grunted. He stopped moving.

He lay on top of her in silence. Eventually he got up. He left Odina alone without saying a word.

Soon enough, Odina was pregnant.

Her cycle stopped being a cycle, her body in thrall of the life that was growing inside her. She was cared for throughout the pregnancy by Fala, an elder village medicine woman who had overseen almost every Powhatan birth for the past sixty years. She had seen everything.

Odina had not been pregnant long when she got a foretaste of the future. Powhatan's men returned from an expedition. They brought with them a little boy of around two or three. Listening in on the men's conversation, Odina understood that they had called upon another tribe on their way back: the Arrohatoc. There, another one of Powhatan's infant sons was being raised until 'readiness' – which, evidently, had now arrived.

The boy toddled forwards on stubby legs, wide brown eyes taking in the sight of his new home. Fala took his hand. She fussed and cooed over him as she led him away. She told him that he would soon be meeting his father – and wasn't that *exciting?*

'How did the mother take it?' one of the men asked another.

'Same way they always do.' He shrugged.

Same, Odina thought. *Just the same. It was what it was.*

Rubbing her hand over her belly – she was about a third of the way along now, according to Fala – Odina thought more about the mother. Would she sleep tonight or would she cry her way through the darkness? Would she take solace in her existing family or retreat into herself? Pragmatism dictated that she should have been expecting this day... but pragmatism and motherly love did not mix.

Odina had a gut feeling that they never should.

Time passed. Seasons passed. Crops and harvests flourished and failed alike.

Odina gave birth to a beautiful baby girl.

The pain of childbirth was beyond anything she ever imagined. During the ordeal, Odina had briefly been lucid enough to notice highly concerned glances from Fala – sure indications that not all was well. Nonetheless she made it through. So did the baby. The pain she couldn't comprehend was replaced by a love she couldn't comprehend.

She was visited by Powhatan. She watched as he held the baby. She had seen him handle the newborns before. It was always a curious duality: one part of him was dispassionately checking the infant over to see how healthy and strong it was, the other part of him was lost in the wonder of fresh fatherhood.

'Have you thought of a name?' he asked.

'Yes.' Odina said. 'Matoaka.' Odina adored the name... but was there really any chance Powhatan would agree to it? The literal meaning was stark: *favourite daughter.* Would he see it as arrogant or unbecoming? Odina readied herself to think of something else.

'Matoaka,' Powhatan said. He rocked the little girl back and forth. 'Yes. Yes, I like it.'

She didn't want to think about it. She knew it was there – a sickeningly unavoidable ending to all this. At every step of little Matoaka's development – those days after birth, travelling back to the Paspahegh, adjusting herself to life in her old village with a new daughter – the future was waiting: *she won't be with you forever, you know. In fact, Powhatan's men will come calling for her a lot sooner than you expect. She'll just be starting to walk and talk – maybe on the cusp of saying that first ever blessed 'mama' – when she'll be ripped away from you.*

She dug into her reserves of strength.

Odina managed to put things into perspective. If her time with Matoaka was limited... if the endgame was inevitable and the present just fleeting – then she would make the *most* of that time.

She would fill those years – two, possibly three if the child was a late bloomer – with joy and love and glee. Odina would overspill her life with happiness to make up for the fact that, when the time came for Matoaka to go, she would never be truly happy again.

And she did exactly that.

It was a habit of villagers across the *Tsenacommacah* not to get too close to the infants Powhatan had sired. They were only temporary members of their tribe, after all: not much different from an animal they were fostering. Nonetheless, many in the village came to adore Matoaka. The girl was as strikingly beautiful as her mother and had a strangely mature temperament. She hardly ever cried.

When she looked up at people her wide brown eyes seemed to be full of scrutiny and absorption.

Odina was shocked when Askook came to see the infant – in a good way. He looked happier and healthier than he ever had. While Odina had been living with Powhatan, Askook had married a sweet young Paspahegh woman named Tayen. He seemed like a contented man for the first time in his life. He had no need to fixate on his flaws anymore.

'You and Tayen will surely be having one of your own soon,' Odina's mother said as she watched Askook handle the baby.

'Maybe.' He smiled.

There was no maybe about it. Soon enough Tayen was pregnant – and soon enough it was time for the child to enter the world. There were complications: bloody, tragic complications. The baby was stillborn. Tayen died while giving birth. All the changes that had happened to Askook vanished in a heartbeat. He was not a man anymore. He was a dead-eyed husk. He was the world's perpetual sufferer, awoken from a daydream.

Odina wished she could help. But really – what could she say? What could she do?

Another tragedy: time passed way, way too quickly. The seasons blurred by. Reddened autumn sluiced past like a nosebleed. Winter's grip seemed only to pinch for a heartbeat. Summer came once more and filled the village with a sense of promise – except, to Odina, the promise was an unthinkable one.

It's not fair, Odina thought, as Powhatan's men came to claim Matoaka. *Surely she can't be ready to go just yet? It was only yesterday when I brought her back home to the village, wasn't it?*

Matoaka was taken. She cried, a rare occurrence. Odina desperately wanted to comfort the little girl but couldn't bring herself to watch as the canoes sailed off down the bend of the river, taking Matoaka out of sight.

Odina fell into a black depression. The rest of the village seemed to join her, a cheerless maelstrom. Odina stopped getting up in the morning. She stopped leaving her bed altogether. She would not bathe nor eat for days on end. The villagers hated to see her like this – yet concerns for her well-being soon gave way to more practical ones.

Odina was not the first surrogate mother the Paspahegh had ever seen. Far from it. The long-established routine was a clear one: once their temporary motherhood duties were over, the woman in question would return to helping out with tribal duties. Odina was not special. She would not be exempt. She was rapidly becoming seen as an outcast – and dragging her family's reputation down with her.

One morning – or afternoon, or evening, Odina didn't care, they all felt the same now – her mother came to her.

'We must talk,' her mother said.

'Must we?' Odina sighed.

'This cannot go on. You are destroying yourself and destroying our good name in the process. Your father and I have been discussing things. We know that neither will be easy for you, Odina... but there are two things you must do.'

'And what are they?'

'Firstly, you need to resume your duties. We all must work, you know that. I have promised people that you will be active again soon. We cannot let that promise be broken.'

'And what is the second?' Odina asked.

Her mother took a deep breath.

'You have fulfilled your service. You are no longer betrothed to Chief Powhatan. You are free to remarry. We feel it would be beneficial if you did.'

'*What?*'

'Most other girls your age have taken a husband.'

'Yes. I did too. You might have noticed.'

'You know what I mean,' her mother snapped. 'People are talking. They say you are willing to throw your life away. That you have resigned yourself to loneliness.'

'And what exactly do you have in mind, Mother? I just pluck a husband out of thin air?'

Odina's mother looked at the ground. She knew that her next suggestion would not be a welcome one. But she said it anyway.

'Askook.'

'Askook?'

'He has recently started to mention the possibility of remarrying.'

'And you... *what?*' Odina snorted. '*Suggested* me? Bartered me? Plotted out the rest of my days while I lay here?'

'Yes.' Her mother's reply was blunt. So was her face: the unyielding glare of the harsh realist. 'Should I have left that to you? It would never get done. *Nothing* would ever get done.'

'Am I supposed to be delighted by this, Mother? By the idea that Askook would take me on as a... *consolation bride?* That he would give me children we could raise while he secretly pines for the one he lost?'

'Delighted? No. Accepting? Yes.'

'No.' It was all Odina could bring herself to say. The pragmatic part of her understood her mother's approach. It was perfectly rational: if Odina remarried it would help ease her back into normal Paspahegh life. But... *pragmatism? Rationality? Wisdom?* What had those ever got her? 'I don't want to.'

'Life is not about what you want,' her mother said. 'You of all people should know that.'

Odina began to cry.

'They *took her*, mother,' she wailed.

'Yet you still live. You still breathe. This world is not done with you yet. What I'm suggesting... marrying Askook... it is not just for you. It is for your family. It is for your people.'

'*Duty.*' Odina scowled through her tears. 'I have seen enough of duty.'

'No.' Her mother gently ran a hand along her face. 'You haven't. Do this for *us*, Odina. For the mother and father who raised you. I cannot promise a life of unfettered joy. But I can promise a *life*.'

Odina sniffled. Her tears stopped.

Pragmatism. Rationality. Wisdom. Yes... she hated these things. They had indeed rewarded her with nothing.

But they were part of who she was.

'I'll do it,' Odina said.

Quiet relief framed the wedding day itself. This was at least some form of salvation: rescuing both Odina and Askook from lives of isolation and despair. The elder villagers were particularly impressed. The pair were making a hard-headed union, casting aside flowery ideas of romanticism in a marriage that was for the good of the whole community.

'I know I am hardly the man you dreamt of,' Askook had said when they first met to discuss the marriage. 'I will be kind to you. I will be an honest husband and a good father. I can be sure of this... because I was in the past.'

'I know,' Odina finally said. She offered him a smile. He smiled back.

She felt awash with empathy: he no doubt *was* a good man. There were a lot worse who could take her hand in matrimony and give her another child. The hole in her heart was never going away – but Askook shared the same pain. He would *understand* her at least. That was a rarity in itself.

The ceremony came and went. Odina moved into Askook's household. The place was unavoidably barren – Tayen had clearly worked to make the home her own, and Askook had stripped away all her decorative touches as part of this new beginning. Odina began to add some flourishes of her own.

One ambition came to the forefront quite quickly: Askook was ready to start a family again. And... although the thought of her distant daughter made Odina's heart swell with sadness... she slowly grew accustomed to the idea that she was ready too.

She began to realise she had an abundance of love still left inside her, untouched by her despair. What better thing to do with that love than lavish it on her future children?

They began to try for a baby. They made love regularly. While at first it seemed awkward and almost procedural, they both soon began to find pleasure in the act. The more time she spent with Askook – the more she saw his outer walls of aloofness crumble – the more she began to entertain the once unthinkable: maybe she *could* fall in love with this man. A different kind of love than she had ever imagined existed, of course... but she had long since accepted that expectations were the quickest way to make the gods laugh.

A while passed. A question arose. She could tell it was troubling Askook. Why wasn't Odina getting pregnant?

Askook did not speak of his concerns. He gradually became more sullen again and put all his energy into village tasks. He barely spoke when he got home, preferring instead to sleep his anxieties away. Odina had no such gift: her anxieties always kept her awake.

She began to think back to her time in the Powhatan village. To Fala. To the way she had looked at Odina during birthing. Her expression. Her concern.

Odina always avoided Powhatan's men when they visited – not that she had any real reason to deal with them anyway – but was troubled enough by her thoughts to approach them the next time their canoes pulled up on the riverbank.

'I must ask you something,' she said to one of the men.

'If it's about the girl...' He looked genuinely sympathetic... but he could not break the rules. 'You know I cannot tell you anything. I'm sorry.'

'It's not about her. Not exactly.'

'Not exactly?'

'When you return to your village, I would like you to speak

to Fala. Ask her about Matoaka's birth.' Odina felt a frisson, a prickle-tinged shiver. It was the first time she had said the girl's name out loud in a long, long time. 'Ask her if she noticed any unusual complications.'

'Like what?'

'She will know what I'm talking about,' Odina said. Of course she would. *Her face. Her expression.* 'I know that I am asking a favour of you. And I am painfully aware that I have nothing to offer in return. But if you could see it in your heart to...'

'I will speak to her,' the man said, holding up a hand, a little unsettled by Odina's openness. 'But you will need to be patient. We are not due to come back here again for a while.'

'I'm a patient woman.' Odina smiled. 'Thank you.'

And she *was* patient, more or less – right up until the last days before another Powhatan visit was due. She had still not fallen pregnant. Askook had retreated further into speechless brooding. Outside their marital home, things were very different indeed: he was becoming something of a local hero as he put endless hours into his duties. His charming, chatty exterior with the villagers was an illusory device worthy of any trickster god.

When Powhatan's men arrived Odina went to meet them. The man she had asked the favour of was present – but he noticed her and merely gestured towards an additional passenger. Odina looked up and was astonished to see Fala: a domestic stowaway among the warriors.

'Why did you come?' Odina asked.

'I was told of your question.' Fala looked mournful, ridden with guilt. Odina felt her stomach lurch. 'I wanted to come here and speak to you myself.' Fala took Odina's hands in her own. 'Sweet girl. Sweet, sweet girl. I'm sorry. I hope you will one day forgive me.'

'Forgive you for what?' Odina managed to ask.

'I was a coward. Pathetic.' Fala closed her eyes for a long moment. Opened them again. 'I knew that it would destroy you if I told you. I couldn't bring myself to put such pain upon you.' Tears welled in her eyes. She clutched onto Odina's upper arms with her fragile quivering hands. 'Please, my girl. *Please*. Forgive me.'

'Tell me,' Odina said.

So: Fala did. She told Odina everything. She told her of the complications during the birth: the excessive blood loss, the tearing of tissue that would heal but no longer function properly, the internal injuries that were never life-ending but always life-changing.

'A woman's body is both strong yet fragile,' Fala said. 'I have seen this happen many times before. Sometimes the first birth causes damage that cannot be repaired. Sometimes the first birth makes a second birth impossible. You will never bear another child, Odina.'

Odina fell silent. No tears came. She was beyond weeping now. She was hollowed, a walking ghost. Fala, meanwhile, had taken on the mantle of crying for both of them.

'See?' Fala sobbed. 'I *knew* it would do this to you. I knew that I might as well be sticking a blade in your chest.'

'I would have found out.' Odina's tone was dull, distant. 'One day I was going to learn the truth. Did you not stop to consider that?'

'I'm sorry.' Fala continued to cry, bereft of her flimsy justifications. 'Sweet girl. I'm sorry. Please forgive me.'

'No,' Odina said. She walked away.

Odina told Askook. She gave him the facts outright. There was no way to alleviate the blow.

He stood in silence for a while, the roof of the domicile casting a shadow across his deadened face.

'Does anyone else know?' he asked. 'Your parents? The village?'

'No,' she said.

'You have to tell them. As soon as possible.'

'I don't...' Odina floundered.

'My good name is at stake here. I know what people say. I have heard the whispers: they wonder if Tayen and the baby were taken from me as punishment from Okeus for some transgression I had made. Now what will they say – that Okeus has also seen fit to take away my virility? My fertility? They must be told that *you* are the burdened one here.'

'That...' Odina laughed: a bitter, humourless discharge. '*That* is what concerns you right now? When I have just bared my soul to you? All you can think of is how others will doubt your manhood?' Any sympathetic layers had been stripped from Askook altogether: a man lost in grief or otherwise, Odina could now see him for who he was. 'Wherever Tayen and the baby are right now, let me tell you this. They are better off there than they would be with *you*–'

The slap seemed to come out of nowhere. It was whip-fast, open-handed, carrying enough force that Askook must have been steeling himself to strike for a while.

Red rabbit-trails of pain streaked across Odina's vision. The sting spread across her cheek, a malevolent pulse. And then: the same, a recurrence, the hand slapping her from the opposite direction. Her other cheek burned.

She was shocked. Terrified. But she had had enough experience in holding back tears to deny Askook one small victory.

She wasn't going to cry.

Askook apologised. He told her that he had lost control: that she had purposefully twisted his temper so far he had lashed out without thought. Odina wasn't paying attention to the apology. She knew that platitudes alone couldn't bury something like this. It would just be the beginning.

She was right. Not too long after that – maybe a week later – Askook hit her again. He apologised again. Days passed. Then he hit her again. He apologised again, this time a half-murmured 'sorry'. Days passed. Then he hit her again – and he didn't apologise. That part of the ritual was done with.

Odina grew to expect these assaults. She didn't tell anyone about the beatings. Why would she? Askook had summed it up one evening:

'No one would believe you,' he told her, pacing the floor of their home. 'You know how I am *seen* out there? After rising from the tragedy I've been through? After all the work I've put into my duties, transforming the face of this village? I'm *adored*. I am *essential*. Vital. You, however? They view you as tainted. Now they know of your barren womb, many have started to wonder if you were not cursed by Okeus yourself. Some even wonder if that curse will start to affect the Paspahegh as a whole. To put it bluntly, woman – you are *lucky*. Lucky that I allow you to live under my roof.'

Everything he said was true. Odina had revealed her infertility. All the villagers knew – and had indeed started to consider the touch of Okeus in things. Even Odina's parents began to wonder if their daughter was a wreck beyond salvage. It was pointless telling them about Askook's violence: he had charmed them as wilfully as he had everyone else. Any outbursts from Odina could simply be traced back to her disposition: *she can be difficult. Very difficult.*

As days slid by in a mire of misery, soon turning into years... Odina eventually made a decision. She was going to do something that made her happy.

It was a stupid idea – one that broke more rules than could probably be counted – but she didn't care.

She was going to go and visit Matoaka.

The timing was perfect. Askook would be away from the village for a few days as part of a long hunting expedition. Odina would have ample time to head out to Powhatan and back. The trip there upriver would take about a day, the trip back maybe half a day with the aid of the current. She knew enough of the *Tsenacommacah* to avoid being seen by other tribes she might pass along the way.

Visiting Matoaka wasn't quite the right turn of phrase, Odina had to keep reminding herself. She would be *seeing* Matoaka: positioning herself at a good vantage point near the Powhatan village and hoping to catch a glimpse of the girl. She knew better than to interact – even though she dearly wished she could. But in a world where she could never touch or talk to her daughter again, simply watching her would have to suffice.

Askook left at nightfall. He didn't say goodbye to Odina. He never did. She waited until an hour or so before sunrise. Odina headed out in one of the canoes.

Her journey was entirely uneventful. The river was calm, the weather was clear. She didn't encounter a single soul. She grounded and hid the canoe around five miles from the Powhatan village and began to approach the village through the overgrown forest, hacking away at a new path.

She made sure to stay on higher ground. Eventually she emerged at the top of a hilly mound, breaking the treeline just before a steep grassy slope plunged into more dense forest. Beyond that – just about safely distant, she reckoned – was the village itself. Odina flattened the grass and settled down, lying on her front, propped up by her arms.

She wondered how long she would have to wait before she caught sight of Matoaka. The answer soon came: not long at all. As the village reached its bustling midday peak, Odina felt her heart stop as she saw the girl. It took a moment to recognise her – she was now seven, taller and lither – but something about Matoaka's gait was unmistakable.

Matoaka seemed happy. She looked joyful, full of life. Playing with some of the other village children, Matoaka gleefully did cartwheels, laughing and cheering as she then watched her friends do the same. The wind just about carried the sound. Odina could make out the dim form of distant words. One in particular hit hard: a woman called out for Matoaka to stop messing around and get back to her chores.

The woman didn't call her *Matoaka*.

Odina watched the village for a while longer. Matoaka did not make another appearance. That didn't matter: Odina had already decided that she would return to this spot and do this regularly.

Which she did. Nearly every time Askook was away, Odina made the journey again to watch over her beloved girl. Every time – even when spying from afar – Odina could see that Matoaka was growing up fast, becoming ever more a self-assured and beautiful girl with each trip. These excursions soon became the only thing that kept Odina going. No matter how dismal life with the Paspahegh could be, she always knew that another trip was coming. When the next journey was near, Odina even occasionally found herself *smiling*.

'What are you so cheerful about?' Askook had once asked her.

'Am I not permitted to be cheerful, husband?' she had said. Such defiance normally ended with Askook striking her – but she had long since stopped expecting anything else. Not in this case, however: he merely lapsed into sulky silence and left her alone.

On her next sojourn to the hillside Odina couldn't spot Matoaka at all. She waited for hours and hours. There was still nothing. Odina was about to leave when: 'Who are you?'

She couldn't believe it – yet it was unmistakably *her*, stood at the treeline just a few feet away. Matoaka.

Matoaka stepped forwards. She was a little apprehensive but carried no real fear. Her eyes glowed with curiosity. She took in the view, clearly a new explorer to this part of the *Tsenacommacah* – and gave a slight yelp of delight when she spotted the distant Powhatan houses.

'That's my village! My home!' She looked back to Odina. 'Were you watching it? Why?'

'I... I...' Odina stammered.

Her head was spinning with questions. *What was the girl doing up here? Was she alone or with friends... or relatives? Was she here randomly or had she actively come looking for intruders?*

'Are you all right?' Matoaka frowned.

'Yes. I am fine. Thank you.' Odina managed to compose herself. 'And... yes. I was observing your village. It is a nice place.'

'Yes.' Matoaka eagerly agreed. But now she cycled back to that first question. She would not let it go unanswered. 'Who are you?'

Odina knew it: this encounter marked the end of these journeys. Matoaka was surely going to rush back to the Powhatan village to tell everyone of the strange woman hiding on the hilltop. Even if Odina ran away now, people would soon figure out who she was.

So: what was the point in tiptoeing around anymore? Why

not just recklessly plunge into the inevitable? 'I'm your mother, Matoaka,' Odina said.

Matoaka thought this over for a moment.

'Oh,' she eventually said. 'I've been wondering about you.'

Matoaka was on her own, it turned out. No one knew she was here. She had developed a habit of going exploring on her own, mini-adventures that she kept quiet from her father and assorted guardians.

'Father thinks I am mischievous,' Matoaka said, bowing her head in slight shame.

'I know. I have heard the nickname the others call you.'

'He calls me that when my mischief amuses him. Sometimes it does *not* amuse him though. He doesn't like me wandering off. I'm not supposed to be out here.' Matoaka looked concerned. 'Will he find out? That I was here?'

'Not from me,' Odina said gently. 'Remember. I'm breaking the rules too. I'm not supposed to be here either. You must know of your father's arrangements with his children's mothers?'

'Yes. He says it is for our own good.' Matoaka put on a deep voice, a wavering impression of Powhatan that Odina found adorable. '*To associate with them will dilute your identity.* I don't know exactly what he means by that. But he says it all the time.' She bit on her lip. 'I don't think it's fair.'

'Neither do I.' Odina gave a reassuring smile. 'That's why I come up here to watch you. This is the closest I could get without being noticed and angering your father more.'

'But *why*?'

'I wanted to see you. I needed to know that you were growing up to be strong and healthy and wise. And you are.

Very much so. You are also becoming more beautiful with every passing day.'

'Thank you.' Matoaka blushed. Despite her tomboy theatrics she also had a certain delicacy about her: a girl who was unmistakably being raised as royalty. Matoaka was struck by another thought. 'Do you come up here a lot?'

'Not as much as I would like, but... yes. I visit often.' Odina's fluttering heart suddenly pitched into darkness again. *Well... I did. But once Powhatan gets word of this, these little excursions of mine will be as dead as last week's fishing haul.* To her surprise – glorious surprise –Matoaka immediately proved her wrong:

'I won't tell about you. And maybe... maybe...' She did a little dance of excitement. 'Maybe we could meet up like this *again*? Whenever you are back? We could talk... and tell stories... and... I could learn about you and you could learn about me...' Her ten-words-a-second flurry trailed off. She looked uncertain. 'If you want to, I mean? Would you like that?'

More than anything, Odina wanted to scream. *I would leap off the edge of Creation to share just ten more words with you.*

'That would be nice,' Odina slowly said.

'How will I know when you're here?'

'Well...' It was a good question. Odina feared she would not have an answer – until she noticed something. Between two sturdy oak trees nearby there was a thick but hollowed dead trunk, maybe six feet high, pitched up during a storm, heavily laid to an angle against the left oak. 'Look. That trunk. What if every time I am up here I do this?' Grunting with exertion, Odina pushed all her weight against the trunk – until it gave way, falling in the opposite direction, now resting squarely against the right tree. It could go back and forth with relative ease. 'You would be able to see that from the village, wouldn't you?'

'Yes.'

'Then that's what we'll do. And it'll be our secret.'

'*Secret.*' Matoaka murmured the word to herself, delighted, infusing it with starry wonder. 'That will be fun.' As she looked back down at the distant village her enthusiasm stalled. 'I must be going now. Father will be wondering where I am.' She backed away into the treeline – but stopped to ask one more question before she left. 'What is your name?'

'Odina.'

'*Odina.*' She toyed with the word, just as she had done with the *secret* a few seconds earlier. She gave a tiny frown. 'I would prefer to call you *mother*. If that is all right with you?'

Odina nodded.

The edge of Creation, my girl. The edge of Creation.

This was how it went for a couple of years. This was what kept Odina sane when everything with the Paspahegh was rotten. She would arrive. She would move the dead oak. Matoaka would show up a couple of hours later.

What did they talk about? Anything and everything. Matoaka had begun her training as a medicine woman, she revealed. She had also helped her father with some important ceremonies and been gifted some brightly coloured shells when some of the Mattaponi tribe came to visit.

Odina told Matoaka a few tales from her own life – ignoring the grim turn things had taken – but mostly stuck to regaling the girl with tribal legends and stories of the gods. Matoaka had heard most of them before – but that did not dull her enjoyment. She loved to hear stories nearly as much as she loved to tell them.

Occasionally they sang. They danced. They played.

The edge of Creation.

One day Matoaka arrived with some bad news.

'There is a man called Yanisin.' She said the name with uncharacteristic spite. 'He's always been the nosiest one in the village. Eyes bigger than clay plates. He has noticed your signal with the oak trunk. Word has got around. No one has come to investigate yet... but they will.'

'So we'll meet–'

'Somewhere else.'

Odina laughed when she heard Matoaka finish the sentence. The same idea, spoken at exactly the same time. The pragmatic rush to solution. Like mother, like daughter.

Matoaka smiled back. 'Where?' she asked.

Odina told her. There was a clearing where she occasionally camped and rested during her secret journeys here. It was hidden deep within the dense forest: the sort of thing that someone could stagger by, only a few feet away, and not even realise existed.

Odina had traipsed to and from there enough times that the route was embedded in her mind. She shared it with Matoaka: exact directions, relevant landmarks, detailed enough to navigate with ease. They set a date.

So: that was how things went for a couple more years. More talking. More playing. More singing and dancing.

Until a meeting when – unknown to Matoaka – Odina had company.

Odina knew that Matoaka would want to talk about the white men.

Word had spread of their return. Talk would be rife in the Powhatan village about how the leadership should react.

Matoaka was way too young to remember previous visitations from the white men – but now the invaders were back. No one knew what they wanted – or even if they were from the exact same place as the last group. On early impressions alone, Odina had heard these white men seemed less outwardly hostile than the ones who came before. That counted for something, she supposed.

All of which led to the issue of the moment: the white man who was lying asleep mere feet away.

Odina had never encountered his kind face to face – and she didn't know exactly what to think. His strange odour and odd mannerisms aside, the weirdest thing about *Ch-awn* was how inexpressive he was. These men were not as open as the Real People, as though they harboured only emptiness in their souls. Like dark spirits.

But... Ch-awn was not a dark spirit, was he? He had abandoned the rest of his people, after all. That must mean they had certain bad values Ch-awn did not want to stick by.

Ch-awn, on his own, seemed like a good man. He had made a great effort not to frighten Odina on his first approach. He had kept her presence secret from Askook and his search party. And she had found his talk of *protection* oddly charming: he naively thought he would stand a chance if the search party came back. Misguided or not, Ch-awn had a code of honour about him.

What, however, would Matoaka think if she spotted Ch-awn?

Odina half-regretted letting Ch-awn sleep at her camp. True, she owed him the favour after he helped her – but this meeting with Matoaka was destined to be an important one. It was a meeting they needed to have alone.

The undergrowth rustled nearby. The sound was too light to be Askook and his lapdogs.

Matoaka was here.

Odina glanced over. Ch-awn and his belongings were down past a grassy slope, out of sight unless someone purposefully ventured round there. She made the quick decision, there and then: she would leave him be. She would let him sleep and hope that Matoaka did not see him.

If he stirred or woke up... or if Matoaka *did* notice him... well, she would deal with that as and when it happened.

Matoaka emerged from the trees. She flung her arms around Odina. Excitedly, she announced that she had *a lot* to talk about. Grinning, Odina ushered her a little further away from the camping spot. They both sat on the opposite split logs of a huge felled oak. The ground rose slightly here, putting the fire and the camp out of sight completely.

'The white men have returned,' Matoaka said.

'So I've heard.' Odina nodded.

'Everyone is worried. They say this does not bode well.' Like everyone in the *Tsenacommacah,* Matoaka knew of the Prophecy. 'I don't like being scared. But I am.'

Odina wished – more than anything – that she could tell Matoaka not to be frightened. But how could she go about explaining herself? To say what she now believed would be to share the unthinkable.

The Prophecy isn't real. It isn't going to happen.

So much of what you've been told isn't real, my girl.

No. She could not share such thoughts with Matoaka. Odina was a complete outsider, an apostate from her tribe – and could therefore afford to dismiss the Prophecy as nonsense. Matoaka, however: the girl *needed* social capital, perhaps more so than anyone else as the daughter of a chief. She had to maintain respect and keep her kinship. So there was no other choice: Odina had to let Matoaka keep believing.

Matoaka looked up to the pink dawn sky, pupils contracting in the growing light. It was almost time for her to go.

This is it, thought Odina. *The last time I will ever speak to her. But she cannot know that.*

Odina took Matoaka's hands in her own. 'I want you to know something,' she said.

'Yes?' Matoaka smiled.

'I want you to know that I love you more than life itself. I always have and I always will. You are my entire world. You are my *manito aki*. You are my All-That-Is.'

'Thank you, Mother.' Matoaka hugged Odina. Then she withdrew. She looked puzzled. 'Why would you say these things?'

'Am I not allowed to tell my daughter how much I love her?'

'It was just...' Matoaka bit her lip. 'The *way* you said it.'

Damn your perceptiveness, girl, Odina thought. *Why can't you let just one thing slip you by?*

'I don't know what you mean,' Odina said.

'You sounded so *final*.' Matoaka sprung to her feet. 'Mother. What is going on?' Before Odina could stop her, the girl had scurried up to the top of the slope. Odina sighed.

Now she's going to spot the white man, isn't she? Now she'll have endless questions about him. This is not how I wanted it to be.

This is not how our final encounter should play out.

Matoaka did not notice Ch-awn. Instead, she simply looked at the camping spot: the paraphernalia scattered there. Signs of long-term habitation.

'Mother.' Matoaka sounded strict as she walked back over to Odina – like she was the elder one interrogating a wayward youngster. 'Are you *staying* out here? Living on the land? Have you left your tribe?'

'Of course not.' Odina tried to make the very notion sound ridiculous. 'Calm down, little one. You know that my journeys to see you can take a couple of days. I need to sleep somewhere, don't I? You've seen my campsite before.'

'Yes, but...' Matoaka struggled. 'This time, it just... well, it looks so... *permanent*. Like you've been here weeks.'

'Where do you get these ideas from?' Odina forced a laugh.

'I'll find out, you know.' Matoaka folded her arms. 'Father knows everything that is going on in the *Tsenacommacah*. He will learn the truth eventually. And so will I.'

'There is nothing to find out.'

'Do you promise?' Matoaka was losing her authority. Now she looked like a worried young girl again.

'I promise,' Odina said.

'And... we will see each other again? As we always do?'

'I promise.'

The lies wrenched her apart inside.

Matoaka hugged and kissed Odina and then scampered back into the forest, eager to get back to Powhatan before her absence was noticed.

Odina sat still on the felled trunk. She waited until she was absolutely sure Matoaka was gone – she couldn't handle it if the girl came back – before unleashing a torrent of tears.

She exploded with grief.

She sat there and wept, burying her head in her hands.

When she looked up again, she saw that Ch-awn was watching her.

When it became clear that Odina was safe from the campsite visitor, Guy had remained in his bedroll. Guy tapered his breathing, staying as still as he could. He lay there and listened to their conversation.

When the girl had left Guy finally got up. He headed past the fire and up the sloping knoll.

He froze.

Odina was sobbing, lost in despair. Guy had no idea what to do – and when she looked up at him he just about managed to say:

'Sorry.'

'It is fine,' Odina lied. She sniffled, wiping her face with her sleeve. 'You have just woken up?'

'I've been awake for a while. I heard you talking with the girl. I figured you didn't want her to see me.'

'Oh.' Odina seemed taken aback. Surprised by Guy's honesty. 'Yes. That's right. Thank you.'

'She is your daughter?'

'Yes.'

'But you do not live with her?'

'I do not live with anyone.' Odina got to her feet, brushing thorns and brambles from her mantle. She said nothing else.

Guy had managed to figure out a few things by listening in. The people here had a joint leader, it seemed. A powerful man who took many wives from his kingdom... had a child with each... then sent the mothers back to their own tribes. It was forbidden for mothers to have direct contact with their children.

Hence: this. All of this.

'She sounds like a sweet girl,' Guy said.

'She is.' Odina managed a smile.

'Her name is...' Guy tried to repeat what he had heard. '*Ma-took-a?*'

'Close. Matoaka. Although...' Odina now looked very distant. 'I think I am the only person who calls her that. Her father has given her a new name, you see. A Powhatan name. His own term of endearment. It means *mischief*.'

Odina told Guy what the new name was.

Guy swirled the word around in his mouth, trying to get to grips with the pronunciation. From the nod Odina gave, he guessed that he did a good job. Guy tried it again for good measure.

'*Pocahontas*,' he said.

CHAPTER EIGHT

1607

It didn't quite happen in an instant. But it was close enough.

Guy had been packing up his bedroll, idly enjoying the novelty of saying a new word over and over – *Pocahontas, Pocahontas, Po-ca-hont-as* – when he noticed that Odina was nowhere to be seen.

Her belongings were still here. She hadn't quietly gathered everything up and darted away.

But the fire had been put out. Trampled into embers. Dusty ashes fanned out towards the west of the treeline, starting off as footprint shapes before fading away.

Guy didn't like the feeling that gave him.

Guy began to follow Odina's tracks. The ground began to rise, sloping uphill, the gradient getting steeper and steeper. He grunted, struggling to keep going. Years ago – before he'd had to rebuild his body after the Tower's torture – he could have cleared this hillside without breaking a sweat.

He winced as sunlight hit his eyes. He emerged into a sparse clearing, patchy shrubs dotting the grass as the land spread out to the edge of a sheer drop. The view from up here would have been quite breathtaking in normal circumstances: the sun-dappled river, the massed trees looking tiny and toylike. Guy guessed the drop to be about fifty feet.

Odina stood on the edge, swaying back and forth.

What is she doing? Guy asked himself. *Some sort of ritual? Some kind of–*

He suddenly realised.

Odina was lost in her last moments.

She was taking one final deep breath before ending it all. Before hurling herself over the edge.

'Odina!' Guy yelled.

Odina whirled around, confused; puffy, reddened eyes widening as she spotted Guy. Her right foot – the one she had been tensing to leap from just seconds earlier – slipped on the dewy grass.

She fell.

Guy howled, charging towards the cliff edge. He flung himself down on the grass, arms extended, reaching out in a move he knew would be futile – Odina had pitched over the side, she was *gone*, he was going to see her body smashed against the rocks below – when he let out a gasp.

There was an outcrop about twenty feet below. Had Odina leapt with all her might she would have overshot it, plunging to her death. Instead, she had fallen down the edge of the cliff itself, scrabbling at rocks and brambles as she went and–

She was dead anyway.

Guy still hadn't managed to save her.

He pummelled his fists against the dirt in anger, bloodying his knuckles, enraged with himself–

Odina was moving.

Her eyes had fluttered open.

'Stay there!' Guy shouted. He was about to start climbing down when he noticed that the outcrop tapered to a sloping trail, a thin yet navigable ledge that jutted from the rock face. He made his way to the trail, speedy yet cautious, loose rocks occasionally breaking free beneath his feet and splashing into the river below.

He reached Odina. He knelt by her side. He had seen similar injuries in battle when men had fallen from high barricades. The roll call of injuries was likely the same: fractured skull, a shattered rib or two, a broken arm. One soldier under Guy's command had survived and – apart from a lifelong limp – recovered well. That, however, was with the swift care of a battlefield surgeon to hand.

'Why...' Odina strained to speak.

'Don't talk,' Guy said, slipping back into pidgin Algonquian. 'Keep your strength. Focus on breathing.' Odina paid him no attention. With weak anger in her eyes, she wanted her question answered.

'Why... did you save... me?' She closed her eyes. 'I... wanted to go. To go... even if...' She passed out again. Guy wondered for a second if that was it – if those had been her final words – when Odina stirred once more, letting out half-conscious moans of pain.

Guy thought back to that injured soldier. They had been scouting the edges of enemy territory when it happened, some distance from the surgeon's tent. Guy and the others had constructed a stretcher upon which they securely bound the man. A stretcher needed two people to carry – but Guy realised he could probably fashion something similar from Odina's sleeping mat and his own bedroll, a dual-layered cocoon that could keep her in place as he pulled her along the ground.

'I'll be back,' he said to Odina, trying to soothe her, not sure if she could even hear him. 'Don't worry.' Guy hurried back up to the ledge and returned to the campsite. He gathered up the mat and the bedroll and headed back down to Odina. She was still drifting in and out of lucidity – but, for want of a better word, she was stable. Stable enough to keep up the accusations:

'Should have... let me... go...'

'Hush.' Guy prepared the bedroll. He tore out a strip of the mat and tightly wound it around one end; a rudimentary handle.

'Should... have... let... me... die...' Odina lapsed into unconsciousness again. She woke up briefly and howled in pain when Guy moved her onto the bedroll – but her eyes almost immediately rolled up into her head and she passed out again.

Guy had no idea where the nearest tribal settlement was, let alone whether they would be friendly. Even if he could find some tolerant natives, would they be able to help Odina in this condition? What if they turned out to be the very people she had fled in the first place?

Guy only knew how to get to one area. And he knew there was a surgeon there who could give Odina a fighting chance.

He would have to go back to Jamestown.

If he pushed himself to his limits – taking on minimal sleep – he could feasibly make it back there in two days. Would Odina even still be alive if he did? He had no idea. But he had to try.

He carefully pulled Odina along the ledge, up the slope towards the forest. There was one small mercy: the ground was mainly flat in the other direction, all the way between here and Jamestown.

Guy began to haul Odina along. About an hour or so into

the expedition, he heard her voice croaking weakly from behind him. She was looking directly at him.

Amid the delirium of pain she had somehow managed a bitter smile.

'Looks like... you're... protecting me,' she muttered, 'whether... I like it... or not.'

Guy reckoned that they had made it a third of the way back when he could take no more: he needed to *sit*, to let his aching muscles get even a small taste of respite. He rummaged through his supplies for something to eat. He gave Odina some water. He had also used his scant medical supplies on her, bandaging Odina's broken arm and collarbone. Odina began repeating something, over and over.

'*Wake Robin. Wake Robin. Wake Robin.*'

It wasn't just half-sentient babble. There was purpose behind it. 'What's Wake Robin?' Guy asked.

'For... pain...' Odina explained.

Guy managed to eke out more details: it was a medicinal plant, a whitish-pink flower atop a thick long stem with mottled leaves. Guy went to find some. It did not take long: the Wake Robin grew in thick patches almost everywhere. He brought it back and prepared it as told: making a poultice and an infused liquid. As Odina sipped at the concoction, she looked visibly relieved. The effect was immediate. She even managed to speak coherently for a short while: explaining how Matoaka had told her of the Wake Robin, how it was part of the girl's education as a medicine woman.

They moved off again.

As they went, Guy spoke to Odina. It was a one-way

conversation: she was unconscious most of the time. But that didn't stop him sharing his thoughts:

'I didn't actually *see* her, you know. Your girl. I only heard her voice while you were both talking. But that was enough. Enough to realise what a remarkable child she is. And yet... you were content to leave her without a mother.' He took a flummoxed breath. 'I don't understand it, Odina. Doesn't she make you want to go on living? Even if your moments together are rare and fleeting, isn't it worth *fighting on* just so you can see her again?' He sighed. 'I'll tell you this. I would not be so eager to leave this world if I had a daughter like that. Even if I yearned for death, I would grit my teeth and seethe through every sunrise purely to keep watch over her.'

'Ch-awn,' Odina weakly said.

Guy craned his neck around. She was awake. She had been listening. She may only have been meekly clinging on to life... but her condemnation *glowed*. She did not like being judged. Not one bit.

'You... know... nothing...' she said. 'About... anything.'

She passed out again.

Jamestown had changed. Altogether it had been just over a week since Guy's desertion – yet the construction had now spread to roughly an acre, the church and domiciles now mostly completed.

Guy wasn't in the mood for admiring the architecture. He was now just a creature of exertion – sweat dripping from his lank hair as he strained to pull Odina further along. She hadn't stirred or spoken in a while. She was still alive – he had checked – but needed medical attention soon.

A young man named Morton stood atop a short guard tower.

A chubby unkempt type, he had already shed masses of weight. Any hopes Guy had of expecting a feast inside Jamestown – or even just something other than leftover oats to eat – immediately vanished. Morton's jaw dropped as he pointed a finger. With a bellow of disbelief he announced:

'*Johnson!* Johnson is back!'

The gates opened. Wingfield and Newport were the first to step outside. They cautiously glanced to the surrounding treeline before heading out. Both looked uncharacteristically grubby and dishevelled – Wingfield in particular. Seven days in the real world had not been kind to him.

Wingfield and Newport marched over towards Guy, Newport looking bewildered, Wingfield looking furious. A number of men had gathered by the gates to observe. Newport waved for some of them to accompany him. They glanced to each other before slowly joining the approach. Guy scanned to see if Smith was among them: anything even close to a friendly face would be useful. He wasn't.

'Well.' Wingfield stopped a few feet away from Guy, putting his hands behind his back and puffing his chest out. Even on starvation rations the man couldn't ditch his pomposity. 'Looks like our intrepid explorer has returned from the wilderness. Did you find anything on your travels, Mr Johnson? The remains of the Ark, perhaps? The Fields of Elysium? Or maybe – just *maybe* – did you find life out there so impossible that you decided to come crawling back to...' Wingfield stopped. He gaped, much as Morton had moments earlier. He spotted the bedroll that Guy was pulling. Spotted Odina. 'What... what in *God's name...*'

'No Ark. No Elysium.' Guy dropped the makeshift reins. Red scabby skin criss-crossed his palms. 'Just a new friend.'

'You brought a savage,' Wingfield spluttered. '*Here?*'

'She is gravely wounded. In need of help. Wotton is an able surgeon, I'm sure he will be able to–'

'I don't care if she is Mother Mary incarnate.' Wingfield seethed. 'To bring one of the natives right to our doorstep–'

'The more time we bicker,' Guy said, 'the less chance of survival she has.'

'You presume to dictate to *me?*' Wingfield yelled. 'You are lucky, Johnson, that I didn't order Morton there to shoot you on sight.'

'Would that speed things up, Wingfield?' Guy yelled back. 'If you were to cease your blathering and put a bullet through my skull, would that at least enable you to *get this fucking girl to a doctor?*'

'You...' Wingfield was trembling with rage. He was still a stranger to insubordination. 'You... you...'

'Mr Wingfield.' Newport stepped forward. 'We may have an opportunity here.'

'Excuse me?' Wingfield sneered.

'It is clear the natives are not fond of us. We have managed to avoid attack so far – but they will come. I have no doubt of that. If we show that we were willing to nurse one of their own back to health, it could be a demonstration that we are here in good faith.'

'There are multiple tribes out there,' Wingfield said. 'According to what little they know, they all have their own customs – and presumably rivalries. Who is to say that helping one of a certain tribe might not mark us out as an enemy to another?'

'That is a risk, yes.' Newport nodded. 'But one worth taking. Besides...' Odina writhed in unconscious fever on the stretcher. Newport stooped down to get a closer look at her. 'This is a young woman in grave condition. Politics and partisanship aside... who would we be if we refused to help her?'

Wingfield mulled the question over. He was a man for whom politics and partisanship came as naturally as breathing, a freak with ink for blood. And yet... he saw the logic in Newport's plan.

'Fine. You, you, you.' Wingfield pointed out three of the men. 'Take her inside. Get her to Wotton. Tell him to use whatever resources he sees fit.'

The three men carefully picked up the bedroll. Odina moaned gently at the sudden movement. Guy watched, feeling strangely helpless.

'As for you, Johnson?' Wingfield fixed his gaze on Guy once more. 'You have returned to Jamestown – so you can now be subject to the laws of Jamestown. We'll dispense with the frivolities of a trial in this particular case. After all, the evidence is stood right before me, is it not? John Johnson, you are guilty of desertion to your duties and, by proxy, treason to the King of England. You are also guilty of stealing supplies and disrupting the course of a valuable diplomatic mission. You are nothing short of a traitor.' Guy could almost see the blood rushing to Wingfield's head. He had been denied his first scalp on foreign land so far – but the perfect opportunity had just strolled right up to him. 'And here in Jamestown, Johnson... traitors hang.'

Smith's would-be hanging had been a solemn and quiet affair. The onlookers had remained silent, tinged with existential unease. That was not the case now. Guy had made no new friends in Jamestown by running away. As Wingfield, Newport and a cavalcade of lackeys prodded Guy along through the town square, the other men made their hatred known. Shouts of *traitor* and *thief* and *scum* hoarsely filled the air.

'Get back,' Wingfield insisted to them all. 'Get *back*.' He had no concern for Guy's safety. He just wanted to make sure that the bounty was his to deal with – and his alone.

Guy looked around for Smith once more. The man was nowhere to be seen. He did, however, see something that eased his mind a little as he passed the medical station: Wotton, the surgeon, leaning over Odina with intense scrutiny. If nothing else, Guy had given her the best chance of survival.

There were worse ways to go than hanging. Guy had seen most of them inflicted on his Parliamentary co-plotters. Jamestown had not purpose-built a scaffold yet – presumably much to Wingfield's chagrin – but one was cobbled together swiftly enough, made from loose struts of timber. Guy was shoved to the front of the assembled crowd: a miasma of tired and hungry faces.

He was struck by the irony. He had wanted to leave these men behind... yet had now given them a focal point to rally behind.

He had united the camp in hatred.

Chaplain Hunt tentatively made his way to the front of the crowd, his face laden with worry. He opened his mouth to speak to Wingfield. Wingfield stopped him, shaking his head. He knew exactly what Hunt was going to say.

'I'm sorry, Chaplain,' Wingfield said, sounding anything but. 'I will not reconsider. This behaviour cannot be tolerated. A message needs to be sent.'

'You have the council's approval?' Hunt asked.

'*Yes*.' Wingfield snapped. 'We have set down our laws. Each ranking council member has the authority to carry them out. Do you seriously expect us to reconvene for every decision like this?'

'I would suggest, at this stage in our development, that yes, that is exactly what you sho–'

'Enough.' Wingfield raised a hand. He softened his tone, an

attempt at appeasement. 'Not everyone can be saved, Hunt. If you want to focus on righting a wayward soul, throw a rock in the air. You'll hit a man who needs your help.' Hunt knew that protesting was useless. He gave a defeated nod. He turned to Guy.

'I'm sorry, John,' he said.

'Don't be.'

'Would you like me to pray for you?'

'If it makes you feel better.'

Hunt frowned – but took the answer as a 'yes'. As Hunt closed his eyes and clasped his hands together, Guy could see two men constructing a noose behind him.

Hunt finished. The men finished. Wingfield looked out to the crowd, inhaling sharply, ready to begin his condemnatory address–

'This,' a voice said, 'is a council matter.'

Smith approached from the east, dressed in dirtied clothes, clearly just back from a scavenging mission. The crowd parted as he closed in on Wingfield. The respect was palpable. Automatic.

'Ah.' Wingfield gave a bitter smirk. 'Smith. If there's anyone we can rely on to completely dismantle a civic proceeding–'

'Oh. I see. So *that's* what this is.'

'Watch your mouth.' Wingfield attempted a threat. Smith let it slide.

'This is not a mere legal incident, Wingfield. This is an *execution*.' Smith looked around. 'One that will affect every single person in this settlement.'

'Really? And how do you figure that?'

'You've seen how much we're struggling,' Smith went on. 'We can barely gather wood or source water without half-killing ourselves. We'd be forty men short of a functioning colony even if three more packed ships turned up.' He waved a hand in

Guy's direction. 'We have here an able-bodied man capable of any manual labour we give him. A resource. An *asset*, to use the financial excess of insects like you.' Wingfield scowled. Smith continued. 'And your solution is to kill him?'

'What, then, would you advise, Smith?'

'We set him to work. We watch him closely. Lock him up at nightfall if need be. Look...' Smith turned to the crowd. 'I understand your anger towards this man. He ran away while I was on an expedition with him. No one here wants him to suffer more than I do. But we have to ask ourselves: is venting our rage more valuable than an extra pair of hands?'

The men began to mutter to each other. The bloodthirsty tumult of minutes earlier had dissipated. They were stuck in grim unrewarding reality once more – with grim unrewarding choices.

'I say we put this to the settlement as a whole,' Smith announced. 'Those in favour of execution. Raise your hands.' A smattering was flung into the air. Wingfield was among them. Newport, notably, was not. 'Now. Those for using him as labour?' The majority of hands were raised. Smith turned to Wingfield. 'It looks like we have an answer.'

Wingfield was silent for a long moment. Guy noticed that his fists were clenched. Tight. Very tight. Eventually he breathed again. He flexed his hands. He took one last stab at authority.

'I agree,' Wingfield said, 'on one condition.'

'Name it.'

'I know that many of you are keeping records to be sent back home. Diaries. Journals. Unofficial or otherwise. I want there to be *absolutely no mention* of this in any of them. Not a word of Johnson's treasonous antics. Not a word of letting a savage girl recover *inside settlement walls*. We are supposed to be an outpost of trade and exploration. I will not have England viewing us as a laughing stock from afar. Are we clear?'

'We're clear,' Smith said. 'Not a word.'

'Very well.' Wingfield relaxed a little. 'But I warn you, Smith. If this man escapes again, I am holding you personally responsible.'

'If he tries to escape again,' Smith said, 'I will personally shoot him dead.' Wingfield nodded at this: it was scant satisfaction... but all he would get. He motioned for the men restraining Guy to let him go.

'I'll leave you to figure out where Johnson can stay,' Wingfield told Smith. 'The rest of us have a colony to run.'

The crowd slowly began to disperse.

Soon enough, only Guy and Smith were left.

'Thank you,' Guy said.

'Of course.' Smith nodded.

'That was a nice touch, by the way.'

'What was?'

'The bit at the end,' Guy said. 'About shooting me if I run out on this place again.'

'Word of advice, Johnson? Don't be so keen to find out if I mean it.'

If Galicia was hot, *la Florida* was an inferno.

Francis had not even been ashore for a full day and already found the heat intolerable: a billion or so degrees in the shade, humidity turning the air to soup, mosquitoes swarming around every creature living or dead. Francis had already been eager to head north as soon as possible – maybe after scoping out the settlement for a while, gathering the resources he and Alonso would need. Now? Now he was half-considering running off with only the clothes on his back.

Three days passed. Things did not improve.

'I never thought I would say this,' Alonso told Francis, drenched in sweat and struggling to breathe. 'But I think I might have preferred life on board the *Magdalena*.'

Francis grunted: an affirmation. He was thinking the exact same thing. The journey on the *Magdalena* had been an overcrowded farce but at least the sea air was fresh. Francis also had his work to keep him occupied: he had been forever busy charming his way into the good books of the ship hierarchy. His disfigurement unsettled people at first – didn't it always? – but he soon worked around that. He made friends with the ship cook and got extra rations. He manipulated the right supply people and made sure he got the softest bedding. He earned the respect of the military officers and was given privileges few others had.

Technically, certain areas of the ship – most notably military stocks – were off-limits to civilian crew members. Francis would often 'accidentally' find himself down there. He would be politely moved on – but not before he had taken stock of the munitions. Not before a mental inventory had been recorded.

The behaviour of the crew soon wore him down. They may well have prayed every night with the ship priest – but they were also uncouth heathens, drinking and swearing with godless lack of grace. Francis entertained himself with thoughts of how they would all be punished in Hell. When that particular well ran dry, he turned to dreaming of all the tortures he would inflict on Fawkes when he finally tracked him down.

Every now and then – awake at night, surrounded by snoring and the noise of the ocean sloshing against the stern – Francis wondered if Fawkes even *was* waiting in Jamestown. These worries soon left his head.

Of course Fawkes would be there. Francis was on the right path.

The behaviour of the Spanish colonists in *la Florida* was just as ill-mannered as those on the *Magdalena*: a bunch of barnyard animals who occasionally saw fit to do an hour or two of work. Still... just like barnyard animals, they could be easily controlled. Francis flittered between them, ditching in and out of conversation, learning exactly where certain resources were kept... how and when they were guarded... and what the safest routes out of the settlement were, for anyone who just so happened to be wandering further afield. Francis was often bewildered at how these cretins acted with him: so friendly, so trusting, speaking one-on-one *as though he and them were somehow the same*. Unbelievable.

The clerical busybodies in *la Florida* were a little more bearable. These were the men who were tasked with helping Francis set up his new *Inquisición* outpost.

Francis spent a few days working with them: an exercise in building his reputation, fooling them into thinking he cared about their plans for blasphemy fines and community snooping. Whatever. He wouldn't be around to see them happen anyway.

Word had gradually been seeping through from various spy networks about the Jamestown project. While the Spaniards were certainly worried about English incursions into the New World, the rumours painted a picture of a colony in crisis. Did you know that they set up camp on a sinking marsh? And what about this absurd notion of 'making England proud'?

Francis wasn't surprised at this. What else could you expect from a bunch of Protestant baboons? What *did* shock him, however, was learning of the colonists' approach to the savages. From his various readings and his talks with Alonso, Francis understood that the New World natives were simply soulless animals.

One could either convert them to the glory of God – if indeed that was possible – or put them out of their misery with a mass mercy killing. But to *engage in diplomacy* with these 'people'? To actively take their well-being and sovereignty into consideration? It was literal insanity. Jamestown was spitting in the face of the Lord.

Which, quite frankly, was very fitting for a place that harboured Guido Fawkes.

After just under a week in *la Florida*, Francis had extracted all the value he could. It was time to move on. He told Alonso to meet him early the next morning at an empty barn on the cusp of the settlement. As the night fell and the settlers mostly slept, Francis went around gathering the things he needed.

Transport was first. He went to the stables where the horses were kept. The man who watched over them at night was a young recruit named Diego, a simple-minded soldier who was reportedly good with a rifle yet terrible at understanding words with more than three syllables. Francis had considered spinning some elaborate yarn to get what he wanted from Diego. He decided that it wasn't worth the effort. It was easier just to bribe him.

'I want two horses,' Francis had told him a couple of days earlier. 'I'll head out just before dawn breaks on Thursday. I'll be gone for a couple of hours. By the time I'm back, you'll still be on shift, the boys in the barracks will still be in dreamland and no one will notice that they were ever gone.'

'What do you want them for?' Diego asked. 'Where are you going?'

'I'm an explorer at heart, young man. I just want to take a

ride with a friend. A brief excursion around the outskirts of the settlement.'

'There's nothing out there.'

'Oh, I'm sure there's something.'

'Not for miles. Only mosquitoes.'

'I *adore* mosquitoes.'

'But...'

'Look.' Francis cut him off. 'Do you want the money or not?' Francis flashed him the gold *escudos*.

'Yes,' Diego swiftly said.

Francis carefully gathered the things he needed for his trip – eight particularly important items included – and stashed them in a hiding place. When the time came he loaded up some saddlebags with the items and went to the meeting place. Alonso was waiting.

'No going back once we leave,' Francis told him. 'Are you in?'

'I'm in,' Alonso said, mounting his horse.

Good for you, Francis thought. *Because I'd have slit your throat like an abattoir pig if you'd said anything else.*

'Right,' Francis said, clutching the reins, getting used to the sway and pitch of the trotting horse. They were a good few hours out of *la Florida* now. Even if the Spaniards sent out men to pursue them, no one at the settlement had any idea which direction they had headed. The two men might as well have vanished into the wind.

He had outlined the basics of his 'plan' to Alonso. They would, Alonso had been led to believe, head to Virginia on horseback before ditching the animals and making their way through the dense woodland on foot. They would scope out some of the excavation sites the Jamestown gold-diggers had prospected. They would figure out a way to steal as much gold as they could. Then they would steal one of the shallops that had been dissembled and stored on the main Trading Company ships – standard practice, Francis knew for a fact – and sail back along the coast to *la Florida*, making sure to steer clear of military attention once they arrived. A few bribes here and there – hardly difficult with their new-found riches – and they would be on the next vessel back to Spain.

Until then, there was the ride ahead.

'I'd estimate that we'll be travelling for twelve days, maybe thirteen,' Francis mused. 'We'll camp for six hours each night. Meaning that for at least eighteen hours a day we will both be wide awake and travelling. And I have no intention of leading the conversation during that time, Alonso. I intend on listening to *you*.'

'What do you mean?' Alonso frowned.

'The dialect. The tongue these savages use. Algonquian, is that what it's called? I want to learn it. And you're going to teach me.'

'What?'

'You spent considerable time with these people, didn't you?' Francis steadied the reins. 'You learned their language. You can share your knowledge with me, can't you?'

'If we encounter any natives,' Alonso slowly said, 'then I would *strongly* advise you let me do the talking.'

'Of course.' Francis nodded. 'But what if we're split apart for some reason? Accidents can happen. What if I find myself alone, surrounded by a group of savages, only able to flap my tongue uselessly? Precautions are important. I need the ability to converse with them if needed.'

'It makes sense,' Alonso admitted. 'I suppose.'

'Damn right it does. Besides...' Laughing, Francis swept an

arm to take in the expansive view: nothing but swampland to the east and clusters of palm trees to the west. 'How else are you going to pass the time? A quick game of Blind Man's Bluff?'

So: Alonso spoke and Francis listened.

Within the space of the first day they had covered verbs and nouns and basic phrases. Francis knew the names of common items and geographic features. *Wakwehša*: a fox. *Napewa*: a man. *Ahkwatwi*: a weapon.

On the first night they set up camp. Alonso searched through the contents of the saddlebags, finding the food he needed – when he froze.

'Tresham,' he said, a low even voice. 'Are these what I think they are?' He was holding up a leather-crafted pouch, stuffed and heavy. He dug into the saddlebag and produced another. And another. And another. Eventually he laid them out across the ground: all eight of them.

'If you think they are gunpowder flasks,' Francis answered, idly poking a stick at the campfire, 'then you are absolutely right.'

'You stole *gunpowder? Munitions*? Do you have any idea what the army does to men who–'

'Who *what?* We're officially marked as traitors, Alonso. If they catch us we'll be put to death anyway. So – yes, I took some of their munitions. Might as well wade into the swamp a bit further if you're already neck-deep, eh? What are they going to do, kill us twice?'

'What do you need it for?'

'You may harbour ambitions of straining on your knees and panning your way through the soil. I have a more direct approach in mind.' Francis rolled his eyes when Alonso still looked confused. 'Excavation, Alonso. If we're going to look for gold properly, we may well need explosives.'

'Oh. I see.' Alonso calmed. And then, for the second time that day: 'That makes sense. I suppose.'

'Good man. Now join me. Dinner is ready.'

They sat together and ate.

Alonso was right: there was perfect sense in bringing the gunpowder. Just not for the reasons he thought.

Francis had been hearing more and more about this 'Jamestown' project – this pustule, this boil, this affront to the Almighty shat into the very soil of His earth. He found himself hating the whole settlement as much as he hated the man who hid there.

Guido Fawkes was not alone in his wickedness. They all had to go.

Francis Tresham was quite literally going to blow Jamestown apart.

CHAPTER NINE

1607

Recovery was slow. But it happened.

Odina was barely conscious for the first few days of her arrival. She soon managed to piece a few things together, slivers gleaned from brief jaunts into the waking world.

Just as mentioned in the rumours circling the *Tsenacommacah*, the white men had built a settlement of wood and steel. They had made a few stupid decisions – erecting the whole thing on swampland, for instance, or not realising that any nearby drinking water would be overrun with scum and bugs come high summer – but they had most definitely staked their presence.

They had their own version of a medicine man. In their babbling tongue they referred to him as a *doc-ta-wah* or a *surge-eh-on*. His name was Wotton. Wotton was kind and attentive, fixing up her wounds, utilising methods and potions Odina had never imagined existed.

She weakly tried to speak to him. He could not understand her. Yet – like an apparition she first thought was a dream – Ch-awn soon began to appear, looking over Wotton's shoulder with concern and compassion. He would translate some of what Wotton was saying for her.

This was how she learned the true scale of her injuries. She had a broken arm, collarbone, ribs and pelvic bone. She had a mass of fractures and torn muscles and swollen bruises. Yet – somehow – Ch-awn's people would be able to help her. These men may have had no idea how to live off the land but they were clearly not incapable.

Yet... for all their prescience... for all their advancements... they could not read an expression nor a simple desire.

They were not giving Odina what she truly wanted.

As soon as she could, she told them as much. She forced out some fragile words.

'What did she say?' Wotton asked Ch-awn.

'She said,' Ch-awn sighed, '"*you should have let me die*".'

'Always nice to work with a grateful patient.'

Ch-awn was the one tasked with bringing her food and water. Odina still didn't want to go on living – but hunger and thirst always got the better of her. When she was lucid enough, she also noticed that Ch-awn slept in the doctor's building every night, sprawled on an unrolled canvas against the opposite wall. From the outside, the door was always barricaded shut behind him.

Ch-awn left Odina to rest. The man called Wotton stopped by a couple of times a day to check up on her, balancing his medical duties with much-needed labour around the rest of the fort. Even through a slight haze, Odina developed a sense of time and place. The white men regularly gave her something called *laud-a-num*: a concoction that was good at easing pain but which often meant she slept in fitful bursts, alternating with long and lonely stretches of wakefulness.

When Odina noticed that Wotton left his kit of medical implements mere feet from where she slept... she knew that she had to seize the opportunity.

Weakly, she reached for the kit. She took out a scalpel.

Her body was refusing to co-operate. It was never going to just lie down and die by itself.

So: she just had to take some initiative.

There was just one small problem.

Odina couldn't do it.

She had imagined – as she held the scalpel to her left wrist – that it would be all too easy. She would slice across her wrist, letting the blood flow out of her. She would take the scalpel in her teeth – she knew from having seen Paspahegh injuries that hands could not grip after certain tendons in the arm had been cut – and would slice across her opposite wrist that way. More blood would flow. It would be painful for a little while... but then the pain would slowly ebb to nothingness along with everything else.

But she just *couldn't do it.*

The desire was there – at least she thought it was. She was not afraid of the pain. So *why* couldn't she do it? Why did she stop herself when the pressure of the scalpel was about to break the skin? Why could she not just *take the leap* and open up her veins?

No matter how hard she willed herself or how often she tried, her trembling fingers would just not finish the job.

Odina was furious. It was not just her body that was mocking her. Now it was her mind as well.

She put the scalpel back in the case.

Of all the moments to figure out I don't want to die, she ruefully thought, *it had to be this.*

Turns out I'm stuck on the edge of Creation. And going nowhere fast.

She was soon strong enough to talk properly again. One night as Ch-awn lay nearby, Odina slowly turned as much as she could to face him, sharp stabs of pain firing through her ribcage.

'You are a prisoner?' she asked.

'More or less,' Ch-awn replied. She noticed that his language of the Real People was improving.

'You work for them all day?'

'Yes.'

'Doing what?'

'Oh. Always a surprise.' Ch-awn snorted.

'This is your punishment?'

'This is my punishment.'

'How long will it last?'

'I don't know,' Ch-awn said. He was silent in the still night. '*You know nothing about anything.*'

'Excuse me?'

'That's what you said. Isn't it? That's what you think of me?'

'I was... defensive, I think.' Odina felt a little ashamed. 'You were speaking as though you understood me, Ch-awn. You imagined yourself to know what it was like in my shoes.'

'Then tell me.' He leant forward. 'Neither of us are going anywhere. All we have is time. Why *did* you leave your people, Odina? Why *are* you so determined to end your life?'

'I...' She lay back. There was another sudden rush of pain as she did so. She gritted her teeth until it subsided. 'I would like to hear about you first. You left your people too. You must have reasons.'

Ch-awn slipped into slow methodical breathing. Odina wondered for a moment if he had fallen asleep. Then:

'We have a word, Odina.' Ch-awn said something in his native tongue, a language that Odina had gathered was called *Ing-leese.* 'Promise.' He reverted to Algonquian. 'Your people must share this concept. All people do, I imagine. You must have... things you say you will do. And if you *don't* do these things when you have said you will, then...'

'Then bad things happen?'

'Not always. But often.' Ch-awn propped himself up on one arm. 'If I promise you my story, Odina... do you promise me yours?'

'Yes,' she said.

For the next few nights – when his servitude was over – Ch-awn would lie down and fill the hours before sleep with his recollections. He told Odina of *Ing-lann* itself, a place on the other side of a near-endless ocean. He spoke of needing to escape *Ing-lann* forever, of schemes and machinations that snared him a place on one of their mighty ships, of his plan to abandon the fellow white men of *Ch-aymes-ton* to their own devices.

Ch-awn's story was fractured and wandering... but Odina pieced the threads together. Whatever he had done in *Ing-lann* had made Ch-awn want to slip away from the world of man: to melt as one into the spirit of nature. She found it odd that he saw this as a punishment. The *Ing-leese* were a truly alien breed.

'What was it you did,' she finally asked him, 'in *Ing-lann?*'

'Something bad,' Ch-awn said.

'And you are a different man now?'

'Very much so.'

Motes of dust danced in the half-light of the roof struts. They both watched them for a short while.

'A promise is a promise, you know,' Ch-awn said.

'Yes. I know.'

And Odina took her turn.

Even when speaking for such a long time began to make her injuries throb, she let her ruptured past spill out into the night air, a cathartic torrent of bliss and bile combined. The tribes of the *Tsenacommacah*. The rules they lived by. The chiefdom of Powhatan. Becoming his bride. Bearing his daughter. Secret meetings with Matoaka.

Right up until one summer morning in the Paspahegh village.

Nothing looked unusual. And when the revelation happened, nothing looked unusual afterwards – not the becalmed river or the gently swaying grass. Odina had simply stood by the water, pail in hand, hair fluttering in the mulberry-scented breeze. No veil of darkness, no demon's red fire, no angry lashing-out from the earth.

The world did not care if part of her mind had just dropped away. That knowledge was both sickening and liberating.

The world didn't care and it never had.

The day had started like any other of the season: with dappled sunlight and a dull headache. Askook had been in a particularly violent mood at the time. He could get angry at the slightest thing, usually in the evenings. He'd mastered the technique of not leaving bruises – an almost instinctive knowledge of *just* how hard he could strike – and any reddened traces usually faded from Odina's skin by the morning. The pain stayed, of course. That was bone-deep and beyond. But Odina was used to it.

No one ever quite knew why, but communal talk among the Paspahegh always turned to the Prophecy around this time of season. Maybe it was something in the air: a quirk of the climate affecting the village mood. *It's that time again,* people would say. *I guess we'll be talking of nothing else but The End again.* They always sounded despairing: they didn't want to talk of death and destruction.

They didn't want to be reminded of The End of All Things.

But Odina did. Odina loved it.

She adored the notion. It was an inbuilt expiration point, a sand timer pouring away. The more that the Paspahegh became convinced the Prophecy was getting closer, the more Odina felt joy swell in her heart.

If the Prophecy *finally* came true, she would not have to deal with her pain anymore. She would not have to suffer Askook or her infertility or her yearning for Matoaka. She had, in her own mind, made a deal with the Prophecy: she would let the days drift by – enjoying the odd meeting with Matoaka to make things bearable – and accept The End when it came, whatever form it took.

There would be no more of *this*. It was, frankly, the only real thing in her future she looked forward to.

Until it hit her.

It came in silence, flowing through her like a new tributary from the river, a wave of coldness that crashed over her with noiseless fury.

No visions or voices accompanied the revelation. No world-shattering celestial display followed suit.

She simply *thought* it.

And she knew, more than anything, it was the truth. There was no Prophecy.

No, no – not just that. There were no deities, no spirits: no Okeus or Ahone or Great Hare, no Mannit or Squannit or Nikomis. There was no world before this, or world beyond this. This world – this sick reality – was all there was.

It was so obvious. How could the villagers... no, worse, how could everyone in the whole *Tsenacommacah* not see that? How could countless generations have grown up thinking anything else?

No apocalypse would ever put her out of her misery. She would be stuck with Askook for the rest of her life. She would spend her days mired in drudgery and violence. She would always mourn children she could never have as well as the one that was stolen from her.

No, Odina thought.

That was not a life worth living.

The decision was instant. She had nothing to fear from ending her own life. She would not be punished in the next world. All that awaited her was emptiness. And emptiness sounded like bliss.

Odina gathered some things and left the village that same night. She had no goodbyes to say, not even to her parents: she just wanted to blink out of existence. It was not long until her next planned secret meeting with Matoaka. It would be their last.

Odina would live in the forest until then. When the time came she would savour every second she spent talking and laughing with Matoaka. She would tell the girl how much she loved her. She would tell a heartbreaking lie: *I'll see you again soon.* And – when Matoaka had gone – Odina would head to the nearest cliffside and do what needed to be done. She would depart this squalid existence for good.

'Do you know what that realisation does to a person?' Odina said to Ch-awn as she shared her tale. 'Can a man like you even begin to imagine how it feels? To have all your gods and spirits and very foundations of belief just *swept away* in a cruel heartbeat? To be left believing in nothing? Do you have any notion what that feels like?'

Ch-awn looked at Odina with solemn eyes.

'I think,' he said, after a moment, 'I might have some idea.'

Odina was about to ask him exactly what he meant – when the corrugated outside wall thudded with the noise of multiple impacts. Ch-awn sat up sharply. He settled again almost instantly.

'Hailstorms now.' He sighed. 'This weather never disappoints.'

'That's not hail,' Odina said.

The impacts became more pronounced: the *th-wick* of sliced air followed by the *twang* of flexing wood. Arrows. Arrows bouncing off the iron wall but very much sticking into the ground outside – and anything else they happened to hit. That was when the shout went out.

'Attack!' someone screamed.

Anyone who was outside ran for the first shelter they could. For many people that was the medical station: Guy and Odina's makeshift dormitory. Six men unlatched the door and staggered inside.

A howl echoed through the night. A seventh person had not made it.

Moments later – as descending walls of projectiles blotted out the moonlight – a young man also dragged himself inside, arrows protruding from his back, blood trickling from the corners of his mouth. He managed to pull himself along another foot or so. His limbs gave way. His eyes glazed over. Gone.

Guy recognised him. He was a labourer called Unger. Guy had not spoken to him much but he always seemed like a decent man.

Guy glanced around at the other men huddled inside the shelter. He recognised one of them instantly: Morton, clutching his arm to stem the blood from a grazed arrow wound. He quickly assessed the others, putting half-remembered names to faces. A carpenter called Todkil. A self-regarding *gentleman* – named Smethes. Pising: another carpenter. Profit: a fisherman. And the sixth man, face hidden as he slumped against the wall in the darkness–

The sixth man was laughing.

'Pull yourself together.' Guy was a commander now. This was combat and these men were his battalion: not the men he would have chosen, but when had *that* ever been the case? He could not – would not – allow one of them to slip into jabbering lunacy. 'For god's sake, man, *wake up*–'

He reached out and pulled the man into the light. It was Wingfield.

The reason for his laughter immediately became clear. He had been grazed by an arrow, just like Morton – except this had been on his chin, a bloody streak carving a horizontal cleft. Wingfield kept touching his hand to it, pulling away red droplets on his fingertips, marvelling at his lucky escape. The laughter was nothing intentional. It was just a reflex. Coping.

'Breathe, Wingfield,' Guy said. 'Deep and slow.' Wingfield did so. He settled.

This was the price of natural authority: all eyes were now on Guy, awaiting further instructions. The only gaze that really concerned Guy was Odina's. She struck a stoic figure as the thud of arrows reverberated outside. Howls of pain and frantic yells from around the fort did not make her flinch. It was what it was. That left only big decisions: what *now*?

'You saw them?' Guy asked Wingfield. The man had zoned out again. Guy shook him by the shoulders. 'Wingfield. The natives. The attackers. You saw them?'

'Ye... ye... yes.'

'How many?'

'Ab... abou... about...'

'How *many*?'

'About tw... tw... tw...'

About twenty, thought Guy, jumping ahead. *Right. Fine.* The attackers had the element of surprise but they certainly didn't have the numbers. He began to plot out tactics in his head – conjuring a top-down projection of the settlement – when Wingfield finally managed to spit it out.

'About two hundred,' he said.

A new noise had joined the cacophony of swishing arrows: the occasional pistol shot, reeled off into the darkness with a fevered shout. Guy took some solace in this: men were fighting back from around the camp. But something wasn't quite right.

He only heard pistols. Not muskets.

'Where are the weapons?' he asked Wingfield.

'Storage.'

'*Storage?*'

'They're in the supply shed to the east of the fort. Right on the opposite side. They're in the dryfats – the casks, the waterproof casks.' Wingfield looked on as Guy rolled his eyes. 'We need to keep them in good condition, Johnson! Protected!'

'Wonderful. And what exactly is protecting *us*?'

'Not *her*, that's for sure.' Morton had suddenly spoke up, grabbing Odina by her injured arm. Odina gave a surprised yelp of pain. 'Let's face it. The savages are here for their girl. I say we give them what they want.'

'Let her go,' Guy said. Calm. Level. 'She stays.'

'Is that right?'

'That's right.'

'And what if we all decide otherwise, Johnson?' Morton closed in on Guy. 'What are you going to do then? Kill all six of us with your bare hands?'

'Yes.'

Morton stared at Guy for a moment. He slowly stepped back. Let Odina go.

'Wingfield,' Guy said. 'Tell me the swords aren't in the dryfats too.'

'Some are.'

'And the rest?'

'There's some in the main barracks.'

'That's what, twenty feet from here?'

'Thereabouts.' Wingfield nodded.

'Right.' Guy nodded back. 'Closer than the dryfats. Much closer.' He began to point people out. 'Morton. Smethes. Profit. I want you all to run over there. As fast as you can. Stop for nothing. Arm yourselves. Be prepared to fight close quarters if the natives breach the fort.' Now came the rest. 'Wingfield. Todkil. Pising. You're coming with me.'

'And just where exactly are *we* going, Johnson?' Wingfield asked.

'I have an idea.'

'*Kapawihšiwa vai*,' Guy told Odina before he left.

Stay here.

She didn't want to – but she knew it made sense. She had

been recovering well but was still too weak to be of any use out there – especially since Morton had nearly re-broken her arm when he grabbed it. Wide-eyed and sweating in pain, Odina gave a grim nod.

'*Walwini*,' she said.

Come back.

Guy nodded – *I will* – and charged out into the fort. Behind him, Wingfield, Todkil and Pising followed. Morton led the others in a separate charge towards the barracks. As Guy pelted across the well-trodden grass he noticed how quiet it had suddenly become. No arrows flew. No pistols fired. Was it all over?

A breeze picked up. A wind. Except: it wasn't.

'Down!' Guy yelled.

Displaced air *whooshed* as arrows thudded into the ground around Guy. He gestured for the men to dive for immediate cover. They flung themselves behind an upturned supply cart in the middle of the camp. Guy hunched down, shrinking into himself, watching as a barrage of arrows peppered the surrounding grass, the closer ones taking wooden splinters out of the cart.

'Brilliant work. *Majestic*.' Wingfield was hunched beside Guy. 'So what now, Johnson?'

'We wait it ou–'

Guy felt a pistol settle against his cheek. More men were hiding behind the cart.

'Remember what I told you about leaving?' Smith asked.

'Hard to forget,' Guy said.

'Good. So let's give you the benefit of the doubt...' Smith lowered the pistol. 'And let's assume that you're heading in the same direction as us. Straight to the dryfats. Straight to the muskets.' Guy caught sight of the *us* in question: five other men following Smith's lead. They were tougher soldier-types than

Guy's own impromptu army – save for Chaplain Hunt, who was crouched with his head in his hands, whimpering pleas to the Almighty.

'Actually,' Guy said, 'I had a different plan.'

'And what might that be?'

Guy told him.

'You're insane, Johnson,' Smith said. 'You're an absolute nickel-plated utter fucking lunatic.'

There was a lull in the arrow fire.

'I suppose so.' Guy nodded.

'Well then. Just as long as that's cleared up.' Smith readied his pistol. 'Good luck.'

'We're going to need it,' Wingfield muttered. Everyone took off running.

Guy had made an assumption. It turned out to be right.

The majority of treeline cover was to the north of the fort – and that was where the natives had emerged from. They were mainly still clustered around that area, a few of them darting forwards in gaps between arrow assault, sometimes darting back when pistol fire ricocheted around them.

They were exactly where Guy hoped they would be. And so was the *Susan Constant*.

The *Constant* was the closest of the transatlantic vessels. Maintained on and off by caretakers who checked them over daily, all three ships were harboured towards the mouth of the James River, a jumping-off point for shallops to explore further inland. Most essential items from the *Constant* and its sister ships had been carried onto land. Some of the heavier items remained: more elaborate relocations yet to be arranged.

The cannons were among them.

The *Constant* was primarily a merchant vessel. While fully rigged, it wasn't equipped with a full-on ninety-one-gun broadside – but it needed some method of defence should it encounter Spanish enemies at sea. The Virginia Trading Company had made sure that the *Constant* had a primed cannon in good working order.

The sounds of pitched battle grew louder behind them.

'Almost there,' Guy said to his followers – when he noticed an extra man had joined his party. It was Smith. He had sent the others to unpack the muskets and then come running after Guy.

'I thought I was insane,' Guy said.

'Oh, you *are*,' Smith told him. 'But even insane men need a helping hand.'

'Christ alive.' Wingfield snorted. 'It just gets better.'

They made it on board the *Constant*. Guy didn't know if the attacking natives had seen them. It didn't matter by this stage anyway.

Wingfield – to what little credit Guy could give him – put aside his moaning and immediately joined Guy and Smith in manoeuvring the cannon around the ship's bulwark. When it looked like Wingfield and Smith could handle the movement themselves, Guy clambered atop the cannon and swabbed out the barrel. He nodded to the others: *it's clear*.

'Todkil. Pising,' Guy shouted, 'we should still have some munitions below decks. I'll need gunpowder propellant. And crossbar shot.'

'Crossbar...?' Todkil looked confused.

Guy remembered: the man was a carpenter. Such terms were utterly alien to him.

'Cannonball shots,' Guy explained. 'With spikes embedded.'

Todkil and Pising nodded and ran below. They emerged moments later with the necessary supplies. Guy told the others to stand back as he and Smith handled the rest: packing the parchment cartridge into the touch hole, ramming in the shot with a cloth wad, priming the breech by lighting the quill.

In the moment of anticipatory silence that followed, both Guy and Smith looked back to the fort. Most of the natives were still in their original spot, firing arrows from afar – yet some had broken further through. Many of the colonists had now grabbed muskets and were firing off shots: some well-judged, others less so. A group of men – Morton among them – had taken up swords and were fighting up close with blade-wielding attackers.

The men of Jamestown could not hold out much longer.

'Do you think this will work?' Smith asked.

Guy didn't have time to reply.

The *Constant* rocked violently as the cannon fired. The men were knocked off their feet. Back on land both sides of the conflict froze and glanced up – like two separate packs of distracted animals – as the noise split the air and the crossbar shot made impact.

It slammed into the treeline where the natives were gathered, causing both instant destruction and instant panic. A couple of towering oaks were uprooted completely, veering like toppled deities, crashing to the ground and sending many of the natives scattering. They had never seen a display of such firepower before. They were not anxious to see another.

Guy heard some of the natives shouting. It was a word he didn't recognise, said in a frantic questioning tone.

Opechancanough?

Guy realised: it was a name. Opechancanough was their leader. One of his men was asking him what to do.

A voice bellowed back – presumably Opechancanough himself.

Wanipahewa, he said.

Run away. Retreat.

Guy clambered to his feet to see the natives were doing exactly that. In remarkably quick unison the attackers backed off and rushed into the dark forest. Jamestown was alone again. For now.

Guy turned around. The other men were hugging and slapping hands on backs and shoulders: the shared relief of congratulation.

Everyone but Wingfield.

'Don't think this makes any difference between you and I, Johnson,' he said, his arms folded. 'Don't think that for *one second*.'

Most of the men gathered in the main square in the aftermath. A few of them were having their injuries tended to by Wotton. Odina had been moved to the chapel for the time being. Unger, meanwhile – astonishingly, the only fatality among the many wounded – had been covered with a sheet, awaiting removal and burial once it was deemed safe enough to leave the compound.

Guy was among the assembled men. They hadn't bothered to bind his wrists or anything like that – what kind of escape could he make when surrounded like this? He was there as an emblem. He was the totemic incarnation of their woes. A beacon of blame.

'We need to remain calm,' Wingfield addressed them all. 'We have fought them off, they show no indication of coming back–'

'*Yet*.' Morton stormed to the front of the crowd, all but shoving Wingfield out of the way. 'They have shown no indication *yet*. But we all know they'll be back. They'll come and they'll kill more of us.'

'If you please,' Wingfield said, trying to wrest back control. 'Let's keep a level head here. We were lucky in that our casualties were low. We–'

'Lucky?' Morton spat the word back. 'Go and tell that to Unger. Tell him how fortunate he is that he'll be worm-food by this time tomorrow. You know as well as I do he'll be the first of many.'

'We have no idea,' Wingfield attempted again, 'why the savages chose to attack as they di–'

'Course we do.' Morton pointed a damning finger straight at Guy. This was when Wingfield stopped interrupting. He stepped back, giving Morton the floor. Any assault on Guy was something he welcomed. 'They came because *he* brought that bitch back here. He finds some whore out in the woods, gets all teary-eyed and drags her right to our doorstep. They probably all followed him, didn't they? Watched to see what we would do. And we *took her in*. White knights on our steeds. Now we know what they think of us. They think we're *soft*.' He was whipping up the crowd.

The men began to murmur: mass affirmation. 'She's one of them. They want her back.'

'Quite.' Wingfield put a chummy hand on Morton's shoulder, trying to foster paper-thin camaraderie. 'I would say that Mr...' He faltered. He had no idea what Morton's name was. 'I would say that our exuberant friend here has captured the spirit of the whole camp quite well. Would the council agree?' Wingfield looked through the crowd, catching the gaze of his fellow council members – yet not giving them time to respond. Instead – barely hiding his elation – he galloped down the route Morton had begun. Wingfield looked straight to Guy. 'Johnson. Happy now? Or did you have anything else in mind? Want to send them written invitations next time?'

'They didn't come for Odina,' Guy said. There was a disbelieving groan from many of the men, including some mocking swipes at his closeness with her: willowy parodies of her name, *Oh-dee-nah* said in clipped mock-regal tones.

'*Shut UP*. All of you.' Everyone awkwardly obeyed. 'Listen to me, Wingfield. She ran from her people. Hid out in the wilderness. She tried to kill herself – I *saw* her. They don't know she's here, I guarantee it.'

'As the gentleman said.' Wingfield looked like he was doffing an imaginary hat to Morton. 'They may have followed you.'

'For three whole days? Are you serious? If they wanted Odina back, they could have taken her from me anytime.'

'They wanted to follow you *here*.'

'Why? They *know* where this place is, Wingfield. They didn't need my help to find it. They've been watching us build our settlement since we first stepped on dry land.'

'*Exactly!*' Wingfield clicked his fingers. 'And if they have been watching us, they will have seen us take the girl in–'

'They haven't been here for days. They haven't *needed* to observe us. What would they have seen? Men arguing and floundering. They know everything about this place they need to. They have likely been plotting this attack for a while between themselves–'

'And maybe that plot involved an injured girl. Hmm? Something to tug at our heartstrings? Lower our defences? Maybe they picked one of their own as a sacrifice? Did you ever think of that? Maybe they took one look at you, Johnson, and thought: *we can use this gullible fool for our own ends. He finds a pretty girl in need of help, he wants to play the hero, he takes her back to white-man-land and while they're all cooing and fussing, we seize the moment and–'*

'She was hiding from them,' Guy said, keeping his voice firm. 'Her injuries were her own. I stopped her from killing herself. I brought her here for Wotton's help. I have told you this a thousand times by now. Did it ever occur to you, *Edward Maria,* that maybe if you hadn't pissed away your time here and done more to engage with the natives, Jamestown might not be in this situation in the first place? Maybe if this colony's so-called President had acted in any way *presidential*–'

Wingfield seethed. 'I will not be lectured by a *deserter* on the merits of my condu–'

'Enough!' Emboldened beyond himself, Morton shoved Wingfield again, even harder this time. Wingfield reeled backwards, only just keeping his balance. 'We may never find out for sure what's going on. But I say – on the chance that the savages do want their bitch back – we give them what they want.'

'You suggested that before.' Guy glowered. 'Remember what I said.'

'There's a lot more than six of us here now, Johnson.'

'What would you suggest, then, Morton?' Guy hissed. 'Just hand her over? Is that it? Odina fled her people for a reason, you know. They would do terrible things to her if she returned.'

'She wants to die anyway,' Morton sneered. 'Doc said so.'

'On *her* terms, maybe. Not the Paspahegh's. But you wouldn't understand that, would you, Morton? A maggot like you could never grasp integrity or virtue–'

'*You*–' Morton lunged forwards to strike Guy. He stopped himself at the last minute. He had refused the bait – and allowed himself a sadistic smile as reward. 'Here's what I think we should do. We give her back to the *Passa-whatever* and we throw you into the bargain, Johnson. If this is all some big manoeuvre, you're the one who caused the whole thing. You can be a peace offering. They can do what they want with you.' His smile widened. 'I mean, I know why you're doing this anyway. So just look on the bright side. Maybe once you're both dead, you'll get a quiet moment in the afterlife to fuck the bitch in every ho–'

Guy leapt at him.

By the time Smith had pulled him back, Guy had rained down blow after blow on Morton's face. Morton blinked, dazed, the flesh around his eyes and lips already swollen. He spat out a couple of teeth.

Smith flung Guy back. Guy skidded across the ground.

'Jesus Christ!' Smith yelled. 'Jesus Christ Almighty! Look at us! Acting like barbarians. Are we not Englishmen? *Are we not Englishmen?*' He glanced around the crowd. No answer was forthcoming. The other councillors – even a natural leader like Newport – were glumly silent. Chaplain Hunt just stood, vacant, numbed by a kind of base violence he had never seen before. The men who were supposed to be in charge were just as defeated as everyone else. No solutions. No big ideas. No arguments. It all felt like the opening strings of a mad symphony. 'If we are to survive for longer than another evening – *if* – then we need to stop squabbling like drunken vagrants outside a tavern. We need to *pull ourselves together*.'

'You always seem chock-full of ideas, Mr Smith,' Wingfield piped up, re-entering the fray.

'Someone needs to be.'

'So what now? Go on. Let's hear it. We have one dead colonist, several injured, a traitor and a complete and utter *mystery woman* to attend to. What's the proper course of action?'

'I believe Johnson,' Smith said.

Some of the surrounding men snorted in derision. Most of

the others were now beyond that. They were tired: so weary they simply wanted guidance.

'The natives don't know the girl is here,' Smith went on. 'The attack was a show of force. It would have happened whether Johnson had returned or not.'

'Fine.' Wingfield threw his hands in the air, exasperated: *what am I to DO with you people?* 'But you still haven't answered my question.'

'What we do now,' Smith said, 'is rebuild. Bigger. Stronger. Safer.' He gestured to the damaged walls and the toppled palisades. 'We make sure that any future attacks don't even scratch the surface of this place.' Smith looked to the men. 'I hope none of you are too fond of sleep. Because you won't be getting a wink until this fort is rebuilt at least three times larger than before. That applies to you more than anyone, Johnson.'

'Fair enough.' Guy rubbed his sore knuckles.

'Oh, it's not fair,' Wingfield said, his voice oddly melodic. 'It's a *farce*.' Yet he intended to do nothing about it. Neither did anyone else. Mumbling between themselves, the men slinked away from each other, back to their various parts of the settlement. Wingfield walked over to Morton, who was just about regaining consciousness on the ground. He held out his hand. Still dazed, Morton took it.

Wingfield helped him up.

'Still alive in there?' Wingfield gently tapped a finger against Morton's forehead.

'Yes,' Morton said.

'Good. Stay there for one moment.' Wingfield left Morton standing where he was. He strode away a few paces and picked up a nearby abandoned pistol. He shot at the ground, inches away from Morton's feet. He calmly walked back over to Morton, who was now shaking. Virtually nose to nose with the man, Wingfield whispered, 'You ever shove me around like that again, whatever-your-name-is... and the next one goes in your head.'

Wingfield walked away. Morton soon followed suit.

Chaplain Hunt was left. Stood alone. Eyes sealed shut. Hands clamped tightly together. Praying.

A few days had passed since the attack. Now able to walk again, Odina attempted to leave the medical station a couple of times to take a look at *Ch-aymes-ton* from the inside. The door was barricaded shut. She realised that she shouldn't have been surprised – they kept Ch-awn locked up in here, they would keep her imprisoned too. They both posed their own hypothetical risks to the fort.

When he finally returned after countless hours helping refortify the settlement, Ch-awn had a question for her.

'Those men,' he said, 'had a leader. Name of Opechancanough. Ever heard of him?'

Odina nodded gravely.

'The leader of the Pamunkey tribe. He is Powhatan's younger brother. He has been known to cause trouble like this before. He is a bitter man, jealous of his brother's authority. He will often take foolish action to prove himself powerful or undermine Powhatan's chiefdom.'

'And I thought politics was a home-grown disease.'

'What?'

'Nothing. Figure of speech.' They fell silent for a moment.

'The men here,' Odina said. 'Are they talking about what to do with me?'

'Yes.' Ch-awn sighed.

'What do they say?'

'No one can decide.'

'What about you?'

'Well. I assume they're going to keep me as a workhorse for the time being. If the English are good at anything, it's maintaining slave labour.'

'You have slaves in *Ing-lann*?'

'Figure of speech. Again.'

'I don't understand, what is this *figure of spe–*'

'Never mind.'

The corrugated walls rattled. It was a gusty night, replete with occasional flurries of rain. Every time it started, Odina wondered if arrows were firing again... if the colony was back under attack.

It would more than likely happen soon.

And maybe next time it would be Askook leading the pack.

'I'm able to move now, Ch-awn,' Odina said. 'I am not speedy by any means... but I'm getting there. I know these surrounding forests better than any of your men could ever dream of. It is likely that nothing good awaits us out there... but I'm *certain* that nothing good awaits us by staying here.'

How could she possibly explain what she meant to say next: that she could no longer go through with her desire to die? That she was stuck among the living once more... and...

... wherever she went from here... maybe... maybe...

... maybe a companion of some sort would be useful?

'Ch-awn. We can leave here. Both of us. Your men think they can detain us – but I have fled my people before and you have fled yours. We'll get out. We will head somewhere completely unknown to anyone.' She swallowed. 'We can do it *together*. You and I. What do you think?'

She waited for an answer. She heard only snores.

Utterly exhausted, Ch-awn had passed out. He seemed more alert the next morning.

'I remember you were talking last night.' He was dressing for the day, waiting for the door to be unlocked and to head out into another day of back-breaking servitude. 'I must have drifted off. I'm sorry. What were you saying?'

Odina smiled weakly.

The moment had passed. The time was not right. Would it ever be again? She didn't know.

'Nothing,' she said.

From the angled slats of light stretching across the floor, Odina guessed that it was just after noon. The man who had just entered the building – ushered in by the familiar sound of the barricade being lifted – must have been drinking since he woke at dawn, possibly even carrying it over from the night before. Odina had discovered that the white men drank intoxicating liquids brewed from rye and wheat – and some of them liked to drink it in huge amounts.

'Doesn't it make you sick?' she had asked Ch-awn when he first told her. 'And dizzy? And weak?'

'Yes.' Ch-awn had laughed. 'But in a good way.'

Strange, strange men indeed.

The *whisk-ee*, as she had heard it called, was very valuable to the *Ing-leese*. The other colonists would not be happy if they found out this man – stockier and rounder than the others – had been drinking so much. He didn't look like he cared. With uneasy gait and flesh-stripping breath, the man wedged shut the door behind him and began to stagger towards Odina.

'You. *You*,' he snarled, pointing his finger at her, foamy spittle around the corners of his mouth. Odina picked up on a few of the words he said. The others just streamed into a slurred mess. 'Look at that.' He took his finger away from her and pointed at a faded dry bloodstain on the floor: where traces of the man they had called *Unn-ger* could not fully be removed. 'Gone. Because of you. Who'll be next? Who'll die with his skin shredded to pieces... all because some traitor wanted to stick his cock in a local brown girl?'

'No.' Odina spoke one of the few *Ing-leese* words she knew. She backed up against the wall as the man advanced on her. 'Please.'

The man stopped.

It was nothing to do with Odina's plea. It was so he could lean to one side and vomit on the floor. He arched back up, wiping his mouth with his sleeve as though nothing had happened. The toxic stench of half-digested corn and bile filled the air.

'Way I see it,' the man said, his stubby fingers unbuckling his belt, 'is that you're living off our good graces. And that's not enough for me. I want something proper in return. Something *tangible.* You've got something you're going to give up for me.'

'No.' Odina tried again. She scrabbled for the right words. 'I... I no want. I no want.'

'I've got more than enough *want* for both of us.'

Odina managed to get to her feet – her injuries still hurting as she did – and opened her mouth to yell.

She was a problem to many of the men here. Unwanted. A burden. But still – they would not allow *this*, would they?

She was about to scream when the man seized a grubby hand around her neck. With his other hand he snatched up a scalpel from Wotton's medical kit. Odina recognised it – it had been the very blade she had failed to cut her wrists with. The man held it against her neck.

'Try to scream,' he said, 'and you won't have a throat to scream out of.'

Odina frantically tried to think of more *Ing-leese* words. She wanted to say: *they'll know you did this. If you leave me alive,*

I'll tell them. If you kill me, they'll figure out it was you. She looked into the man's glazed eyes and realised that he didn't care. He was just a creature without causality – driven by a terrible instinct that was now prodding against her thigh. Odina tried to flinch away. The man pushed himself closer to her. He took the scalpel and began to cut away at her clothing.

He stopped.

'Just... just one second...' he said.

He hunched over to vomit on the ground again. Odina quickly grabbed the scalpel from his hand.

'You...' The man's eyes widened. 'You fucking *bitch*, give that back or I swear to God I'll...'

He got no further.

Odina had only meant it as a warning swipe. Just a *swish* of the scalpel to break the skin: a defensive ploy from a trapped animal, like a hiss from a wildcat or growl from a racoon. That was all.

She hadn't meant to tear the man's throat wide open.

Pulsing red spurts gushed out of the man's neck. He tried to clutch his throat and stem the tide. His fingers were soon slick with blood. He grew paler until he became almost translucent. He managed to mouth a couple of tortured words – *help me* – before he keeled backwards. Blood pooled out, thick and viscous. He was soon dead.

Odina was left alone with the corpse for a moment. Then the door opened again.

'Morton,' the other man casually said as he walked in. 'I hope you're not–' He froze. He saw his friend bleeding out on the ground. His body seemed to shut down for a moment, devoid of autonomy. Everything from that second on played out in a slowed-down operetta, each action a crescendo: the new man noticing Odina's shadow, turning round to see her, his eyes snapping down to the glint of the metal scalpel in her hand.

She was weak and tired... but this man was nowhere near the size of his friend. He was a skinny wretch.

She could take him. Or at least try to. She *had* to.

She leapt at him, her body screaming with pain as she did so. He was quicker than she thought. He lashed out, a lighter blow than anything *Mor-tunn* had offered... yet one that took her by surprise nonetheless.

Odina crashed against the far wall. Within seconds the man was looming over her. He clamped both of his hands around her throat. Again, the strength was not as great as *Mor-tunn's*... but he made up for it in determination: a very different kind of sober madness glowed in his eyes.

Odina felt strangely placid.

Time to give in. This was The End. The man was going to finish the job–

The man's hands slackened. Odina gave a wheezing gasp, her throat feeling like a pinhole.

The man looked confused. He reached around to the back of his head and pulled out the axe that had been thrust there.

He spent his last seconds examining the axe curiously. The blood. The fragments of skull. The flecks of brain matter.

His eyes upturned and he fell backwards.

Odina's gasping breaths became more steady. She looked up to see Ch-awn, hand still poised from where he had brought down the axe.

Ch-awn took in the vista. His handiwork. Odina's too. There was no coming back from this. No matter the justification: *Ch-aymes-ton* had birthed its first killers. They would both be marked as demons.

'Can you get up?' Ch-awn asked her.

'Yes.'

'Can you walk?'

'Yes.'

'Can you run?'

'It will hurt. But yes.'

Ch-awn grabbed her hand. Hauled her up.

'Then we're running,' he said.

They fled the fort. No one spotted them. It was the height of the working day. Not a single man could afford to be distracted.

They kept on running, never slowing, ploughing through any obstacles that the forest threw their way. Even when their bodies screamed for them to stop, they kept on going. When one of them stumbled or looked like quitting, the other pushed them onwards.

Guy had no idea how long and how far they went: ten to fifteen miles maybe, enough that when the inevitable end came they slumped to the ground almost as one, sapped even of the energy to raise their arms and break their fall. They lay flat, face down, side by side, drawing in rasping breaths like their lungs would never fill again. Leaves stuck to their mouths. Dirt clogged their noses.

'Shall we go on?' Odina finally said.

'No,' Guy answered, unsure of whether he was right or not. 'I think we're far enough from Jamestown.'

'If they chase us–'

'They will. But they're slow. Indecisive.' Again: he hoped this was the truth. 'We can rest. For now.'

They stayed there for a few hours. They both slept, deep and dreamless. Guy woke to Odina shaking him by the shoulder.

'Enough rest now. We must go on.'

He couldn't argue with her this time. They began to walk on, plagued by limps and aches and bruises. Odina led the way.

'Do you know where we're going?' Guy asked.

'Roughly, yes. I think we're just by Weyanock territory. If we move carefully around there we should be able to avoid them. Then we just have to skirt around the Appamattucks. Beyond that are the waterfalls. They are difficult to cross. Our tribes do not venture further.'

'What happens when we get there?' Odina had no answer.

Guy didn't press for one.

They kept on walking in silence. Their wordlessness was comfortable: a chance to recoup their thoughts. Occasionally they rested, eating grubs and berries, carefully drinking water from springs that marked nearby villages. They walked some more. At night Odina set up a firepit. They sat together. Close.

'Your people have promises,' Guy said. 'Do you have *confessions*?'

'What are they?' Odina frowned at the new English word.

'Things you have kept close to your heart. Secrets. They burden you and weigh you down when you keep them inside. So you tell another person and... you feel lighter. Stronger even.'

'Oh. Yes.' Odina smiled. 'We have those.'

'I have two,' Guy said. 'Would you like to hear them?' Odina nodded. 'My name isn't John. Not my real name anyway. That is Guido. Guy.'

'*Gh-ai*?'

'Guy.'

'*Guy*.'

'That's right.'

'And your second confession?'

'I lied to you,' Guy said. 'Back in Jamestown. I told you that I'd fallen asleep while you were talking the night before. I told you I couldn't remember what you said.'

'And you could?'

'Yes.' Guy nodded.

The fire crackled. Animal noises filled the air: chirruping insects, distant howling wolves.

Guy was closer to Odina. His hand was upon hers. She did not move it away.

It had been *so long* for Guy: multiple lifetimes it felt like, enough for him to assume this part of him was dead. Enough to forget altogether what men and women could do.

He had not known another woman since the death of his wife. He had felt it would be wrong: a betrayal of her memory. Feelings like this were for other people. Weren't they?

No. They could be his too. They could be anyone's: man or beast alike.

'I have lost any faith I once had,' Guy said. 'I have been stripped of my god and my beliefs. As much as I wish I could go back, I simply cannot imagine a world beyond this. There is just *us*, Odina. But... when I first stumbled across you... I don't know. I felt that maybe something was guiding me. I don't believe in fate but–'

Odina kissed him.

He was surprised. His instinct was to draw back. But another instinct soon took its place.

He melted into her.

Soon they were kissing on the ground, lost in each other, unfazed by the leaves that crackled below or the rocky stones that prodded against them.

This was an outpouring of *everything*: lust slaying repression, desire culling restraint. Guy had wondered if Odina shared the same feelings: now he *knew* she did, also somehow knowing – a psychic braid, a connection of minds, he didn't understand exactly how – that an act like this had been a long-forgotten ghost for her as well.

Both had been trapped in loveless voids. Once-bright stars of passion had flamed out completely, leaving nothing but dead black epitaphs. They had each become less than human – and had been too deadened to even realise it.

Guy pulled back slightly. His brow was against Odina's. Their sweat mingled. His hair stuck against her skin – and hers against his.

He could feel it burning: his very last cinder of rationality. But he still had just enough composure to say:

'This is... this is...' He couldn't pinpoint the right Algonquian words. He didn't have to. Odina knew what he was trying to say.

This is reckless. This is mad. This is dangerous.

'I don't care,' she said.

And – as it turned out – neither did Guy.

Odina woke up.

Something had changed. Her night with Guy had made everything different. She chided herself for such flutter-headed romantic nonsense – but it was *true*, wasn't it? Even the very air took on a different scent this morning–

Smoke.

She bolted upright. Guy had fallen asleep beside her but now he was nowhere to be seen.

As she looked around the clearing – *no*, she thought, *oh no, no, no, no, NO* – she saw what Guy had done. The fool. The idiot. Even with all the military experience he had spoken of,

Guy had made a stupid rudimentary mistake. The fire he had built was not a buried firepit like Odina's had been. Instead, Guy had kindled together some wood and lit it above ground. He might as well have raised a flag. There was every chance the fire would attract–

She noticed Guy. He was looking at her with pained apologetic eyes. He was on the ground, his hands bound behind his back, head pinned under someone's foot. Barely an instant later Odina felt the same thing happen to her: pushed mercilessly to the soil, her wrists swiftly tied, her head forced into place so she could see what happened next.

This was not just a capture. It was a show.

That's typical of the bastard, she thought. *So, so typical.*

A stream of urine fizzed onto the campfire, putting out the flames. Hissing acrid smoke coiled into the air. And above everything stood the culprit: he who had just quite literally pissed all over someone's dreams and was very pleased with himself about it.

'Hello, Odina,' Askook said.

They had set the horses free. When they had arrived at the edge of the Virginian woodland – somewhere they could only traverse by foot – Francis had suggested a far superior option: they shoot the beasts, carve and cure the meat and keep it as food reserves. Alonso, however, had grown attached to the animals. Not willing to have such a stupid and superficial argument, Francis held his tongue. He allowed the man a small victory. Alonso was still useful, after all. He had taught Francis a lot of Algonquian and could teach him a lot more. No point causing a rift over some dumb animals.

Once the horses had bounded off, Francis and Alonso began

transferring essentials from the saddlebags into their bedrolls. The gunpowder was the most important. They shared the pouches between them.

They set off in the direction of Jamestown. The plan was to watch for signs of occupation and then covertly observe the place from afar.

'We need to get a good feel for their routines,' Francis explained. 'If we're to pull this off, we need to know exactly who these men are.'

'I suppose so,' Alonso said. 'Makes sense.'

There it was: Alonso's stock response to anything. Francis wondered if the man ever said anything else. He let it go. It was another argument he couldn't be bothered having. They needed unity if they were going to get to Jamestown.

Francis was somewhat surprised, then, when Jamestown came directly to them instead.

'Quick!' Francis gestured for Alonso to throw him his bedroll. He had already dropped his own to the ground, removing the gunpowder pouches. He was frantically trying to bury them. Alonso had frozen, bewildered. '*Quick! Now!*' He finally got the message. He flung the bedroll over to Francis. Francis pulled out the other pouches. He had to work fast.

They had been navigating the dense forest for about a day. Alonso had been taking Francis through some more advanced Algonquian phrases – when Francis had stopped him. He had heard something. At first he'd been worried that the nearby rustling could be a bear or some other fearsome predator – then he realised it was something worse.

Voices. Male voices.

English-speaking male voices.

They had heard Francis and Alonso's panicked movements. Horribly familiar phrases filled the air: *someone is out there, I heard them, could it be him?* Francis tore at fistfuls of soft dirt, digging madly, angling himself to get better leverage – when his knee nudged against the gunpowder pouches and sent them rolling down a nearby steep slope.

He almost whimpered as he watched them go. He instinctively began to stumble after them, his heart sinking as they rolled out of view–

'Stop!' A man yelled. Francis turned around.

A group of four Englishmen had their muskets raised. Alonso already had his hands in the air. Francis followed suit. All four of the Englishmen gaped in horror as they saw Francis's disfigured face. The leader of the group edged forwards, weapon primed. He squinted, making sure Francis's malformation was not just a trick of the light.

'What in the name of Christ *happened to you?*' he asked.

'My name is Tresham. Francis Tresham.'

'You're English?' The man looked even more shocked.

'Yes.'

'You're not one of ours. I'd remember someone who... looked like you. Who are you?'

It only took Francis a second to think of his response. Later on – bedded down on a straw mattress in a cosy hut inside Jamestown – he would look back on this with immense gratitude. *God's inspiration. That's what it was. A moment of ingenuity powered by the Divine.*

'Please!' He began to weep.

Francis fell to his knees. He grabbed at the bedrolls – at *both* of them, the crux of his deceit. Then he pointed to Alonso.

'He made me carry them both! Treated me as a packhorse! A slave! I was captured by the Spanish while at sea. They took me to one of their colonies. But... this man... he abandoned his own army. Took me with him... tortured me... *burned* me... did *this* to my face...'

The Englishmen were listening with horror.

Perfect, Francis thought.

'He was going to use me as a hostage,' Francis babbled on. 'He had heard of your Jamestown settlement. He wanted to exchange me for some of the riches you may have found...' Francis put his face in his hands and sobbed: the very image of crushed defeat. 'Please. *Please*. Save me from him. He is a monster, do you understand, nothing more, *this man is A MONSTER–'*

Alonso had no idea what Francis was saying.

And he had no idea why the Englishmen were glaring at him. 'I think we should all calm down,' Alonso said.

None of the Englishmen understood Spanish. They merely knew what it meant: an *enemy*, the kind of man they had all battled before. A man whose army aimed to defile all that made England great.

'I think–' Alonso tried to repeat himself.

Four simultaneous musket shots tore his body apart.

The gunfire smoke ebbed away. The noise echoed deep into the forest. The lead Englishman approached Francis and helped him to his feet.

'It's all right,' the Englishman said. 'You're safe now.'

'Thank you.' Francis kept up the tears. *'Thank you thank you thank you–'*

'Calm down. We will take you back to our settlement. But...' The man cast a wary eye over Alonso's blasted corpse. 'We have many questions. We will expect answers.'

'Of course.' Francis wobbled to his feet. 'Please. What is your name?'

'Smith,' the man answered. 'John Smith.'

'Then I thank you again, Mr Smith.' Francis clutched tightly at Smith's lapels. 'I will forever be in your debt.'

They began to head back to Jamestown. As they left Alonso's body for the foxes and the fowl, Francis snuck a look at him.

Should have let me kill those horses, my friend, he thought. *Maybe the Devil would let you ride them in Hell.*

Francis's first impression of Jamestown: it was a curious fusion of brutality and banality.

Life was tough for the colonists, almost entirely without luxury – and with that came a sense of boredom. Men needed more than mere work for intellectual nourishment – yes, even *these* men, this dragged-together assortment of reprobates and apes.

A new man in town – especially one with a story such as Francis's – was a very big deal. People gawked at his face when he arrived. In England or Spain onlookers would at least try to hide their fascinated horror. Not here. All the fat had been trimmed: civility and manners hacked off at the edges.

Francis told his story to the one called Smith. Not that there was much competition... but Smith seemed to be among the most intelligent of the bunch. He had a sharpness and verve that Francis almost admired. Almost.

A crowd gathered around Francis and Smith's conversation. He soon took to addressing the whole settlement, a performing minstrel regaling them with tales of his abduction from a merchant vessel by the Spanish Army, of being the only survivor after they looted and pillaged the ship like rabid pirates, of his further kidnap and disfigurement by the sadistic deserter known as Alonso.

They lapped it up.

Story time was all good fun, of course – but any joy Francis gleaned from being an entertainer soon faded.

Guido Fawkes was nowhere to be seen.

Two other men named Wingfield and Newport joined Smith in dealing with Francis. Francis had seen men like this countless times before. Newport was the reliable type: salty, earthy, a donkey with enough common sense to be easily trained. Wingfield, meanwhile, was just a donkey: an ass with a plummy accent and all the 'right' breeding, but an ass nonetheless.

Newport, Wingfield and Smith went briefly to talk to some other men, clearly a council discussing things between themselves. Their decision did not take long. Wingfield walked back over to Francis, flashing a toothy smile.

That's a good smile, Francis thought. *Nice and persuasive. I used to be able to smile like that.*

'Captain Newport will be taking our vessels the *Constant* and *Godspeed* back to England in around a month,' Wingfield said. 'He will be happy to take you back home. In the meantime, you are more than welcome to stay here – although we do ask that you carry your weight, so to speak. It gives me no pleasure to ask this of a man who has endured as much as you, but...' Wingfield glanced around the place. It was an obvious shambles, barely held together. 'As you can see. We need all the help we can get.'

'Of course. Of *course*.' Francis grabbed Wingfield's hands. 'Anything I can help you fine gentlemen with. Anything at all. It will be scant payment for saving my life.'

'Our pleasure.' Wingfield awkwardly pulled his hands loose.

'I must warn you. Some of the men are a little on edge. We had an incident a few days ago.'

'Really?'

'Yes. A rather bloody affair, I'm sorry to say. Turns out that one of our own had been conspiring to run off with a savage girl, of all things. Killed two good men who got in his way: Morton and Herd, two hard-working labourers. The murderer goes by the name of Johnson. John Johnson.'

Francis felt a jolt. A fizz of triumph. He hid it well.

'How awful,' he said.

'I never liked the man myself. We've been sending out search parties hoping to capture him. That's why Smith and the men were out there in the first place, when they stumbled across you.'

'Any luck yet?'

'We're sending parties out daily. We'll get him. I'm sure of that. And when we do, I swear as President of this colony, I'll...' Wingfield's eyes glistened. For the first time Francis saw true malice in there: a thirst for revenge, anger beyond words. Had he underestimated this man?

'You'll what?' Francis asked.

'Nothing. Never mind.' Wingfield smiled again. It was a disappointment. Everyone should let their mask slip once in a while, Francis reasoned. It was good for the spirit. The fact that Wingfield couldn't was very telling. 'Enough talk of our problems. There's goodness here too, you know. Optimism. Hope. An outpost of England's soul in a new Creation.' Wingfield sounded like he didn't believe a word of this. 'Anyway. Let's get you some food... set you up with somewhere to sleep. Oh – first, we'd better get Wotton to take a look at your injuries.'

'My injuries?' It took Francis a moment. His face. The burnt flesh supposedly inflicted by his 'kidnapper' Alonso. 'Oh. Of course. Yes.'

Francis was soon alone with Wotton, an apparent surgeon who happily distinguished himself by being less of a troglodyte than the average Jamestown dweller. Wotton frowned as he prodded at the scarred flesh.

'Well. It's not pretty. But it's clean. It's healed well.' Wotton leant back. 'When did you say this happened again?'

'I don't know exactly. I lost track of time out there.'

'But... recently?'

'Recently enough, yes,' Francis said.

'Remarkable.' Wotton examined the flesh for a moment longer. Francis began to worry: was he going to have a problem here? Was Wotton going to start asking questions he might later regret? Francis calmed slightly as Wotton moved away, returning a moment later with a dose of laudanum. 'For any residual pain. Best I can offer, I'm afraid.'

'I appreciate it.'

'Not at all. Welcome to Jamestown.'

Francis was thinking.

The men here were already hunting for Fawkes. They were unwitting sub-contractors seeking out Francis's target. If they brought Fawkes back, he would no doubt start babbling about how he knew Francis... but everyone would dismiss this as lies from a desperate killer.

Here was what really mattered: if Francis could spend his days here twisting the knife... taking the men's hatred for 'John Johnson' and fine-tuning it into something truly fearsome, a collective venom... then, by the time they dragged him back here, Fawkes's punishment would make the slaughter of the

Canaanites look like child's play. Francis would be in the centre of it all: a ringleader in a circus of blood.

It would be beautiful.

After that, of course, the heathens in Jamestown would have served their purpose – and Francis could dispatch them however he saw fit. Until then: there were threads to be woven.

Souls to steer.

CHAPTER TEN

1607

The Paspahegh village was a curious mix: part organised, part organic. Multiple acres had been cleared of brushwood to create a central thoroughfare.

Regimented field boundaries lined off various crops: planted arrays of sweet-smelling tobacco seeds and squash. Fenced stretches of tall poles palisaded the area. The houses – which Guy already knew were called *yihakans* – were solid and practical, lashed together with sapling cross-pieces and deerskin thread, a smoke hole centring every roof. The houses took no defined path like an English street: instead, they spread out in random formation under dotted groves of mulberry trees.

At a glance Guy guessed there were around fifty houses – including some larger constructions, clearly temples or lodgings made for senior rulers.

The journey had not been comfortable. Guy had being dragged over unforgiving terrain like a bound animal carcass.

Now here, Askook had taken him and Odina into the centre of the village. It felt like a skewed reprisal of his time in Jamestown: on display as a loathed curiosity. Villagers – caught in the midst of hunting or cooking or weaving – looked on in surprise.

'I call upon Chief Wowinchapuncke,' yelled Askook.

There were assorted gasps. This was not a request to be made lightly. Wallowing in the attention, Askook cast a self-satisfied glance at Guy.

Guy stared right back. There was a flicker in Askook's bravado. Seeing the man again – after hearing every grim story Odina had to share about him – painted him in a diseased new light. He was cruelty in human form: crookedness made flesh, a gnarled serpentine manifestation.

Odina was nearby. She was stood under the watch of Askook's loyal envoy. An older woman howled Odina's name and tried to run over to her. Guy guessed this was Odina's mother. Some of the other villagers stopped her. Askook gestured for her to step back.

'No interaction,' he warned. 'Not yet. We wait for Wowinchapuncke. He'll tell us what to do with them.'

Wowinchapuncke did not take long to arrive. A tall and haggard man in his sixties, his apparel set him out as a leader: fine leather garments, yellowish-silvery body paint daubed across his face and shoulders, a curious double-horned decoration atop his head. He spotted Odina first. His stoic face betrayed a mix of emotions: relief that she was safe, sadness at the wayward conduct of a Paspahegh daughter. He could not hide his emotion when he set eyes on Askook's other captive. He looked at Guy with utter shock.

'He is one of them,' Wowinchapuncke starkly said.

'Yes.' Askook nodded. 'And he knows our tongue.'

This provoked unsettled murmurs from the villagers.

Wowinchapuncke held out a firm hand, a motion to quell the spreading panic. The onlookers quietened down.

'How is it that you speak our words?' Wowinchapuncke asked Guy.

'I learned,' Guy said.

The nearby murmurs turned to outright gasps. To look upon a white man was one thing. To hear one speak Algonquian was beyond imagining.

Wowinchapuncke motioned for calm once more. 'You have fled your people?'

'Yes,' Guy said.

'Why?'

'Differences.'

'I see.' Wowinchapuncke's eyes narrowed. He wasn't used to this kind of monosyllabic defiance. He turned to look at Odina, hurt and confused... then back at Guy. 'And what were you doing with *her*?'

Guy said nothing.

'You will answer, white man.' Askook slapped Guy across the face. Guy still said nothing.

'Do not play us for fools.' Askook produced a hunting knife and held the serrated blade towards Guy's throat. 'You will answer the Chief when–'

'I can answer,' Odina suddenly said.

'Well.' Askook looked at Odina too – but he had none of the tortured rift shown by Wowinchapuncke. He could barely contain his glee. The source of his humiliation was now under his heel. Honey-sweetened vengeance. 'That is entirely up to Chief Wowinchapuncke, isn't it?'

Wowinchapuncke thought for a moment. Then nodded. 'Very well,' he said. 'Let's hear from the girl first.'

And with that, Guy's life was in Odina's hands.

'He saved me,' Odina said.

'Go on.' Wowinchapuncke motioned.

'I was camping alone. Some of the white men had gone exploring, far from their colony. They found me and... I couldn't tell what they were saying, but I think they intended to take me. Keep me.'

'Keep you?'

'Yes. As a slave. But not for labour. A...' Odina looked embarrassed. 'A different sort.'

'They are monsters.' Wowinchapuncke spoke quietly but anger simmered hotly within him. 'They brought no women of their own. So they think they can take *ours*?'

'They tried to remove my clothes,' Odina went on. 'To have their way with me. Right there and then. I cried and begged but they would not stop. If it had not been for...' She caught herself. She made sure to use Guy's other name. 'If it had not been for Ch-awn here, they would have continued.'

'What did he do?'

'He dealt with them.' Odina lowered her gaze, trying to project the image of a meek young woman who had never been exposed to violence. Wowinchapuncke – woefully unaware of the things she had seen, remembering only little Odina who had been known as Paspahegh's most refined child since her birth – did not need much convincing. 'It was terrifying to see. I wish death upon no men. But Ch-awn had no choice.'

Wowinchapuncke let the story hang in the air. He looked to Guy. 'White man,' he said. 'This is how it happened?'

Odina held her breath as she waited for Guy's answer. Her story was far from perfect, she understood that. It would paint a dark picture of all the men in *Ch-aymes-ton*. It would almost certainly result in further attacks upon the settlement – maybe not now, but soon. Speaking of which:

'Do you see now, Chief Wowinchapuncke?' Askook chimed in. '*This* is surely why the Pamunkey saw fit to attack. The rest of the *Tsenacommacah* may have frowned upon their actions. But now we know that Opechancanough was acting wisely in his command–'

'We will get to that later.' Wowinchapuncke silenced Askook. He was still waiting for Guy's answer. Odina desperately hoped that Guy would see what she had done, what little choice she had: the lesser of two evils, a lie told to save Guy's life at the expense of his people's reputation. 'I need to hear it from you, invader. Tell me now – is this how it happened?'

Odina tensed.

'Yes,' Guy said.

Odina exhaled again.

'You had no hesitation in killing your own people,' Wowinchapuncke asked, 'to save a Paspahegh girl?'

'I do not see them as *my* people.'

'And yet you came here with them. Across an ocean.'

'I always intended to vanish. Leave them behind. But I never intended to trespass on your land or that of any other tribe in the *Tsenacommacah*.'

'You pose me a lot of dilemmas, white man.'

'I can only imagine.'

'I'm sorry, Chief Wowinchapuncke,' Askook interjected again. 'But there is something else I feel we are failing to address.'

'And that is?' Wowinchapuncke looked to Askook with waning patience. 'Why did Odina leave the Paspahegh in the first place?' Askook turned his vindictive scowl to Odina. 'Why did she leave her parents worried and heartbroken? Why did she leave her husband in distress? Why would a young woman choose to tear the heart out of a community like that? I think we deserve answers, don't you?'

Wowinchapuncke didn't like Askook's attempts to steer the conversation. Yet he agreed.

'Your absence has indeed torn a rift through this village,' Wowinchapuncke solemnly told Odina. 'Askook is right. You must tell us why you did what you did.'

Odina kept her shameful gaze tethered to the ground. She had already turned into a performance.

Now it was time to unveil another one.

She had always been able to cry on cue. It was something she had used to get her own way as a little girl. She'd always been reluctant to seize its manipulative power as an adult – but there was no better time than now.

Bursting into tears, Odina flung herself at Askook's feet. His conceit turned to surprise. He hadn't expected *that*.

'Please forgive me, husband,' Odina bawled. 'I'm sorry. I'm *sorry*.'

A number of the elder women from the village – Odina's mother among them – closed in on Odina. Askook was too shocked to deter them. They gently helped her up, soothing hands patting down her arms and shoulders, glaring daggers at Askook for causing this breakdown.

Askook stiffened, his hackles raised. He wasn't going to be offset by such emotive nonsense.

'Sorry for *what*, Odina?' he asked. 'You still haven't explained.'

'I was by the river one morning.' Odina sniffled. 'And then... I think... I think that something possessed me. A dark spirit. A nameless and evil thing.' The onlookers gave each other worried glances. For spirits to intervene in mortal affairs was never a good sign. 'It told me that I was a barren wretch. That I did not deserve a man like you. It whispered into my ear and said...' Odina feigned being unstable. The surrounding women held her upright. 'It said that I should just crawl off into the forest and vanish. It told me that you would find someone else... someone to bear you children... while I should free you from the burden of my presence. It told me that my punishment was to live alone in the wilderness. And every time I felt like returning the spirit would say no... no... *NO*...'

'My girl.' Odina's mother tearfully wrapped her arms around her. Odina fell into the hug for a moment. She then slithered free, leaving her weeping mother as she stepped forward, arms outstretched to Askook.

'Husband,' Odina said. 'I beg your forgiveness. To earn the forgiveness of the Paspahegh, I must hear it from you first.' Despite protests from the women behind her, Odina sank to her knees. 'Please say I have it. *Please.*'

Askook looked around, lost, uncertain. Everyone looked back at him expectantly – including Wowinchapuncke, visibly moved by Odina's story.

Askook knew, of course, that the whole thing was a lie. During particularly heated arguments with Odina – when she no longer cared if he hit her or not, only he knew exactly what she thought of him – she had screamed at him with honest bile: *I'm glad I could never have your children! I'd rather die than have your demon seed planted in me, you heap of dung!*

Askook stared at Odina as the whole village awaited his judgement. He knew that Odina had the upper hand here. He could not be seen as a callous and vengeful man. He needed to be seen as a protector.

Do not expect this to end well, his fevered glare said to Odina. *This is just one more humiliation I will be repaid for. And repaid in full.*

So be it, came her silent reply.

'My wife.' Askook put on a display of fake emotion almost as profound as Odina's. He let Odina sink into his arms. 'My beautiful wife. Of course I forgive you. I will forever be here for you. The spirits will never take you from me again.' He hugged her tighter. He hissed into her ear, 'I will be away from this village for a few days. But we will discuss this – in *great* detail, I promise – when I get back. Try to flee again and–'

'You think I am afraid to die by your hand?' Odina hissed back, her grateful face at odds with her venomous tone. 'I would welcome it.'

'Oh, I'm well aware of that. That's why I'll massacre both your parents if I even get the slightest *hint* of you strolling off again.' Askook let her go. Odina felt her mother pulling her back: desperate to keep hugging the girl she had missed so much. Askook watched the embrace, his warning echoing heavily in Odina's heart. *Massacred. I warn you. Gutted and filleted.*

Odina was so shaken she almost overlooked the other thing Askook had said: *I will be away from this village for a few days.*

What was he talking about?

'If I may suggest something,' Askook said to Wowinchapuncke, 'that we can do with the white man?'

'I will make that decision.' Wowinchapuncke waved a hand. 'You have done enough for one day.'

'Actually, Chief Wowinchapuncke... I don't think I have.'

The onlookers mumbled. This wasn't exactly full-on defiance – but refuting orders like this was more than Wowinchapuncke was ever used to. Many flinched, awaiting an outburst. Wowinchapuncke was feeling generous. 'Explain yourself, Askook.'

'I captured this Ch-awn man,' Askook said. 'I feel it is only right my suggestion should be heard.'

'You captured him on behalf of the Paspahegh. Not for yourself.'

'I did *both*.'

'Watch your tone.'

'I apologise.'

'Get to your point.'

'I know that you and the other chiefs have discussed the arrival of the white men with Powhatan. Powhatan himself would surely be most interested to speak to Ch-awn.'

'You're saying we give him our captive?'

'In exchange for Powhatan's undying respect? Yes.'

'Powhatan can be fierce,' Wowinchapuncke reflected. 'Even if this white man is... less savage than the others, Powhatan still may not be interested in simply *talking* to him. He may wish to do far worse.'

'Powhatan gets what Powhatan wants,' Askook said. 'Is that not the way things work? Ask yourself, Chief Wowinchapuncke: what would it be worth to the Paspahegh if we became Powahtan's most favoured tribe? It would be greater recognition of your own glory. Recognition you deserve.'

'Recognition for you too.' Wowinchapuncke gave a knowing smile. 'Powhatan has no idea you even exist as of now. This would certainly bring you to his attention. Along with all that entails. Power. Riches. Rewards.'

'That,' Askook returned the smile, 'would simply be an added benefit.'

'I'm certain it would. What do you have in mind?'

'There's no point in wasting time,' Askook said. 'I can leave with my men immediately. We'll have this Ch-awn creature in Powhatan's hands within the day.'

'Very well.' Wowinchapuncke nodded. 'Do it. But just make sure Powhatan knows: this is a gift from *me* to *him*.'

'Of course.' Askook motioned for his two lackeys to get moving. Without hesitation they grabbed Guy, spears prodding at his lower back, moving him along with his hands securely bound.

At least I get to walk this time, Guy mused. *Beats being dragged.*

Any gallows humour he could muster vanished when he met Odina's eyes. She was stuck in Paspahegh now: a prisoner in all but name.

Darkly certain that he would never see Odina again – that she was condemned to a life of misery he could once have helped her escape – Guy deliberately looked away.

He had failed her.

And the shame was crippling.

With Guy bound and sat behind Askook in one of the canoes, they made the journey to Powhatan without stopping. It was a long jaunt during which no one spoke a word. Guy knew what Askook wanted: the native was hoping the foreigner would plead for his life... or at least beg to know exactly what was going to happen to him. Guy refused to give Askook the satisfaction. And if the man became enraged by this and plunged his blade through Guy's chest? Guy would not show a glimmer of fear. He had suffered worse.

The four men travelling down the river occupied their own private kingdom. Guy had nothing to do but watch the scenery drift by. He started to suffer defeatist thoughts: would this be the final time he would ever gaze upon nature like this? Had last night's sunset been the last he would ever see?

He ditched the fatalism. It would do him no good. Even if he was to die trying, he had a new mission. He would return to Odina. Somehow.

They approached the Powhatan village. In unspoken unison, Askook and his men drifted their canoes over to the riverbank. Villagers who were hauling in fishnets stopped and stared.

They had arrived.

They blindfolded Guy as soon as they made it to land. He knew their reasons. If he had been able to scope out landmarks on the way to Powhatan, that could help him if he attempted to escape.

He was surrounded by noise: mainly the chatter of villagers. The acoustics were vast and sparse. The village seemed a lot bigger than the Paspahegh's. The scent was a little different too: hints of raspberries and cherries and roasted nuts.

There were none of the theatrics that had accompanied Guy's entrance into the Paspahegh village. Everything was oddly subdued.

Askook reined in his arrogance – no small feat, Guy understood – and spoke quietly to a couple of Powhatan's intermediaries. Amidst the bustle Guy managed to catch a few words: *offering* and *gift* and *tribute*. He felt like a crate of goods being haggled over by men like Wingfield: living cargo of the Virginia Trading Company. For a while, Guy stood alone, still blindfolded, feeling prods and nudges from curious onlookers who wanted to get up close to this strange white invader.

Askook returned. The deal had been done. Before he left he leaned in closer to Guy, sealing off their communication forever with a gleeful missive.

'Whether you live or die from hereon in,' he whispered, 'your life is no longer your own.'

Askook slid away, taking his entourage with him.

Guy felt various hands grip around his arms. Silently, a couple of indeterminate aides ushered him along. The ground was level and smooth beneath his feet.

Through the fabric of the blindfold he saw the light dim – they were heading under some overhanging trees, he guessed – and then the outside air turned into the smoky tang of an interior.

He was made to sit down, his legs crossed over each other. His escorts left. He was alone for a brief moment before he felt another presence nearby. He could feel the man's bulk in the shifting air. His scent alone indicated power: the musk of dried sweat and decorative warpaint. Guy blinked as large hands slowly removed his blindfold.

The hut was a lavish and imposing structure. The man before him lowered himself onto an intricately carved throne. It couldn't be clearer if his name had been announced via courtesan fanfare. This was the Chief of Chiefs. This was the man who ruled over the *Tsenacommacah*.

Powhatan.

'The Paspahegh man who brought you here.' Powhatan spoke in gravelly tones, a voice worn down by a lifetime of robust duty but still filled with authority. 'He tells me you are different from the other pale men. He says that you know our language, for a start.'

'He is right.' Guy nodded.

'Remarkable.' Powhatan was a man who had seen much in his life – yet was still capable of surprise. He took long drags from an ornate smoking pipe, a ceramic object decorated with off-white shells.

Guy watched with curiosity. He wasn't going to die. At least that was apparent. The ruler of the kingdom had deemed him a subject of interest – for now anyway – and wanted to find out more.

It was leverage. Not much. But some.

Powhatan had lots of questions. There were things he demanded to know. Guy revealed what he thought was prudent: his need to escape his homeland, his ulterior motives in joining the voyage over here, his flagellation-spurred drive to vanish into the wilderness. Powhatan wanted to know lots more about Guy's homeland – 'and I *will* get my answers' – but first he focused on the crux of recent events, the turning point in the *Tsenacommacah's* new history:

'You massacred your own in order to save a Paspahegh woman. You have made an enemy of your people.'

'In a way,' Guy said.

'Your people are violent? Savage?'

'They are like all people.' Guy saw an opportunity. He still needed to work with Odina's story – that he had saved her from a pack of white would-be rapists – but he could also wheel back the condemnation of Jamestown as a whole. He could maybe convince Powhatan that an attack on the colony might not be necessary. 'There are violent and savage men among them. I battled three of them. But there are also good men too. Many of my people want nothing more than peace. To learn from you. Trade. Forge alliances. And, truth be told, my enemies in Jamestown were my enemies long before that... incident.'

'You are a man who makes adversaries easily?'

'Yes.'

'I know the feeling well.' Powhatan smiled as he toked on his pipe. Guy was struck by how surreal this all was: how a meeting with a warlord was shifting into conversational repartee. He compared it to his confrontation with King James – back when he had been *another* Guy, one willing to slaughter hundreds for imaginary men in the sky. James had been a rich boy out of his depth. He had deserved Guy's scorn. Powhatan, however, was a man who had earned his leadership. 'A man without any enemies is a man without any principles. Would you agree?'

'I would.'

'I get the feeling that your Paspahegh captor' – Powhatan had not bothered nor cared to remember Askook's name, which gave Guy a small tinge of delight – 'wanted me to make an example of you. "He may be a more noble invader than the others, Chief Powhatan", he told me. But he is still an "invader".'

'That man and I were not on good terms.' Guy held his tongue. He could not reveal the truth about Askook and Odina – and certainly not his desire to get back to Odina. Powhatan already had enough power over him without adding that to the mix.

'I gathered that. Your name – Ch-awn, is that right?'

'Yes.'

'I am a fair man, Ch-awn. I have not been in the past, maybe, but no one builds an empire through fairness. I'm sure that applies to your homeland too.'

'Very much so.'

'You have come uninvited to the *Tsenacommacah*. Yet you've shown me that you are not a threat. The rest of your people... even though you claim there are decent men among them... I am not so sure of.' He drew thoughtfully on his pipe. 'You can be a valuable resource to me, Ch-awn, if you are willing to co-operate. While I decide how to approach the issue of your people, you may stay in the village as my guest. You will be on hand to answer any questions I might have about *Ing-er-lend* and the *Ingleesh*. Rest assured I will have many. You will be given food and shelter and taken care of. You will be forbidden from straying beyond the bounds of the village – I strongly urge you not to try it – but otherwise you will enjoy the same basic freedoms as any Real Person.'

'Your people may not take kindly to me.'

'They will take to you however I say they will.' He tapped out his pipe and laid it on the ground. 'Now. Do you agree to my plan?'

'What's the alternative?' Guy asked.

'It is best not to ask.' Powhatan's smile was calm and polite. But the iron will of his younger self still shone through.

'Then we have a deal.'

'Excellent. Now – the tribes of your homeland. Tell me all about them.'

Guy explained much to a fascinated Powhatan. On the first day alone he took the Grand Chief on a descriptive tour of England: explaining that the closest things to tribes were called *cities,* that the climate was a more temperate version of the *Tsenacommacah*, that the chiefdom of the nation was occupied by a King named James. Powhatan mentioned that a council of elders would often meet in his village to discuss new rules and laws. Did Ch-awn's nation have something similar?

'A place called Parliament,' Guy said.

'This *Parl-ee-a-ment.* It is full of knowledgeable and honourable men, yes? Those who have done and seen much with their lives? Those who have gathered much wisdom they wish to share?'

'Sort of,' Guy said.

When Powhatan tired of asking questions – for now – Guy was allowed to wander the village. He wondered how Wingfield would react if he set eyes on this place: knowing that his infernal 'savages' were living a far more civilised existence than the Virginia Company's finest.

Reactions to Guy were mixed. Some just gawked in hapless bewilderment. Some – mainly men – glowered at him, clearly wishing this imposter did not have Powhatan's favoured status. Some of the younger women giggled, especially when Guy smiled at them. Guy was so swept up in this new world that he almost forgot the sorrow gnawing at his insides.

Odina. She was still out there... back in Paspahegh, stuck with that *thing* of a husband. Every second he spent here was–

Odina.

She was here. In front of him.

It took a second or two for his senses to focus. No, no, it wasn't Odina: that was impossible. But it was, bizarrely, a miniature version of her: Odina's features and mannerisms compressed into the frame of a ten-year-old girl. As the girl called out to a passing friend – *see you tomorrow, Enola* – her voice even sounded the same. Guy knew he had heard it before.

This was Matoaka.

He didn't realise he had stopped in his tracks – frozen, a human icicle – until the girl bumped into him, spilling some of the clams she had collected in her basket.

She looked irritated, about to snap at Guy. Then she saw him.

'I'm sorry,' Guy said. He stooped over and started picking up the clams. 'Let me help you with these.'

'You are the foreigner.' Matoaka slowly joined him in retrieving the clams. 'The one who knows our ways and words.'

'Some of your ways. Some of your words.' Guy smiled.

'My father speaks a lot about you.'

'I'm sure he does. He speaks to me of you too. You must be Matoaka.'

'Yes.' She frowned. 'But my father calls me Pocahontas. So everyone else calls me that too.'

'Well. *I* would like to call you Matoaka. If that is acceptable to you?'

'I...' Her frown deepened, as though she was turning over the world's greatest dilemma in her mind. Finally she gave a presumptuous nod, looking every inch the tiny princess allowing a favour to a commoner. 'Yes. I will allow it.' She frowned as she gathered up more of the clams. 'Some of these are spoiled now. Ruined.'

'Sorry,' Guy said.

'You say sorry a lot.'

'Is that right? Some people might think that I don't say sorry eno–' He noticed something on the girl's arm. A curious sheen rubbed into the skin. It seemed familiar.

'Matoaka. What is that?'

'This?' She proudly held out her forearm. A thick coal-black grain was matted in the light downy hair. 'It's pretty, isn't it? I do like the body paint that our women wear... but the colour can fade so easily. I like how vivid this is. Dark and strong.' She suddenly became protective, drawing her arm away. 'But it's *mine*. I found it.'

'Found what?'

'The strange black soil. The special dirt. Down by the river. I've never seen anything like it before.' She began to look upset. She regretted saying anything. 'But you have to keep it *secret!* Don't you understand? I don't want anyone else wearing it, it's mine, it's *mine* and–'

'I won't tell anyone,' Guy said. 'But... please. I just need to take another look at it.'

Warily, Matoaka held out her arm again. Guy ran his finger along it and accumulated some of the coarse black dust. He raised it to his nose and then – only confirming what he now already knew – he touched his finger to his tongue. The scent: a fusion of sulphur and burnt steak. The taste: a curious metallic saltiness.

It was gunpowder.

'I *told* you,' Matoaka said, after Guy asked for the fifth time. 'There was a small mound of it. By the riverside. There were some sort of little sacks nearby too. Do you think someone must have been trying to collect it? The special soil?'

'I think so.' Guy nodded.

'I couldn't bring the little sacks though.' Matoaka gave a sullen pout. 'I had too much to carry. Clams. Stupid clams. I *hate* clams.'

'That's all right. Can you remember where it is?'

'Yes.' She nodded, full of pride. 'Exactly where.'

Guy's head was spinning. The gunpowder *must* have come from either English or Spanish soldiers – but how the hell did it get out there?

He knew that Jamestown had a middling supply of the stuff – nowhere near enough, to be honest – and that it was safely procured in the dryfats and on the ships. No one would remove it and ditch it in the forest. Which was not to say any Spaniards would do the same as well: gunpowder was a valuable commodity wherever it came from.

Could it have been the casualty of a shipwreck, goods washed upriver after a disaster? Possibly. But word got out: such a wreck could not be kept secret for long. And Guy had not seen any other telltale signs during his excursions on the river: no floating wooden debris or homespun paraphernalia.

But. It was definitely gunpowder.

'Do you think you could go out there,' Guy asked, 'and bring it back for me?'

'No,' Matoaka said firmly, a territorial verve she had adopted from her father. 'I already said. It's *mine.*'

Guy sighed. He really didn't want to do what he was about to... but he had no other choice.

'Matoaka.' He took the basket and gently put it to one side. 'I have to tell you something. I *know.*'

'Know about what?'

'About your meetings. With your mother.' Guy watched as Matoaka's face morphed into shock. He powered through the guilt – was *this* what he had come to now, a grown man blackmailing a child? – and carried on. 'You meet often, don't you? It's all very nice. Talking and laughing and singing. Such fun. But your father would be furious if he found out what little *Pocahontas* was up to, wouldn't he?'

'How...' Matoaka stammered. 'How do you know about that?'

'It doesn't matter. I *know* and I can tell Powhatan any time I choose. Unless you make an agreement with me, Matoaka. You head into the forest today and bring me back the sacks filled with the special dirt – and I won't let your father know what you've been doing.'

'That's not *fair*!' she blurted.

'I know.'

'You're *mean!*'

'I know.'

'I...' She understood she was out of options: maybe the first time, as a chief's favourite daughter, she had ever felt like this. 'I'll do it.' She kicked away her basket – clam-gathering forgotten amidst her frustration – and stormed off. She turned back briefly to say one last thing. 'I *hate* you.'

'I know.' Guy sighed.

It had been a joy to find out about the gunpowder stashes in Jamestown. It had been a huge disappointment when Francis actually saw them.

There was a mere smattering kept on the *Discovery* and the *Godspeed*. A much larger stock was kept on board the *Susan Constant* – but Francis learned that two imbecile carpenters called Todkil and Pising had left the containers open following a recent cannon-firing incident. The powder had reacted with the air and decayed – as it always did when left unattended for a while – therefore becoming useless. There was also a strictly regimented amount kept in storage in the fort itself – yet this was kept near the food supplies. That meant, like the ever-decreasing food rations, it was guarded constantly and measured daily. It would be near impossible for Francis to swoop in and pilfer a handful – let alone the amount he would need to carry out his divine plan.

He needed the pouches. Out in the forest. Some of the powder may have spilled, yes – but most would still be kept safely inside.

Francis had a decent sense of direction; he was sure he could track to the point where he had lost the pouches. Alonso's corpse would be a giveaway, assuming the wildlife hadn't totally devoured it. And the pouches themselves couldn't have got too far, could they?

As requested by Wingfield, Francis had begun 'pulling his weight' in Jamestown. He had noticed that men were often sent exploring for gold deposits: sifting through riverbank soil for the telltale off-yellow gleam. Nothing had been found so far. It was a job the men always complained about: thankless, tiring, crushing. Francis was all too happy to make it his regular assignment. The others were all too happy to let him: in fact, his apparent readiness to take it on only made him more popular in the colony.

After a few days searching – he couldn't stay gone too long to avoid suspicion – Francis began to think he was on the right track. Then, when he came across Alonso's bloated corpse, he *knew* he was there: at the edge of the slope he had watched the pouches roll over.

He clambered down. The noise of the river only got louder – and his hopes started to grow dimmer. If the sacks had hit the water, the goods were gone: dissolved, dispersed, clogging up the gills of unlucky fish for miles. He kept on looking around the area but gave himself a caveat: *expect disappointment*.

He saw them. He let out a joyous laugh. *Thank you, Lord.* The pouches were partially ripped and half-embedded in the wet soil – but the powder itself was still plentiful, and it had still yet to start decaying. From afar Francis reckoned that maybe a quarter of it had been lost to the river – leaving a good amount he could sift back into the pouches and carry with him. Then he–

What in the name of Hell was this?

There was movement. A partial silhouette cast against the dappled light through the trees.

A figure, hunched over, scrabbling and sifting.

It looked like someone else had had the same idea.

Not just someone else: a girl. Young. Ten or eleven, he would say. One of the savages.

She was keeping herself entertained as she took grainy black handfuls of the powder and stuffed them back into the pouches. She was singing a lilting tune, occasionally stopping to grumble when things got difficult. Francis recognised some of the words.

She seemed to be cursing someone. *Can't believe he made me do this... hate him so much... thinks he can order me around just because he's Daddy's new pet...*

She looked up.

Francis did not have time to hide. The girl caught sight of his mangled half-face. She was about to scream.

'Wait. Wait!' Francis said in Algonquian.

It was enough of a surprise that the girl held her scream. She clutched the stuffed pouches to her chest, much like an English child would cradle a doll for comfort. Her hands were quivering. She was trying to keep her fear under control.

Francis had always hated children. Even when he was one. But now he needed to pretend otherwise.

He needed to be a kind, benevolent uncle. Only then could he deal with this little bitch.

'Please don't be scared.' Francis held up his hands. 'I'm not here to hurt you. I'm just looking for something that belongs to me, that's all.' He motioned to the reddened dirt that stained the girl's hands. 'What you have there, see? It's mine. And it's something very precious to me.'

The girl looked to her hands. To the pouches. Back to Francis. 'Are you... a demon?' she asked.

'No, no, no.' Francis shook his head. 'I'm not.'

'Yes you are!' The girl was now more agitated. Still clutching the pouches tightly, she shot to her feet. 'You can't fool me!' Francis tentatively moved closer. The girl flinched back. 'Get away from me!'

'You're right.' *Fine,* thought Francis. *Whatever works.* He knew his menacing leer was more effective than his 'friendly' grin anyway. 'I am a demon. And unless you give me what's mine, I'll–'

The girl took off running. Still holding the pouches.

'Get back here!' Francis yelled. *'GET BACK HERE YOU*

LITTLE WHORE!' He began to run full pelt after her. She was tiny and lithe and knew her surroundings – but he was faster. He chased her down the riverbank and through a mass of spiky brambles and thistles that shredded his skin. The girl vanished from sight for a second – but then he *had* her. Francis dived forwards, fingers outstretched. His hand clasped around the girl's ankle, taking her to the ground as well. She dropped the pouches in front of her. Francis began to drag himself along, intent on throttling the child.

'Just... give me... the... *fucking... powder,*' he grunted, 'and... I'll... leave you... *alone...*'

The girl lashed out with something: a small blade of some kind. Francis howled in pain as he felt it slash across the ruined side of his face. A second later there was another slash, one that tore along nose to temple on the right side of his face. Blood seeped into his eyes, a thick flow he couldn't stem. He wiped it away. More came. He couldn't see a thing.

But he could hear her: oh yes. He heard all too well as – gasping, crying – the girl gathered her bounty once more and darted off into the forest.

Francis staggered around, flailing blindly. It was useless. By the time the blood had stopped oozing so thickly down his face, the girl was gone. He ran his fingers along the skin on the right side of his face, now freshly torn. The girl had meant business. He had almost lost his right eye.

He made up a story when he got back to Jamestown. While sifting for gold he had lost his footing and taken a humiliating fall. Wotton had taken a look at the wounds, washing them out. They were mainly superficial, he told Francis. They would heal well on their own.

'Not that I was particularly handsome anyway,' Francis joked to the others at mealtime that evening. 'I mean, how can you make this face look worse anyway? That's like putting a hat on a hat.' The other men roared in laughter. Even Wingfield – normally above bawdy jokes – cracked a smile.

'Like putting a hat on a hat, he says.' Pising snorted, before clapping a chummy hand on Francis's shoulder.

One thing was now obvious to Francis: the men at Jamestown admired him. They saw him as a compatriot, a brother in arms of their shabby new enterprise. They genuinely liked him.

And he despised every last one of them.

'*Pocahontas!*'

The shriek went up from a startled woman as she saw Matoaka staggering back into the village. Sobbing like a newborn, exhausted, cut and bruised and smeared in mud and dust, Matoaka dropped the pouches to the ground in front of her.

Guy was among the crowd who rushed over to her. Despite being a weeping wreck, she managed to throw him a glare through the tears. *There. Your precious bounty. Happy now?*

Village elders demanded to know where she had been. She refused to tell them. The arguments grew so fierce that eventually Powhatan himself emerged to take stock of the situation. Voices were immediately lowered. Deference reigned. An appearance like this was far from the norm.

'Pocahontas.' Powhatan spoke with gruff tenderness as he ran a hand along the girl's face. 'What have you done *now*?' He noticed the pouches lying on the ground nearby. He took a handful of the powder and let it drift through his fingers. 'What is this? Why did you go out to get it? Did someone tell you to?' Matoaka still refused to speak. Guy knew what had to be done.

The girl was strong-willed but not immortal: they would eke the truth out of her eventually.

It was better coming from him.

'I did,' he said.

Fifty pairs of silent eyes simultaneously landed on Guy. But he only saw one. Powhatan's angry glare was a sunbeam burning right at him.

'Take the white man to my *yihakan*,' Powhatan said.

Guy was waiting for a while in the hut, alone and cross-legged. Eventually Powhatan entered.

He sat on his throne, not taking his eyes off Guy as he did so.

'My girl has quite the imagination about her,' he said. 'She claims she saw a demon of some sort out in the woods – a powerful dark spirit who wanted to take her away. I told her that such a thing was impossible. A spirit like that would only ever reveal himself to a great warrior or a tribal leader... not a little girl. Yet still she insists. Hopefully one of the medicine women will be able to talk her round.' Powhatan picked up his ceramic pipe, turning it over in his hands, deciding whether or not he was in the mood to smoke it. He wasn't. 'But I'm not particularly interested in her fantastical tales right now. I would much rather know why you asked her to go and collect this... material for you.'

'Chief Powhatan,' Guy slowly began. 'You have shown me great hospitality while keeping me here. You did not have to do this. As such, I am eternally grateful. The material you speak of is called *gunpowder*. It is an invention we have, across the ocean. I believe that it could be of great use to you – and, unable to leave the confines of the village myself, I needed someone to go and retrieve it.'

'So you chose the daughter of a chief.' Powhatan's stare was unyielding. 'To act as an errand girl.'

Guy lowered his head.

'I noticed that she had some of the powder on her hands and arms. She told me she knew exactly where it was. I just thought she would be the best person to find it.' Guy swallowed. 'But you are right, Chief Powhatan. What I did was ignorant and foolish. An insult to you and your people. I beg your forgiveness. I accept whatever punishment you see fit to lay down.'

Powhatan sat motionless for a while.

'This powder,' he said. 'What exactly *is* it?'

Guy looked back up.

'If you could accompany me outside, Chief Powhatan... I will happily show you.'

Once Guy's demonstration was over – once the villagers had yelped and cheered with triumphant delight at the things he showed them, once Powhatan's earlier concerns had vanished and left only a look of exultant wonder on the tribal chief's face – Guy felt his future slipping away.

True, it was a good thing that the Powhatan villagers now celebrated his presence.

True, he had further aligned himself with the most powerful forces in the *Tsenacommacah*.

But any chance of leaving Powhatan and getting back to Odina was now an even smaller prospect.

Guy was going to be here for a long, long time.

By the time the chapel was fully decorated and Chaplain Hunt was able to carry out his first service, Francis's contempt for Jamestown had tripled in magnitude. It was an Anglican Communion service, the type of insult to the True Faith that had made Francis want to see England burn in the first place. Francis did not fear God's judgement for sitting through the abomination – He would understand that Francis had no choice but to play along, outwardly hamming it up, ever the jolly heretic – but he did feel the pressure of His calling increase.

Finding Guy Fawkes and killing him would not be enough. Razing Jamestown to the ground would not be enough. Fine as first steps in a grander plan, yes – but now mere aperitifs to what lay ahead.

This untouched New World – so perfect as a blank canvas to spread the word of God – was now clearly at risk of infection. The virus was called Protestantism. It was a turbulent malady, easily transmitted. Once it had a foothold it did not die off easily. And – as by far the noblest custodian of this fresh continent – it would be Francis's lifelong task to keep it at bay.

All of this was why – on June 22, when Captain Newport and twenty other men loaded necessary supplies onto the *Susan Constant* and *Godspeed* to travel back to England – Francis refused the passage he was offered.

He wanted, he told the men of Jamestown, to stay with them.

'You all saved my life,' he told the assembled colonists as the *Constant* and *Godspeed* sailed off towards the horizon. 'I have no kinship as strong as this back home. I am one of you now.' He smiled. 'A brother.'

The men cheered. Wingfield looked on – not quite approving of this raucousness, but also grateful that something had finally lifted the men's spirits. Francis held his arms aloft, basking in the camaraderie.

Brother, the men chanted.

Brother. Brother. Brother.

CHAPTER ELEVEN

November 1607 – January 1608

It was like she had never left.

Once the initial flurry of sympathy was over, Odina was pitched back into the routine chores she had always known. Every day was the same. Sometimes she honestly wondered if the whole episode with Ch-awn – no, *Guy*, his real name was Guy – had been a fever dream.

Askook had predictably taken out his frustrations on Odina. At first he no longer even cared about the traces of his tirades: leaving Odina visibly bruised whenever his temper snapped and he lashed out.

She made up stories. He made up stories. The stories were believed. Soon enough even Askook's violence against her returned to 'normal', subdued attacks that deliberately left little bruising. More than ever before, Odina's parents now saw Askook as an ever-patient ward looking after the welfare of a mad and broken woman.

And who was Odina to argue with that judgement? She was as mad and broken as they came.

One thing was different now, however: Odina no longer had the comforting lure of The End of All Things to see her through. Now that she knew the apocalypse of the Prophecy was never coming, she also knew that she was stuck here forever. She didn't care one bit about what happened to her – but she knew that Askook's promise to butcher her parents if she fled the village was no bluff.

'You know,' she had told Askook in one of her more defiant moments, 'if you *did* do something like that, Wowinchapuncke would sentence you to death. You'd have your skin flayed off with sharpened shells. To start.'

'I'm sure I would,' Askook replied. 'But that wouldn't put your mother and father back together again now, would it?'

So: things were terrible and they kept on being terrible. Odina went through the motions, a reanimated corpse whose inner spirit had vanished long ago. Weeks went by in a maelstrom of nothingness. Odina barely paid attention to life as it passed her by. The only consolation she had was that her constant misery was predictable. At least her ordeal was consistent.

Until, when the seasons changed, Odina was denied even that.

The *matchacomoco* was coming. It was the time of year when representatives from across the *Tsenacommacah* travelled to visit Powhatan for a meeting of discussion between all the tribal councils – adjoined to a few days of festivities, including dancing and singing. Powhatan had smartly turned this officious business into a partial celebration of family: something everyone could look forward to. The men who visited were encouraged by Powhatan to bring their loved ones along. Hence Askook's stomach-churning dictate:

'I'm going there,' he told Odina. 'And you're coming with me.'

She began to laugh. It was all she could do.

'Something funny?' Askook scowled.

'You never stop, do you? Never reach a depth you won't sink beneath.'

'I don't know what you're talking about. I'm going to the *matchacomoco*. You're my wife and you're coming too. It's tradition.'

'You know she'll be there. You know that I'll see her but I won't be able to talk to her. You know what that will do to me.'

'Oh. Yes. Of course.' Askook nodded, drawing the whole charade out with sadistic theatricality. 'Matoaka.'

'Don't you *ever* say her name in front of me–'

'It'll be tough. But you're a fighter. You'll pull through.' Askook pretended that he had just realised something else. 'Maybe you'll see your friend as well. The white man. Word is they're keeping him as their charge. Like some sort of domesticated animal. Reunions are always fun, aren't they?'

'You'll never meet the Great Hare,' Odina said, invoking an afterlife she no longer believed in. 'You will be turned away from his world. Your soul will wander lost and alone between the earth and the sky. You do know that?'

'Possibly. But until then? We're on my time.'

'But that wouldn't put your mother and father back together again now, would it?' It was a powerfully threatening question from Askook – but he didn't realise just how apt it was. When Odina stopped by to visit her mother and father on the night before the *matchacomoco*, it became clear that they were, in fact, already in the process of falling apart.

Her father's disintegration came from his mood. Over the past few weeks he had become despondent and withdrawn, a far cry from his usual gusto. For whatever reason, a social animal had been muzzled – and he wouldn't share the reason why with Odina. Whenever she asked what was wrong, he simply waved her away, on the verge of tears. *I don't need to tell you*, he seemed to be saying. *You will find out soon enough.*

He was right.

Odina had been worried about her mother's cough for a while now. She had insisted her mother go and see one of the local medicine women for treatment. Her mother had kept putting it off – but had elected to finally go when she woke up gasping, unable to breathe, phlegmy chunks of hawked-up blood on her straw bedding.

'I am dying, Odina,' her mother gently told her.

'What?' Odina couldn't process it.

'The medicine women have seen this before. It is a growth inside me: the cancer. It is growing near my heart and lungs.' She pitched into a sudden coughing fit.

Her condition wasn't getting worse day by day: it seemed to be declining minute by minute. 'Remember what happened to Nittowosew a few seasons ago?'

Yes. Odina certainly did. Nittowosew had been a woman only a few years older than her: friendly, kind, well-liked within the village. Her cancer had eaten her up from the inside. Towards the end of her life she was little more than a bony half-sentient cadaver, unable to speak or eat or eventually swallow, the tumours inside her seizing their dark territory. She had clung to life much longer than anyone had expected. Many wished she had given in earlier to save herself the pain. Odina trembled at the thought of her mother suffering the same fate.

'How...' Odina held back her tears. 'How long do you have?'

'Not long.' With a sad smile, Odina's mother took her

daughter's hands. 'I had wanted to wait until after the *matchacomoco* to tell you. But...' She began to cough violently, as though her body was providing a demonstration of her point. 'How could I go about hiding this longer?'

'I must stay,' Odina said. 'I will tell Askook I am not going to the *matchacomoco*. You need me, Father needs me–'

'I *will* need you. And your father will too... possibly even more than I do. Once I am gone you need to be his rock, Odina. He will look to you for strength. You must provide it.'

'I...'

'You *will* go to the *matchacomoco*. A few days makes no difference to me. I will still be dying then. You have tough times ahead, Odina – so I want you to make the most of the *matchacomoco* and the joy you will find there. Take respite in the wonder of the Real People before your next trial begins.'

Odina couldn't argue. Her mother thought that she was being selfless – and didn't realise that Odina loathed the idea of attending the *matchacomoco* with every cell of her being. Odina thanked her mother and hugged her. She didn't want to poison the love that glowed from her mother's gesture.

She crept around the back of her parents' domicile and cried for what seemed like hours. Before she went home she stopped by a nearby stream to splash her puffy eyes with cooling water. She didn't want Askook to see that she had been crying. The bastard seemed to thrive on her misery, after all.

And she was determined to let him starve.

The Lord was clearing house.

An outbreak of malaria had taken hold in Jamestown. It had been a prelude, an initial assault that soon let through a host of other sicknesses: dysentery, typhoid and scurvy among them.

Already weakened by starvation and fatigue, the men of Jamestown began to drop dead in their dozens. Short and Clovill and Asbie were among the earlier victims; Galthrope, Martin and Morish some of the more recent ones. Names that would be lost to history, save for some scribbled entries on a ship roster.

Barely a few days could pass without another meagre funeral ceremony being held just outside the colony gates. Some of them were a little more lavish than others – social status was still perhaps the most potent import from England – and the coffins of 'gentlemen' were often decorated and gilded.

One such coffin belonged to Bartholomew Gosnold: the man who had captained the *Godspeed* across the ocean. This proved to be a turning point for Wingfield. So far he had fought off any attempts to depose him as President – and there had been plenty – but growing hunger and resentment from the men meant that thin ice was getting thinner. While Wingfield clung to his position, something about Gosnold's death – perhaps the proof that disease cared not for family titles or good breeding – made him give in. He handed over the Presidential reins to his fellow councilman Ratcliffe: the one-time captain of the *Discovery*.

'I earnestly hope you can turn this mess around,' Wingfield had told him. He hadn't meant a word of it. Hope was futile against such damnation. Wingfield was left to wander among the others, keeping his lower rank as a councilman. There was no punishment meted for his ruinous leadership. What could be done to him? His punishment was that he was *here*.

Francis, meanwhile, held no fear of falling sick.

Even if plagued by illness he knew he would recover. He was too vital a part of God's plan for a feeble disease to kill him. As time passed Francis became more and more convinced that some divine shield had rendered him immune. Other men had dropped dead at the slightest hint of contact with the infected. Francis did not get so much as a headache.

Chaplain Hunt, when possible, tried his best to be at the victims' sides as they died. He would clutch their hands and utter soothing words and pray with them. Hunt was moved to tears when Francis asked if he could assist him in this process. Whenever Hunt left the room Francis would lean over the dying man and whisper in their ear something about how their Protestantism was going to see them disembowelled while nailed to an upside-down crucifix in Hell.

Sometimes the men heard him.

'This is a cruel malady,' Hunt observed. 'When I look at the faces of the men who have just passed... they have such an expression of abject fear. Sometimes I worry that they are taking no comfort from my words.'

'I'm sure they are, Chaplain,' Francis said, putting a supportive hand on his shoulder.

The men in Jamestown – with typically brutish lack of imagination – referred to it as 'the dying time'. Despite the overall atmosphere of defeat, they nonetheless tried to rally back together and recuperate. Ratcliffe's new leadership was a slight boost – he was, at least, more competent than Wingfield – but as time passed his own arrogant foibles became obvious. The men's bodies were failing. The malaria might have eased off – but hunger had not.

One clear night Francis saw that a huge bundle of wood had been stacked high in the town square. It had been set alight, burning, thick acrid smoke willowing up into the cold clear sky. Many of the men were sat around drinking the final dregs of their whisky rations. Smith was among them.

As Francis approached from one side he saw Wingfield approaching from the other. While no longer President, the man still liked to cling to whatever pockets of authority he could find.

'What's all this?' Wingfield asked. 'What's going on?' He watched as the fire intensified. 'These are our reserves. Fuel for the winter months.'

'If we don't find a good supply of food shortly,' Smith said, slightly drunk, uncharacteristically flippant, 'we won't *last* the winter.' He took a slug of whisky and wiped his thick moustache and beard. His swept back reddish-brown hair was beginning to tumble across his forehead. 'If we are to starve here, should we not at least get nice and toasty and enjoy ourselves?'

The surrounding men laughed. Wingfield shook his head in disgust and stormed off. Francis stayed where he was, oddly hypnotised by the rising flames.

'The stacked fire is a new tradition, of sorts,' Smith said to Francis, an explanation that had not been asked for. 'Something that started last year back in England. I thought it would be prudent to bring it over here as well. It's November 5th, see? The anniversary of the botched attempt to murder our King. You are aware of the events that took place, aren't you?'

'Somewhat,' Francis said.

Later in the night the fire fizzled out. Jubilation did too... possibly, many of the men grimly thought, for good. The next morning – and every morning after that – the daily grind returned, bringing diminishing returns each time. Little food went hand in hand with little hope. A sense of collapse pervaded.

There were noises coming from far away, distant sounds that echoed through the forest, dimly yet definitely audible through the walls of Jamestown. Francis had heard them before and he was fairly sure he would hear them again. He liked to head to the marshland whenever the noises began, staring out into the treeline and the imaginary horizon beyond. He had a very good idea what those noises were.

'They're back,' Smith said, sidling up to Francis as he stood listening to the latest bout.

'Yes.'

'Do they sound the same to you as they do to me?' Smith asked. 'It's foolish, I suppose... it shouldn't be possible... but they sound awfully like...'

'Explosions,' Francis said.

'Yes. Exactly. Which leads me to believe one of three things. Either our native friends out there have suddenly invented gunpowder... or they've taken it from somewhere. God knows where.'

'What's the third?'

'That the Spanish are coming. And they're shooting their way through the New World as they go. Which do you think is the most probable?'

'I couldn't possibly say.'

'Well,' Smith said. 'I intend to find out. It won't be the primary reason for my journey – but I will be endeavouring to do it nonetheless.'

'Your journey?' Francis raised his one remaining eyebrow.

'We are, quite frankly, dead men walking here.' Smith cast a glance back towards the main fort. 'Mouths to feed and nothing to put in them. Our only hope, I would say, is to pray we can still forge an alliance with some of the natives. Trade some of our goods for food. I'm taking a few men and we're going to travel upriver. We're going to try to meet one of the larger tribes. True, they could just massacre us on sight... but if we stay here, we're doomed anyway. I'd rather go out on my feet than scrabbling in the dirt.' He fell silent as more of the distant noises emerged from the trees. 'There's always extra room for a level-headed man such as yourself. We could use your talents. What do you say, Tresham? Will you join me on this last-ditch expedition? Are you in?'

More muffled explosions echoed from the world beyond.

'I'm in,' Francis said.

Guy knew what most of the men in the village – Powhatan included – had been thinking. The flammable powder would be perfect for weaponry. They had already figured out that the 'exploding sticks' and 'deadly pellets' utilised by the white men had some sort of powerful catalyst inside them – and now they knew what it was.

'This *gunn-powd-ah*,' Powhatan had said. 'It is common where you come from? Easy to make and procure?'

'Common enough, yes,' Guy explained. 'But no less valuable for that.'

'It fetches a good price when traded?'

'Very good.'

'So it must have been left out in the wilds of the *Tsenacommacah* accidentally. Lost rather than abandoned. No one would simply ditch something of such great worth.'

'They certainly wouldn't.'

'Then *whose* is it?' Powhatan frowned.

'It's almost definitely not from Jamestown, I can tell you that,' Guy said. 'Which means it probably belongs to the Spanish. As for how it ended up out there... I don't know.' Powhatan looked concerned. He understood that the *Spaneesh* were another faction of pale men from across the ocean – and previous encounters between them and the *Tsenacommacah* had been bloody and regretful. If both the *Spaneesh* and the *Ingleesh* were circling the *Tsenacommacah* at the same time... then things were worse than he could ever have imagined.

Guy's very first demonstration had been to blow up a troublesome patch of buttonweed that was growing in the village square: a stubborn plant that made walking difficult yet grew back more rapidly after being torn up at the roots. He had piled a small amount of the gunpowder into a furrow, ignited it using one of the nearby torches and motioned for everyone to stand back. The crowd had been astonished when the buttonweed was instantly blown apart.

The gunpowder had mainly been deployed since then for similar purposes. First up had been an effort to clear some burdensome felled trees around the village. Then detonation met expansionism: Powhatan ordered that previously uninhabitable areas surrounding the village be cleared with haste. Guy often oversaw a lot of these excursions – and soon earned the grudging respect of both normal villagers and Powhatan's inner circle alike.

Matoaka was particularly fascinated by the gunpowder. Having realised she could trust Guy – he had made good on keeping her meetings with her mother secret, after all – she took to trailing him around like a puppy dog. Powhatan found the whole thing amusing: *you're burdened with Pocahontas and her mischief now, white man.*

'I have decided something,' Matoaka told Guy, shortly after his first demonstration of gunpowder to the villagers.

'What's that?' he asked.

'I have decided that I no longer hate you.'

'Well. I'm honoured.'

'I think, in fact, that I might *like* you.'

'Even better.'

'But I need to know.' She had taken on the air of a junior diplomat again. 'How did you know about my mother and I?'

'I will tell you that another time,' Guy answered. And – every time Matoaka put forth the same question, which was many times over the following weeks – he gave her the same answer. Eventually – despite her impatient frustration – she stopped asking. She was willing to wait. Just about.

Guy enjoyed having Matoaka around – yet her presence also caused him undeniable pain. So many of her gestures and quirks reminded him of Odina. The bitter irony never failed to gnaw at Guy. Odina couldn't have been more than fifty miles away yet might as well have been in the basement of *Hurleyford House*.

Any thoughts of biding his time for an escape still rung hollow: Guy might have been appreciated in the village but he was very much still a prisoner here, a man under constant observation.

Still. He did what he could. He observed his captors well, taking note of their routines and traditions and daily rituals. It was when he started to notice mild variations – extra space being made, rehearsals for elaborate dances taking place – that he raised the question to Matoaka.

'What's going on?' he asked.

'Don't you know? It's the *matchacomoco*.' She giggled. Guy guessed this was the same as forgetting about Christmas back home. 'They're preparing the village. We'll be getting visitors from every tribe in the *Tsenacommacah*.'

'Every tribe?'

'Yes.'

'Even the Paspahegh?'

'Even the Paspahegh.'

The day of the *matchacomoco* came.

Guy watched as they arrived: the people of the Mattaponi and Arrohatoc and Chiskiack among others. Word had spread of the pale man being kept in the Powhatan village so they weren't totally shocked to see him – but they all eyed him up with suspicion as they entered the grounds. Guy took stock of them in return: surveying potential enemies with a soldier's eye.

He knew the Paspahegh were coming before he even saw their faces. Looking down the river from afar he could see the telltale decorations on their canoes, the same vessels that had ferried him here. As they banked to shore the occupants themselves became visible. With a wave of helpless fury Guy spotted the man himself: Askook, no doubt the self-appointed leader of this envoy, his poise bolstered by his rapid self-importance. He noticed that other men among the delegation were accompanied by their wives.

Guy felt his heart thud.

Did that mean... did that *mean*...?

He saw her. Sat behind Askook on the canoe. Tired. Defeated. A woman who seemed to have aged sixty-odd years in the last sixty-odd days.

Odina.

Odina did not see Guy at first. She followed Askook in obedient silence as the envoy was led from the canoes to the village square, taking their places among the other assembled tribes. Greetings were exchanged. Civility was maintained. Truces were honoured. Powhatan would stand for nothing less.

Guy was out of view but had a good vantage point for proceedings. He watched as Powhatan was introduced. A convoy of his sons and daughters took part in a ceremonial introduction. Matoaka was among them. Guy noticed Odina's lifeless glare: she was trying to hide any trace of emotion as she watched her daughter from afar, knowing this was the closest to contact she would now ever get.

Occasionally the façade broke, a heart-rending glimmer of despair breaking through. Askook sat beside her. He was keeping his reaction in check too... but anyone could tell he was revelling in the power he held.

Powhatan took to the centre of the square and began to address the spectators. He spoke of his gratitude for their loyalty and his pride in overseeing the years – long peace of the *Tsenacommacah.* He spoke of the Prophecy and how the gods had still seen fit not to unleash The End of All That Is – and how important it was to keep the gods unoffended. He eventually moved on to the burning topic of the moment: the arrival of a new set of invaders into the *Tsenacommacah,* the most substantial such appearance for over a generation.

'Many of you will know that I have been keeping one of the invaders under my supervision.' Powhatan waved for Guy to step forward. Instructed to remain silent, Guy stood motionless as the various tribes analysed him, feeling more than ever like an exotic animal dragged out of hibernation for paying visitors. Odina finally saw him. His eyes met hers. As before, she just about managed to stay impassive – save for one solitary tear that rolled down her cheek.

Askook reached out. Wiped the tear away with his thumb. He looked to Guy. Smiled.

I could take the fucker, Guy thought. *Right here, right now*.

It was entirely possible. With surprise on his side he could launch himself forwards, grabbing a spear or blade as he went, thrusting it into Askook's neck and leaving the man dead before anyone could drag him away.

But what *then*?

That would be a death sentence for Guy. And – if the reasons behind it ever emerged – possibly one for Odina too.

No. He had to wait.

Powhatan gestured for Guy to go and stand to one side again. He did as he was told.

'This white man has told me much about these invaders and their aims,' Powhatan continued. 'He seems to have no allegiance to them and is therefore free to speak honestly. Many of you may be sceptical... but having observed Ch-awn's conduct, I believe him. From what he says, the foreigners are somewhat torn between their approach to us. Many of them are eager to be diplomatic.' There were no groans of disbelief from the audience – such disrespect to Powhatan would be unthinkable – but their quiet cynicism was visible to all. 'Many of them seek the opposite. Conquest. Territory. They wish to–'

'Chief Powhatan!'

Powhatan glanced up. For anyone to dare interrupt, it needed to be exceptionally important – and it was.

Many had already wondered about the empty spaces within the ceremonial area. These were reserved for people from the Pamunkey. They had yet to arrive... and, as their men finally approached the square, it was clear why. They were fresh from battle: clothes dirtied and bloodied. Behind them were two captives, hunched as they walked, hands bound behind them, heads completely covered with sacks.

One thing was clear.

The captured men were no natives. They were white. Invaders. The lead Pamunkey tribesman spoke up.

'Forgive me, elder brother,' he said, 'for our absence so far.'

'No need to be sorry, Opechancanough,' Powhatan said, eyeing the curious tableau. 'It looks like you have been preoccupied.'

'We were attacked, brother,' Opechancanough explained. 'The white men came to our village. There were ten of them. It was clearly a planned assault. We battled. All but two of them were killed.' He motioned towards the hooded prisoners his men had in tow. 'These two.'

'*Okeus*,' Askook muttered – and soon found himself surrounded by assenting murmurs. Chief Powhatan had been talking about the invaders – then two of them were delivered to his town, trussed and bound like this? What else *could* it be but the work of Okeus? Emboldened, Askook stood up and addressed Powhatan.

'With respect, Chief Powhatan,' he said. 'How much do you trust your pet white man now? Should you perhaps not have slaughtered the sacrificial turkey I gave you?'

'Funny.' Powhatan glared. 'I do not detect much respect in your tone *at all*, Paspahegh man. I will assume you are not quite feeling yourself. I will forgive you now and spare you the need to beg for it.' Silenced, Askook sat down again.

Powhatan turned back to Opechancanough. 'Who are the two men you captured?'

'One of them seems to be their leader,' Opechancanough replied. 'A strong man, a dangerous fighter. As for the other...' He trailed off.

'Yes?'

'I've never seen anything like him, elder brother. He resembles more monster than man.'

Concerned chatter began to rise from the crowd. Powhatan raised his hand. He wanted silence. He got it.

'I will speak to the leader in private,' he said. 'As for the other one... take him to the pit. Detain him there.'

'Chief Powhatan.' Askook shot to his feet again. Odina winced. Would this cretin ever learn *anything*? 'With respect...'

'There are those words again.'

'With *respect*,' Askook emphasised, showing that he meant it this time, 'I think it might also be prudent to imprison the other white man as well.' He gestured over to Guy. 'At least temporarily. I am aware that you trust him, but... is it not possible he could have exploited your good nature? That he could be planning some sort of attack of his own?' Powhatan frowned. As much as he hated to admit it, this arrogant Paspahegh upstart was right. 'I will be happy to oversee the detention of the prisoners. A task I will carry out to make up for my earlier disrespect.'

'Very well.' Powhatan nodded.

The Pamunkey men prodded the second prisoner along as the hooded white leader was taken directly to Powhatan's temple. Askook approached Guy, blade drawn.

'Do I have to bind your hands too, invader?' he asked. 'Or will you proceed without protest?'

'I'll proceed,' Guy said.

'Good.'

'Are you enjoying yourself?'

'What?'

'This display,' Guy said. 'This preening. This pompous arrogance. Like the strut of a peacock. It's not enough for a "man" like you to win, is it? You have to show it off like a petulant child.'

'If you must know, *Ingleesh*,' Askook said, 'yes. I am enjoying myself.' He leaned in closer. 'But not as much as I'm enjoying my time with Odina. She still has a little... impetuousness to her, now and again. But I think that's something I can iron out without too much trouble.' He forced Guy around and made him march forwards.

Guy and the other captive were taken to the pit itself: a circular hole of around ten feet in depth and twenty in diameter, lined with irregular wooden struts to keep the structure in place, clearly designed to keep captives or war prisoners in. Guy was shoved over the side. As he groggily staggered to his feet he saw

Askook and a couple of Paspahegh lackeys lowering themselves into the pit as well.

The Paspahegh men took Guy's hands and tied them, looping the binding around one of the upright wooden slats. They then repeated the process with the other man: throwing the hooded prisoner into the pit and then tying him to a slat on the opposite side.

When Guy looked up he saw that Odina was standing by the edge of the pit. She was a forced witness, a helpless spectator to Askook's pedantry. Askook motioned for the other Paspahegh men to leave. They did, cautiously climbing out of the pit and heading back to the *matchacomoco.*

Guy met Odina's gaze. She looked down to him with defeated sorrow. Guy desperately wanted to speak to her: to mouth something, *anything*; soundless words that might possibly reignite the spark she had lost.

He couldn't think of anything. His own spark – the one he didn't even realise he had until he met her – was gone too.

'Right then.' Askook clutched at the sack that was draped over the other captive's head. '*More monster than man,* is it?' He whipped off the sack. 'I'll be the judge of–'

And suddenly: yes. He *was* the judge. A shocked and silent one.

The *Ingleesh* man was disfigured beyond anything Askook had ever seen. In an act of almost primal revulsion Askook leapt back and scrambled up out of the pit. The man glanced around, a tendril of drool swaying from the ruined side of his mouth, his one remaining eye struggling to focus on the influx of light.

Guy was just as horrified as Askook – but this was purely the horror of recognition.

The disfigured man looked over to Guy.

'Fawkes,' said Francis Tresham. 'Fancy meeting you here.'

'Friendly bunch, aren't they?' Francis glanced up to Askook and Odina, both of whom remained speechless at his unveiling. 'I won't lie. I'd have preferred a welcoming party of food and wine but... when in Rome.' He took a better look at Askook and Odina. 'Do you reckon the poor bastards even know what Rome is? Think they have the slightest idea of what *true* civilisation looks like?'

'You're...' Guy struggled. 'You're...'

'Well, I'm not *dead*, if that's the achingly predictable way you were going to finish that sentence.' When he grinned – or did the closest thing he could – Guy saw that this was not just Francis Tresham. This was the creature he had suspected lurked inside Tresham for a long time: now summoned and set free, a Djinn powered by venom alone. 'Although that's not for your lack of trying, is it? You know, for a military man – a trained killer – one would think you'd do a better job of finishing people off.'

Guy took it all in. A timeline flashed up: improbable but the only logical route here.

The musket shot. *His* musket shot. It had been non-fatal. Non-fatal but nonetheless destructive for it.

And it had opened up a portal for *this thing* to slide through.

'You should have let me go,' Guy said. 'From the *Guadiana*.'

'Is that right?'

'I didn't want things to end that way.'

'Oh. I see. You were *pressured* into trying to kill me.' Francis laughed. There was no humour in it. 'Well. Who can blame you? I mean, how *dare* I burden you with an escape from public execution and a new life overseas–'

'It was not a life I wante–'

'It doesn't *FUCKING MATTER WHAT YOU*

WANTED!' Francis screamed. His sneering faux-detachment was gone. Now his words were as warped as his physique. He twisted and strained at the wooden post in a fit of frenzy. 'I *own* your life, Fawkes. You understand that? I could easily have let you go to that gallows. I could have watched from the palace as your grubby little heart was held aloft. I wish I *had*, more than anything. But I *didn't*. I saved you because I thought you were different to the others.' His laugh was genuine now: real disbelief at how stupid he had once been. 'I thought you were a man of God. A *true* disciple. So I put everything on the line for a so-called Brother in Christ and then *THIS'* – he arched back his neck, bringing his desiccated half-face up to the light for Guy to see in full – *'IS HOW YOU REPAY ME!'* He settled again, breathing heavily. 'No. I see now what I always should have. You are no man of God, are you, Guido Fawkes?'

Francis's rasping breaths steamed into the cold air.

'No,' Guy said.

'You never were. Were you?'

'I believed that I was. But no. I wasn't.'

'*Now* you discover honesty. Maybe you should ditch it again. It doesn't fit you well.'

'You came out here to find me?' Guy asked.

'Naturally.'

'How did you learn I was here?'

'With ingenuity.'

'How did you get here?'

'With difficulty.'

'And what was your intention, Tresham? What did you plan to do when you finally caught up with me?'

Francis sighed: the weariness of a man who wanted to rest yet still had much to do.

'It's funny, really,' he said. 'I've been playing out this scenario in my head for almost a year now. I had never quite imagined these sort of circumstances of course...' He briefly glanced up to Askook and Odina, both of whom were still enthralled at the unfolding theatre below. 'And I really hadn't imagined myself talking as much.'

'What had you imagined doing?' Guy asked.

'Oh. You know.' Francis began a shrug – which then instantly turned into a larger motion. His constant shuffling against the wooden post had not just been a spasm of rage. His wrists whipped free and frayed ends of rope flapped in the air between them, cut apart by a jagged wedge that poked out behind him.

Francis lunged across the pit.

He clamped his hands around Guy's throat.

'This,' he said.

He shouldn't have been surprised by the attack – but he *was*, and now he was paying for it.

The force of Francis's assault also wrenched Guy's hands free from their bounds, the wooden post which he was tied to breaking on impact. Guy tried to tear Francis's hands away but they were seized tight, fuelled by pure hatred. Instinctively he raised a hand to claw at Francis's face. Instinct made him choose the wrong side. He tried to scratch at flesh that was already scarred and nerveless. He tried to wedge a thumb into an empty eye socket. By the time Guy realised his mistake his vision was turning red. Sounds were getting distant. He could hear Odina pleading with Askook – 'Stop them, please, *stop them*' – and the hollow reverberation of Francis's laughter growing louder and louder, closer and closer–

Guy could breathe again.

Francis had been flung aside. Now Guy understood: the

laughter had not belonged to his attacker. It came from Askook, now back down in the pit with them both, delighted at the show that was being put on for him. *When in Rome*, Francis had said. He was right. Askook looked like an Emperor revelling at a bloody Colosseum spar, a tinpot Commodus astride his kingdom.

'You weren't lying after all, were you, Ch-awn?' Askook held out his spear, motioning for Francis and Guy to back away. The two men edged apart, neither taking their glare from the other. 'There really is a big rift between your people. I wonder why? Are *you* the one who turned this man into a freak, Ch-awn? Because that would explain–' He arched around as Francis tried to scrabble back towards Guy. He held out his spear. 'Ah, ah, ah. Where do you think you're going, half-man? *Back*.'

'You can't let them fight,' Odina said.

'What?' Askook snapped.

'Powhatan will be angry if one of them gets hurt. Or killed.'

'Will he now?' Askook reached into his mantle and pulled out a couple of items. He dropped them onto the soil, one of them landing right next to each poised Englishman. A blade and a blade. One for Guy, one for Francis. 'It's possible that they could have had their own weapons, isn't it? Possible that one could have gutted the other before I had the chance to intervene. And if that possibility *happened*... who here would tell Powhatan?'

'I would.' Odina folded her arms. Her defiance was weak. But it was still defiance. And that angered Askook.

'You–' He was about to climb out of the pit and deal with her. He stopped. His gloating amusement returned. 'You know what? Go ahead. Why would he believe a word you said anyway? Some dumb barren bitch who imagines dark spirits telling her to die?' Now he did climb out of the pit – but with slow assurance rather than lost temper. He stood beside Odina, looking back down at the two men. '*You can't let them fight.*' He put on a whiny and insulting impersonation of her voice. 'I assure you, wife – I can. In fact, it looks like the only entertainment I'm going to get from this lousy *matchacomoco*.'

Askook dropped a hand: a universal gesture to proceed. The ultimatum did not need to be spoken.

Two men. Two weapons. One fight. One survivor. Francis grabbed his blade.

Guy grabbed his.

'We don't have to do this,' Guy said.

'Course we do.' Francis tightened his grip on his blade and began to stalk sideways, treading a half-circle around Guy. 'Don't play the pacifist, Fawkes. It's another lie that doesn't quite work.'

'This won't end well for you.'

'You sound very sure.' Francis took a swipe forward with the blade. Guy stretched back, out of its range, now mirroring Francis's circular sidesteps. The two men shimmied around the perimeter of the pit, adjacent predators waiting to strike.

'I've seen combat,' Guy said.

'So have I.'

'Not like I have. Do you really think you can win this?'

'I *was* doing. Before our erstwhile ringleader jumped in.' Francis took another swipe. Guy dodged it again. 'Or had you forgotten?'

'You got lucky.'

'Oh. Right. That must be it.'

'We can put these knives down. We can–'

'What? Talk it over? Let bygones be bygones? Turn a blind eye?' Francis leapt forward. He struck out with a flurry of moves, dashing the blade back and forth: untrained and undisciplined but no less dangerous for it. One frantic swipe cut a red gash across Guy's arm. Francis looked on with delight. He caught his breath before beginning to stalk around the pit again. 'There's no world in which this wasn't going to happen, Fawkes.'

'You're going to die, Tresham. Unless you stand down *now*.'

'Go on. Talk. Talk, talk, *talk*. Hollow words, hollow man.'

'I'm warning you–'

Francis dived for Guy again. This time Guy was ready.

Guy grabbed Francis's arm and twisted it around his back, fully intending to break it. Francis dropped the blade – but had enough composure left to swoop his right foot back under Guy's. The two fell to the ground. Guy straddled Francis's chest and rained down a succession of punches upon him, blow after blow, until–

A sharp pain. An upwards surge of agony.

Francis had reached out with desperate grasping fingers and seized the blade again. He had taken an upward swipe along Guy's torso. Guy fell back. Francis kicked him away. The two men scrabbled apart.

Guy put a hand to the wound. The cut was not too deep: bloody but superficial. He let the blood seep into his clothes: an arcing crimson line.

'Should have stabbed me,' Guy said.

'There's still time.'

They both got back to their feet.

'You ever think, Fawkes,' Francis said, sidestepping in a cautious half-circle again, 'that you're maybe not the man you used to be? You spent time on the rack. That changes people. Joints get weak. Muscles don't work the way they once did. Oh, and I really doubt the food out here is up to much. Face it. You're wasting away.'

'Last warning, Tresham.' Guy stood poised to attack.

'Get on with it.'

So Guy did.

He managed to get in a decent swipe of his own: almost mirroring the injury Francis had inflicted on him, a slash upwards from pelvis to ribcage. Francis howled as Guy took advantage of the distraction – and slammed a fist upwards, connecting with Francis's chin, sending the man's head snapping back. Francis staggered away, falling, eventually slamming head-on into the jagged wooden edge he had used to cut his bonds. A recently healed gash across his temple – admittedly hard to notice amid the rest of the carnage – opened up again.

Bloodied and battered, Francis hauled himself to his feet. He started to laugh.

'Must sting you a little, mustn't it, Fawkes?' Francis spat out a wad of bloody sputum. 'Such a brave noble soldier like you, brought down to the level of a street brawler.' He lunged at Guy, blade aloft. He missed. 'So you've really got to ask yourself.' Another lunge. Another miss. 'What do you have left that separates you from the likes of me? *What do you have that I don't?*'

Francis took another unwieldy swipe. He missed again – but looked shocked when Guy's arm whipped forward and seized his own.

'Depth perception,' Guy said. This time Guy broke the arm.

Francis screamed. He blindly whipped out with his blade.

Francis's eyes widened. Chance, it was: pure chance. His slashing move had arced right over his previous one: opening up Guy's torso gash further. Guy staggered back, lost in pained disbelief. He briefly glanced down. Blood was flowing, thick, fast. Not enough to kill him... or even stop him fighting...

But enough for Francis to act.

Francis charged at Guy, diving on top of him, ignoring the

pain of his broken arm as he clamped his fingers around one side of Guy's head, half-pushing Guy's face into the slick red dirt.

Guy struggled to move.

Francis put the blade against his throat. Guy stopped.

'You want to know the irony of it all, Fawkes?' Francis whispered. 'You were right. That day in Barnet – your instincts were correct. I didn't write that letter. I had no intention of letting that prick Monteagle know anything. Truth is, we'll probably never know who *did* write it. But when the other plotters accused me of doing it? When they were ready to *kill me* for it? I had no other choice. I needed to mete out some justice in return. So I spurred things along. I made sure the letter was read. Catesby, Wintour, Percy, the lot of them – I made sure they paid for their disrespect. Maybe one day Parliament *will* burn. But I want it to be destroyed by true Men of God. Not pretenders.'

His grip on the blade wobbled for a moment. An emotive tremor.

'The worst thing though? It all revolved around you. I thought I was saving a friend.'

'You thought wrong,' Guy managed to wheeze.

'Do you accept Christ as your Lord and Saviour?' Francis pushed the edge of the blade against Guy's skin. The first droplets of blood began to pool around the serrated edge. '*Do you?* I'm giving you the chance not to burn in Hell, Fawkes. More than you deserve – but what kind of Soldier of God would I be if I didn't?' Keeping the knife where it was, he leant in closer. For a second Guy wondered if he could bite the man's nose off – leave him howling, with blood pissing out of his even more ravaged 'face' – but he could not even move that far.

He had messed up. It was over.

He had tried to vanish like a beast but now he was going to die like one.

'See, *that's* the main difference between me and you, Fawkes.' Spittle flecked from Francis's ruined lips. 'You were content just to shoot me and scuttle away. Me? I want this moment to *mean something*.' He began to press on the knife again. 'Now. *Do you accept Christ as your Lord and Saviour?* You just have to blink, Fawkes. Blink to say yes. Blink and you may be forgiven for everything you've done. Just *blink*.'

Guy didn't blink.

He was going to die with his eyes wide open.

'Blink,' Francis urged. '*Blink*.'

Guy kept on staring. Wide hateful eyes. Orbs of defiance.

'Blink,' Francis said.

'Just *do it*!' Askook yelled. Francis looked up.

'What are you waiting for?' Askook sneered. 'Do it, man! Don't just crouch there babbling! Kill him. *Kill him!*'

Francis exhaled.

He released the pressure on the knife.

'*You*,' Francis said, revealing to a stunned Askook that he could speak fluent Algonquian too, 'presume to order *me*?'

'You... you...' Askook could not quite process what was happening.

'I take orders from God. And God alone. Not some worthless savage like you. You stand there, a creature as base as any worm, and you *dare* to imagine you can dictate instructions to me?' He held up the knife and pointed it at Askook. 'I suggest you shut your mouth, boy. Before I slice you a new one.'

Guy took in a desperate retching gasp. This was his chance. He was about to fight every weary impulse in his body and fling himself at Francis when – Askook leapt down into the pit. He jabbed his spear at Francis's hand. Francis howled in pain, dropping the blade. Francis howled even louder when Askook seized hold of his broken arm, twisting it around his back as he threw Francis across the pit. Francis slowly rolled onto his back, groaning, spitting out dirt and clutching his arm.

'You could have lived,' Askook told him. 'You know that? Maybe Powhatan would have executed you in the end... but you would at least have survived *this*. I swear... the stupidity of you white men is boundless. Now you're going to die as well. Now Powhatan will hear how the two *Ingleesh* fools took blades to each other and neither pulled through. A futile act by futile men.'

Askook saw Guy struggling to get back up. He sent Guy's head to the ground with a brutal kick. Dazed, Guy could only watch as he saw the blurry outline of Askook picking up Francis's discarded blade.

'Please, Askook,' Odina screamed from nearby. '*No! Don't–*'

'Shut up, cunt,' Askook hissed. He brought the blade to Guy's neck. 'Always the way, isn't it? You want a job done properly, you have to do it yourself.'

'Askook. I beg you. *Please,* let him live–'

'*Do you want to be next?*' Askook yelled, turning to glare at Odina. 'If you don't shut up, you'll be joining these two in the ground.' He smiled at Guy. He seemed almost grateful for the interruption. 'Come to think of it – I'm not going to slice your throat. I'm taking your heart, white man. And I'm going to feed it to the hunting dogs.'

'*No...*' Odina softly cried, lacking the energy to scream.

Askook raised the knife in the air, eyes filled with triumphant malice, ready to bring it down between Guy's ribs. Guy was filled with the same resistant rage as with Francis. He was not going to look away. He was not going to flinch. He would look at Askook with pure hatred right until the very end.

Askook brought his arm down. He only made it halfway.

He gurgled. Blood pooled from the corners of his mouth.

Like a chick poking its beak through an eggshell, the sharp glint of an arrowhead slowly sluiced open the middle of his throat.

He reached around the back of his neck. Tried to pull the arrow out.

Another one thudded into place. It pinned his hand to his neck, gliding through the bone and flesh and tendons, coming out just below his jaw.

A final one thudded into his heart.

He turned and stared with livid surprise at his assailant. He fell backwards. Just before he died – a scratchy whisper straining to escape his shattered throat – he spoke his killer's name. He left this world wholly unable to believe who had taken him out of it.

'Po... ca... hon... tas...?'

Matoaka lowered the bow.

Askook had been amazed. And she was too. Her actions had been instinctive... but as that instinct faded and reality set in, tears welled in her eyes.

She dropped the bow, hands trembling with shaky panic. She was not a warrior or a deity-sent avenger. She was a scared little girl.

And she wanted her mother.

Matoaka ran to Odina and flung her arms around the woman. Odina hugged the girl so tightly it was as though Matoaka vanished.

Still wheezing – now spattered with the blood of two other men as well as his own – Guy stumbled to his feet. He ignored the pain racking his body – he'd felt it before, he'd no doubt feel it again – and hauled himself out of the pit. He staggered over to

Odina and Matoaka. It was his turn to throw his arms around them.

'Are you hurt? Injured?' He frantically looked them over. They seemed fine – physically, at least.

'I killed him.' Matoaka was sobbing, her face buried in her mother's mantle. Odina ran a soothing hand through the girl's long flaxen hair. Odina looked down to Askook's body: a spiritless husk gazing dead-eyed up at the clouds. Her face communicated nothing. She was not going to waste any emotion on him.

'You had to do it,' Guy said. 'You saved me.'

'But he's *dead*!' Matoaka wept. 'Now Ahone will strike me down–'

'No.' Odina took the girl's face in her hands. 'No god nor anyone on earth will punish you for this.'

'But...'

'You told me a story once. Remember when that wild dog attacked the village? That rabid creature? And your father took his spear to it?'

'Yes.' Matoaka sniffled.

'That is all you did,' Odina told her. 'That and nothing more. You put a crazed animal out of its misery.'

Crazed animal. The words made Guy snap out of his reverie. Tresham.

Tresham was still here and he–

He had vanished. Francis Tresham was nowhere to be seen. Guy frantically looked around for signs of his departure – fluttering leaves, echoing footfall – but could see nothing. When Matoaka spoke up next Guy realised: that didn't matter. At least not for now. There were more important things to deal with.

'Father... and the villagers...' Matoaka was caught in a wave of panic. 'What about when *they* find out? What will they–'

'They won't find out,' Guy said. Both Odina and Matoaka

looked to him, puzzled. 'We're alone here. Everyone is busy with the *matchacomoco*. No one knows what just happened. And if we do this right, no one will.' He crouched down, hands on Matoaka's shoulders. 'Your father. He is dealing with the other man from Jamestown. The leader. I know this man. His name is Smith. He is decent and good. What does your father intend to do with him?'

'I don't know...' Matoaka faltered.

'Powhatan will more than likely kill your friend,' Odina said. 'Even if the attack has been exaggerated... even if he was not among the aggressors and strived to resolve things peacefully... that will make little difference. Powhatan has a reputation to maintain, especially when it comes to these invaders. His decision to keep you in the village set tongues wagging. He cannot afford any more shows of weakness.'

'Your father will listen to you, won't he?' Guy asked Matoaka. 'You're his favourite, after all. His little *Pocahontas*.'

'Yes...' Matoaka sounded unsure.

'I need you to tell Powhatan: *Smith cannot die.* Do you understand, Matoaka? He cannot kill that man. You need to run to your father's temple – run *now* – and stop him. Throw yourself over Smith if you have to. Say what you must. Tell him...' Guy plucked a justification out of thin air. 'Tell him you sense goodness in the man. Say you want to keep him around the same way Powhatan kept me. Anything. You do that... and your mother and I will make sure that Askook disappears. We'll bury the body, hide it well. No one will ever find him. Can you do this for me, Matoaka? Can you win your father round?'

Matoaka thought the question over. She sighed. Her brow corrugated: the leaden weight of duty.

'Yes,' she said.

Odina remembered the layout of the village well from her time as Powhatan's temporary bride. There was an area of particularly dense forest just on the outskirts of the village. It was the most realistic option for getting rid of a body. Odina ran back into the village and stole a couple of digging implements. She and Guy then dragged Askook's corpse to the makeshift burial site. They frantically dug through the soil until they were straining and drenched in sweat. There was no time for ceremonial quirks or last-minute eulogies – not that Askook deserved either of these. They rolled his body into the grave and immediately began shovelling the dirt on top of it.

Neither of them exchanged a word as they worked. It was only when they had finished that they slumped against the trunk of a nearby cedar tree.

'You're sure they won't find him?' Guy asked.

'I'm sure,' Odina said. 'No one heads into the forest this way. They have no need to. The woods soon turn into dead marshland. There's nothing to hunt, nothing to scavenge.'

They lapsed into silence again.

Guy placed his hand on hers. This was the first moment of real connection they had had since Askook discovered their campsite: months ago in real time, countless lifetimes ago in spirit.

'Come with me,' Guy said.

'Where?' Odina gave a tired smile.

'I don't know. Does that matter? It didn't before. We had no destination in mind. We still don't need one. I just know that I want to be with you.' Guy felt a sudden pang. Uncertainty crept in. 'You still feel the same way, don't you?'

'Yes,' Odina said. She closed her eyes. 'But...'

But.

Guy rested his head against the tree.

'Askook is gone,' she explained. 'But I cannot leave the Paspahegh.'

'You did it before. You can do it again.'

'My mother is sick. I don't know how long she has. I need to stay and look after her. Then... my father. He won't be able to cope once she is gone. He will be destroyed. He'll need someone to look after him too.' Her tired smile remained. There was a tiny glimmer of triumph in there, despite everything. Was she still bound to life with the Paspahegh? Yes. But the binding came from choice rather than force.

'In that case, let me stay with you,' Guy said. 'Let me live with the Paspahegh. Become one of you.'

'The Paspahegh would never allow that. And even if they did, you could never *become* one of us. That is why all this conflict began in the first place. That is why I suspect it will never end.'

'Yes.' Guy knew it was true. There was no point in arguing. He thought for a moment. 'I am sorry to hear of your mother.'

'She is a brave woman. She will face her end with strength. But my father may live for many seasons yet. He will need me.'

'And... what if I *wait* for many seasons?' Guy asked.

'What do you mean?'

'You will do a fine job of looking after your father,' Guy said. 'But he will not be around forever. So – I will stay in Jamestown for however long it takes. I will live there and wait until you are ready – no matter how many seasons I have to endure. When you are free of your obligation to the Paspahegh... come to find me. Then we will leave on our travels together. We will go wherever we want.'

'You will hate it in Jamestown.'

'I will cope. As long as you are waiting.'

'I...' Odina blinked. The enormity and scale of what Guy was suggesting was just beginning to sink in – as was the possibility of it. 'Do you mean this? You would do this for me? Truly?'

'Truly.'

'We could be old ourselves by the time I am free.'

'Then we will be old together.'

And that settled it.

They kissed. They basked in their determination.

'You would do the same for your family,' Odina said. 'Wouldn't you?'

'Yes.'

'I know you would. Because you are a good man.'

'Am I?'

'You are.' She planted another gentle kiss on his lips. She looked back towards the village. 'Whatever happens with your friend, Smith, Powhatan will want to address the *matchacomoco* again. We need to rejoin them.'

'Right.' Guy nodded, struggling to focus on pragmatic issues rather than his shattered heart. He looked down. His clothes were torn and bloody. 'They'll notice me looking like this. They'll have questions.'

'The other man. *Fran-ceese*, was it? We can tell everyone he attacked you. He made a break for it, ran off into the woods. Askook chased him. Neither of them came back. That will explain things.'

'Yes.' Guy nodded. It was a good plan. 'Two birds, one stone.'

'What?'

'Nothing. Never mind. It's smart. It makes sense.'

'It does...' Odina was now thinking it over. 'Unless *Fran-ceese* comes back. He could tell everyone what actually happened.'

'No.' Guy gave a firm shake of his head. 'He'll steer clear of the Powhatan village. The Paspahegh too. Any tribes. It's me he wants.'

'And if he comes for you? Will you be ready?'

Guy didn't answer.

He got to his feet. Helped Odina up.

'Let's go,' he said.

When Smith had been captured by the Pamunkey – after days of travelling upriver – he had tried to curry favour with his captors by impressing them: a demonstration of the civilisation from which he came. It was one hell of a gamble. When he and his followers had stumbled across their village they had tried to approach peacefully – but the Pamunkey had attacked immediately. Only Smith and Tresham survived. Smith had fired off his pistol several times over, making sure to avenge the deaths of his own men with deaths of the enemy. All of which made conversation following his capture a little... stilted.

He showed the Pamunkey his compass. At best, he figured, they could take him as some sort of deity endowed with magical gifts. At worst, they could see him as a resource for other such useful items. While they were intrigued by the wobbling needle and Smith's explanation, neither turned out to be true. They saw Smith as leverage: something to pass on to a much higher authority.

That had led him here: kneeling inside a temple, bowing before the High Chief they called Powhatan. Closest to Powhatan was the one they called Opechancanough, a man who Smith understood to be Powhatan's brother. They were all surrounded by sitting observers, a selection of powerful leaders from varying tribes.

Smith was fed: a platter of food, some of it identifiable to him, some not. That didn't matter. He wolfed it down, only slowing when hit by a twang of self-consciousness. If he was hoping to bargain with Powhatan, he didn't want to appear overly desperate. He cursed himself. He might have ruined everything already: showed his empty hands before negotiations even began.

Powhatan asked Smith a simple question.

Where do you come from?

Smith gave his reply. He told Powhatan of his own Great Chief: a King named James. He told of the endless vessels and thundering cannons of the navy and – with a little embellishment of course – told Powhatan that he was in charge of the whole fleet. He gave vivid depictions of the sheer military might of his homeland – yet also the people who lived there, the ordinary souls just trying to get on with their ordinary lives.

Powhatan was fascinated. He clearly yearned to hear more. Smith – happy to have the chief in the palm of his hand – was more than happy to continue.

Then Opechancanough leaned in.

Opechancanough whispered something to Powhatan. From both of their expressions, Smith knew what they were talking about.

This man does not seem like an enemy, Powhatan's face said. *I wish to learn more from him.*

You cannot be seen as weak, Opechancanough's face said. *I know that you do not want to... but you know what has to be done.* Opechancanough nodded to the other onlookers. Smith took in their expressions too: anticipatory ire. They had not come here to see some pseudo-diplomatic exchange. They had come here to see an invader punished for his transgressions.

I know, Powhatan's face sadly expressed. He gave Smith an almost apologetic look. Kings did not obey their subjects – but they always needed their subjects' respect. It was a thin line. Smith had unfortunately crossed it.

A couple of bulky guards grabbed Smith by the arms and forced him to the ground. He looked on in terror as some other guards entered the temple – carrying with them two huge stone boulders.

One boulder was placed on the ground. Smith's head was rested upon it. The other was held aloft by a guard.

Ready to come crashing down. Ready to dash Smith's brains out.

Smith closed his eyes. He wondered what the end would feel like. Would it be immediate? Would he still be conscious as his life ebbed away: dying in a dark red haze, like sunlight shining through tightly shut eyelids?

He heard another voice. A little girl.

'*Stop!*' she yelled.

Smith opened his eyes. The girl was pleading with Powhatan – pleading, he suddenly realised, with a mixture of relief and amazement, for his own life. Her pleas flowed from her with conviction; impassioned words that affected Powhatan deeply. Smith suddenly realised something else from their dynamic: they were father and daughter. No one else would be able to speak to a chief like this.

Powhatan nodded to the guards.

The guard with the rock backed away. He gently lowered it to the ground.

The little girl wanted Smith alive. And the wishes of Powhatan's daughter took precedence over the social machinations of other tribe leaders. They didn't like Smith surviving? Tough luck. Powhatan's own flesh and blood had spoken – and the verdict was on Smith's side.

Opechancanough immediately began to argue. Powhatan gave him another look that Smith found instantly readable: *do not do this in front of the others, brother. Let us take this elsewhere.*

Opechancanough and Powhatan left the temple.

Guy and Odina were heading back to the *matchacomoco* when Odina spotted something. She held out an arm in front of Guy.

'Wait. Look.'

It was Powhatan. He was outside the temple, deep in heated argument with Opechancanough. Odina and Guy slinked back, out of sight.

'You needed a *show of force*,' Opechancanough ranted. 'And this is how you choose to act? To show some feeble notion of mercy because... because *what?* Your daughter begged you to? Is this how things are going to work from hereon in, brother? Are you to base all decisions affecting the *Tsenacommacah* on the whim of hysterical young girls?'

Powhatan jabbed a rigid finger in Opechancanough's chest.

'You are my brother,' he said, just about keeping his tone level, 'but you are also my subject. I suggest you watch your tongue.'

'No.' Opechancanough batted Powhatan's hand away. He had no time for hierarchy anymore. His rage had shredded any sense of caution. 'You are old. You are weak. You will be dead long before I am. And when you're gone... when I step up to your throne and take your place... I tell you this: it will be the *end* of pathetic decisions like this putting the *Tsenacommacah* at risk. There will be no half-measures. I will make sure every single invader is culled. The river will flow red with their blood. Their skins will be nailed to trees along the coast as a warning sign. I will treat 'peace' like the children's story it is and ensure that we *are strong and proud*.'

Powhatan looked like he was about to explode with anger. After a few seconds, however, he settled. He now seemed vaguely saddened.

'You will likely get many of us killed,' Powhatan said. 'Maybe the whole *Tsenacommacah.* We know very little of where the white men come from – but I suspect there are many more. An endless number. Like insects swarming, like grains of sand spilling through your fingers. They will come and keep coming. They would seek revenge for such slaughter. Maybe they would wipe out the Real People altogether.'

'Then at least,' Opechancanough snarled, 'we will go out fighting.'

'I have seen more battles than you have seen sunrises, little brother,' Powhatan said, his tone still sad and weary. 'Let me tell you something. Fighting can end more things than it starts.'

'Hypocrite,' Opechancanough seethed. 'You conquered the entire *Tsenacommacah* by fighting. You made a kingdom from it. And you have kept it in order ever since.'

'Yes.' Powhatan nodded. 'But I am Powhatan. And you are not.' Opechancanough turned away in disgust.

'Enjoy your reign while it lasts, brother,' he said as he walked away. 'Because I'm what comes *after* the Prophecy.'

Guy was captivated by the argument yet also relieved – it seemed that Smith had been spared after all. He and Odina then tried to sneak around Powhatan once Opechancanough had gone. Despite his own distraction – his jaw clenched, lost in bitter contemplation – Powhatan noticed them. A lifetime of vigilance could not be suppressed so easily.

'Ch-awn. Odina.' He frowned. 'Where is the other white man? Where is the Paspahegh man?'

Odina explained everything to him, using the cover story she and Guy had fabricated. Guy listened, impressed at Odina's storytelling prowess: the shock she felt when the white prisoner made his violent escape and attacked Ch-awn en route, the pride she felt when her Paspahegh husband immediately took up chase into the forest.

'A brave move by this... Askook,' Powhatan reflected. 'Perhaps I underestimated him.'

'Perhaps,' Odina managed to say through gritted teeth.

Powhatan called out a few names, his voice echoing to the other side of the village. Like well-trained servants three men soon appeared. Powhatan ordered them to go and find the prisoner and Askook.

'Track them until sunrise tomorrow,' he told them before they went. 'If you do not find them, return to me. We will discuss the next steps from there.' When he was alone again with Guy and Odina, Powhatan turned to them. 'Keep this to yourselves. I have enough to contend with right now without explaining this to the *matchacomoco*.' He looked into the distance; in the direction of the gathering in question. 'Come on. Odina – join me, sit back with your people. Ch-awn, stay out of sight.' He let out a frustrated sigh. 'And if anyone else interrupts this celebration of togetherness, I'm going to kill them.'

Opechancanough and the Pamunkey had left. They made a big show of their departure. Just before heading off Opechancanough had yelled to the other *matchacomoco* attendees:

'Be wary of this "leader" of ours. Ask yourself if your tithes and tributes are going to a man who deserves it.'

This had provoked the biggest murmur of unease yet: *no one* spoke about Powhatan like that, not even his own brother, and especially not while seated as guests in the chief's village. The chatter subsided when Powhatan strode back into the centre of the gathering. No one noticed Odina returning to her place – save for a couple of the other Paspahegh men, who glanced at her quizzically, wanting to know where Askook was.

'I'll explain later,' she whispered.

'My brother is a troubled man,' Powhatan said to the assembled crowd. 'And while I am quick to forgive mistakes, there will be consequences for his actions. Just not today. Today I am tired of discussing the problems that blight our land. There will be no more talk of invaders or what to do with them. There is more to the *matchacomoco* than dry and stale debate – there is also singing and dancing and celebration. And I think it is time that was underway, don't you?'

There was a gleeful response from the crowd. The tribes united in a moment of reprieve. It was time to forget the dread of the Prophecy and everything it entailed – if only for an evening. They all got to their feet upon Powhatan's signal and began to make their preparations.

Watching from afar, Guy noticed that Matoaka was now standing next to him. 'Thank you,' he said. 'You did it.'

'It was easier than I thought,' Matoaka mused.

'Very modest of you.'

'Father is a cold man sometimes. But I can crack the ice.'

'What did you tell him?'

'I did as you told me. I told Father that I sensed a noble spirit inside *Sm-ith*. I said that to kill him would leave me in despair... that a dark cloud would follow me around for as long as I could imagine. I begged him to spare his life and let *Sm-ith* prove there was goodness in him.' Matoaka winced. 'That wasn't all though.'

'Oh no?'

'No.' Matoaka shook her head. 'Father can be swayed but he

also has a fondness for material goods. I told him that *Sm-ith* could prove his loyalty to us by making things: some hatchets for him, some bells and beads and copper for me.'

'A servant for his darling daughter.'

'Only for a couple of days. Only until the *matchacomoco* is over. Then he will be free to leave.' She gave another wince. 'There's just one other thing.'

'What's that?' Guy asked.

'I said that you would be joining him.'

The songs outside the darkened hut were joyous and imbued with freedom: chants and yelps set to the beat of rattling drums. Occasionally – like two men staring at the wall of Plato's cave – they caught a glimpse of dancing shadows, feather-headed entities writhing in unison.

Other than that, Guy and Smith were alone with their work.

They didn't speak a word to each other for several hours. They just sat – looking for all the world, Guy thought with surreal amusement, like a pair of naughty schoolboys trapped in detention – and carried out their tasks, moulding hatchets and threading decorative jewellery.

'It's not what you think it was,' Guy finally said. Smith put down his half-carved hatchet.

'Two men dead, Johnson.' Smith stared at Guy. 'Cut up like ribbons in a tailors shop. Followed by a swift departure from you and your lady friend. Care to tell me what I'm supposed to think?'

'We had no choice.'

'Interesting turn of phrase. You didn't *have* to escape.' He picked the hatchet up again, ready to continue working on it – but then dropped it once more in frustration. 'Or, if you *really* wanted to... good God, Johnson. You're a man of cunning. You're resourceful. I half-expected to wake up one morning and find that you'd somehow broken out and sneaked away in the night. Did you really have to turn into a killer on your way out? Morton and Herd got in your way, I get it – but did they really have to die?'

'Yes,' Guy said.

Smith waited for an explanation.

'Morton tried to rape Odina,' Guy went on. 'He was drunk and he was violent and she fought back. I won't shed any tears for the bastard. He got what he deserved.'

Smith took this on board.

'I see. Morton was always a problem. Argumentative. Spiteful. Drinking too much.' He was willing to let that one rest – but there was another name to be accounted for. 'And Herd?'

It was Guy's turn to down tools. He gently laid down the necklace he was beading together.

'Herd only saw the aftermath. Maybe he thought Odina had killed Morton unprovoked – you know, acted like the "savage" Wingfield kept calling her. I'm not sure. All I know is that Herd had his hands around Odina's throat when I walked in. I did what was necessary. I didn't plan on killing him. But plans rarely work out in Jamestown, do they?'

'Plans rarely work out *anywhere*, in my experience.'

'Fair point.'

'Jesus Christ, Johnson.' Smith shook his head. 'Jesus Christ Almighty. It's cut and dried. You could have stayed. Could have explained yourself. It was an act of self-defence. People would have listened.'

'Right.' Guy snorted. 'Sure. Course they would. Come on, Smith – if *you* were out for my scalp afterwards, what hope would I have had appealing to anyone else? Chances are someone would have just shot me on sight and Wingfield would have commissioned them a medal. Same for Odina. We had to run. You know it, I know it.'

Smith slowly picked up his hatchet. He resumed work. They continued their duties in silence for a moment.

'I've done well, you know,' Smith said. 'At least I think I have. Even if I say so myself.'

'What do you mean?' Guy raised an eyebrow.

'Chaplain Hunt always talks about resisting temptation. Not that there's any of that in Jamestown. What am I going to do, treat myself to two daily handfuls of grain instead of one?' Smith gave a gentle snort. 'But *you*. Every time I talk to you I have to restrain myself from asking the same question.' He leaned forward slightly. 'What *is* your story, Johnson?'

Guy finished beading the necklace. Calmly – with the dextrous fingers of a man who learned quickly – he immediately started another.

'I don't think it is my story anymore,' Guy said. 'The man who did those terrible things back in England... I think he's dead. Gone forever.'

'And the man who replaced him?' Smith asked. 'Is he any better?'

'That's a matter of opinion.'

'Put it this way. Look at the man who is no longer here. Would he have done the things you have for this Odina girl? Saved her life? Made sacrifices?'

'No. I don't think he would.'

'Then his replacement is already winning, I'd say. He has his flaws, yes. They are profound and numerate. But no one is perfect except God Himself.' Smith had finished the hatchet. He turned it over in his hands, briefly admiring his work. 'Still. I'm starting to think you hold no stock in the Almighty... or any other gods for that matter. Am I right, Johnson?'

'You might be.'

'Look. Your sins are yours alone. If your guilt is a burden you want to carry in private, I cannot stop you. I expect my curiosity means nothing to you. But I would like you to show me one courtesy.'

'What's that?' Guy asked.

'Your name,' Smith said. 'Your real one. That's all I want to know. After all we've been through, I simply want to know what you're called. Nothing more.'

Guy was about to fall silent again – but something compelled him to speak. There might be consequences, sure... but he was willing to risk them. This was the way he lived now: to *not* be at risk would be an anomaly.

'Fawkes,' he said. 'My name is Guido Fawkes.'

'Guido Fawkes.' Smith muttered the name to himself. There was a hint of distant recollection in his eyes, as though he had heard the name before: something dropped in barroom chats or alleyway banter. Guy waited grimly for him to remember. He didn't. Smith shrugged away the feeling as a random quirk of memory. Instead, he repeated the name and smiled. '*Guido Fawkes*. Well. Now I can see why you kept it hidden. John Johnson is *much* better.'

'Fair comment.' Guy laughed. 'Can you do me a courtesy in return, Smith?'

'Of course.'

'Make sure that name is never uttered again. Please.'

'Noted.' Smith nodded. 'And what of this Tresham fellow? Did he escape as you said? Or... is there something more about him that I should know?'

'I am hoping,' Guy said, already a third of the way through the necklace he was beading, 'that you will never need to find out.'

'Ah. A plan, eh? And what were we saying about *plans* just a moment ago?' Guy didn't reply.

He finished off the necklace without a word and started another.

Guy and Smith left the Powhatan village without any ceremony. Powhatan had granted them use of a canoe each.

As they sailed away Guy spotted Odina on the shoreline.

They hadn't been able to say a proper goodbye to each other. They had only seen each other in glimpsed passes since the day of the *matchacomoco*. To get any closer would be to raise suspicions.

Yet mere words were irrelevant. Odina's look said it all.

Guy felt his heart sink. The last time he had been taken away from her like this, he had assumed – at least briefly – it would be the last time he ever saw her. Now he knew that wasn't the case... but instead it would be a nigh-on unbearable amount of time before he could touch her again. He wasn't sure which was worse.

Nilawa tepatamwa, Odina mouthed.

I love you.

Nilawa tepatamwa, Guy mouthed back. They both managed to hold back their tears. Both would sob to the heavens when they were alone later, Guy was sure of that – but for the time being they remained strong. If they couldn't share their tears with each other, then no one else could have them.

He and Smith drifted round the river bend.

'I have a fairly good idea of what will happen to us back in Jamestown,' Smith said, roughly a day and a half into their journey. 'But... in case I'm wrong... I'm happy to reinstate my old offer. The colony could use a man like you. I will support you against any enemies if you decide to stay.'

'I'm happy to accept it,' Guy said.

Smith looked astonished.

'I had imagined it might take more persuasion than that,' Smith said.

'Quite the opposite. In fact, I intend to stay in Jamestown for a very long time indeed.'

'Would you mind if I ask what inspired this change of heart?'

'Yes. I would.'

'I thought as much.' Smith smiled. They drifted along for a moment.

'It all depends, of course,' Guy said. 'What if you're right?'

'Sorry?'

'Your prediction. Of what will happen to us when we get back. What if it turns out to be right?'

'Then none of this matters anyway.'

Smith was right. Gruesomely, horribly – yet inevitably – right.

They arrived back to discover that President Ratcliffe had been taken ill and – while not quite at death's door – was incapable of carrying out his duties. As such Wingfield had resumed command – or at least a creature that partially resembled Wingfield.

Skeletal and chittering, Wingfield's clothes hung loosely off his dilapidated frame. His eyes seemed too large for his head, his face now resembling a paper mask that had been stretched awkwardly over his skull.

He was not alone. When Guy and Smith arrived at the colony entrance and were seized by a group of men, Guy marvelled at how bony the arms looping around his own were. He resisted pushing the men away for fear the slightest nudge would break their bones. Their weakness was soon mollified as their number swelled – and soon Guy and Smith were being marched into Jamestown by an angry escort of twelve starving colonists.

Starving. That was an understatement. Many men were simply slumped against the fort walls, having given up on survival entirely. Jamestown was not just on its last legs. It had snapped them off at the kneecaps. It was scraping along on bloodied stumps.

As Guy and Smith were hauled to see Wingfield, Guy noticed just how empty the colony seemed. He tried to tally up exactly how many men were left alive.

Wingfield clocked him.

'A headcount, is it, Johnson? Is that what you're hoping to do?' Wingfield limped along, his mania the only thing about him that had expanded. 'Let me save you the trouble. There are thirty-eight of us left. *Thirty-eight* men out of one hundred and four.'

'There must be some mistake...' Smith faltered, disbelieving.

'Oh, no mistake, Smith. The only mistake here was trusting you to return from the natives with supplies. What was it you said before leaving? *I'm going to set up a trading route. We're going to make bonds and we're going to grow our civilisations together*. And then – nothing. You vanish for weeks. Now you come back empty-handed. Oh, apart from bringing a murderer back into town. Another mouth to feed would be too simple, wouldn't it? You had to make sure he was a killer as well.'

'Wingfield.' Smith tried to make a pointless plea for rationality. 'Things aren't what you think. Johnson here–'

'*Johnson here* looks like he's been eating well,' Wingfield snapped. 'As do you. Maybe you did manage to wrangle some food from the savages, eh? If only you'd been so kind as to include us in your deal.'

Guy and Smith glanced around. The men were powered by pure spite. Hunger had brought them together: the only thing that could make them rally behind Wingfield.

'You left us to die, Smith,' Wingfield said. 'It's as simple as that.' He looked out, past the trees, as though staring at the ocean beyond. 'Just like that bastard Newport. *I'll be back*, he told us. He was supposed to be here months ago. But he's *not coming*, is he? Oh no. He's back in England, living the high life, no doubt laughing over a brandy as we drop like flies.'

'You don't know what you're–'

'Enough. *Enough.*' Wingfield scrunched his eyes tight shut and threw his hands in the air. He rubbed his temples. 'These headaches. Such headaches.' He opened his eyes again. They reignited with righteous fury. 'Treason. That's what it is. Now... in the past, you've both escaped what you had coming. Almost made a habit of it, in fact. But that habit is *over*. It is time to finish what should have been done a long time ago.' He raised his voice, his hoarsened pitch battling his own fatigue, nonetheless managing to stir the other men into communal action. 'No circumstance will give you reprieve now. Fortune will not whore herself out for you anymore. This time, by Christ... *this time* you both shall hang.'

Smith looked to Guy. A sad yet accepting glance. There was nothing they could do.

'Mr Wingfield.' Smith lowered his head, almost appearing as defeated as the skeletal men surrounding him. 'I'm aware that it is probably futile to try and talk you out of this–'

'Not probably, Smith. *Unequivocally*.'

'Fine. Then I have one last request.'

'I'm listening.'

'Bury me beyond the outskirts of the fort. Closer to the sea. Looking towards the horizon.'

Wingfield said nothing. He gave a slow nod. Smith took it as confirmation. Guy, however, picked up on something else: a hesitancy in Wingfield's conduct, a nagging guilt.

Among the many things that were not quite right, something in Jamestown felt doubly wrong.

He suddenly knew what it was. 'They're not going to bury us,' Guy said.

'What?' Smith looked puzzled.

'Look around. They have no crops, no meat, no supplies. Not a thing. The only harvest Jamestown has to offer is the dead.' Guy swallowed. 'What do you think they've been eating?'

It took a moment for Smith to understand. When he did his face contorted with horror.

'Oh my God. Oh dear Christ. Oh no.' He looked to Wingfield with disgust – and an abstract sort of pity. Wingfield's guilt was now reflected in the faces of all the other men. 'Tell me you haven't. Look at me and tell me before God that you did not–'

'You *cannot judge us!*' Wingfield shrieked. 'You think I have not prayed for forgiveness? If you have been faced with the stark choices we have, Smith – instead of filling your belly and getting serviced by native whore girls – you would have done the same. We did what was necessary to survive. We did what *your actions* made us do. If anyone should feel sick with remorse, it should be you.' He motioned for the surrounding men to grab Guy and Smith and follow him. 'No more delays. No more talk. This is the end for you both. Face it like men.'

'Men do not eat other men,' Guy said.

Wingfield spun round. He looked like he was about to strike Guy – but he settled. He gave a warped smile instead.

'Out here, Johnson... men are something different altogether.'

With that – with their feet being dragged over the soil, over the earth of a New World that had been baptised in blood and hunger and showed no signs of retracting its claws – Guy and Smith were taken to the gallows.

Neither man said a word: not to each other, nor to the emaciated crowd. Guy felt a strange peace that he had never known while waiting for death in the Tower of London. His time in the Tower had been marked by failure: his plot thwarted, ambitions in ruins. Now, at least, he knew that he had achieved something great. Odina was alive. Safe. It was a victory against all of *this*.

With the noose slipped around his neck – with Smith suffering the same indignation by his side – Guy looked to Wingfield. The man was a despot in his own realm, a tyrant of this crumbling fortress. Wingfield's eyes shone with destiny reclaimed: *third time lucky, gentlemen. History will see you both as my conquests. You tried to alter that. You failed.*

But Wingfield would be wrong.

'*Constant!*' A shout went up from one of the men. 'It's... it's the *Constant!*'

Soon all the others echoed the shout. Soon Guy felt his body buckle as the rope around his neck was cut. Soon he was slumped on the ground, Smith next to him, his rope also cut.

The men who cut them down had forgotten about everything that seemed so important mere seconds earlier. Even Wingfield did not care that his final attempt to hang the unhangable duo had been scuppered. He was doing what all the other men were doing.

He was crying. Weeping tears of relief and joy.

Looming in the mouth of the river – back from England,

several months late but now very much here – the *Susan Constant* headed towards Jamestown.

Details began to get clearer, etched outlines against the churning grey sky. Guy could see Newport, stood on the bow, telescope raised to one eye as he chartered a path. He could see the stacked crates of supplies bound atop the deck. He could see other people: sailors, men who looked robust and strong and would bring with them the trappings of civilisation.

The men of Jamestown were all on their knees, hands aloft, shouting messages of praise and glory to the sky. Stripped of his faith but not stripped of his gratitude, Guy joined them. He sunk to his knees and let out a primal howl.

Salvation pitched its sails and angled towards land.

CHAPTER TWELVE

January 1608

Matoaka struggled her way through the undergrowth. As the vegetation began to thin out she saw the familiar signs that Odina was waiting for her: the carefully hidden firepit, the remnants of cooking. She scratched her legs on a few of the brambles as she trampled ahead. This was the trouble with finding a new spot for their regular meetups: the ground hadn't quite been tamed by human feet yet. They were on the cusp of where the large patch of marshland began – closer to Jamestown than either of them would have liked.

That was a small price to pay. All that mattered was that Matoaka could regularly see her mother again. It was still their secret, of course – but it also felt like their burdens had been lifted. Odina seemed lighter and happier these days. She still carried grave sadness about her – Matoaka felt that, for whatever reason, this was something forever ingrained into her mother's spirit – but it did not seem to purely define her now.

Something big had changed. Matoaka guessed it had something to do with Askook. She had only rarely encountered the man before the incident at the *matchacomoco*. While she never quite trusted nor liked him, she had never considered him a monster. His savage display at the pit had changed that.

And yet... she had killed him. She had taken a life.

Despite Odina's reassurance – that it had to be done, there was no other choice – the guilt still plagued Matoaka. Occasionally she would hear talk from the adults about the curious Paspahegh man who had chased the foreigner into the woods and vanished: the fact that many people had looked for him and found nothing, the fact that one of the Great Winds might simply have swept him out of this world. Matoaka hated the weight of the secret. It played on her mind and it infected her dreams – so much so that Odina's first question was:

'You are still having the nightmares?'

'Yes.' Matoaka briefly considered lying; putting a brave face on things. She abandoned the idea. 'Less than at first. But they still come. I see Askook a lot. He is dead but also alive. He does not speak to me but I can see it in his eyes: he is angry. He wants to know why I did what I did.'

'Do you tell him?'

'Sometimes. I say that he was a bad man and he had to be stopped. He looks even angrier when I tell him that.' Matoaka shivered. It was not cold. 'Do you think it is Askook himself speaking to me? That he has stepped into my dreams from beyond this world?'

'No.' Odina took Matoaka's hands as she reassured her. 'Wherever Askook is now, he cannot hurt you.'

'Where do you think he is now?' Matoaka asked. 'Would the Great Hare have welcomed him? Forgiven all he did wrong?'

'That is a complicated question,' Odina said carefully. 'A

very serious one too. And I think – today – we should talk about less serious things. I think we have earned that, don't you?'

'Yes.' Matoaka smiled.

So they spoke of the less-than-serious: they talked of darting foxes and leaping salmon and scurrying bugs. They joked and they played. They sang and they danced. As Odina watched Matoaka she noticed something that saddened her slightly: hints of self-consciousness in the girl's demeanour, a sense that such frivolity might soon be behind her. She was growing up fast. Soon she would have her first blood. After that, womanhood would embrace her.

But... the dancing and singing would not end just yet. There would be more. And when Matoaka grew beyond that? Then their meetings would continue – except now Odina would talk to her of womanly things. She would be a much-needed mentor as Matoaka glided into adulthood.

Odina noticed that Matoaka had brought something with her: a leather satchel the girl had crafted herself – with some skill, Odina noticed – that was slung around her shoulder.

'Is this a gift?' Odina joked. 'For me?'

'Actually, yes. A gift for you, Mother.' Matoaka patted the satchel. 'But not for now. You can open it later, when you return to your village.'

'What is it?'

'It's a *surprise.*'

'Give me a clue.' Odina frowned. 'Matoaka. You didn't steal anything from your village, did you?'

'Maybe...' Matoaka looked to the ground.

'*Maybe?* Surely there's only a yes or a no–'

'I didn't take all of it. And it hardly ever gets used anymore. I think my father has forgotten about it anyway. No one will notice it's missing!' Matoaka patted the satchel. 'You can have it later, like I said. If you don't want it, then give it back to me the next time we meet.'

'All right.' Odina folded her arms. 'But no more stealing. Understand?'

'And when you open it...' Matoaka had already moved on. 'When you open it... you can think of me... and I'll be doing *this* dance...' The girl broke out into a comical display of flailing limbs, poking out her tongue and crossing her eyes as she did so. Odina laughed.

Odina loathed herself at having once yearned to die. How could she have left *this* behind? How could she have thrown away the chance to watch her beautiful girl grow and flourish over the coming years? It was insanity. Selfishness. In many ways the story she had told the Paspahegh – possession by a dark spirit – was true. The spirit had been despair. The summoner had been Askook. And somewhere in that whole maelstrom she had been lost.

She still thought of Guy all the time. Racked with confusion and longing, she felt like – as her life had intertwined with his – she had briefly stepped into an alien world. She had tolerated Powhatan. She had loathed Askook. Guy was the first man she had genuinely loved.

Just as she had once told Guy – an outburst for which she would never forgive herself – Odina felt like she *knew nothing about anything*. She had imagined such tortured romance to be her story alone: a path wholly unique to her. During the time Odina spent looking after her dying mother – time where she got to know the woman like never before – she learned that it was anything but. Her mother told Odina of her distant past: of the men she had wooed and loves she had known before her father. Some of them had ended gracefully. Some disastrously. Most of them, however, had fizzled out confusingly. Most of the time love did not follow a straight path – if it stuck to a path at all.

'Why can't anything be *simple*?'

Odina was plucked out of her thoughts. She was amazed. It was as though Matoaka had read her mind.

'What did you say?'

'Everything makes me tired.' Matoaka folded her arms. 'I miss being little. I miss having nothing to think about but playing and singing. Father used to grab me and swing me around and sing songs to me. Now all he does is sit and frown and think about the invaders. I have heard him saying to his council: *I worry for the future Matoaka might have.* He thinks the *Ing-leese* are bringing about the Prophecy. And... what if the Prophecy arrives after Father is no longer here? What if I am the one who has to face it?'

Odina tried to think of a platitude, something to soothe Matoaka's worries. She suddenly realised that was the wrong way to go.

Only the truth would suffice.

'The white men are going nowhere,' Odina said solemnly. 'They are going to be a part of this land and your life. Your father is right. Dealing with them is a burden you will have to carry, perhaps long after both he and I are gone.'

'I don't want to.' She pouted.

'The world is not invested in what you want.'

'Yes.' She sulkily agreed. This was something she had suspected for a while – but now had that all-important adult confirmation.

'But... I don't think the Prophecy has any bearing on this.'

'No?' Matoaka's eyes widened.

'No. I think things will change drastically. You've seen an animal running, haven't you? When it gathers speed and cannot stop or change direction without tumbling over? Something like that is happening here. Worlds have met and whatever happens next cannot be stopped. I feel that you will be at the centre of all this, Matoaka. You are too special to be anything but.'

'What will become of me?'

'I don't know exactly. But I think your name will be remembered across this land for countless generations. Maybe even more so than your father. Than *anyone*. And I think those beyond the *Tsenacommacah* will know of you too. Across the oceans. Beyond the world of the Real People.'

'They will?' The idea seemed insane to Matoaka.

'I think they will. And when the two worlds begin to fuse further... your legacy will shine upon the world that emerges.'

'What if that *doesn't* happen?' Matoaka asked. 'What if the *Ing-leese* decide to go home and never come back? The others too – the *Span-ee-ards*? What if our world stays our world and their world stays theirs?'

'Less blood would probably be shed that way. Less people would suffer. Less lands would be conquered, less histories burned. But that is the future you *want*, Matoaka. Not the one that may be coming.'

Matoaka retreated even further into pouty sulkiness, still unevenly walking the tightrope between girl and woman. She kicked a pebble. It thunked off a nearby tree.

'I wish I could just *stop* everything,' she said. 'Right here, right now. No more days, no more seasons. I wish that we could stay here, just you and me, forever, like... like...'

'Like a lake frozen for the winter,' Odina said, with a sadness Matoaka did not notice.

'Yes!' Matoaka was delighted at the metaphor. 'And we wouldn't have to leave, *ever*, and we could...' She stopped, her nose twitching like a curious rabbit. Odina sniffed the air too. Something was not quite right. Nothing immediately apparent – almost imperceptible even – but somehow *off*.

Matoaka looked around. She pointed, finger jutting towards the sky. 'Mother. Look.'

Odina saw it: the thick acrid smoke of a fire churning into the sky, a blaze beyond mere campfires and indeed anything else the *Tsenacommacah* had ever seen. It did not carry the natural heft of a brushfire or the result of a lightning strike: it was wholly unnatural in scope, a man-made atrocity.

That meant it could only be coming from one place.

'Ch-awn,' Matoaka said. 'He might be in danger.'

'We should–' Odina did not finish.

'Help! Yes!' Matoaka darted off into the woods.

Odina had meant to say *be careful* – as in *we should proceed with caution, we don't know exactly what is going on.* But her daughter had never been one for cautiousness or hesitancy. She never would be.

Odina took off, running after Matoaka.

Towards the unknown. Towards the fire. Towards the *Ing-leese.*

The order had been dropped like a stillborn whale and with half the subtlety. Newport – tired from his time at sea yet deeming himself fitter than any half-mad, fully-starved colonist at taking command – had temporarily adopted the role of President.

'We are going to do what we did before,' he said to the assembled Jamestown men, both new arrivals and beleaguered long-timers. 'Except this time we are going to make it work. We are going to *strike off the past altogether.* I don't care what was happening when I arrived. I don't care who had betrayed who, who had stolen what, who was due for twenty lashes or an appointment with the hangman's noose. We are starting afresh. So I suggest you see our arrival as redemption in more ways than one. Think of this as a fresh new dawn for Jamestown. We are all Adam and this is our Eden.'

Even among a bunch of cynical hard-living toilers, the words offered some genuine inspiration. Everyone knew that the colony would descend back into bickering factions soon enough – but the settlers were so enamoured with fresh food supplies that pessimism briefly died. Men who had been moments away from lynching Guy and Smith – and then doing far, far worse afterwards – now broke bread with them like families at harvest.

Wingfield was among the reformed revellers – and even took it with good grace when Newport reinstated Ratcliffe to President instead of him. For now at least, Wingfield had been granted a sense of perspective. Survival was worth much more than status ever was.

Guy took on guard duty, standing watch outside the fort every other day. He felt particularly attuned to the task. It offered him the chance to continue doing what he mostly did anyway: scanning the treeline and marsh beyond the colony, determined to spot a returning Francis Tresham – or any signs thereof – before the man spotted him. Until he knew for certain that Tresham was dead, Guy was a pilgrim being stalked by a lion. His best weapon was awareness.

Weeks passed. No sign of Francis emerged.

'What would it take,' Smith eventually asked Guy, 'for you to believe that that lunatic is dead?'

'His head on a fucking pike,' Guy replied.

'I cannot offer you that. Instead, I can gift you with evidence. The man has not been seen in well over a month. You say he was badly injured when he vanished. Coupled with the fact that he seemed to be descending into madness... I don't think his prognosis is good.'

'You shouldn't underestimate him. He's resourceful. Smart. He fooled you, didn't he?'

'He's not dealing with me. Out there, he's dealing with nature. And she's a lot less forgiving.'

'We'll see, Smith. We'll see.'

Forty days and forty nights.

It all seemed so obvious now. A precedent had been set: just when Francis assumed that everything was going to plan, something always came along to cripple things. He always pulled through. Learned. Adapted. Accepted that these were simply trials sent by God to further test his mettle.

But... this. *This*. He knew in his heart that it was the final hurdle.

Once Francis had completed this last and most demanding task, he would be granted his divine goal of destroying Guido Fawkes and those who protected him. He had come close, yes – but he just hadn't earned it yet.

It was so wonderfully appropriate, wasn't it? *Never let it be said that the Almighty doesn't have a fine sense of irony*, thought Francis. Just as Jesus was sent out into the desert to survive his solitude, so was Francis Tresham. He would be in pain but his body would heal. He would be hungry, yet – like the kind of meek soul set to inherit the earth – he would live on humbly foraged scraps. He would possibly suffer the same Devil's temptations as Christ – offered bread from stones, offered the rulership of all the world's kingdoms – but he would throw them back in Satan's face.

And to what end? He wasn't quite sure about that. He suspected that he would know when his trial was over.

It may have been less than forty days or it may have been more. Francis lost track of reality: he was running simply on Francis Time, a slow hallucinogenic blur. Some hints of chronology slipped through: his broken arm was setting, for instance, healing at an unusual angle. He felt like a puppet under the control of someone else. He occasionally caught sight of his own reflection in puddled water. He looked worse than he ever had – truly, a beaten-down martyr – but he did not care. He would be rebuilt from this low point. It would be glorious.

He began to get glimpses – visual and aural – of his ultimate reward. Whispered voices began to drift through his head. Strange silhouettes appeared at the edge of his vision, watching him with great interest, only to vanish when he tried to look at them directly. Their disappearance grew more prolonged every time: becoming slow fades that left wispy traces.

Francis was encouraged by this. They were angels, he was sure of it – and they were getting ready to deliver their message to him.

Soon they began to take on a glowing blue tinge. *Closer to corporeality,* Francis thought. *Closer and closer.*

Eventually – when Francis was still optimistic but starting to wonder exactly how long this vision quest was going to take – one of the glowing figures emerged from the forest, gliding directly towards him, no longer dissipating upon his gaze.

This was it. It was time. Francis threw back his head and cackled in triumphant laughter. He had done it. He was worthy. Some microscopically small voice at the back of his head whispered tiny reservations – *aren't people who see apparitions insane? Doesn't this mean that you've completely gone over the edge?* – but he silenced it, knowing it would be gone forever once he did.

He held his arms aloft. The glowing figure floated ever closer.

The apparition was faceless to begin with – a crackling void that soon began to fill. The faces that came were ones from his past, cycling and turning, long-forgotten and forever-remembered people drifting in and out of each other.

Francis gaped in amazement as he watched. He had not expected this – but it was absolutely perfect. Who better to serve as the mouthpiece of the Lord than incarnations of those Francis had encountered on earth? He began to weep tears of gratitude.

All this for him.

'Tell me,' he begged, dropping to his knees, 'what I must do.'

You already know, the shifting figure said, lips unmoving, a timeless and genderless voice beamed directly into Francis's skull. The melding line-up of revolving faces continued. His father. His mother. Uncles. Aunts. Old teachers, old schoolfriends, old workmates. Catesby. Wintour. Percy. Alonso.

'Do I?' Francis whimpered.

Fawkes must die. Jamestown must die with him.

'But...' Francis lowered his head in shame. 'I have squandered the resources.'

What do you mean?

'The gunpowder is lost to me.'

And?

'And...'

Francis's eyes widened.

He suddenly knew where the spirit was going with this. He couldn't believe he hadn't seen it himself; that he had let his mind cloud over with such a blinkered single purpose. His tears of gratitude returned.

You wanted the destruction of Jamestown to be a gift to the Heavens, the apparition went on. *You wanted it to be something that literally shook the world. A righteous blast. A detonation.*

'Yes... yes...'

You wanted the gunpowder to do to Jamestown what it had never done to Parliament. An explosion. A statement.

'Yes...'

You wanted a flash of Holy Fire to wipe out evil where it stood.

'Yes! That is what I wanted!'

But you became fixated on this gunpowder, didn't you? You yearned for this single great explosion so badly. So you forgot one simple and honest truth: something that men have known for many thousands of years.

'Yes.' Francis couldn't believe how stupid he had been.

What is that truth?

'You don't need gunpowder to destroy something.'

And?

'You don't need gunpowder to start a fire.'

Exactly. Put your pride aside, Francis Tresham. Abandon your dream of a single glorious moment of chaos. Understand that all you need to do to turn Jamestown into ashes...

'... is to start a fire.'

Take the fire of a torch. Set it to the wooden balustrades. Watch as the flames spread and consume everything in their wake. The voice was filled with love: forgiveness for Francis's short-sightedness. *Will it be spectacular as your ideal of a gunpowder blast? No. Will as many die? Almost certainly not. But countless heathens WILL die – and Jamestown WILL burn. You will still have secured a victory for the Kingdom of Heaven, Francis. Now – tell me. Tell me what you have learned.*

'The gunpowder was just a distraction,' Francis sobbed. 'It was...' He was struck by the revelation. 'It was a distraction sent by God Himself! That was my final test, wasn't it?'

Yes.

'To realise that everything I needed was in my possession all along?'

Yes.

The apparition reached out and placed its hand atop Francis's head. He quivered in ecstasy.

Now. Go. You are ready to fulfil your mission.

It was January. It was cold – but everyone in Jamestown knew that the bitterest extremes of winter were yet to come. And with a welcome break from tradition, it just so happened that the colonists were actually well prepared for the upcoming season. They had pre-rationed their existing supplies and pulled themselves together for a couple of successful hunting expeditions. The domiciles in the settlement were all completed and fully insulated. The protective triangular wall around the fort was reinforced and sturdy. The upcoming winter would by no means be easy – and spring was sure to bring new challenges – but it looked like the colony just might pull through.

Everyone in Jamestown had made an agreement not to waste firewood: it was going to be needed during the cold months ahead. So when Guy – a few hours away from guard duty – woke from an afternoon nap to the nearby smell of burning, his immediate reaction was anger.

He stormed outside, looking for the culprit. Who was that? What the hell did they think they were playing at? It was a cold day, yes – but it wasn't *freezing,* and anyone unable to cope with the weather today frankly needed to deal with it.

Guy glanced around the inner fort. He couldn't see any men huddled round impromptu fires. Yet he could still make out that smoky nip in the air. He checked to see if anyone else had noticed it. No – not yet. That didn't matter. He had always been the first to pick up on things like this.

Smith spotted him. Frowned. 'Everything all right, Johnso–'

Guy held up a hand to silence him. The smell was getting

stronger, carried on the wind. It was near. Nearer than Guy had expected. That was when he saw it: a curling wisp of smoke coming from the south-western corner of the fort, growing in density and thickness right before his eyes, the alarmingly fast prelude to an inferno that would soon be out of control. The noise came next, gaining volume just as quickly: the crackling and popping march of destruction. That was how it began – the first recorded structural blaze on American soil.

'*Fire!*' Guy yelled.

They had plans in place for such an eventuality. Aside from a few panicked onlookers – who soon had their gawking slapped out of them – the men of Jamestown immediately sprang into action. They rushed with empty pails to the nearby river, scooping up water and running back to the fort with it slopping over the sides. Wingfield took it upon himself to start directing them: waving his arms, yelling. Smith ran over and thrust an empty pail into his hands.

'Shut up, shithead,' he told Wingfield, 'and get to work.'

The flames had already crept up the balustrade. Glowing embers leapt like orange ticks to the rooftops of the nearest huts. The bundled straw immediately caught fire, spreading with alarming speed. As the first to grab a pail of water, Guy was the first back at the scene.

He put his shoulders down and charged ahead, getting as close to the blaze as he could – dangerously close, his hair and eyebrows getting singed – and threw the water over it. Freshly damp wood sizzled like overdone cooking. Steam mingled with the smoke. The fire continued to spread. The pail of water had hardly made a dent – but it was a start. More men with more pails were coming. Guy could not afford to give in to defeatism now. *We can do this,* he told himself. *We can stop this thing–*

A large strut from the balustrade crashed onto the ground behind him, blocking his path back to the river. The grass caught alight. Guy's view of the other men was obscured by a churning veil of smoke. He was considering the odds – could he make it through, could he leap over the wooden strut and escape unscathed? – when a rasping voice made him spin back round:

'It was only a spark.'

Francis Tresham was stood watching the fire spread.

He was stood in profile, his left side facing Guy as he surveyed the flames, an amber glow bathing his disfigured features. Guy immediately put the picture together. A dropped torch lay burning the grass by Francis's feet. He had been hiding out in the nearby forest where he had started a campfire. He had snapped a thick branch from one of the trees and set one end on fire. Then he had wandered out here: holding the flaming torch to the balustrade and waiting for the inevitable. So simple yet so destructive.

'Just a tiny spark, Fawkes,' Francis said, marvelling at his handiwork. 'That was all it took.'

Guy felt the rush of fresh ignition behind him: more of the fort catching fire, the grass lighting up. He wanted more than anything to back away from this creature but he couldn't. Francis was an apparition of angular bones and hunched decay: a walking corpse, a bit-player in a Bosch triptych. He was skirting the very edge of his species.

Guy wanted to kill him. More than anything. And he knew he *could*: the kind of advantages that Francis could muster during the pit battle were now long gone. But... he had to deal with the fire. He had to somehow make his way back to the river and join the others in tackling the blaze. He had to save Jamestown.

He didn't have time to stomp on this insect.

'Go,' Guy said. 'Run.'

'Excuse me?' Francis asked.

'I'm giving you a chance, Tresham. You can leave. Now. You can run back into that forest and keep running. You can stay out there. You can die out there. Alone. That right there is a thousand times more than what you deserve.'

'Well.' Francis pretended to mull it over. 'That's a very interesting offer, Fawkes.'

He turned to face Guy, full on, no longer just an abstract side-profile against the fire. It was the blade Guy noticed first: the dull gleam of filthy metal, the same weapon that Francis had tried to kill him with during the *matchacomoco*. The next thing Guy spotted took a longer moment to register: as though it *just wasn't possible*, as though the limits of this disaster should not be able to stretch any further.

The girl was trembling in the grip of Francis's other arm, eyes saucer-wide with horror. Francis's grimy hand was clamped over her mouth. The blade was pressed against her jugular.

Matoaka. He had Matoaka.

'I think, however,' Francis said, 'I'm going to decline.'

Decisions before actions, Powhatan would often tell Matoaka when she was in trouble for her impulsive behaviour. *If I can only get three words into that head of yours, my little Pocahontas, it will be those. Decisions. Before. Actions.*

So what would her father think of this? Matoaka wondered. She hadn't given a second thought as to what she would actually *do* when she reached the white men's colony. She had only known that someone – very possibly Ch-awn – might need help. Her father would understand her brash rush to action in *that* case, wouldn't he? He would see the value in ditching hesitant scruples if someone was in danger, surely?

She honestly didn't know – and she didn't know about her mother either. Odina could be running right behind her now... or she could have stayed back at the meeting spot. Matoaka didn't have time to check. All her focus was on what lay in front: the fort in flames.

When she spotted it from a distance the fire had just been starting, a skinny twisting column of smoke rising into the sky. Now that column had become a sky unto itself: leaden black smoke that appeared almost as a shifting solid mass. It was everywhere.

Matoaka emerged from the treeline, dazedly walking out into the marshland clearing. She had been hoping that a plan would drop into her head as soon as she got here – or at least that she would immediately see someone in need of help. Confusion reigned. She could hear the voices of several men, distant, almost lost below the crackling *whoosh* of flames. She couldn't see anyone, however... apart from what *looked* like a lone figure battling through the smoke. She squinted to get a better look. She was about to raise her hand and call out when–

Someone grabbed her.

She tried to scream but a hand covered her mouth.

She looked up. It was him. The man from the forest and the pit. The demon with half a face.

'Let her go, Tresham,' Guy said.

He remained where he was. The heat of the flames behind him was getting more oppressive – but he couldn't risk moving and provoking any hair-trigger reaction from Francis. Matoaka looked to Guy with wide terrified eyes. Guy tried his best to look reassuring: *it's all going to be all right*.

It didn't work.

He didn't believe it himself.

'It's probably difficult for you to grasp, Fawkes,' Francis said, seeming to thrive in the heat, 'but you're not best placed to give orders right now.'

'You want me. Not her.'

'Maybe I want you both.'

'Why?'

'Maybe I want to make your last moments just that little bit more unbearable. Maybe turning your tiny friend inside out would be the very thing. One last meal before execution.'

'You're still in there.' Guy took a slow step forwards. 'Somewhere. You hate me and you want me dead. I get it, Tresham. I do. But...' He coughed. Smoke was billowing close over their heads. 'But you can still act like a man seeking vengeance rather than a monster. You want me, you can have me. But let the girl go.'

'Are you *implying*,' Francis asked, enjoying drawing this out, relishing his new-found power, bolstered by the glow of the nearing flames, 'that you would trade your own life for hers?'

Guy swallowed.

'If that's what you want,' he said. 'Yes.'

Francis nodded, taking this in. It looked like he had genuinely intended to slaughter Matoaka – but now a new and more tempting sadistic route had opened.

'I would be willing to honour that deal,' Francis said. And – even though the man was a gargoyle sculpted of pure dishonesty – Guy saw that Francis really meant it.

'Good.' Guy crept forwards again. 'That's good. Now–'

'*Now...*' Francis pressed the knife against Matoaka's neck. Guy stopped where he was, holding up his hands in a plea for mercy. Francis nodded over to the nearby blazing fort: now a sheer wall of fire just ten feet away. 'Now is when you see yourself out, Guido Fawkes.'

'What do you mean?' Guy asked. But he knew.

'Walk into the fire,' Francis said. 'Walk into it and stand there and *let me watch you burn*. I want to see you leave this world in flames. No redemption this time. No offer to commit yourself to the Lord anew. No. You'll be trading in this fire for an eternal one – and I want to *see your fucking face the second you realise that*.'

He coughed, hawking up black sputum. 'I will allow you one small mercy though. The last thing you see will be me letting the girl go. The question is...' He leered like a rapist in Sodom. 'Do you trust me to keep my word?'

'It looks like I don't have a choice.'

'Then entertain me, Fawkes.' Francis swept his free arm towards the fire. 'Bring me joy.'

Guy turned to the fire.

He meant what he had said. He really didn't have a choice. He had to do this.

He didn't want to look at Matoaka. He knew the damage that an uncertain last glance before death could cause to an onlooker: endless internal questions. *What were they trying to say? Were they saying goodbye or were they begging me to save them? Was there something they wanted me to know?* No – he would keep his gaze fixed firmly on that bastard Tresham. He would give the man what he wanted.

He would endure the pain for Matoaka to survive. He took a step towards the fire.

His outer layer of skin would peel away. That's how it would start. He would be in agony. The fire would then burn through to the flesh beneath. It would start to split open. Fat would begin to leak out, bubbling and boiling.

He took another step.

His muscles would shrivel and contract, charring inside like cuts of overdone meat. His organs would roast. His eyeballs would melt.

Another step.

His nerve endings would burn. After that he would no longer be able to feel pain – but he would still be conscious of everything that was happening. One more step.

For Matoaka, he told himself, a mantra that he began to run through his head. *For Matoaka. For Matoaka. For Matoaka.*

Just a couple more steps and he would be–

'*Get OFF HER!*'

He spun around when he heard the voice. Odina was here.

She had never seen a fire like it. When Odina had been running after Matoaka she had convinced herself that it might not be as bad as the thick curling smoke implied – but when she emerged from the forest she realised that it was far worse.

She was overcome with horror.

And then – when she saw the *Fran-ceese* creature with a blade to Matoaka's neck – she was overcome with rage.

She pelted across the clearing, not caring about the rising heat, not caring about the floating embers that whipped across her face and burnt her as she went. She just knew that this man had to die.

'*Get OFF HER!*'

She screamed at him. She threw herself through the air.

Francis arced around, taken by surprise – and threw Matoaka to the ground so he could turn his blade on Odina. Matoaka grunted as she hit her head, knocked out cold. One of her sandals flew off, as did a bracelet. Her leather satchel was cast to one side.

Odina charged into Francis. Seething, Francis thrust his arm forward. They connected: a crunching union of bones and bile.

Odina tried to inhale. It was an ungodly wheezing rasp.

The smoke, she frantically thought. *It's choking me. It's going to kill me and it's going to kill Matoaka before the fire even gets a chance–*

Her chest felt like it was caving in: a pain beyond pain. Then she understood. It wasn't just the smoke.

Francis pulled his arm back, letting out a cry of triumph as he did so. The blade in his hand was slick and red with fresh blood.

Odina looked down. The stab wound was in the middle of her chest, directly between the ribs. Blood – so much blood – was oozing out and staining her clothes. She felt her heartbeat thud in her ears – and then begin to weaken. Dizziness hit. A black tunnel began to grow around her vision. She could not stay standing much longer. She staggered backwards.

'*No!*' she heard Guy scream.

She didn't know he had been watching. And – even though this was *it*, even though she was dying – Odina felt a surge of relief. Guy would make sure Matoaka was safe. Guy would make Francis pay for what he had done.

Guy was running towards her. Then he wasn't.

Another huge flaming strut from the balustrade teetered off, crashing to the ground, a behemoth of wood and fire blocking Guy's path. For the first time Odina saw true helplessness in Guy's eyes.

Her vision continued to darken. Her dizziness was unbearable. Staying upright was the hardest thing she had ever done.

In front of her, Francis looked to his blade and then to

Odina's wound. He then looked over to Guy, trapped mere feet away, a tortured observer who could do nothing but watch. He began to laugh. He laughed like a spoilt child getting a second helping of cake – then a third, then a fourth. He laughed and laughed and laughed. It was all so perfect for him.

Francis turned away from Odina. She was forgotten now: already dead, a piece of flotsam he could let float away. Blade in hand – and his taste for killing clearly piqued – he began to head towards an unconscious Matoaka.

No, Odina managed to think.

I cannot let him. I will not let him.

With a last burst of energy she flung herself at Francis again. Surprise gave her the advantage – at least to begin with. She fell to the ground, taking him with her. As she hit the grass, Odina knew: she would never stand up again.

She gripped her fingers around Francis's ankle, a feeble attempt to restrain him. He kicked her in the face. Odina rolled onto her back. Within seconds Francis was on top of her. His face was a mess of irritated disgust. *Why couldn't this woman just die? Why did she have to keep bothering him, like some sort of mosquito buzzing round a banquet?*

Francis thrust the blade into Odina's chest again. This time he did not pull his hand back.

Odina heard Guy scream again: another futile howl of anger and despair. Her head lolled to the right. She could just about see Guy. He could just about see her. It was enough for her to mouth seven words.

The last three were *I love you*.

'Come on then.' Francis pressed down the blade. Odina felt herself going cold: her pain turning to icy numbness as the blade went deeper and the life flowed out of her. Francis's face was just inches from hers. 'Let's see it, you worthless fucking savage. Let's see the lights go out. *Let's see it*.'

They were right next to the burning fort.

Odina reached out with her right arm, ripping off a loose piece of fabric from her mantle. She let it flop against the ground, hoping that the strip of clothing was close enough to catch fire.

It was. Flames licked at the edge of the fabric. She reached out with her other arm.

She found what she was looking for. Matoaka's satchel.

Odina heard the girl's voice in her head one last time. *A gift for you, Mother... I didn't take all of it. And it hardly ever gets used anymore. I think my father has forgotten about it anyway...*

Odina's weak fingers reached inside the leather satchel. They rested around something. A small pouch. Small but powerful.

The stuff they called *gun-pow-derr.*

Francis let go of the blade. He glanced between Odina's hands. Saw the bundled-up burning fabric. Saw the satchel and the pouch. Saw the flames enveloping Odina's hand. Saw her calm expression.

His sadistic glee wiped from existence, Francis had only one remaining desire. It was the need felt by any man about to die.

He wanted a reason.

'For your people?' he asked.

Odina spat in his face.

'For my daughter,' she said.

And – with a clap of hands, a one-and-done round of applause to mark the end of a show that had gone on far too long – the powder met the fire.

Odina's last three words to Guy had been *I love you.*

The four before that were *Take her and run.*

Guy got the message. He knew that it was going to hurt – both him and Matoaka alike – but there was no option.

He had mere seconds. He dived forwards, through the flaming balustrade, through the fire – and grabbed Matoaka, pulling her back through the flames and to the other side. Her clothes and hair caught fire. She woke up immediately, screaming – which turned to muffled yelps as Guy grabbed her and rolled them both along the ground.

He took a second to check her over. Her hair was singed and her clothes were smoking. Light-red burnt patches formed fresh welts on her skin. But apart from that – a miracle in a world he had long known didn't harbour any – she was fine. Guy quickly patted down his own hair and clothes. They had escaped without too much damage too. His arms had taken the brunt of the flames – but he could see to those later.

He grabbed Matoaka and ran.

The explosion came a second later. The thrust of ignited air lifted them off their feet. The sound was everything: unimaginably loud one second, drowned out by the ringing in their ears the next. Guy and Matoaka thudded to the ground. Guy immediately threw himself over the girl, protecting her as a shower of flaming debris rained down.

They stayed like that for a moment.

The debris stopped falling. The echo of the explosion faded. There was just the roar and crackle of the burning fort: a sound which had seemed so unbearably loud just minutes earlier... but which now felt like unremarkable background noise.

The other men were yelling. Some of them had been frozen in their tracks when the explosion happened. They remained stock-still, pails of water held uselessly in their hands.

'What the hell are you doing?' Smith yelled at them. 'Water on the fire. Now. Now! *Now!*'

They snapped back to reality. They snapped back to action.

'I need to put this fire out,' Guy said, words that scraped out of his red-raw throat. 'I need to help the others.'

'In a moment,' Matoaka said.

Guy nodded.

And, for a short while – with arms that were already beginning to blister – Guy held the little girl as she sobbed.

CHAPTER THIRTEEN

January 7th – April 10th 1608

The men at Jamestown were, as a rule, not a sentimental bunch. They valued action over idealism, solutions over hugs. Yet – nonetheless – they managed to scrape together enough communal empathy to console Guy in his sorrow. They made sure his wounds were dealt with first. He was allowed to rest while the others immediately began to rebuild. He had dearly valued the native woman who lost her life – the woman who had come running from the forest to try and help the colonists – and was granted time to mourn.

No one apart from Guy had seen Francis. No one knew of his involvement. Everyone assumed that the blaze had started out of random carelessness – someone covertly sparking up a small fire to keep warm – and the explosion came from some gunpowder that had dropped out of the relocated dryfats. Odina's death was a tragic accident that befell a brave woman.

Remarkably there were no other fatalities in the Jamestown

fire – or what could now charitably be referred to as Jamestown. While the colonists had eventually managed to get the fire under control, they had only been able to do so because the blaze had torn through all available fuel. It had burned itself out by burning Jamestown to the ground.

Now the heat had vanished from the air – leaving only a mass of smoking cinders where the fort once stood – the colonists, fresh without shelter, soon began to notice the opposite extreme in temperature.

It was cold. It was damn cold. Winter was tightening its grip.

Guy wished he still had faith to lose anew. It would have been a lot easier to focus his anger on a God who had betrayed him. As things stood, he could only look inwards: he only had himself to blame. Everything that happened – everything with Francis and Odina and Matoaka – was on his head. Without him, Jamestown and the *Tsenacommacah* would certainly have had fractured relations… but he had brought misfortune here like a bad smell leading rats from the sewers.

Matoaka knew this too. Guy could tell. She was sat nearby as she recovered from her ordeal, swathed in blankets, shivering, given medical attention from Wotton with what little resources he had left. She stared vacantly at Guy whenever he caught her eye. If hatred and resentment had not grown within her yet, they would soon.

And rightly so, Guy told himself.

'How are you coping, Johnson?' Smith asked him.

'I'm coping,' Guy said.

'I'm sorry about the woman. Your friend. She gave her life trying to save others. Her sacrifice will not be forgotten.'

'Thank you.'

'There's something I need to ask you.' Smith sighed. 'Not something I *want* to ask. But there's no other way around this.'

'Go ahead.'

'Rebuilding the fort will take time. It will be tough. But we'll get there. We're not short of materials.' He glanced over to the surrounding woodland. 'But we lost a lot of our food supplies in the fire. There's no way we'll be able to restock them before winter hits in earnest.'

'So what do you suggest?'

'The girl. The chief's daughter. Can you speak to her? She could convince Powhatan to help us. I've no doubt his tribe could spare some supplies to get us through the next few months.'

'The girl has just lost her mother, Smith,' Guy said.

'I know.' Smith looked genuinely remorseful. 'But she is our only hope right now, Johnson. And no one is better placed to talk to her than you.'

Guy echoed Smith's words when he approached Matoaka. It was as good a sentiment as any.

'I do not want to ask you this,' he gently said to the girl. 'But I have to.'

He told her the plan. Guy and Smith would take Matoaka back to Powhatan. While there, Matoaka could sweet-talk her father into giving the colonists some food supplies: helping to build a bridge between the two worlds, a display of benevolence that would leave the colonists forever indebted. If anyone could persuade Powhatan the value of this, it would be his favourite daughter Pocahontas.

Matoaka thought it over for a moment.

'Why,' she finally asked, 'would I do such a thing?'

'That's a good question,' Guy said. 'After what you've lost... you would be forgiven for wanting the exact opposite. You could take joy in watching Jamestown starve. You could even request that your father's men march into town and slaughter us all wholesale.'

'Yes.' Matoaka's tone was flat. 'I could.'

'But that's not *you*, is it? To do that would be the actions of men. Stupid men, violent men, wicked men. The Treshams and Askooks and Opechancanoughs of this world. You are different than them, Matoaka. Something new and hopeful. You could save the lives of those souls with your words alone, whether they deserved your help or not.'

Matoaka lasped into silent thought again. 'I will do it,' she said, 'on one condition.'

'Name it.'

'One of your chiefs. The man with one arm.'

'Newport.'

'*Neu-port*, yes.' Matoaka nodded. 'He sails back to your land every now and then, does he not?'

'He does.'

'When will he be going again?'

'I'm not sure,' Guy said. 'But shortly, I assume.'

'Then I want you to go with him. Go and never come back.' Guy looked down. Matoaka had placed her hands on his.

He looked into her eyes. He had been wrong about her simmering anger or resentment. To his surprise – which maybe shouldn't have been the case, given the girl's eerie maturity – there was something else. A sad pragmatism.

'I know you did not mean for my mother to die.' Matoaka was filled with sorrow. 'You did not mean for any of the bad things you've caused to happen. But you *did* cause them, Ch-awn. You are not a dark or evil spirit... but I do think you are an unfortunate one. A lost one. I think you bring chaos and madness in your wake no matter what your intentions. I think you harbour a curse. I dearly wish this was not so – but the longer you stay in the *Tsenacommacah*, the more death and destruction you will bring.' She let go of his hands. 'I will persuade my father to help your men. But only if you leave.'

Guy slowly nodded.

'Then we have an agreement,' he said.

The Powhatan village was a different beast altogether now the *matchacomoco* was over. The approach to the territory itself seemed sedate and tranquil. Guy and Smith and Matoaka banked their shallops to land. Matoaka led the two men into the village.

Powhatan's guards immediately surrounded them. Matoaka told them to back off. They obeyed – and also seemed somewhat shocked at her newly authoritative tone. This was not the playful little girl they knew. This was a young woman who knew her power.

Matoaka took Guy and Smith to see Powhatan. Powhatan listened solemnly as Matoaka recounted everything. He looked particularly distressed to hear of the death of Odina; distressed enough that he held no anger to learn of Odina and Matoaka's regular covert meetings. He was increasingly aware that the Real People were edging towards extinction – and every one of their number lost was one too many. Matoaka outlined her deal to Powhatan: food supplies in exchange for Guy's departure. Powhatan agreed.

'I am ready to accept this agreement,' Powhatan said to Guy and Smith, 'but I have one condition.'

'Very well,' Guy said. 'What is it?'

'I want one of the Real People to accompany you on your travels back.' Powhatan gestured for one of his men to step forward. One did so: a rangy and alert-looking man who Guy had seen in action before, a fiercely loyal acolyte to his chief. 'Namontack here will join your voyage. He will spend time in your world. When your ships return, he will return with them. He will tell me of the things he has seen.'

'That can be arranged.' Guy nodded.

'I've always believed that those who control the past control the future,' he said. 'I fear that Pocahontas is right about you, Ch-awn. Through no fault of your own, perhaps, your very presence brings endless disaster.'

'I'm inclined to agree,' Guy said.

'This will be the last time I see you, Ch-awn,' Powhatan mused. 'I wish you well. I hope that wherever you go next you can redeem yourself of what haunts you.' Powhatan looked to Smith. 'As for you. Let us treat this as a new beginning. If we are to live alongside each other, let us become allies rather than enemies. Let us trade both goods and knowledge.'

'Let us do that.' Smith gave a nod.

Neither of them sounded entirely convinced. But it would work for now.

As Guy and Smith left – with both a bounty of food supplies and new human cargo in the shape of Namontack – Guy looked to the edge of the river. Matoaka was watching him go.

She raised a hand. *Farewell.* Guy raised his hand in return. Other than that, Matoaka showed no emotion.

It was what it was.

The colonists rebuilt as quickly as they could: enough shelter, at least, for them all to sleep inside during the cold nights. The winter came. They bunkered down. They saw it through.

Guy realised for the first time that Smith had been keeping a journal of his time in Jamestown. He noticed Smith one night, working by candlelight, making additions and revisions and tearing out old pages.

'What are you doing?' Guy asked as Smith carefully burned the pages.

'I'm doing what I promised.' Smith gave a weak smile. 'You may have brought your fair share of chaos to this place, Johnson. But I'll never let it be said you were anything less than interesting.'

'Good to know.' Guy returned the smile. 'The question is – how will your story go now? Everything we did, everything we saw. What are you going to replace me with?'

'Oh.' Smith shrugged. 'I'll think of something.' He carried on burning the pages for a moment.

'I think the girl was right, you know,' Smith eventually said. 'Maybe you are... *haunted*, in a way. Maybe you do need to cleanse yourself somehow. Find some sort of redemption. A way to exorcise the demons that follow you.'

'Believe me,' Guy said. 'There's no maybe about it.'

It was on April 10th 1608 – the end of a harsh winter, the green shoots of a life-giving spring to come – that Captain Newport loaded up the *Susan Constant* with goods and men and began the voyage back to England. There were two additional passengers to the planned crew. One was Namontack: an emissary from Powhatan, a native whose command of English was coming along well, the first of his kind who would ever traverse the ocean to the land of the white men. The other – never to be noted on any manifest, past, present or future – was 'John Johnson'.

Goodbyes had been direct and to the point. Terse and pointed for some, calmly polite for others – but never less than genuine. That was all that Guy could have hoped for.

'Take care of yourself, John Johnson,' Smith said over a firm handshake.

'You too, John Smith.' Guy gave the settlement one last glance. 'And take care of this place too.'

'I'll do my best.'

And that, Guy noted with a strange relief, felt genuine too.

The *Constant* set sail. The ocean opened up. When not helping out with crew duty, Guy spent most of his time above deck. He had spent countless months at sea over the course of his life – but he had never before stopped to marvel at how *vast* it was... how vast the world itself was... how full of possibilities and opportunities and paths to take.

'We're making stops at Dominica and the Canary Islands en route,' Newport had told him. 'We'll also be skimming the west coast of Africa. Southern Europe too. I'm not completely averse to making a brief detour while we're there. There's no pressure for you to be on board when we arrive in London. After all...' He gave Guy a knowing look. 'You can't account for a man who doesn't exist, can you?'

'No,' Guy agreed. 'I don't believe you can.'

He did not make his decision immediately. He had plenty of time to decide. He spent his days on the *Constant* either busy at work or deep in thought.

At night he dreamt. He dreamt of strawberry fields and still rivers – and, in the middle of it all, something that shouldn't be there but also *should*.

He dreamt of a clearing and a campfire and a woman sat

waiting for him. The woman would look up to him as he approached. She would smile. He would smile back. They never managed to get any further than that. That was the moment everything always vanished: dissipated in a haze of unearthly smoke.

The smoke got in his eyes.

He tried and tried to blink it away. It was useless.

And whenever Guy woke, those same eyes were filled with tears.

THE END

A NOTE FROM THE PUBLISHER

Thank you for reading this book. If you enjoyed it please do consider leaving a review on Amazon to help others find it too.

We hate typos. All of our books have been rigorously edited and proofread, but sometimes mistakes do slip through. If you have spotted a typo, please do let us know and we can get it amended within hours.

info@bloodhoundbooks.com

Printed in Great Britain
by Amazon